TUMMY
LOVE

Sarah Orten

Cover design by Simon Hartshorne
Designed & Typeset by Simon Hartshorne

ISBN 978-0-9929294-0-4

Printed and bound by Copytech (UK) Limited, Peterborough.

Edvard Munch's *The Scream*. From *The Violet Journal* (MM T 2760, fol. 56r) in the Munch Museum. Printed with permission from the Munch Museum.

www.SarahOrton.co.uk

TUMMY
LOVE

SARAH ORTON

To my precious children Sophie and Harry
and the 'fourth emergency service' – my husband Steven

PROLOGUE

One year, two weeks and three days (+ 13 nights without her)

Melanie walked over to the empty cot.

"Elizabeth, Elspeth, Bess, Betsy Boo, Li-ly-bet…"

She reached over the bars and with her finger traced the outline of where one year, two weeks and three days of life had lain (and still counting, counting, counting). The sheets and blanket were gone. They were pulled away in a hurry, in a rush to pick Elizabeth up, in a scramble to carry her far, far away and over the hills.

Hey diddle, diddle
The cat and the fiddle
The cow jumped over the moon
The little dog laughed to see such fun
And the dish ran away with the spoon

In the silence of the night, Melanie watched the clock creep to eleven o'clock, groan past midnight and wail at one o'clock. *A late feed* her swollen breasts protested.

Hickory, Dickory, Dock
The mouse ran up the clock
The clock struck one

The mouse ran down

Hickory, Dickory, Dock

Melanie's head spun from thirteen broken nights – the endless passage of the past two weeks dripped dark and slowly like black treacle. A fortnight of being ousted from her nest, Melanie's baby snatched from her, the family barred from entering their home as the forensic team scoured the house and grounds in search of clues as to Elizabeth's whereabouts.

Melanie's body grew heavy and weary from the hours of waiting, hoping – hoping, waiting. Her head spun from the lack of sleep and the endless questions to account for 'the missing half hour' between arriving home and Melanie's desperate call for an ambulance for her husband who lay bleeding to death on the nursery carpet. Unable to steady herself she grabbed the bars of the cot. They were the bars that had been crawled over by the SOCOs who had stripped everything else away, swooping down like locusts to snatch Elizabeth's toys, her dummy and mattress cover – leaving a trail of silver aluminium fingerprint dust in their wake... ashes to ashes... dust to dust.

She held on like a sailor gripping the rails on deck in a violent storm. The first waves of panic swirled around her feet and legs, pulling her off balance. She tightened her hold. Then the cold sinister fear, that rose like flood water seeped in through her pores. Dark and relentless, it grabbed and knotted her stomach and squeezed her lungs, until she gasped for air. The fear stabbed into her heart with a force that made her collapse to the floor, her body covering the unsightly blood stain which emanated from her husband the night of Elizabeth's evaporation from the surface of the earth. After some time, she opened her eyes, her vision crawling erratically up the wall and resting wildly on a large photograph showing baby Elizabeth squeezing a teddy bear twice her size.

"Chocolate," she yelled, calling the bear's familiar name into the silent nursery.

The threadbare teddy had been fortuitously scurried away in need of urgent attention, only the day before Elizabeth's disappearance. It was the only toy to have escaped the efficient swoop of the cot by the SOCOs. Frantically she pushed a chair over to a high storage cupboard and retrieved the bear, clutching it so tightly the toy was in danger of losing its worn limbs altogether.

The soft toy had first lost its growl in 1977 when Melanie was aged ten. But it was not until her sixteenth birthday in 1983 that Melanie's mother placed Chocolate into hibernation for the 'grandchildren'.

Melanie remembered the teenage pull at her heart strings when the bear disappeared from her bedroom one day. She could not have imagined how *this* would feel – the yank of her own flesh and blood being taken from her. She stumbled over to Elizabeth's chest of drawers. Her mind focused on the small task she was about to undertake. It would be a distraction to fill a few moments of the long night ahead, when sleep was impossible. Melanie hurled the contents of the drawers onto the floor, as she searched for fresh cot sheets and an outfit to dress the bear. Her eyes fell on a cheery yellow babygrow – the large grinning clown was painfully at odds with the tragedy of the empty cot.

Again peculiar short, rasping, snatches of air replaced Melanie's attempts to breathe normally as she lifted her leg and broken heart over the bars of the cot. She folded her legs and arms into the cramped but familiar space, relaxing her body into the mattress, as it jolted and creaked in protest. Melanie pulled the cotton sheets over her body like an Egyptian priest preparing his royal Pharaoh for burial. Round and around shrouding her head, her shoulders and body. Then she pressed her nose into the teddy bear inhaling the scent, pulling Elizabeth's smell into her nostrils, retrieving the memory of her skin, her smile, her breath. Melanie willed her baby back into her mother's embrace – to suckle, to feed, to need her.

Another suffocating wave of panic swept over her. She inhaled deeply again, this time longing to draw Elizabeth back into the safety of her womb. But her uterus had already been taken, robbing her of the chance of more children.

Elizabeth's scent was exquisite, but Melanie's decision to smell her baby's aroma came at a terrible price. It unleashed the full wrath of her pain. Like a coil unravelling, it whipped everything in its path. The grief oozed up from the pit of her stomach and rose into her chest. It kicked and curled out of her mouth in a fearful earth-splitting moan. A moan of a mother who fears her child, her flesh and blood, her heart and soul has been torn away from her forever and ever... Amen.

One year, two weeks and three days (+ 14 nights without her)

Melanie stood in the middle of the nursery. In the one year, two weeks and three days since Elizabeth took her first gasp of air (and still counting, counting, counting) her second born had acquired an extraordinary number of names. Melanie let her lips and tongue roll and click and feel their way round each of the whispered pet names.

"Elizabeth, Lilybet, Elspeth, Bess, Betsy."

She repeated the names over and over again, as she rocked herself to the comforting mantra. It was just as her grandmother had whispered and mouthed her prayers to the Virgin Mary, the Father, the Son and the Holy Ghost. She remembered the rhythmic click, click, click of her rosary beads passing through her worn fingers, hands which were big, lined and beautiful. Fingers that had loved much, served many, prayed for an eternity; hands that had cooked, washed and scrubbed a thousand times over for her four sons and two daughters; hands that had buried her youngest daughter Isabelle, who died from a twisted bowel.

Hail Mary full of grace...

Each name seemed subconsciously ready to be hung on the pegs of the daily routine of motherhood.

"Betsy Boo, smelly pooh," said Elizabeth's big sister Hannah, who was strangely drawn to, yet repulsed by the "yucky stuff" that strained and blew and oozed and farted itself out of her baby sister.

After bath time, Hannah chanted "Bess, Bess no longer a mess."

Melanie blew an enormous, vibrating raspberry into her daughter's rotund tummy and then returned to look at Bess's liquid blue eyes as the baby squealed in a playful, wordless banter.

Then Bess became Elspeth as Melanie sought out her favourite place, the soft folds of skin on Elspeth's neck. She nuzzled her baby with her nose – as a mare encourages her foal to take its first steps.

"Oh sweet Elspeth," she whispered, "Do you know how long we waited for you?"

The more formal "Miss Elizabeth Abigail Maloney" was reserved for the daily application of cream. Every night Melanie ran generous, sweeping dollops of zinc and castor oil ointment over her daughter's Churchillian creases, to ward off nappy rash and eczema.

"Never has fat looked so beautiful Miss Elizabeth Abigail Maloney," said Melanie.

As she lay her daughter down to sleep, Melanie curled the baby's fingers around her index finger and soothed her...

Elizabeth, Elspeth, Betsy and Bess,
They all went together to seek a bird's nest,
They found a bird's nest with five eggs in,
They all took one, and left four in.

But Melanie's favourite pet name, princess Lilybet, was

reserved for the most intimate hour of all, their midnight hour. It was a private collusion between mother and daughter. By her first birthday, Elizabeth's cry for milk came sometime after midnight and always before one in the morning. Nothing could steal this silent, unseen moment from mother and child.

Melanie thought... until her baby was cruelly snatched from her cot (and still counting, counting, counting) that *Elizabeth* would decide when to take her last suckle from her mother – just as Hannah had more than four years before her younger sister.

A short while after midnight Elizabeth's stirrings and gurgles seeped their way into Melanie's dream, just as the steam rose up into her nostrils as a child, when her French grandmother invited her to lift the lid on her heady rabbit and Cognac stew.

Melanie peeled herself away from the warmth of her husband's chest.

"The safest place on earth," she smiled dreamily at Harry.

Seventeen steps along the long gallery landing and nine across the nursery to Elizabeth's cot. She could do it blindfolded and in her sleep. Melanie wiped the hot tears of wanting from Elizabeth and melted into the menagerie of bean bags and sheep skins with her baby. Sliding the child across her tummy, Melanie gently guided princess Lilybet to her nipple. As the milk flowed and she heard the gentle 'tat-tat-tat' of sucking, Melanie ran her finger across her baby's cheek – reserving her favourite name for their intimate night-time meeting.

"Lilybet, Lilybet, princess Li-ly-bet."

Melanie's midnight feeds for Lilybet were rolled out for her like a long red carpet laid out for a princess. As Elizabeth's head crowned between Melanie's legs at 5.42am on Monday 1st November 2004, she wondered in the crescendo of blood and pain, could this faceless, sexless, nameless child command the love she already had for Hannah – her firstborn.

An overwhelming need to bear down saw Melanie roll onto all fours, as the midwife struggled to pull on her gloves for the impending expulsion of the child. The exit came uncommonly quickly, with Melanie's cry of "I need to PUUUUUUUUSH," accompanied by three almighty convulsing and contracting tremors, that began in her brain and worked their way down her body. The midwife caught the anonymous blob of flesh, heart and soul, just as she had finished negotiating her left thumb into her surgical glove.

"Oh I'm so sorry," said Melanie feeling a large amount of solid passing between her legs, "I think I've had an accident… I need the toilet."

"Congratulations," said the midwife. "You've just 'crapped' out a baby girl."

Melanie rolled over and the buxom midwife slid the new life onto her tummy. She marvelled at this fusion of love and passion between Harry and herself, this sacrifice of flesh splitting pain. As her eyes ran down the cord that disappeared between her legs and still anchored her second child to the now redundant placenta; she knew the answer was 'yes', she knew she could love Elizabeth as much as Hannah.

Even before the blood flowed; before her head swam hard and fast, spiralling down the tube of unconsciousness; before she saw her husband Harry crying and heard "post-partum haemorrhage" echo and ricochet along a hollow tunnel; before a doctor's face peered at her, distorted through a goldfish bowl and her eyes disconnected and rolled into the back of her skull; before all this, Melanie's heart trembled with love for her second born child.

Pat-a-cake, Pat-a-cake
Baker's man
Make me a cake as fast as you can
Pat it and prick it and mark it with 'E'
And put in the oven for Harry and me

When the blackness came and the doctors removed her uterus, she understood that she wanted to make hundreds of Elizabeths and Hannahs, she wanted Harry Maloney to fill her over and over again, she wanted girls and boys, and twins and triplets, to carry and feed and love.

…A big brood of Maloneys forever and ever

…Amen

PART I

2005

Chapter One

Friday 18 November – 2pm

Elizabeth Maloney's destiny and life (one year, two weeks and three days on the night of her disappearance) was sealed during a fleeting conversation on an intercom between her loving but misguided parents. The wireless intercom system linked Melanie Henriksen's studio-come-kitchen on the ground floor of the main house, with Harry Maloney's private orthodontic practice, located in a long, single storey brick building in the grounds of The Oast.

With their flu-ridden nanny unable to babysit Elizabeth and Hannah on one of the most important nights of Melanie's career, the dice was thrown for last minute childcare cover. Shake and throw. Melanie's parents were out of the equation as they lived in Norway, whilst Harry's were just far enough away to make "a sudden change of plan difficult dear… sorry."

The orthodontist made another roll of the dice. The regular babysitter in the village divided her time between The King's Head and the care of young children. She was pulling pints that night.

Yet another roll: played more with hope than luck. This time Melanie tried a friend's recommendation, but drew another bum deal.

Then in desperation, Melanie called friends-of-friends' babysitters in nearby villages around the Weald of Kent. But one by one, they fell away, like the house of cards Melanie used to build with her French grandmother in her garden by the sea.

Darius Sorokin then, was the ninth choice, the same lucky number that brings the black cat nine chances of life. Darius Sorokin was the final deal, Melanie and Harry's 'trump card' to take care of their children that evening.

In fact, Darius was *not* Melanie's choice at all. *She* would have preferred to ask her London friends Angelica Mayhew and Sophia Haverstock, to step into the breach. But the sisters were both committed to attending 'The Art of Food' book launch with celebrated food photographer Joshua Haverstock.

'The Art of Food' photographic food book was a unique collaboration between Melanie Henriksen OBE, TV's top children's cook and the fastest selling children's recipe book author in the UK, and photographer Joshua Haverstock. Quite unlike any of Melanie Henriksen's other cookery books, this lifestyle book was a photographical masterpiece featuring food landscapes created by Melanie and Joshua and now bound for the coffee tables of the millions of fans of the nation's 'kiddie cook'.

Minky Sloane of Sloane PR, the doyenne of food PR and publicity and the powerhouse behind her most lucrative client, had planned and orchestrated the fantastical launch, book signing and VIP party in London. The launch had been in everyone's diary for nine months (the same period Elizabeth had lain safely in her mother's womb). Now the PR guru would not entertain the "minor headache" of finding a babysitter, endanger the prestigious red carpet launch of 'The Art of Food' in Oxford Street.

"Be on time Melanie and look bloody beautiful darling," said Minky Sloane during Melanie's last call to her publicist at midday.

"Why doesn't Harry stay at home to look after the girls... I *could* just come on my own," Melanie suggested.

"What... and leave 'the dishy dentist' behind?" said Minky indignantly.

"Orthodontist Minky, remember Harry is not a dentist, he's an or-tho-don-tist."

"Well darling it's all bloody teeth as far as I'm concerned – whether you're pulling, filling or straightening them – besides the papers love the 'dishy dentist' tag. He's fifty per cent of the golden 'kiddie cook' couple and we need photos tonight for the paps. Call in the fairy godmother if you have to. See you at six o'clock sharp darling."

Melanie smiled ironically. Obstacles didn't exist in Minky's 'darling' world. They *had* to find a babysitter.

The couple undoubtedly faced a multitude of distractions as they counted down to Melanie's big night, which perhaps went some way to explaining why they (why Harry) gambled Elizabeth's life away on a thirty second intercom conversation.

For her part, Melanie was halfway through an hour long session with her hairdresser in the kitchen. On one knee she juggled her sick baby and on the other an endless stream of special limited edition copies of 'The Art of Food' book which still needed signing for the VIP party.

"Try to keep your head up Ms Henriksen," said the hairdresser with a fistful of hair grips and a head full of resentments.

The mobile hairdresser was brushing, spraying and gripping Melanie's long, dark hair into a sweeping Audrey Hepburn creation, to complement her stunning 60s-inspired red dress which she'd had designed especially for the book launch.

Hannah, meanwhile, played with her doll's house close to her mother, with the occasional piece of plastic furniture crunching under the hairdresser's heel.

Elizabeth began crying and writhing around on her mother's lap.

"Oh you're burning up," said Melanie as she put her hand on Elizabeth's flushed forehead. She lifted the baby's mouth under her nose and smelt her hot, toffee breath. She knew the familiar smell, fiery and sweet, the early indicator of a fever without the need to consult the doctor. The crying rose to a frenzied, ear-bursting scream and Melanie asked the hairdresser to pass her the paracetamol syrup from the dresser.

Normally reserving her breast for princess Lilybet's midnight feed, she tried to comfort her baby on her nipple. The hairdresser raised an eyebrow and muttered something about a "career change into nursing or child care". She wanted to be home for her favourite 'soap' and the fraught hair styling appointment with the usually calm and collected 'kiddie cook' was beginning to run over.

Across the lawn in the orthodontic practice, Harry faced a different set of challenges. He was without his nurse for half an hour whilst she ran to the dry cleaners to collect the designer suit he'd forgotten to pick up ready for the evening's book launch and party. A double booking by the receptionist, who had caught the nanny's flu, meant the surgery was running 45 minutes behind schedule.

So the offer of Darius Sorokin to babysit Elizabeth Abigail Maloney (the eighteen-year-old patient who lived just across the green from the Henriksen/Maloney household) seemed too good to be true.

"If something's too good to be true dear, it usually is," Harry's risk-averse mother always cautioned from the safety of her house on the coast.

It was only days after Darius Sorokin had stolen Elizabeth from her cot that Melanie discovered Сорокин, the Russian for Sorokin, was derived from the word soroka (сорока) meaning magpie – a bird known to steal young chicks from other birds' nests.

On paper "Harry's choice" of Darius Sorokin looked sound enough. After all he had virtually watched the boy grow up in his orthodontic chair, he reasoned.

"How's my most challenging orthodontic case?" Harry asked Darius every time he came to the practice during his eight-year treatment plan.

Harry posed the question in an all smiling John Wayne kind-a "Let's go get some Indians" voice, with a hint of a Southern drawl and the gaited walk. The mothers loved Harry's dishy smile and play-acting. The teenage patients and his nurse usually squirmed. Harry was passionate about Westerns, or the 'Bang Bangs' as he affectionately called them, but when he confessed his obsession to friends or colleagues, he was met with derision or feigned interest in the dated genre and the dead film star. So he kept his pastime in a closet on his side of the bed and only brought out the DVD's and old videos late at night when Melanie and the children were asleep.

By the age of ten, when Darius's treatment began in earnest, the boy had manicured an outwardly polite demeanour, but internally was excruciatingly shy. The psychiatric reports later said 'withdrawn'. The sharpness of Darius's features was exacerbated by thin, mean lips and a peculiar smile. It was a smile that hovered halfway between awkwardness and what appeared to Harry Maloney to be the hint of a sneer. Harry put the strange expression down to the unfortunate and challenging arrangement of his teeth. He was confident a full and normal smile would be restored to his face on completion of the treatment.

The awkwardness of Darius Sorokin during his appointments with Harry Maloney was compounded by the presence of his cosmetically-enhanced and gushing mother, who was constantly by his side. Natasha Sorokin, a retired Russian gymnast, stood at six foot tall with her heels, whilst her plunging neckline and garish polka dot dresses clung to her surgically enhanced breasts.

Darius quickly mastered the English language, but developed an unfortunate habit of over-emphasising the 's' consonant, which gave his speech patterns a peculiar hissing quality, and made his impeccable politeness seem staged and insincere.

"How ni-ccc-e to sss-see you Mi-sss-ter Maloney," said Darius after the customary stroke of his hair from his doting mother.

8

When Harry asked Darius to "Open wide little soldier" at the start of his treatment plan, he noted the severe Class II division 2 malocclusion, on a moderate Skeletal II base with significantly decreased lower face height. Added to this he observed that intra-orally there was severe lower arch crowding and moderate upper arch crowding, complicated by a palatally displaced impacted canine.

The intensive treatment plan began with the removal of two premolars to relieve the crowding, performed by Dr Maloney under local anaesthetic. Some children wriggled and squirmed, other kids clung to their mother's hand for reassurance, whilst some gave their nervousness away by their wide-eyed expression through the protective eye glasses. Darius however was one of Harry's "bravest little soldiers". The boy remained utterly impassive (the psychiatrist later observed a tendency towards 'detachment') as he listened to the clicking and cracking of the premolars being extracted from their sockets.

It was the cleaner who noticed a *Brave Soldier* sticker and certificate had accidentally been left behind by the "little Russian boy" when she cleaned the toilets that evening. In contrast, Darius kept his premolars in a jar by his bed throughout his childhood. The treatment continued with upper arch expansion, functional appliance, traction to the canines and fixed appliance detailing of his occlusion. The checkups and indefinite wearing of a retainer at night would ensure Darius didn't "fall at the last hurdle".

"Orthodontics is all about team work Darius and you've been a good team player," said Harry, patting Darius on the shoulder. The "brave little soldier" analogies usually hung around in the trenches till about thirteen and were superseded by numerous sporting phrases like, "Let's be on the winning side Darius" and "We're in training now for the final whistle". But Darius, the joker with the sneer, would be the one blowing the whistle and he was happy to play dirty.

On the afternoon of 'The Art of Food' book launch, Harry stepped back to admire the years of treatment. The end result was perfect in every way, except for Darius's smile. Despite the now perfect alignment of his teeth and correction of his bite, the boy's smile seemed to have developed into a pronounced and unattractive sneer.

At 18 years of age, Darius's body stretched the full length of the surgery chair. He had grown tall and athletic like his mother and had become an exceptional talent in the art of fencing. Unlike his mother, however, Darius also showed "outstanding academic potential" according to his masters at Eton College, as five straight 'A' grades in maths and the sciences saw Oxford and Cambridge University falling over each other to offer him a place to study Engineering Science. Now on his gap year and with the rest of his Eton peers already headed for distant shores around the world, Darius opted for the loner's trip. His plans for the year were vague... he was at a loose end. So the bum hand was laid out on the table. Darius Sorokin, the quiet, gifted student, with a perfect set of teeth, and a smile that looked like a sneer, was free to babysit Hannah and Elizabeth.

"Darius would *lerve* to save ze day Dr Muzloney, wouldn't you sweetie," said Natasha volunteering her son to babysit for the night, as she stroked his hair.

She leant towards Harry, with her low cut dress now revealing the edge of a lacy polka dot bra and with the distraction of Natasha's enormous breasts and recently filled lips sliding towards the 'dishy dentist', Harry hadn't thought to double-check the babysitting offer with a glance at Darius.

"I'll just let Melanie know the good news, she'll be so relieved we've solved our babysitting crisis," he said.

Lifting his eyes from Natasha's voluptuous cleavage, which hovered alluringly at eye level, he turned on his dental stool to press the intercom. The buzzer sounded in the kitchen just as Melanie closed the door on the hairdresser-in-a-hurry.

"Hello gorgeous we've found a babysitter," said Harry, his voice chirping cheerily through the intercom. "Do you remember Darius Sorokin?"

Silence…Melanie was distracted by Elizabeth writhing in her arms and put the back of her hand on Elizabeth's forehead.

"You know, the boy I always call my 'most challenging orthodontic case'. Well Darius is standing right here and he's generously offered to watch the girls for us tonight."

The polka dot offered dickhead not me, thought Darius.

Without really listening Melanie cut in: "I'm really worried Harry, Elizabeth's burning up. She's not well."

Natasha smiled and winked at Harry, mouthing silently and seductively: "Everyzing will be just fine Dr Muzloney."

Buoyed up by the reassurance from Natasha, he placed his cards on the table and put all his money on the joker with the sneer.

"It's a done deal then. If there are any major problems I can always dash back early from London on the train and my wife can follow in the chauffeured car," said Harry.

Elizabeth's fraught screaming emerged through the intercom and punctuated the air in the surgery.

WHAH – WHAH –WHAH!

"Don't worry Melanie, everything will be just fine... won't it Darius?" and the orthodontist turned for the first time to look directly at the newly hired babysitter.

Darius nodded silently, his thin lips slightly curling up to one side and he hissed a slippery and insincere "Yes-sss."

CHAPTER TWO

Saturday 3 December – 12noon

Melanie felt a hot, impatient five and three-quarter-year old flop across her tummy. Hannah pulled open her mother's swollen eyes, puffed up and red from the relentless crying and her fight to sleep. The family had transferred from the confines of the guest-house in the garden, back to the family home, once the police had completed their fruitless forensic search of the house and garden during the fortnight since Elizabeth had first vanished with the babysitter. The familiar surroundings of Elizabeth's nursery and their home failed to deliver Melanie's desperate search for sleep.

"Here have these," said her doctor.

"Will it take the pain away?" she asked numbly, her eyes pleading for someone, anyone, to give her an answer... to give her princess Lilybet back.

"No – it's not magic Melanie – but it will calm things down a little for you – it'll bring you a little peace and quiet."

QUIET she yelled inwardly. *I have all the quiet I need.* She had a silent coffin instead of a cot, a mausoleum for a nursery, a high-chair that was "good as gold" and a baby carrier that didn't make a sound.

Give Lilybet back Darius, she's MINE!

Hannah let go of her mother's eyelids.

"Where's 'lizabeth?" said Hannah, still struggling to get her tongue around the E-li part of her baby sister's name. "Where *is* she Mummy?"

What to say? Your baby sister's gone on holiday, to the hospital, to stay with Bestemor and Bestefar in Norway. She's lost Hannah, just lost. They've got hundreds of people looking for her. Everything will be fine with the keystone cops and the village of well meaning search parties. Now millions of people know about the mysterious disappearance of the 'kiddie cook's princess Lilybet and the Russian babysitter' they're sure to find her... she is simply lost.

Melanie forced her dried out, cried out eyes open and pushed herself to a sitting position.

"Yucky Mummy, your eyes are all red like Drakooolah."

"Elizabeth is playing hide and seek darling. She's hiding somewhere and we just need to find her," said Melanie.

"Well why don't you help look for her *now* instead of just lying there all the time and crying?" said Hannah bossily.

Melanie hid her face of despair behind her hands.

"'lizabeth must be hiding in a wee-ally good place Mummy," said Hannah ready to join in with her baby sister's game.

*Please let it be a **good** hiding place*, Melanie screamed inside, *please God.*

Hannah took a second look at her mother and realised she wasn't going to get out of bed.

"Well *I'm* going to find her," said Hannah, huffing loudly.

She stomped out of the room wearing her Snow White dress and favourite pink wellington boots, "Coming ready or NO-OT."

The room fell silent. *Tread water Melanie. You don't have to move forward or look backwards, just get through the next minute, the next hour, keep your head above water, don't drown Melanie.*

❀ ❀ ❀

"Mum-mee," Hannah said, shouting impatiently across the room at the mound of duvet covering her mother's form. "Rachel's here to take me to my Christmas party."

"Pardon darling," said Melanie, as her head emerged from under the cocoon-like security of the duvet. Melanie tried to pull her mind back to dry land, kicking to the surface unsure how many minutes or hours had slipped by.

"Rachel. My nan-nee," she said again, this time with her hands on her hips.

Melanie dragged herself out of bed and walked morosely down the stairs. It was the first time Melanie had seen Rachel since she'd called in sick with flu, the day of the book launch, the night Elizabeth was taken. Rachel was standing in the huge, vaulted living room. It was the part of the oast that had once been used to dry and store the estate's hops. They were the hops that were transported to the powerful British breweries by generations of the Davenport family, the previous owners of the property, before the family's tragedy and scandal choked the hop fields surrounding the village green. Rachel appeared very small in the big, echoing space, dwarfed by the galleried landing that led to Hannah's bedroom and Elizabeth's nursery. Her eyes and nose were streaming and red. Pearls of perspiration gathered on her forehead, despite the icy temperatures outside. The guilt that Rachel's 21-year-old, flu-ridden body was now feeling over Elizabeth's disappearance caused her to talk to Melanie's feet.

"I can come back and help around the house once I've taken Hannah to the party Ms Henriksen."

Rachel never calls me Ms Henriksen, it's always Melanie, she thought.

But the barrier of formality made the awkwardness of the moment seem a little more palatable.

"What with?" said Ms Henriksen, not realising how sharp her tone sounded.

The desperate pain of waiting for news of Elizabeth had drained Melanie's effervescence away – her heart was shattered into lifeless pebbles on the beach.

"Perhaps you could start by helping me with the 'Welcome home' banner," she said, spitting the words out angrily. Melanie's uncharacteristically harsh words shocked her as they left her mouth, but she couldn't hold back the anger that was bubbling up inside her like a burning pan of milk spilling over the stove. "Or maybe we could scrub down the bars of the cot... because they're covered in the fingerprint powder the forensic team left behind. Or perhaps we could make up Elizabeth's cot with some fresh sheets and find some new toys, because CID sure as hell stripped my baby's cot bare."

Melanie shielded her face behind her hand, as her face crumpled in agony. She moaned, rocking to and fro.

"Oh I'm so sorry – I'm so sorry Ms Henriksen. I wish I knew what to say."

The nanny reached out to touch her employer's arm, but was too embarrassed to make contact with her skin. She continued to mumble at the floor.

"I'll be back with Hannah at four thirty sharp," she croaked, finally summoning the courage to lift her eyes to Melanie's face.

Rachel couldn't conceal her shock. Melanie's bubbly, pretty face, the nation's popular 'kiddie cook' was now hollow and gaunt. Her sunken eyes were framed by wild hair that appeared as though it hadn't been tamed by a brush for a week or more. She must have lost a stone in weight in a fortnight, Rachel thought. Hannah pulled on Melanie's hand – trying to bring her mother back to shore again.

"Don't cry Mum-mee," she said, frustrated and perturbed by her mother's peculiar behaviour. "Please make something choc-co-let for me today – you're always happy when you cook something choc-co-let."

The little girl savoured the taste of the word as it left her mouth.

"We'll see Hannah. Mummy is very sad... Mummy doesn't feel very well. I'll try my best..."

❀ ❀ ❀

"I just want to reassure you Melanie and Harry that everybody is doing everything they possibly can," said one of the family liaison officers assigned to the case, shortly after Hannah left for her party. Melanie stared numbly at a photograph of Elizabeth.

The cruel finger of suspicion that pointed at the couple during the initial fortnight of Elizabeth's disappearance gradually shifted away from them. Separate questioning at the station about the 'missing half hour' on their return home, the broken front window, Harry's trail of blood around the house, delivered carbon copy accounts from both parents, whilst the endless witness statements from 'The Art of Food' launch gave them a watertight alibi before they arrived home to the house of horror.

DC Saunders explained: "Obviously we can't share many aspects of the investigation with you, but we can tell you that one of the Sorokin's cars vanished the night Darius and Elizabeth disappeared. The mother, Natasha Sorokin, stalled the lines of enquiry for 24 hours, by claiming not to have noticed the car had been taken. However we have good reason to believe that Darius headed to London. CID has been checking the CCTV and ANPR cameras, sorry… I mean automatic number plate recognition cameras, across the capital. We've identified the family had a number of *interesting* business contacts and acquaintances that stretch all the way back to Moscow. We put out an all ports warning almost immediately, because we think Darius will try to escape back to Russia. So if Darius tries to slip out of the country on a ticket or passport using his name, we'll have him."

"But what about Elizabeth, will you *have* my baby?"
OH GOD, please bring her back.

❀   ❀   ❀

Melanie couldn't remember how the clock in the kitchen had worked its way round to 3.10pm. Despite its age, she knew the timepiece was surprisingly accurate thanks to a trip to the work-bench of a respected clock restorer in Portobello Road. Dazed and listless she listened to the rhythmic, comforting tick-tock, tick-tock, tick-tock and supposed that the station clock must have kept many a lone traveller company over the five decades it had reportedly hung in the waiting room of the long departed Goudhurst station.

Still she couldn't trace the last few hours. She remembered the family liaison officers sitting with her and Harry sometime after Hannah had left for the party with the nanny but she couldn't recall what they had said – it was all a blur, muddled by the haze of the tranquilisers.

She recalled making a cup of tea and sitting at the huge circular marble island in the middle of the kitchen. The substantial island had been the focal point of family life, until Elizabeth's disappear-ance, for this was the place that morphed from the breakfast bar to Melanie's kitchen studio for the filming of 'Melanie's Munchkins'. In the afternoon, the island transformed into the ideal surface for any close up camera work and then by the evening it evolved into her office and recipe development work station and the place to share a glass of wine with Harry. She would often sit up late at the marble island, once the children were in bed, and write up any new recipe ideas for her latest children's recipe book, or study her script for her new weekly primetime chat show 'Henriksen's Half Hour'.

Without fail people gasped when they saw Melanie's kitchen and studio for the first time. The quadruple roundel and farmhouse kitchen created an enormous space that had been imaginatively filled with bespoke, solid oak units. They cleverly snaked their way around the four roundels. Hanging on the raw brick walls of the kitchen was a huge photographic canvas featuring an image of the Davenport family standing outside the oast in 1897 with an army of hoppers, all of whom bore testament to Victorian England's insatiable thirst for English hops and British brewed beer.

A huge, adjustable, Victoriana utensil hanger was stacked with all the very latest cooking equipment. Manufacturers lined up to pay Melanie a generous fee to endorse their brands and have their products featured on the set of 'Melanie's Munchkins', which was on its tenth series and still achieving audience viewing figures of over six million.

Melanie looked up at the row of cookery books and ran her finger across them one by one: 'Melanie's Morning Sickness Survival Kit', 'Melanie's Melting Moments', 'Melanie's Munchkins', 'No more Terrible Twos – with a healthy eating plan', 'Chocolate Heaven for your Little Angels' and her best seller 'Tummy Love – the best start in life for babies and toddlers'.

Then Melanie's mind returned to the terrible present tense as she spotted her latest accomplishment 'The Art of Food' coffee-table book, by Joshua Haverstock & Melanie Henriksen. The '*brilliant collaboration between the hottest food photographer and the star of children's TV cookery*' Minky Sloane's press release had boasted. She thought about the glamorous book launch in Oxford Street, about Elizabeth's temperature, the impending sense of doom that screamed inside her...

Why didn't I listen? She slapped her face. *Why didn't I listen?*

She winced, slid the book off the shelf and dropped it into the paper recycling bin. The celebrity cook forced her mind to turn 180 degrees, for the sake of Hannah.

How can I bear to cook? How can I do something so normal when Elizabeth has been stolen?

She slapped herself again, *something chocolate for Hannah.* Wearily Melanie pulled down 'Chocolate Heaven for your Little Angels'. She could hardly bring herself to look at her bright, smiling portrait on the front cover and flicked aimlessly through the pages till she came to 'Chocolate Crispy Cakes'.

'*Did anybody ever need an excuse to make these all-time party classics?*' she asked her readers in an impossibly effervescent narrative. '*It's one of the easiest recipes to follow with very young children and the combination of puffed rice cereal and chocolate makes it the perfect party partnership of all time.*'

Melanie slammed the book shut unable to stomach her saccharin happiness. She knew the recipe inside-out and back-to-front and instinctively spooned the ingredients into a pan without the need for scales. Once the ingredients had melted into a glossy chocolate paste, she added the puffed rice cereal which popped and crackled. She smiled remembering how Hannah always squealed with delight at this point in the recipe. Spooning the crackly mix into 48 cake cases, Melanie placed the cakes into two containers to set in the fridge.

The heady smell of chocolate reactivated the feeling of hunger and Melanie's stomach growled for sustenance. She ran a spoon around the saucepan and licked off the chocolate sauce. *Delicious* she thought in a blind moment of glibness, and for a brief instant her life seemed as normal as it ever would be... as it ever could be.

CHAPTER THREE

Saturday 3 December – 4.10pm

The idea of returning was irresistible. A fortnight of playing cat and mouse and hide and seek had given his pointed face a sharper edge and his eyes sunk further into the dark sockets that betrayed only snatched moments of sleep. The fake number plates on the car, his changed appearance with his shaved head, had enabled him to drive away from the village green undetected. Now he wanted to go back home to Cranhurst.

Fourteen days of evasion, of ducking and diving, of outwitting everybody helped him to realise what he already knew. He could go back and take a look... *for the sheer fucking hell of it.* He felt invincible. No, he **was** invincible and returning to the scene of the crime would prove it to everyone long after he had disappeared back into the ether, reinvigorated by his mother's love and her Mafioso money.

NO BA-SSS-TARD *WILL CATCH ME,* he thought.

Darius crept past his mother's Georgian house opposite the Maloney/Henriksen household, like a lion stalking a gazelle. He loathed the lewd and garish late-Victorian addition to the otherwise beautiful Georgian mansion. It was an obscene addition to the house, not dissimilar to the lurid addition to his mother – the engorged, surgically enhanced breasts – or her garish, polka dot presence on the arm of an endless string of wealthy country gentlemen. They were all lured into her bedroom with her loud and vile polka dot dresses, her skin-tight dotty trousers and cheap polka dot miniskirts, and her pumped up plastic tits which screamed 'Fuck me – fuck me now.'

He crouched and ran behind the hedge running along the edge of the green, under the early cover of a dark wintry sky. As he ran, the scent of a smouldering garden fire close by filled his nostrils, just as the acrid smell of a fireball had filled his nasal passages when he was six years old, as his father drove his Mercedes down the federal highway in Moscow.

The need to look, to stare at what you shouldn't see, was the same seductive pull that drew Darius back to the crime scene he had masterminded, but as yet was lying undetected.

The 'rubbernecks' on the highway, knew they shouldn't look either, but they couldn't help themselves, just as Darius couldn't help returning to Elizabeth's home. As he breathed in the woody, smoky aroma emanating from a nearby garden, he thought of his mother sat dead ahead of him in the front of the Mercedes, in her stupid fucking polka dot sundress.

"Don't look Darius keep your eyes straight ahead," she said dramatically in Russian.

As they drew closer to the crash scene, the traffic slowed, so that every goddamn sick-o could take a really good look… nice and slow.

More frantically this time, as though she was just about to descend into one of her diabetic hypos, she repeated in her mother tongue: "Don't look Darius, close your eyes this is not good for you to see. Close your eyes sweetie."

Darius smirked as he watched his mother locking her gaze on the crash scene. Without thinking, the drama seeking polka dot hit the electric window to amplify her sensual connection with the crash site – the burning car, the smell of rubber, of petrol, of human flesh.

"поможет нам Бог (God help us)," she said, holding her hand to her mouth, but unable to draw her greedy little Oligarch eyes away. Then she saw it, a split second before Darius.

"О мой Бог (Oh my God)," she whimpered, recoiling and then jutting her head through the open window like some stupid fucking chicken.

As if the dot's pathetic pleading is going to change anything, Darius sneered.

Darius let his eyes roll slowly over the scene, the crumpled car blackened by the fireball that had ripped through the car and blown the roof into the central reservation. Then he stared at the bit that Darius really wanted to see, nobody could help but look at the thing that sat in the driver's seat.

The 24-year-old male was a promising violinist in the Moscow State Symphony Orchestra and was on his way to his wedding. He had discussed a 'surprise diversion' from the order of service with the father of the bride only the day before, as he planned to serenade his fiancé up the aisle on the arm of her adoring father to Bach's 'Air on G String'.

"How cool is-sss that," Darius squealed excitedly as the back of the Mercedes rode slowly past the musician – his father driving a reverential 5mph so those who were brave enough, and sick enough, could take a really good look. Darius stared long and hard at the remains of the 24-year-old violinist and looked at the bit that nobody wanted to see, but couldn't help staring at.... the charcoaled, love-sick pup whose melted form sat upright in the car seat as his blackened, musical hands still gripped the steering wheel.

Now the eighteen-year-old fugitive began scraping around the old rotten window frame that would give him access to the Maloney/Henriksen basement, enabling him to slither back into The Oast, out of sight of his mother's polka dot love nest and any passersby on the green. Slowly, methodically, he scraped (little by little)... he had all the time in the world to kill.

Upstairs in the kitchen, Melanie loaded up her tray with the two containers of the 'Chocolate Crispy Cakes' and walked over to the door that lead to the basement, leaving a couple of the cakes in the fridge for Hannah when she skipped through the door, after her Christmas party, at 4.30pm sharp. She noted the time – 4.28pm – and then looked at the lifeless windows stretching across open farmland behind the oast house – cold, dark and blackened by the long winter night ahead.

Hannah should be home any minute, she thought. *Don't be a second late darling, not a second. Mummy needs you home.*

She thought of the nanny's face and knew her guilt would deliver a resignation letter before the week was over. Melanie opened the door to the basement, balancing the tray on one knee and stretched out into the blackness to feel for the light switch. Having a little girl *and* a baby had turned her into a dexterous juggler.

I still have two children she screamed silently within.

Down in the depths of the house, Darius worked the knife along the side of the window frame, rocking it towards him.

Easy does it.

He silenced the fall of the window towards him with his body, but lost his grip on the knife.

Shit he cursed internally.

The knife disappeared into the darkness and clattered as it hit the floor of the basement, falling behind one of two cabinet freezers.

"Is anybody there?" said Melanie.

Half deranged by the lack of sleep and the constant counting, counting, counting of the hours and days since Elizabeth had been stolen, she cried out once more.

"I said is anybody there?"

She shuffled forward like a bag lady with no particular place to go. Melanie finally found the light switch with her elbow and the light flooded the huge space that ran under her ground floor studio, office and kitchen. The bright white strip lights seemed strangely at odds with the cold damp air that hung in the basement. She stepped gingerly down the stone staircase, careful not to slip. Melanie carried the tray of goodies, the 'Chocolate Crispy

Cakes' that were the marker of lazy, carefree toddler days in the garden, of five birthday parties for Hannah and Elizabeth's first birthday party.

"Give her back you thief," Melanie said, shouting to the nothingness before her. Her right breast dribbled with a little milk and Melanie's heart ached for her baby.

The Queen of Hearts she made some tarts all on a summer's day;
The Knave of Hearts he stole the tarts and took them clean away.
The King of Hearts called for the tarts and beat the Knave full sore
The Knave of Hearts brought back the tarts and vowed he'd steal no more.

Melanie placed the tray on top of one of two cabinet freezers, which were full to overflowing with some of her finest creations. Lifting the lid on the first freezer, she found a space for one container of the crispy cakes by re-arranging the international toddler recipes she had been working on. She closed the freezer lid and then slid the remaining chocolate crackle cakes, from the top of the other freezer. She noticed a superficial scratch on the lid and remembered how pleased Harry was with her bargain purchase, as she skilfully negotiated £100 off the already competitive sale price.

Melanie lifted the lid on the second freezer.

❀ ❀ ❀

Her scream reverberated around the basement, up into the kitchen studio and shot across the lawn to Harry's orthodontic practice. The scream flew upstairs across Elizabeth's empty nursery, Hannah's bedroom, up out of the roof, across the village green and on into the big, wide world, to eternity and back. Then the black curtain dropped across her eyes, like the final curtain at a pantomime. Melanie lost consciousness, seconds before her knees buckled and her head hit the cold, cruel floor. Very slowly Darius eased his face over the high window-ledge. He couldn't resist it. He took one final look, at the thing you shouldn't stare at, inside the freezer cabinet.

CHAPTER FOUR

Saturday 3 December – 4.36pm

"I was walking along a path with two friends – the sun was setting – suddenly the sky turned blood red – I paused, feeling exhausted, and leaned on the fence – there was blood and tongues of fire above the blue-black fjord and the city – my friends walked on, and I stood there trembling with anxiety – and I sensed an infinite scream passing through nature."

Edvard Munch

The Edvard Munch style scream that emerged from Melanie's lungs after the discovery of her baby in the freezer, reached the ears of Darius Sorokin first, given his close proximity to the freezer. It took less than a second for the fearful shriek of the 'kiddie cook' to shoot up the basement stairwell and ricochet around the roundel kitchen, like a wild shot with a pin-ball machine; then a further few seconds to fire across the lawn to smash into the reception area of the practice and ring in the ears of the staff and patients in The Oast Orthodontic Practice.

As Melanie stared at Elizabeth, nestled between her children's soups and purees, Darius was fascinated to watch the scene unfold in slow motion from his prime vantage point at the high window in the basement, like a chemistry experiment in the school lab. He noted the sensory flow of information into Melanie's cortex, data that would transfer to the short-term memory in her brain, even before she fainted. It was clearly information that was causing her an element of distress, evidenced by the ugly and agonised contortions in her face. It was not so very different from the weirdo, zombie masks Darius liked to spook his mother with on Halloween night as a child.

Darius noted in his conclusion, that this was what could be defined as a proper 'Hammer Horror Edvard Munch' scream. It was not dissimilar to the x-rated screams in the movies that filled his bedroom cupboard and swam around the swamp in his head.

Yeh, this was a full on, fuck me kind of scream, that gave him goose bumps, even before he leant over the ledge of the window sill for one final peek at the freak show he'd masterminded and so brilliantly concealed for two weeks.

❀ ❀ ❀

Elizabeth's scream, on the other hand, got under Darius's skin. Like an irritating splinter that won't budge, even with the aid of a pin. Her scream irritated the tits off Darius, all evening, hour after fucking hour. It was a relentless wail, a: "Whah, Whah, Whah, Whah!"

Not even the odd: "Shut the fuck up," or spoonful of paracet-amol syrup lessened the intensity of the "Whah, Whah, fucking Whah". It was only when he picked the writhing blob of flesh up with his gloves on so as not to touch the squirming, squealing slug, that the idea to cool her off once and for all came to him. The "Whah, Whah, Whah" lessened to a whimpering and pitiful: "Merr, Merr, Merr" as he closed the lid on her forever.

❀　❀　❀

The second recipient of the 'Hammer Horror' scream was the receptionist, whose desk was positioned close to the front door of the surgery. It was the first practice that Harry had managed to hold since his daughter's disappearance two weeks earlier, his right arm still heavily bandaged from the accident that had nearly killed him on the fateful night of 'The Art of Food' book launch.

The receptionist had made a full recovery from her bout of flu, unlike the guilt-ridden nanny. Clearly the heavy burden of knowing that Rachel's illness had seen her charges placed in the care of Darius Sorokin, weighed heavily on her immune system, stalling her recuperation. When the scream ran up the reception-ist's spine, the flu-like symptoms briefly flushed through her body again. She sat down quickly, feeling hot and woozy, and put a steadying hand on the desk.

The scream seared across the waiting room, which caused Mrs Jones to spill some coffee on her new, pale lemon skirt and release a dribble of urine, through her weakened pelvic floor.

The urine ran through to the suede sofa and left a small circular stain.

After the scream haunted Mrs Jones in the waiting room, it smacked Harry on the back of the head and then ripped around his skull like a migraine. It slapped the nurse across the cheek and she dropped the saliva ejector. The terrible noise pinned Molly Jones to the dental chair, like a dart hitting a bull's eye. She held her hands to her ears, her mouth dropped in terror and her eyes popped wide open, looking strangely detached from her skull. It was the same agonised look Harry had seen when he'd visited an art museum in Oslo years earlier with his fiancé, to see 'The Scream', by Norwegian artist Edvard Munch.

"It is said to symbolise the human species overwhelmed by an attack of existential angst," Melanie explained to Harry, sounding terribly authoritative. Then she smiled and giggled: "Actually I think it's really creepy."

So they kissed the creepiness away, right in front of the painting in the middle of the Munch Museum in Oslo.

Molly Jones broke out of the painting, left her existential angst in the orthodontic chair, and ran into the arms of her mother.

The blood curdling scream split the atom in Harry's head, as he dropped the dental mirror in his right hand and leapt out of his stool, with the speed of a cowboy fleeing an Apache attack. His dental stool shot across the room like a casualty in a saloon bar brawl. He kicked through the surgery door and bolted past the stunned receptionist. As he sprinted across the lawn Harry cleared the picket fence that divided the practice from the main house, like a seasoned hurdler. Harry tore round to the back door, ran across the kitchen and took the basement flight of steps, two at a time. He leapt down the final five steps in one go, in a move that any John Wayne stunt-double would have been proud of. His chest was heaving and his guns were blazing, ready to shoot the baddie that had caused his wife to scream so fearfully and loudly. But the room was empty. Empty... save for the two large freezer cabinets in the far corner of the room, one with its lid still open, and his wife who lay sprawled on the basement floor, the merciless surface that held her crumpled body with its broken heart.

The chocolate culinary carnage was strewn across the floor. Some of the crispy cakes had landed perfectly, right side up, still in their dainty floral cake cases, whilst others had smashed into pieces.

Snap, crackle, pop!

Harry threw himself across the cold basement floor next to his wife and scooped her floppy head into his lap, checking for a pulse. He cradled her ghostly-white face with his hands, trying to wipe the film of perspiration that ran down her cheeks with the corner of his white coat.

"Shush," he said, like a steam train coming into the buffers at the end of a long journey. He picked her limp body up into his arms and stroked her face, which seemed drugged and lifeless. He rocked her, to and fro, with the comforting rhythm of a hammock swinging on a warm, summer's afternoon.

"Shush," he soothed again, rocking backwards and forwards, as tears of worry and exhaustion trickled down his cheeks.

Rock-a-bye baby on a tree top
When the wind blows the cradle will rock

When the bough breaks the cradle will fall
Down will come baby cradle and all

I love you so much, his heart winced. Melanie looked fragile and childlike in his arms. Her sanity crawled out of her skull momentarily and she murmured incoherently.

"Hey my gorgeous girlie did you fall?" he asked, as she opened her eyes and smiled weakly. "What happened sweetheart, did you hit your head Melanie?"

As Melanie lay in Harry's warm arms and he rocked her worn out, torn out mind, she attempted to recall why she was on the floor. Her mind was fuzzy it was full of fluff – just like her favourite teddy, like Elizabeth's favourite toy. She smiled weakly again.

"Chocolate?" she quizzed hazily, pulling the bear's name back into her head.

Then her eyes refocused on the room.

"Look at all the chocolate cakes Harry, the mess... What happened, why are we here?"

"You must have slipped gorgeous – we heard the most frightful scream in the surgery. Don't worry Melanie as long as you are okay nothing else matters... I'll clear up."

Her eyes crept slowly up the side of the cabinet freezer, which looked strangely out of proportion from her position lying on the floor. She'd taken a bite of the 'Eat me' biscuit and had shrunk down to Hannah's height, like 'Alice in Wonderland'. Her gaze rested at the top of the freezer and she saw that the lid was open. The mental shut down that offered her an oasis, a blank, a brief moment of respite, began to fail. Like a rusty old boiler, the neural paths were firing up, connecting her brain to their final destination – her short-term memory. The memory of what lay inside the freezer. Harry stroked her damp hair, relieved that Melanie hadn't sustained a serious head injury.

She's coming back to me, he thought.

Then he saw the change. The neural paths her brain had previously trodden were found again, like a well-worn path through the woods. Harry saw Melanie's face crumple in on itself, the mask of agony. Then the wild-eyed look of terror, as her pupils bore straight up into the back of Harry's skull.

"Oh my God Melanie, what is it? What's happened?"

"Lilybet," she screamed. "It's our princess Li-ly-bet."

Her agony was his agony and the tears flowed freely now down his cheeks.

"It's okay baby, they're going to find her. It's okay," he sobbed, as he rocked his wife more in desperation than comfort.

But Melanie simply shook her head from side to side, with the mumblings of a drunken tramp. Her eyes crept back up the side of the freezer, which appeared to her more mausoleum-like now. She pleaded with the shiny white box, that she'd got for a knockdown price.

"No, no, no, no, don't take her, don't take princess Lilybet…"

Melanie stared back at Harry, with a look of horror that chilled him to the bone. She nodded towards the freezer, directing him to look inside. Harry gently placed Melanie's head on his white coat, as she covered her broken face with both hands, and whimpered their daughter's name.

Harry shook like a drug addict, out of control and full of fear.

He pushed himself to his feet, his limbs heavy, weighed down and shaking. He grabbed the edge of the cabinet with his right hand and slowly pulled himself up. As his eyes drew level with the freezer he saw Elizabeth's foot first, her beautiful little toes, curled and pudgy, frozen, in a final kick for freedom.

Forcing himself on up, he pushed to standing, shaking 'cold turkey' now. His eyes hovered over Elizabeth's frozen face, which had turned a ghostly bluish-white. But he couldn't bare the aberration and fell to his knees. A violent jerk pulled at his guts and he threw up. The heaving and retching was drowned out by Melanie, who screamed and lashed from side to side. Harry closed his eyes. He didn't want to see anything, ever again. But the image of Elizabeth Abigail Maloney, with her bright, blue eyes and her beautiful face, frozen in a desperate, eternal plea for mercy, was seared into his memory... forever and ever.

CHAPTER FIVE

Saturday 3 December – 4.38pm

"Let's be on the winning side," Dr Maloney had often said to his 'most challenging orthodontic case' before he ran down to the basement and dumped his baby in the freezer.

Now Darius was happy to take the coach's advice and 'go for gold'. But the stakes were higher – the other competitors were catching up. The police, the villagers and the search parties were all closing the net, slowly but surely, drawing nearer and nearer. As Harry raced to rescue Melanie from the baddie in the basement, the baddie slid away from the window-ledge. It was time to begin his sprint to the finishing line, to the safety of his mother's Georgian house, away from Melanie's crowd pleasing scream.

The auditorium was buzzing with the gossip of hundreds of villagers. Everyone was on the lookout and on edge: the dog walkers, the car drivers and the local newspaper reporter Douglas MacIntyre. Even the reluctant child spectators couldn't help staring, but later wished they'd gone home to eat their tea that night.

Darius's racetrack home was to be the 500 metre long village green with its perfectly mown cricket pitch, which ran between The Oast Orthodontic Practice and his mother's polka dot love nest. Despite the raised stakes, Darius was odds-on favourite that night. The tooth man wearing the cowboy hat had already run his pointless Wild West race to the dead-end basement and the end of the line, whilst the athletic, young Russian was poised to run the race of his life, stealth-like and calculating.

He placed his feet in the starter blocks, waiting to run like a leopard. He crept forward, barely moving whilst he sensed everything around him: the exposed areas, the useful patches of cover, the oak trees and the strategically positioned hedge running down one side of the green. He crouched forward, making himself difficult to observe or detect in the dim moonlight. He prepared to penetrate the sophisticated defence shields, to wreak havoc and mayhem from a distance, to fly under the wire silent and unseen.

Ready, steady, go.

Darius set out with a low, fast run. The sneaking, creeping quality enabled him to fly past the nanny and Hannah unnoticed behind the boundary hedge and picket fence, as they walked up the garden path, at 4.38pm. The eight minute delay at the school Christmas party had mercifully spared Hannah the distress of hearing her mother's scream. They were eight minutes later than the "4.30pm sharp" promised by Rachel to her gaunt and jumpy employer, who now lay on the basement floor in pieces. Darius watched Hannah's little legs trying to keep up with the long strides of the nanny, who was planning the wording of her resignation letter, as she hurried up the path to the house of doom, coughing and spluttering from the flu that still clung to her guilt-ridden body.

A stream of cars drove up the road running parallel with the green. A police car at the back of the line of cars slowed the traffic to the official speed limit. Darius flung himself against the trunk of an oak tree, secreting himself into the bark, whilst the cars cruised past at thirty miles per hour. Everyone looked in their rear-view mirrors to track the tailing police car, but nobody thought to take a second look at the shadows on the green.

Darius spotted a dog walker carrying a torch. He leapt behind the long, low hedge and crawled on his belly to avoid detection. The dog back-tracked, then picked up Darius's foul scent behind the hedging. The yappy little terrier was insistent. Barking and digging – willing his master to come and meet the creepy babysitter that everyone was looking for. But with daylight gone and the cold seeping through the dog walker's arthritic hands, he turned to put the terrier back on the lead. The old man drew within a few feet of Darius, as the dog whimpered suddenly and hobbled back to the safety of his master.

"Hey there little fellow, did you pick up a thorn?"

The owner carried the lame terrier home and spent an hour removing the sharp object that had lodged itself in his paw.

Darius was off again and was on the home straight now, as he reached speeds of over ten miles per hour. His breathtaking pace was in total contrast to the young boy nervously trotting across the green to fetch his ball. Zack's mother warned her son about playing with his football in the garden after dark, but an ambitious kick over his garden wall, beckoned the young lad out from the safety of his garden like 'Peter and the Wolf'.

He scampered across the village green to fetch what looked like the promise of his ball, which was barely visible in the pale moonlight. Sadly for Zack, the laws of momentum made a collision utterly inevitable with the babysitter on the run. The high speed thump of human flesh saw the little boy carried for several yards before he was taken down and pinned under Darius's hot, smelly body. It was a rugby tackle any pro would have been proud of. The boy, who had overheard his mother talking about the babysitter and the missing baby to a friend, let out a terrified, strangulated: "'elp."

Darius slapped his grubby hand over the kid's mouth "Shush."

The gentleness of the sound was in stark contrast to the dirty, sweaty hand being held over Zack's mouth. The boy's eyes darted nervously around Darius's head as he searched in vain for his rescue party.

"Come in now Zack it's getting dark. How can you see that ball anyway? Come on in, it's so cold," his mother insisted only ten minutes previously.

As Zack looked up into the clammy, panting face of the man lying on top of him, he longed for his mother to come and look for him now. How he yearned to be at home, curled up by the fire and eating some buttered toast.

"Are you a good boy?" Darius asked the child.

"Emmm," Zack gasped, frantically nodding up and down under the gagging hand, desperate to demonstrate his allegiance to the scary man who looked a lot like Darius Sorokin.

"Well then…sss-say nothing. Do you under-sss-tand," and the long, slow 's' slithered out of his mouth like a snake sliding down the boy's shivering body.

"DO-YOU-under-sss-tand?" Darius repeated, jerking his hand up and down across the child's lips as he spoke.

Zack's eyes communicated that he had understood perfectly the need for absolute discretion. (Indeed, he took his promise of silence so seriously, that after three months of almost no verbal communication, his mother took him to see a speech therapist. After this bore little fruit, he was referred on to a child psychologist.)

Darius picked the boy up and brushed him down.

"Hey look mate," he said brightly, trying to emulate the speech patterns of 'the locals'. "There'sss your ball."

Darius passed the ball to his new chum on the green. In Zack's hour of need, the round inanimate object proved a surprising comfort, as he clung to the football like a hot-water bottle. The babysitter flicked his head towards the boy's house, indicating that he was free to leave. Zack turned and tried to hurry back towards the safety of his house, but he trod through the treacle nightmare that clings to each foot, preventing a rapid getaway.

"Hey you," Darius said, whispering into the still night air, as the child turned back to look at his neighbour. "If you sss-say anything, and I mean a word, you know what will happen don't you?"

Zack froze, waiting for the judge's sentence and Darius ran his finger slowly across his throat. In an instant the athlete had vanished, as Darius made the final dash to the finishing line, the high red brick wall encircling his mother's Georgian doll's house. He climbed and rolled over the top of the wall, then dropped down silently on the other side.

Home sss-sweet home.

He glanced up, his mother's bedroom and bathroom lights were on. *Good,* he thought, and his mean, thin lip curled in the corner at the thought of his mother lavishing some sympathy on her only son.

A police car and ambulance sped up Cranhurst high street passing Douglas MacIntyre's office, as he typed up details of the apparent two-week stalemate in the missing baby case.

Things are hotting up again he thought, as he watched the emergency entourage rip through the tranquillity of the rural high street. The seasoned hack followed his nose and his hunch and jumped in his car to arrive moments behind the emergency services and ahead of the media scrum that would join him again over the next 24 hours.

The emergency services emitted a surprisingly merry dance of red and blue lights across the green, but the light display failed to lift the sense of foreboding in the village, as net curtains fluttered at the front of numerous properties in the vicinity. All at once the doors flew open on the entourage of vehicles as the police and paramedics disembarked and ran towards The Oast... but there was no need to hurry... a slow, mournful procession would have sufficed, as their expertise in resuscitation were now tragically redundant.

CHAPTER SIX

Saturday 3 December – 4.57pm

Darius slid round to the back of his mother's house and tried the kitchen door.

Locked, fuck it

He worked his knife below one of the large, wooden sash windows that led into the kitchen, but his attempts at a break-in was taking longer than the intruder wanted and he started to stab impatiently at the wood. A next door neighbour's door opened and closed.

Shit, he cursed silently.

A manicured poodle was let out for her routine early evening constitution and illegal fouling all over the village green. The dog's doting and besotted elderly mistress, Miss Potts, failed to follow her little ball of fuzz around the communal green each night with her 'poop scoop', much to the annoyance of the cricket team in the summer. The poodle had five minutes to foul the green each night and the time was carefully monitored from an old, but reliable 1940s lime green Bakelite clock on the lady's mantle-piece.

The dog picked up the strange scent of the sweaty boy and heard the hacking sound of the knife on wood. Unlike the terrier that Darius had encountered only a moment earlier on the green, the little, white poodle was alone, without the protection of her owner. Blanche trotted round to the back garden of the Georgian mansion and pushed her pert nose through the wrought-iron gate, she let out a single "Yap" to alert the stranger of her presence.

Darius responded with an equally yappy: "Shut it!"

Finally, the sash window loosened. He slid it up and lifted one leg up onto the window-ledge. But like a dog with a juicy bone, the poodle had latched onto the intruder who reeked of malice, and now it wouldn't let it go.

She barked again. A high-pitched, "Yap, yap, yap," building to a, "RA, RA, RA, RA, RA!"

"I sss-said shut it," Darius said menacingly.

But the relentless, "RA, RA, RA!" continued, like the incessant screaming of baby Elizabeth.

Cry Baby Bunting
Daddy's gone a-hunting
Gone to fetch a rabbit skin
To wrap the Baby Bunting in
Cry Baby Bunting

A light went on in Miss Potts's porch and the old lady opened her front door.

"Blanche dinnertime, come to Mummy," Miss Potts said, cooing into the cold night air.

But the poodle didn't hear her mistress's call, as she clenched the wrought-iron bars and tried to shake the gate with her tiny jaws.

"RA, RA, RA. RA, RA, RA!"

Darius restored the peace quickly and efficiently and slipped into his mother's kitchen through the window. The feral boy grabbed a fork from the drawer and flung the fridge open, stabbing at the food and stuffing it into his mouth. Darius worked his way through a bowl of leftover Bœuf Stroganoff and then grabbed two Blini pancakes, lathered them in caviar, and shoved them in quick succession into his mouth. Darius ditched his fork and tipped a bowl of Rassolnik down his throat. He drained the soup into his hungry, hollow belly, but didn't allow time for the chunks of potatoes and pickled vegetables to work their way through his oesophagus, as it clogged up at the back of his throat like a blocked drain, gurgling and spewing down the sides of his mouth and running onto his neck and filthy clothes. Once his belly was satisfied, he went in search of his mother.

Darius crept to the small cupboard under the grand sweeping Georgian staircase and lifted the powerful torch off the wall hook. Then he tripped the lights and the house was plunged into darkness. Upstairs, Natasha had just drained her second glass of wine and poured another as she sank back down into her watery oasis big enough for two. The pining for her son would soon be over. As he climbed the stairs, he heard his mother let out an overly-dramatic but unconvincing "'elp, zumbudy 'elp me" followed by the sound of a glass smashing on the floor. He stood behind the bathroom door and sneered as his mother scrabbled around helplessly trying to find her dotty bathrobe in the darkened room, whilst avoiding the splinters of glass.

❀ ❀ ❀

Watching his mother strip naked had become something of a habit for Darius, for whilst his teenage friends collected stamps, rocks and football memorabilia, Darius became a neutral observer of his mother's sex life. One night in his early teens, he awoke from his first 'wet dream' to the intermittent sounds of primeval grunting and hysterical screaming punctuating the night air. Darius sauntered down the landing and decided to find the source of the hullabaloo. He opened his mother's bedroom door to no more than a crack and peered in to see Natasha's energetic 'live performance' on top of an elderly gentleman. A few nights later he meandered down the passageway again and pushed the door wide open this time. He saw a giant walrus of a man huffing and puffing all over the dot, as she disappeared under his layers of fat.

"Sweetie, did my son come into ze bedroom last night?" Natasha enquired casually the next morning.

She scraped her overly bleached hair into a high bun, rather too fiercely to ever possess natural class and too harshly to pass as her longed for 'English country lady' status.

"Might have," Darius snarled.

"It's not good for Darius to see doze tings," she said, as if addressing a detached third-party sat in an adjoining waiting room, waiting to be loved.

The third time Darius came to watch his mother, she had forgotten to close the door. Darius didn't creep this time. He simply stood at the door in the shadows to watch the tall, bony man grinding and pushing into his mother. After the scrawny man finished crunching on top of the dot, he flopped on top of her like an empty tube of toothpaste. Light snoring followed almost immediately, as the man's angular hip bones pinned his mother down to the bed. Natasha looked over and saw her son standing by the door. She waved the back of her free hand at him as if she was trying to shoo away a fly.

"Go away sweetie. It's not good for a boyz eyez. Darius needs to go back to bed to sleep."

The next morning the polka dot sought counsel with her son again.

"What's a poor Russian girl to do Darius? It's zo lonely for a city girl like me in a place like this," twirling his hair once more.

After that, there seemed to be an 'open door' policy into his mother's room. So Darius pulled up a ringside seat night after night to watch his mother from the shadows, performing her tricks with the circus ponies. Riding and bouncing on top of a seemingly endless line of men queuing up at her door. The audience of one sat in the corner unmoved by the performance and he always left the show without applauding.

The first time Darius joined the queue of men eager to warm Natasha Sorokin's bed, the mother of one could have been forgiven for her confusion. The light was dim in her bedroom and she was groggy from the red wine and her deep state of REM sleep. The hand that slipped around the dot's waist, between her frilly, dotty underwear, could have easily been mistaken for a grown man's touch, rather than the hand of a 16-year-old boy. There was every reason under the sun why her son's hand could have been confused for the hand of Nigel, James, Charles or any other Tom, Dick or Harry for that matter. But when she rolled over and saw his mean, pointy face, the cold eyes and the sneering smile – and when she let his hand slide down – time and time again – the silent pact of collusion was signed between them.

❀ ❀ ❀

Now Darius waited patiently behind the bathroom door waiting to give the whore who liked to be screwed by her own son the surprise of her life.

"Hallo, hallo, iz anybody der?" the star of her very own one-woman, B-movie droned, as she scrabbled around naked, still trying to avoid the broken glass and feeling for her bath gown in the darkened room. Her theatrical movements, the ostentatious and garish props around the bathroom, the syringes and discarded insulin vials, all added to the low-grade drama that gave away the clues to her sleazy origins.

"Darius…is that you Darius," she whispered into the darkness, her throat strangled by the fear of the dark and what lay in it.

Darius flicked the torch on under his chin, freaky style.

"BOO!"

Natasha let out a hysterical laugh – her relief was palpable.

"Oh my God, it's my sweetie boy. I thought you were an intwuder coming to kill me. Where did all your hair go? I can't believe it's you."

She flung her arms around him still dripping wet and naked.

Darius's arms remained at his side after the two week separation.

"What's happened to de lights?" she asked, returning to her more vulnerable B-movie star status.

"Didn't want the poli-ccc-e to sss-see me," he said morosely.

But Natasha chose not to ask him *why* the police wanted to see him. Even after two weeks without her son, the long police interviews and the intense house search she had had to endure; Natasha held back from asking Darius a single probing question.

"What has happened Darius? Where did you go? Was it you who stole the family car? Where's Elizabeth? Have you killed Elizabeth Maloney? What have you done with Harry and Melanie's baby?"

No, the questions were never asked. The 'I-won't-say-anything-if-you-don't' playground pact was still firmly in place. Natasha looked deep into Darius's eyes and her 'sweetie boy' returned her gaze, the collusion joined them like an umbilical cord. The most searching question Natasha wanted to ask her son was, "What have you done to de lights Darius?"

As he shone the torch on her naked body, he wanted to remind the dumb-fuck dot what she'd let her 'sweetie boy' do to her over and over again.

"You look filthy," Natasha said, as his torch picked up flashes of the food stains down his neck and the patches of mud and grass all over his body.

"You *are* filthy," said Darius as he licked her lips.

"Here come and have a bath," she invited, "let me scrub ze dirt away."

The dot climbed into the bath with her son and rubbed

soap all over Darius's body, paying special attention to the area between his legs, just as her father had taught her to do as a child. Natasha climbed out of the sullied waters and switched back fleetingly into her maternal role as she wrapped Darius in a towel and rubbed oil onto his shaved head.

"I need money," Darius said. "Two thou-sss-and pounds-sss should be enough."

Still there were no questions. Natasha took the torch to the safe. Like an obedient bank clerk, she keyed in the code and counted out two thousand pounds in twenty pound notes. He slapped his hand on top of hers.

"Better make it three thou-sss-and for the trouble I've gone to, to come back and sss-see you," and his lip curled up in an ironic leer.

Just then there was a knock at the front door. Natasha froze for a moment phased by the unusual sound of someone 'dropping by'. Darius assumed it must be the police. Then a second knock followed, louder this time and more insistent.

"An-sss-wer it," Darius ordered. "Act dumb Mum-sssie, act really sss-stupid."

He slid behind a curtain in the hall. Natasha opened the front door and shone the torch into the darkness. She couldn't see anyone and was just about to close the door when an old lady, no taller than five foot stepped out of the shadows.

"Hello dear," said the lady, who had to strain her neck to look up at Natasha in her heels and bathrobe.

"Hello dearz," Natasha reciprocated, trying to sound like a local.

"Have you seen my poodle?" asked the stranger at the door. "She's white. Blanche is her name. That's French for white you know. My sister liked the name, but she died ten years ago from cancer of the pancreas. God rest her soul. So I'm all alone you see, apart from Blanche. She's my best friend she's all I've got. I'm awfully worried because she didn't come home after her late night constitution around the green. It's so unusual, she's never done anything like this before, it's totally out of character and I didn't know who to turn to."

Hardly stopping to draw breath the petite old woman continued, "I'm so sorry to bother you dear, with all the worry of your son and that sweet little baby going missing. But I need to get *my* baby back Mrs Sorokin… you see she's my only friend in the whole world…and… I – I don't know if I could cope without her."

And then Miss Potts began to sob extraordinarily loudly for such a small framed woman.

"I'm zo zorry. How I would lerve to 'elp you but I haven't seen *any-zing*," Natasha said dramatically, over emphasising the final word.

Miss Potts began to dab her tears away with a neatly embroidered hankie and it was only then that she noticed there were no lights on in the house, except for the torch that Mrs Sorokin held in her hand.

"What happened to your lights?"

Act dumb you dumb-fuck Darius snarled silently.

"Oh I think a fuse must have blown. You know how theze old houzes are. Sorry I didn't hearz your name?"

"Miss Potts," she said laughing at her own name. "Now let me help you sort out your lights," she said bustling past Natasha, before she had time to refuse her offer of help.

Stop the old bitch Darius's brain screamed impotently.

"Where's the fuse box?" she enquired hobbling into the darkness. "I used to be in the land army in the war, it's amazing what we learnt. All of us girls were qualified electricians, car mechanics and farmers by the end of the war, when our men came back to rescue us," she laughed, trying to conceal six decades of grief.

She paused…"Oh course I didn't get rescued my dear, because Bertie never came home and men were in short supply. Oh I broke my heart… but my sister was the most wonderful companion. She was a spinster too, we were two Potts together!" Miss Potts twittered with laughter again as she walked further into the darkness.

"Now where *is* this fuse box of yours dear? It's usually under the stairs, or in a cupboard in the kitchen. Let's try under here first. Shine your torch dear, this way if you please."

Like an experienced electrician, Miss Potts located the panel on the wall with the aid of the torch light and opened the flap.

"How lucky are we? Looks like a simple surge that's flipped your trip switch," she said, as the electricity burst into the stunning 19th century Russian chandelier in the stone hallway.

"Voila… that's French for 'lo and behold' did you know? Bertie taught me the odd word, here and there. You know, in his letters home. Ah well, c'est la vie. Oh there I go again," she said, laughing louder than before.

"Anyway dear, if you do see or hear anything of my poodle, please pop round. I'll have to report Blanche missing to the police in the morning if she doesn't come home. Oh I do hope nothing untoward has happened to her."

Blanche's mistress pottered slowly towards the door, rolling from side to side on loose hips that had yet to reach the top of the NHS's hip replacement queue. Natasha walked alongside her as both their shoes echoed on the beautiful, but hard stone floor. Miss Potts was just two yards from the front door. Two yards from the freedom line, where she could return to her familiar daily routine with the hope that Blanche would soon be back by her side, rather than lying dead with her throat slit in the Sorokin's garden.

The light revealed the Georgian splendour of the house, the exquisite cornicing, the elegant balustrade that curved around the 18th century staircase, and the mural that ran across the ceiling above the chandelier. But the light also exposed Darius's shoes behind the curtains. The drapes were a good three inches short of the floor, due to an inexperienced girl measuring up from the local curtain company. Natasha spotted the clue to her son's whereabouts first and attempted a diversion with an unconvincing cough, from her B-movie performance.

However, the old lady was remarkably spritely for someone in her eighties and Miss Potts noticed the shoes too. She saw the outline of a man standing behind the curtains. Then she saw the man with the sneer emerge from the curtain. She saw Mrs Sorokin clearly wanted to say something to the man who looked a lot like Darius, but she saw that her neighbour kept quiet. Then she saw Mrs Sorokin running up the stairs crying, holding her mouth shut with her hand, as if she *still* wanted to say something else.

Miss Potts heard the man say he had seen her poodle in the back garden. She felt his guiding hand on the small of her back pushing her towards the back door, as her wobbly arthritic hips, creaked in their joints. But the hand pushed a little too hard, so that Miss Potts found herself trotting quickly towards the back door, as her heart beat faster and her mouth filled with the dryness that panic brings. Last of all she saw the man open the back door. Still wanting to believe in a happy ending, she looked forward to being re-united with her beloved poodle, but butterflies fluttered in the pit of her stomach and a fearful darkness swallowed her up.

Chapter Seven

Saturday 3 December – 6.05pm

It was time to flee. Natasha Sorokin, the mistress of self-preservation knew it was time to vanish from the crime scene, before the police paid her another visit. Natasha decided against waving goodbye to her son in the back garden, even though she instinctively knew she wouldn't see him for a very long time. Instead, she waited in her room, whilst her 'sweetie boy' saw Miss Potts and the poodle off the premises. She heard her son exit the garden with his new travelling companions, the sound of *bump-bump-bump* and then she heard nothing.

When everything fell quieter than the grave, save for the intermittent hooting of an owl in the distance, Natasha sprang into action – the gymnast in her still buried deep in her muscle memory. She ran downstairs and emptied the safe of £20,000 cash, credit cards, jewellery and her passports – genuine and forged.

Then she brewed a strong black coffee for all night sustenance and began the meticulous planning of an 'extended holiday' back home. Natasha called Aeroflot (Аэрофлот) and booked a one-way ticket to Moscow departing early the following morning using her pseudonym Natasha Yashin and a decoy flight to Grenada on the same day under her real name Natasha Sorokin.

Natasha clumsily negotiated a pair of the cleaner's gloves onto her fingers as she planned to erase any sign of her son's last visit to the house. The alien transaction of pulling on the rubber gloves was achieved with the same awkwardness she had had as a young gymnast when she was coerced into fitting a condom onto her coach's cock for the first time.

The part-time cleaner and former gymnast bleached every door handle, from the ground floor to the attic and then worked her way around each window-ledge and lever. Next she vacuumed the house from top to bottom, wiped all the internal surfaces and continued with a mop and bucket, cleaning the expansive tiled and wooden floors. Finally she gave the bathroom a forensic clean and threw Darius's muddied clothes into a refuse sack, together with her polka dot bathing robe.

Natasha flung open her designer set of suitcases, all of which carried her signature garish polka dot design and threw in her favourite outfits, the inappropriate plunging tops and skimpy skirts, the drawer full of nightwear. Then she opened a smaller case and filled it with underwear and her extravagant accessories, the boas, the polka dot scarves and chiffons, adding in a month's supply of insulin and syringes.

She scribbled a note to her odd-job boy and dated the letter Friday 2 December – 24 hours before Darius had run back home to visit her and 24 hours before Miss Potts had fatefully knocked at the front door.

The sentimentalist in Natasha reached for all her most treasured memories of her early life as a gymnast, the photographs, newspaper cuttings, the programmes, medals and certificates. For it was Natasha's outstanding natural ability as a gymnast that looked set to be the poor little Russian girl's 'golden ticket' out of the two bedroom flat she shared with her four siblings and widowed father, in the grim, grey suburbs sprawling outside Moscow's fairytale onion domes in Red Square. The close proximity of so much human flesh in crowded beds thrust the young prepubescent Natasha unnaturally close to her lonely, grieving father who turned to his 12-year-old daughter to supply the comfort and solace that his wife had once so willingly given him.

Natasha longed to pirouette and back flip in the impish footsteps of the gifted gymnast Olga Korbut and then planned to defect to the material comfort of the West, away from the molestations of her father. The young girl was first plucked from obscurity from a run-down playground outside Moscow, when a talent scout for the USSR gymnastics team spotted her outstanding natural agility and flexibility, combined with a complete lack of fear. By the age of 13, Natasha was already hooked on the adrenalin rush of competing. She lapped up the 'ooos' and 'ahs' of an appreciative crowd as she began winning national competitions with her trademark half-in, half-out double Salto, combining a half twist on each Salto. The crowds were transfixed by her nimble athleticism, the bend and flex of her taut muscular body and her ability to integrate mischievous dance moves into her routines, as Olga Korbut had done before her.

It took Natasha longer to appreciate the 'special attention' lavished on her by her coach when she reached puberty at the age of 13, shortly after becoming the bed-fellow of her father. In time the attention of both men became so normal that her moral compass became little more than a twisted helter-skelter of right and wrong, where boundaries were blurred and rubbed out leaving her free to please any man or boy, and any son or stranger by the time she reached adulthood.

Finally her exceptional early promise as a gymnast was cruelly snatched from her and the USSR's medal tally in 1978 when she reached her fourteenth birthday. First she developed Type 1 diabetes which she controlled with regular insulin shots, but then her hormones kicked in and she shot up to 5ft 11", dwarfing many of the other pre-pubescent and stunted gymnasts that surrounded her.

Natasha headed to the back door just after midnight, her suitcases in her hands, and then paused to look at another gallery of framed photographs charting her rise as a glamour model and pole dancer in the early eighties after her failed career as a gymnast. She walked to the other side of the room to survey a small selection of pictures of her son and plucked a single picture of her 'sweetie boy' aged about eight years old, smiling in the back garden with the gardener. It was a moment when Darius still had the potential of growing into a good looking man and when there was still the promise of a good life, before his teenage obsession with fencing began.

Natasha's son had clearly benefited from his mother's athletic gene pool but rejected his mother's path of gymnastics. Instead the young teenager was instantly drawn to the sport of fencing, captivated by the discipline of sabre, with its cutting and thrusting weapon. Darius rose rapidly through the Cadet rankings performing well at the British Youth Championships and winning the boy's sabre category by the time he was 15. The detached deviant devoted all his spare time at school to training sessions with his Eton coach, but it was the summer training camps in Budapest where Darius was to experience the greatest thrill of his fanatical flirtation with fencing.

The flaming redhead with her ivory complexion, when compared with the peroxide plasticity of his mother, immediately turned Darius's head and stiffened his penis, as he wanked in the toilets by day and under the sheets by night. The girl's outstanding ability in sabre left Darius entranced during the camp, as he obsessively watched her sparring with her female partner. He gradually wormed his way closer to her side during the physical conditioning training and footwork sessions. An inviting, warm smile from the English beauty on a boat trip to Lake Balaton would prove the fatal opening cut in the one-sided holiday romance, as the girl was tagged and followed by Darius during the weekend excursions to the Danube, Szentendre and the spas in Budapest.

The randy teenager began suggesting they train together and, lacking the confidence or maturity to resist, the red-haired beauty laughed nervously, but never actually gave her consent. After that the girl found herself followed everywhere she went during the summer camp, unable to shake the boy off, like a dog owner with a needy puppy. The final corps-à-corps came when the girl went for an early morning run through the woods with the lusty, love-sick pup panting behind – following her into the dark shadows. She stopped to catch her breath and Darius moved towards the girl as she backed up cornered by a tree behind her.

"Can I kiss-sss you," the snake hissed, sneering in his peculiar lop-sided way.

She giggled nervously too shy to say "no", yet not wanting her first kiss to be with the loner who wouldn't leave her alone. But her nervous giggle sealed her fate. He slammed her against the tree and filled her mouth with his slimy tongue, as his braces clattered and crashed against her teeth. The girl was certain this was not how her first kiss was supposed to be, nor was it the one she had watched at the cinema. And as he ripped down her jogging pants and thrust himself upon her, she tried to scream but was prevented from doing so by the snake writhing around in her mouth.

Natasha prepared to flee the broken nest she had feathered with her son. She loaded her sports car hidden from view inside the garage, placing the luggage in the boot and a bag of Darius's clothes on the passenger seat, to be disposed of discreetly on the way to the airport. Then she went to a secret flap in the floor and retrieved a pair of false number plates, noting that the other set had already been taken by her son on the first night of Darius and Elizabeth's disappearance.

After fitting the plates, she slid into the car, turned the key in the ignition, but kept the lights turned off. Natasha drove down a farm path and crawled out of the village in second gear, in the opposite direction from The Oast, away from the parked police cars and the two officers standing guard outside the Maloney/Henriksen property. She looked in her rear-view mirror and caught a last glimpse of the Georgian doll's house that had been home for the past decade and casually blew it a farewell kiss.

She let her mind drift over the memories of the cook who'd filled their larder, Luke the odd-job boy who'd filled her bed and Mr Morris the gardener who'd filled her garden with fresh produce and the promise of a fresh start for her son. Then she mulled over the Toms, Dicks and Harrys that had kept her warm at night. Last of all, Natasha thought of her son recalling how she'd nearly ended Darius's life in a back street abortion clinic in Moscow eighteen years earlier. As she sped away from the village and flicked her lights on, Natasha Sorokin wondered if she'd made a terrible mistake letting her only son be spared from the abortionist's knife.

2005

Chapter Eight

Saturday 3 December – 6.05pm

The darkness of the night and the twisted collusion between mother and son, provided all the cover Darius needed to slip away again unseen from the dot's house. Having reunited Miss Potts with her precious canine companion, Darius propped the old woman and her dog against the wall in the garden, like the 'Penny for the Guy' figures that used to sit motionless on every street corner on the fifth of November.

Darius grabbed a rucksack from the cloakroom and shoved some food into the bag together with the money from his mother and a scrapbook charting his 'first love' with the red-headed fencer. Next he turned his attention to his travelling companions and loaded them into a wheelbarrow. Miss Potts, with her tiny five foot nothing form fitted perfectly into the novel form of transport, with room to spare for her beloved Blanche alongside her. Darius pulled out an emergency blanket from the rucksack and tucked his fellow travellers in – warm and snug and hidden from view. He began his second run of the night, this time in the opposite direction from the village green, across the fields at the back of the house. Darius flicked on the torch again, opened the back gate and stretched out his arms straight and rigid and ran fast and low like a fighter plane skimming the earth.

After opening and manoeuvring the wheelbarrow through a five-bar gate Darius veered from his familiar path to his childhood den in the woods and instead took a right across a ploughed field. The wheelbarrow bumped rhythmically across the furrowed ridges carved into the thick, clay soil. Miss Potts's arm fell over the edge of the wheelbarrow and banged in time to the rhythm of the grooves in the land, banging the drum of encouragement, as Darius ran his second race of the night, away from Elizabeth's frozen grave and away from the dot's house.

The terrain became even rougher and on several occasions the front wheel was momentarily grounded by a large mound of soil and the wheelbarrow reared up like a stallion shying from a busy road. Miss Potts slid down the barrow and an arthritic leg joined the arm in the rhythmic percussion ensemble. Eventually Darius reached his final destination, a small lake. He skimmed the water with the powerful torch, picking up a host of shimmering shadows and a line of weeping willow trees that shed tears over the water, for what they were about to receive.

The lake with a tiny manmade island in the middle was one of Darius's favourite childhood playgrounds – a place to hang out and disappear after the death of his only childhood friend, Mr Morris the gardener. At the age of 12 Darius bought a small, wooden rowing boat with his mushrooming weekly allowance, and had the local farmer deliver it to the lake on the back of his tractor, without the dot ever knowing of the boat's existence.

Darius transferred his companions from the wheelbarrow to the rowing boat and tucked Miss Potts and Blanche's bodies under the warm and comforting fleece. Scanning the area with his torch for a couple of small boulders, Darius dragged them one by one to the water's edge. He created a complicated masthead knot around each boulder with the rope and then attached one rock to Miss Potts and one to the hind leg of Blanche, like matching accessories. He stepped back out of the boat, untied the rope that ran around a willow on the bank and rested for a moment wiping away a single, salty drop of sweat that ran down his right temple.

"Time to sss-set sss-sail," he said to his companions as he prepared to step into the boat.

SNAP.

Darius flung himself onto the bank – a soggy, cold mix of decomposed leaves and watery grassland. The 'snap' was unmistakable – it was the snap of a foot on a branch. He turned the torch off and froze for a moment, straining to hear for any more footsteps. Darius scrambled along the ground on his belly, shuffling fast and furious and then rolled behind a bush.

SNAP. Snap, snap, SNAP.

The footsteps were getting closer and Darius felt his cold heart beat against the icy, dank earth. There was a pause and then again the same sound.

SNAP. Snap, snap, SNAP.

Just then a deer emerged from the trees, heading towards the lake to drink.

Shit he cursed silently as he dropped his head down onto his hands and laughed ironically. The alien sound of laughter startled the deer and the animal immediately fled back to the security of the trees. Darius pushed himself to standing and flicked his torch on again and hurried back to the boat.

But Miss Potts and her poodle had decided to go on a boat ride and the vessel had drifted across the water.

No you devils come back, Darius yelled inside his head.

He tried grabbing branches and stretching them out across the water like a giant claw. The boat was tantalisingly close – just as the oasis is to the hallucinating traveller lost in the desert. In his frustration he hurled the branch at the boat, which wobbled for a moment. The branch momentarily dipped under the water and then bobbed up to the surface again. Darius stood motionless, watching the boat drifting further away still. He slapped the side of his head, in an effort to force an idea to the surface.

Think you bastard, think.

Just then he remembered the extra rope still in the rucksack. He hurried to the bag and pulled it out. His bony fingers worked quickly and methodically, to create a hangman's knot. He whirled the knotted rope above his head and hurled it out into the beam of light. It slapped down across the water, just short of the boat.

Damn his brain cursed and he pulled the wet rope out of the water, feeding it back through his hands.

He prepared the rope again and this time took several paces back. He lunged forward following his throwing action through with his full body, re-enacting the Russian shot-putters he'd watched in the Athens Olympics.

"Yes-sss," he said, hissing quietly, as the rope was caught by one of the ribbed rowlock horns. He pulled gently and the hangman's knot seemed to drop perfectly around its intended target. Darius gave it one more firm tug for good measure. He began pulling, threading the rope rhythmically through his hands, one-two, one-two. Little by little, the boat began to edge back towards the bank. But the boulders had almost doubled the weight of the boat's cargo and the rusty rowlock horn began to come loose from the rotting wooden base of the vessel, which had sat in the water for six consecutive winters. With just three metres to go, Darius suddenly lunged backwards onto his back, as the horn flew free of the decayed wood. The boat rocked mockingly jigging from side to side like the vintage laughing policeman he had seen on a seaside pier – it was tantalisingly close, but just out of reach.

Fuck it his mind screamed as he kicked the earth in frustration. He shone the torch across the water and calculated that with a short run up he could leap into the vessel. Darius placed the torch strategically on a rock, so that its powerful beam shone right across the water to the little island in the middle.

"One-two-three," he whispered as he reversed, taking three large steps backwards for the run up.

One, two, three, four, five
Once I caught a fish alive
Six, seven, eight, nine, ten
Then I let it go again
Why did you let it go?
Because it bit my finger so

Which finger did it bite?

This little finger on my right

Darius took three giant strides and then threw himself out across the edge of the lake in the direction of the rowing boat. His legs and arms flailed wildly in the air as he propelled himself towards the boat. The leap was masterful, athletic and gazelle-like. But he needed to hit the boat dead-centre and that was to ask an almost impossible physical feat of the tall young man, despite his physical fitness. His left foot landed at the nearest end of the boat, crunching down on Miss Potts's face, as it jerked left to the floor of the boat. His ankle gave way under the moving landing platform and the boat creaked wildly from side to side. Darius arched his back in a desperate effort to stop the inevitable forward motion, but the laws of physics dictated that the rest of his long, lean body would continue to catapult forward, until it smacked the rim of the left-hand side of the boat.

The Russian should have known (with his A-grade grasp of physics) that the sudden arrival of a 12 stone, six foot mass on one side of the boat would immediately upset its balance. The unwanted intrusion of the foreigner created a wild lurch to the left, as water surged over one side of the boat and flipped it up and over. The wooden vessel smashed Darius's head down under the thick, black, slimy water. Miss Potts slammed on top of Darius, legs and arms, hair and bones suffocating him, pushing him, down and down as the pond weed gripped and salivated over his legs. The boulders crashed to the lake's bed with a silent, deadly thud-thud, dragging, pulling and squeezing Darius into the glutinous, viscous liquid, thick with slime, as Miss Potts cracked on top of him.

In his panic for air his lungs screamed and the disgusting bile seeped down his air pipe and oozed through his lungs. Darius kicked and riled around at the bottom of the lake that was blacker than tar and colder than death itself. He punched and pushed, his eyes popped open screaming for the surface. In one final epileptic jerk for freedom, he kicked and freed himself from the grip of the arms and legs, the pond weed, the ropes, the anchoring weight that held Miss Potts and Blanche to the deadly depths of the lake's bed.

Darius thrashed and kicked his way to the surface of the water. His jaw dropped into a horrified 'o' as he gasped for the air he had been deprived of for close to 40 seconds. He frantically and spasmodically kicked in the water and dropped his head back gasping for oxygen to fill his water-logged lungs as he retched on the vile, green stew that filled his mouth. The rush of air returned him to his senses and he felt the ice-cold water grip his body like a vice. He also sensed a strange pumping from his head and something thick and warm ran down his cheek. Darius tasted salty, metallic blood drip into his mouth. His body began to shake and his teeth chattered uncontrollably as he pulled himself on to the bank and rolled onto his back, dripping, frozen and his head covered in blood. Delirious from the loss of blood, the depravation of oxygen and the trauma of the murdered seeking vengeance with the murderer in the depths of the water, Darius collapsed and lost consciousness.

Just then a single robin sounded the arrival of the winter dawn and blood red and orange seeped across the horizon.

Red sky in the morning, shepherd's warning.

CHAPTER NINE

Sunday 4 December – 7.32am

Just as Darius closed his eyes, Elizabeth's big sister opened her eyes a mile and a half away. The winter sun trickled its watery light into Hannah's alien surroundings in the guesthouse that stood alongside the family home and orthodontic practice. Hannah remembered the nanny whisking her into the little house that was usually reserved for visitors, as she heard her Mummy wailing louder than ever in the basement with Daddy after she'd returned home from the Christmas party.

Hannah rubbed her nose and reached out for Chocolate, who lay next to her, upside down, with his face pressed into the mattress and bottom stuck in the air.

"Naughty teddy," she berated the bear, who had spent the last year in her baby sister's cot, before 'lizabeth had decided to play her extended game of hide and seek.

"Chocolate always passes to the youngest child in the family," Melanie explained gently to Hannah. "It's the family tradition," as she echoed the words of her mother a generation before her.

With the absence of her younger sister for the past fortnight, Hannah reclaimed the bear after her mother retrieved it from the high cupboard in Elizabeth's nursery. At five and three-quarters and following a recent growth spurt, Hannah now stood a head taller than the cuddly toy. She kissed the familiar, furry cheek and giggled, rubbing her face into Chocolate's tummy, as she had seen her mother do to Elizabeth at bath time.

Hannah ambled out of bed confused as to why she was sleeping in the guesthouse... *again*. She pulled on her sheep slippers, each of which had a tinker bell sewn into the ears. The sheep's faces grinned at Hannah and she grinned back shaking one foot and then the other, like a jester in a royal court. She dragged Chocolate out of the bed by his right paw and toddled across the little box-room, still bleary-eyed from sleep. Hannah grabbed a handful of curtain material and pulled it back clumsily. She looked out at the beautiful sunrise that shot across the horizon, enchanted by the red and orange streaks of colour.

The silence was suddenly broken by a creak behind her.

"'lizabeth ... 'lizabeth," said Hannah, but the room was deathly still.

Hannah padded over to the other bed and got down on her hands and knees to peer under it.

"Where are you 'lizabeth? Where **are** you? Stop hiding now. It's a stupid, silly game."

Looking into the dark and spooky space under the bed she felt a horrid, empty feeling at the bottom of her stomach – not knowing that this feeling was called loneliness.

"Stop hiding 'lizabeth ... it's boring. I want to play with you."

Hannah heard footsteps below her room and the front door creak open and shut quietly.

She tried to call "Mum-mee," but her voice-box felt strangled and constrained and no sound came from her. She shuddered, suddenly spooked by the footsteps and the dark space under the bed. She froze, still and stiff and hung on to Chocolate's paw with a clenched fist. Hannah panicked, just as she had when a spider climbed across her face in the summer and ran to the other bedroom, her slippers jangling like a Christmas sleigh. Panting, she touched the mound under the duvet… it was the side of the bed where Mummy always slept. She lunged towards the person under the covers and, on finding her mother there, nuzzled into her tummy… the place her mother had told her babies come from.

Melanie stirred and rolled behind her daughter. As the numbing effect of the tranquilisers began to wear off, she clamped her arms around Hannah a little too tight and much too desperately to reassure her daughter that all was well. Melanie wanted to keep her firstborn safe forever cocooned between the sheets, warm and protected, where four souls had once cuddled each morning.

There were four in the bed and the little one said
Roll over, roll over
So they all rolled over and one fell out
There were three in the bed and the little one said
Roll over, roll over
So they all rolled over and one fell out
There were two in the bed…

Hannah wrestled her mother's fierce grip a little looser, till she could comfortably rest and doze on her arm. Then Hannah felt wet trickle down the back of her neck and she knew Mummy was crying again… even before she heard the irregular, muffled gasps for air and before the moaning started.

"Lilybet, princess Lilybet."

CHAPTER TEN

Sunday 4 December – 7.34am

Sleep eluded Harry. Without the heavy sedation that Melanie swallowed to hold her sanity together, Harry tossed and turned throughout the first night back in the guesthouse, whilst the SOCOs, FME and pathologist worked late into the night in the bowels of The Oast. The family liaison officers strongly urged Melanie and Harry to move away from the murder scene for a few months, but neither parent could bear to leave their daughter's final resting place. So they "bravely" or many privately said "foolishly" or "weirdly" stayed, just a stone's throw from their daughter's frozen grave.

Harry lay on the sofa fully clothed and sobbed silently as Melanie slept comatose upstairs. Sunrise brought the relief of daylight. He pulled on his heavy overcoat and crept to the front door. He felt sure he would suffocate in the claustrophobic guesthouse and hurriedly slipped outside to get some fresh air. As he stepped onto the porch he collided with the back of a policeman. The skinny, young, new recruit turned suddenly in

74

his crisp, oversized uniform and, already wrong-footed by the collision, the police officer caught his heel on the front step. As he tumbled backwards landing hard on his coccyx, PC Dawkins' introduction to guarding a property during a murder investigation was unceremoniously caught by the press pack gathered behind the police cordon.

The unshaven, dishevelled and heartbroken Harry apologised perfunctorily and offered a hand to pull the bobby up. This was awkwardly refused and PC Dawkins returned to his feet with the ungainly motion of a new born giraffe trying to stand for the first time. Shaken and startled by the clatter of dozens of shutters and flashbulbs in the media scrum, Harry raised his hand to shield his face and strode across the lawn in the direction of the surgery.

"Um Sir," said the twitchy new recruit, calling after Harry and trotting a few paces away from his assigned post. "Um I'm afraid you can't go back into the house now, not until the um bod… well not until… well you know," he trailed off, kicking himself for uttering the unmentionable 'b' word to the father of the deceased.

Harry turned to the clueless officer. "Don't worry I'm not going *home*, I'm going to *work*," and he slammed the door of the Oast Orthodontic Practice in PC Dawkins' face.

Harry walked robotically through the reception, the waiting room and into the sterile, yet familiar surroundings of his surgery. He flicked on the lights, squinting against their luminosity, until his eyes had adjusted to the brightness. There was the customary and comforting hum as the lights warmed up.

The orthodontist walked on auto-pilot to the filing room at the back of the single storey byre that housed the surgery and headed for the 'Active Treatment' section. Harry quickly found the patients filed under 'S', thanks to the efficiency of his nurse's filing system, and almost before he knew it his fingers landed on Sorokin. His hand trembled momentarily before he could bring himself to pull the file off the shelf.

The orthodontist's instinct was to rip the document to shreds, but he forced his body to sit at his work bench and began reading through the whole file from the start to the end of the treatment plan. He needed to refresh his memory, no matter how painful, to look for clues about Darius's life, his likes and dislikes, his interests and hobbies, the progression of the treatment – all of which were meticulously noted down. Harry studied each entry trying to find the sniff of a clue.

He looked at the correspondence with Natasha Sorokin, every bill had been paid on time and the cheques were accompanied by several garish and effusive thank you letters written on scented notepaper speaking of the *'transformation to my zonzs ugly teeths'*. Harry flicked the light box on and hung up Darius's lateral skull x-ray on the screen. He fantasised about smashing the cranium of his baby's murderer on the surgery floor.

Shaking again he turned to the back of the folder and looked at the 'before and after' shots. They always seemed so impressive during one of his lectures – particularly when the case was as severe and challenging as this one had been. But it was the sneering lips and cold, detached look in Darius's eyes that drew and reviled the orthodontist in equal measure. Then he turned the page to study the print-out of his end-of-treatment shots as the sheet wobbled in his jittery hands.

"Where are you, you bastard?"

Harry snarled at the final sneering picture of Darius (still blissfully unaware just how close the double murderer was). He shook with rage and fury and took his biro stabbing at the image with his pen, over and over, until Darius's photograph was indented with ugly pock-marks all over his face.

"I'll wipe that snide look off your evil face, you little shit!" he yelled. Harry lifted the picture to eye level and coldly whispered: "I'm going to find you Darius and when I do, I'm going to kill you, just as you killed my daughter."

Exhausted, Harry slumped into the orthodontic chair. The cowboy was mortally wounded by his 'most challenging orthodontic case'. The good guy had been shot and needed to rest a little, while the sheriff went in search of the rescue party. But, for now, none came. He picked up the controls to the treatment chair and pressed the button up and down, listening to the mechanical climb and its comforting hiss on its descent. The lift and gentle drop calmed Harry momentarily as he closed his red and cried out eyes and thought of Elizabeth.

He recalled how she loved to sit on his lap on the chair and travel up and down whilst he sang the words of one of her favourite nursery rhymes.

Oh the Grand Old Duke of York
He had ten thousand men
He marched them up to the top of the hill
And he marched them down again.
And when they were up, they were up
And when they were down, they were down

And when they were only halfway up,
They were neither up nor down

Harry thought of Elizabeth riding on his lap on the chair, her peel of laughter as he took the chair up and down to the rhythm of the nursery rhyme. But then Harry saw her face again, discoloured a ghostly bluish white, frozen in time. He arched his arms across his eyes and mouth and wept like a baby, like the baby that had been stolen and murdered. The salty torrent ran down his face and forearms and dried uncomfortably, prickling his skin. He walked over to the stainless steel basin and splashed his face. As he stood up again he caught a glimpse of himself in the mirror. The 'dishy dentist' had been drilled away, his warm hazel eyes, were encircled with dark, puffy rings, made red and swollen by the crying. His handsome, broad chin protruded, more angular now, given his significant weight loss over the past fortnight and his once glowing cheeks were sunken and sallow.

Harry slumped down on his orthodontic chair again and swung his legs up onto the chair, as he had watched hundreds of patients do over the years. He pressed his finger on the rinse dispenser and a jet stream of water filled the plastic beaker. He brought the chair to a sitting position and watched the tablet dissolve, swilling the familiar refreshing aniseed and minty liquid around his gums and cheeks. He spat the mouthwash into the spittoon, just as he saw Darius's reflection in the shiny bowl grin and sneer up at him. He jumped and turned around, ready to draw his pistols. But the room was empty. He grabbed the cup again and swigged another large mouthful, like a cowboy gulping down his last desperate drink before a pistol duel at dawn. He pumped his cheeks in and out more aggressively this time, spitting the liquid with such a force that it splashed over the edges of the spittoon and back up into his face.

"Damn you, damn you forever!"

The normally mild-mannered, 'dishy dentist' crushed the plastic cup in his hand, wishing it were Darius's brain squelching between his fingers and hurled it across the surgery.

The broken hearted orthodontist walked across the surgery to a photograph of Elizabeth and Hannah sat on their mother's lap in the long grass at the back of the garden. The three of them wore daisy chains fashioned by Melanie around their heads and smiled broadly. How he yearned to kiss Elizabeth again, as he pressed his lips against the lifeless and inanimate glass.

The forensic swoop of Elizabeth's cot had seen all evidence of his daughter removed. Barred from the house again, he longed to find a little piece of her now, somewhere in the surgery. More in hope than expectation he went in search of one of her dummies. Harry had taken to sterilising the teats and bottles in the dental steriliser when the bottle steriliser had malfunctioned in the house. He prayed that there might be one still left languishing in the machine, but when he lifted the lid the machine was empty.

Harry rummaged through the draws and cupboards. His sense of despair was overwhelming as he walked back into the surgery. Then he spotted one of his white coats hanging on the back of the door. Sifting through the memory of his last afternoon with Elizabeth he recalled heading back to the surgery to lock up, still dressed in his white coat, just moments before Darius arrived to babysit the children.

His hand trembled as he felt the two top pockets… nothing. Then he checked the right lower pocket… but still nothing. Finally he slid his hand into the left pocket and his fingers touched a soft rubbery teat. He lifted the dummy out of his pocket and cupped it in both hands, lifting the treasured relic slowly to his face and smelt Elizabeth's breath – the sweet fiery breath of a fever. Then he touched his lips on the place where Elizabeth had last suckled… and he kissed his daughter goodbye.

CHAPTER ELEVEN

Sunday 4 December – 8.25am

A man of words and not of deeds
Is like a garden full of weeds
And when the weeds begin to grow
It's like a garden full of snow
And when the snow begins to fall
It's like a bird upon the wall
And when the bird away does fly
It's like an eagle in the sky
And when the sky begins to roar
It's like a lion at the door
And when the door begins to crack
It's like a stick across your back
And when your back begins to smart
It's like a penknife in your heart
And when your heart begins to bleed
You're dead, and dead, and dead indeed

The double murderer and dog slayer drifted in and out of consciousness as he lay beside the watery grave of Miss Potts and her poodle. The seductive call of hyperthermia tempted him to sleep some more as he felt a heavy weight pulling his eyelids closed again. Echoing voices from the spirit world called him back to unconsciousness and there were many on the face of the earth, and especially in the village of Cranhurst, who would have been pleased had he succumbed to the call of eternity, in the hope that he would be dragged to the fiery pit of Hades. He saw his mother's face, even though she was already sat in the departure lounge at Gatwick airport, wrapped up in her thick plot of self-preservation.

The freezing December morning seeped into Darius's jaw first and his perfectly straightened teeth clattered and jangled in his head. The noise slowly nudged him back to the land of the living and he pushed himself to a sitting position. His head swam fast and around like the big dip on a roller coaster, with all of the screams, but none of the fun. Darius's stomach lurched with the repugnant contents of the stagnant lake. His body expelled the alien visitor at the pit of his stomach in a violent, projectile vomit, the stench of which left him retching for several minutes.

The Russian pushed himself to standing, as his vision blurred in and out of focus, and he stiffly manoeuvred the rucksack of money and provisions onto his back. The hideous, stinking Frankenstein spectacle began to move one wounded and injured limb in front of the other. His bony, white features jutted out like death itself, as the thick green slime of the lake clung to his six foot frame and stained clothes. The deep gash across the side of his head had oozed blood down one side of his face, creating a repulsive congealed life form. The slayer of souls clanked mechanically away from the lake and away from the weeping willows.

He manoeuvred his long, creaky joints into a crouching position and crawled behind the hedgerow which gave him a degree of protection from the village green, just two fields away. The winter hedgerow was a shadow of its summer cousin, which buzzed with insects and birdlife and was alive with the rich and varied greens of hawthorn, holly, blackthorn and hazel. The bare branches and large holes revealed intermittent flashes of the monstrosity crawling woodenly behind the sparse winter hedge. But that morning nobody was looking across the fields, for everyone's attention was focused around the village green and the macabre discovery of baby Elizabeth. A new shift of journalists and camera crews gathered outside the Henriksen/Maloney household in the hope of the next juicy morsel in the gruesome 'Frozen Baby' case.

So Darius was left undisturbed to worm his way into the woods and, once he was under the cover of the trees, he returned stiffly to his feet moving deeper and deeper into the forest. Then he made a right turn into some dense vegetation and lifted the camouflaged entrance to his secret underground dugout. The loner's childhood place to hang out all alone had been strengthened, deepened and elaborated upon throughout Darius's teens and now provided the perfect hideaway. So he slithered down into the pit like the venomous snake that he was.

CHAPTER TWELVE

Sunday 4 December – 8.27am

Hannah was unsettled by her mother's constant crying. She watched Mummy swallow some more pills and then drift off to sleep again. Her stomach rumbled loudly, so she rolled out of her parent's temporary bedroom in the guesthouse and went in search of breakfast.

There were two in the bed and the little one said

Roll over, roll over

So they all rolled over and one fell out

There was one in the bed and the little one said…

…Nothing

Hannah bumped down the stairs on her rear end and meandered into the kitchen-cum-breakfast room. She missed the warm comforting whirr of the AGA in the "*proper* kitchen where they really lived" and the alluring smell of her mother's cooking that perpetually filled the air and on *really* special days the aroma of *choc-o-let*…

Hannah foraged around the small guesthouse kitchen for

something to eat. The delicious chocolate crispy cakes, the ones that had been flung on the basement floor the day before, were the "something choc-o-let" cakes that she really wanted to eat. However, the cupboards were all bare.

Old Mother Hubbard
Went to the cupboard
To get her poor doggie a bone,
When she got there
The cupboard was bare
So the poor little doggie had none.

Eventually Hannah found an opened, out-of-date packet of plain biscuits at the back of a drawer, which had hung around from an earlier houseguest.

I want to go home. 'lizabeth I want to play with you... where **are** *you?*

There was a single carton of milk, put in the fridge by Rachel the night before, whilst Mummy and Daddy talked to the two nice police ladies. She didn't know what they were saying, because she'd had to stay in the bedroom with Rachel her nanny all evening, but she felt sure they had been talking about 'lizabeth again. She remembered hearing Mummy crying loads and loads until her sobs faded and Hannah fell asleep on Rachel's lap.

Unable to reach the high cupboard, where the cups were stored, she carried the whole carton of milk into the sitting room. Hannah turned on the TV and found one of her favourite cartoons, which kept her occupied for ten minutes or so. After consuming half a packet of biscuits, the first three of which had turned soft and soggy, Hannah began to feel a little sick from the influx of sugar on an empty stomach. She awkwardly lifted the milk carton to her lips to diffuse the saccharin head spin and clumsily splashed milk all over the rug and down her pyjamas.

"Oh bother," she said, as she had heard her father do from time to time.

She tried to wipe up the mess with her doll's blanket but merely created a smeary, white film down her front and across the rug. When Hannah looked up again at the TV, the cartoon was finished and a pretty lady was reading the news. Then she saw a picture of her Mummy, smiling and looking *reee-ally beautiful* at 'The Art of Food' launch in London. She ran over to the television.

"Mum-meeee," she said excitedly, touching her mother's mouth and kissing the screen. She quickly jumped backwards as the static stung her lips.

Then some more pictures came onto the screen showing Melanie smiling and cooking during one of her many TV appearances on 'Melanie's Munchkins'. Hannah sat on the rug with her face just a few inches away from the screen. After that there was some footage of Mummy and Daddy running out of the front of the house with a blanket over their heads... but it didn't seem to be raining. Next she saw a police car and ambulance, then some policemen went into her *real* house and there was a man in a strange, white space suit... but he didn't have a rocket.

Hannah saw a picture of the man with "the hissy way of speaking" flash up on the screen behind the pretty lady inside the television. Then the lady who was telling the story about Mummy said: "Elizabeth Maloney's body was found at her home".

"No she's not, I haven't found her yet!" shouted Hannah. She stood up and placed her hands on her hips, filled with the righteous indignation of a five and three-quarter year old. "'lizabeth's hiding and I'm seeking and I haven't found her yet!"

Hannah poked her tongue out at the silly lady (even though she knew it was very bad manners). Then the television lady told a terrible lie, despite the fact that Mummy said it was naughty to tell 'porky pies'.

"Elizabeth Maloney was murdered at some point during the evening and her tiny body was discovered hidden in the freezer, in the basement of the family home, two weeks after her disappearance. The police have issued a statement to say that a full and thorough investigation will seek to understand how the girl's body could have been missed during the initial search of the house a fortnight earlier."

Hannah slammed her hands over her ears. She felt confused. *What does 'murmured' mean* she wondered?

"Liar, liar, pants on fire," she yelled at the TV screen, as hot tears of frustration and panic ran down her face.

The little girl ran to the window and saw lots of people with cameras looking back at her. They were all standing behind a strip of tape and Hannah assumed that they must have been *very nawty* and had been told to stand behind the line by the policemen. She saw 'P' for panda, 'O' for orange and 'L' for lollipop but couldn't make out the other letters. The cameras flashed in the dull morning light like a fireworks display, but it didn't feel exciting like bonfire night had the month before. She looked across to the house and saw a long white tent had been erected from the front door to the gate and wondered if Mummy was planning a camping party. Then she saw a car reverse up to the fence just short of the entrance to the long white tunnel. The boot of the car was opened, and for a split second, Hannah saw one of the spacemen place a big bag in the boot.

Lots of men and women with cameras started taking pictures and there were loads more flashy lights. But all the camera people were stuck behind the naughty line, so they couldn't see the bag being loaded into the car, not like Hannah could.

What's in the bag?

Hannah stared across the green and back to her house trying to understand what was happening. Slowly she pieced the picture together like her chunky 24-piece jigsaw puzzle, but her mind still couldn't drop the final piece into place and she yelped like a trapped puppy, frustrated by the hole in the picture that stopped her understanding where 'lizabeth was. Hannah turned the TV off and clung to her teddy. Tears splashed down her cheeks as she walked back to the kitchen. How could her baby sister be hiding in a freezer?

"It's ridicuulus," she told the white box in the kitchen. "Everybody knows that only Eskimos and polar bears could live in a freezer."

The little girl shuddered – with the feeling that a spider must be crawling across her face again. She stared at the freezer that stood in the corner of the guesthouse kitchen. It was much smaller than the two giant white boxes that Mummy filled with food in her *real* house. Hannah put Chocolate on the floor, pushed a small plastic chair across the kitchen and scrambled up onto the chair. She tugged on the lid of the freezer and eventually it yawned open and billowed a crystalised, foreign smelling blast of cold – a strange salty smell of the sea and spices, as the seal-on-seal released a ghostly WHAH! The whoosh of cold air blasted up and wrapped around Hannah's face for a split second. She gasped – unprepared for the rush of ice into her mouth and windpipe and then the white condensation evaporated like an aberration. She held onto the edge of the freezer and gingerly peeked over the edge, where she saw a dozen or so boxes filled with different coloured mixes – with Mummy's grown up scribbles on each lid.

"See Chocolate I knew 'lizabeth couldn't hide in the freezer."

She wanted to climb down and retrieve the bear, to show her furry friend that babies didn't hide in freezers, but the icy rim of the freezer gripped her little fingers.

Look out, Look out,
Jack Frost is about,
He's after our fingers and toes;
And, all through the night,
The gay little sprite
Is working where nobody knows.

She attempted to pull away from the freezer but the ice gripped her fingers like a vice. One by one she tried desperately to peel her fingers away, but each time felt as though her skin would rip. She yelped and screamed, "Mummy, Daddy, please help me! Mummy, Daddy HELP ME!"

Hannah's pleading was too weak and too far away to rouse Melanie from her drug-filled sleep, but her screaming and yelping increased in intensity just as Harry walked back in to the house after his fruitless search for clues in the surgery. The 'goodie' was stirred from his steed for the second time in 24 hours and ran towards the now high-pitched screaming. Today, however, Harry had the gait of a wounded old soldier, rather than the stunt double of yesterday, when he ran to his wife in the depths of The Oast.

"Hannah!" Harry yelled, as soon as he reached the kitchen door. "What on earth are you doing?" he shouted. He bent to lift his firstborn into his arms.

"My hands!" she screamed hysterically. "They're stuck Daddy – they're burning!"

"Wait there," he commanded.

Harry ran across to the sink and threw some dead 'condolence' flowers out of a vase. They'd been sent by a patient's well meaning mother after Elizabeth's initial disappearance eight days before her body had even been found. Harry threw the foul smelling green liquid and flowers into the sink. He rinsed the vase with a frantic scrubbing action and filled it with lukewarm water, running back to his stranded daughter.

"There, there," he soothed, as the warm water slowly released Hannah from the freezer's icy grip. Harry swept his 'little elf' into his arms as she buried her face into her father's chest and howled. He gently rocked her to and fro and closed the lid of the freezer.

"Never mind Hannah. Never mind my little elf."

Hannah's hysterical howling gradually subsided to an intermittent sob.

"Naughty freezer Daddy," said Hannah, looking fiercely at the freezer.

"Ve-ry naugh-ty free-zer Ha-nnah." Harry smacked the freezer in the manner of a Punch & Judy puppet delivering his line "That's the way to do it".

Hannah raised a smile through the tears as her father carried her through to the sitting room and tenderly tucked his daughter and Chocolate under a throw on the sofa. He found some almond oil in the medical box and rubbed it into the palms of her hands and fingers. Gradually the fiery tingling subsided, together with the tears.

"I'm not going to be angry Hannah, but you really shouldn't have climbed up on a chair and opened the freezer without asking first."

Hannah nodded a guilty acknowledgement and bit her bottom lip, just as her mother was in the habit of doing to fill an awkward moment.

"I was looking for 'lizabeth Daddy. I was *only* trying to find her. Are the po-wece looking for 'lizabeth too Daddy... are they playing hide and seek?"

They cuddled in silence for a while.

"What does *murmured* mean Daddy?"

As Hannah posed the question she stared up directly into her father's face with the piercing blue eyes that had been inherited from her mother's Nordic line.

"That's a funny big word for a little elf like you."

Harry smiled weakly.

"The lady on the TV said 'lizabeth's been murmured."

Harry dropped his gaze to the ground, trying to hide his swollen, red eyes. But Hannah wanted the comfort of his gaze and cupped her little hands around her father's chin, pushing his head back up. His eyes welled up with tears and Hannah started crying again too, sensing that something was very wrong. Harry stroked Hannah's cheek trying to placate her.

"I'm *so* sorry darling, I'm *so* sorry."

Harry's chest heaved in agony as he gasped for air sobbing loudly. Hannah drilled her little fists on his chest wanting him to say something nice, wanting the crying to stop. She'd never seen her big, strong Daddy cry and it scared her. She knew her father would drop in the last piece of the jigsaw puzzle and soon she would know what *murmured* meant, but she wasn't sure she wanted to know anymore as a feeling of anxiety buzzed around her head like a swarm of bees. Harry cradled his daughter's face in his hands and looked directly into her eyes, his face red and blotchy from the crying.

"What I'm going to tell you now will be one of the hardest, saddest things you'll ever have to hear, but I need to tell you something, so you must try to be brave. Yesterday the police did find your baby sister, but the ambulance men couldn't make her better. She didn't want to die... that's what murdered means, when you don't want to die but you do all the same. Elizabeth wanted to stay with us, but she couldn't because a bad man wouldn't let her, so she's gone to heaven to play hide and seek with the angels. She would have preferred to stay with Mummy and Daddy and her big, beautiful sister, but she's gone. Jesus is looking after her now and she's very, very happy there... it's just so incredibly sad for us isn't it... because we wanted to love and take care of her and we'll all miss her so much...."

Hannah's face collapsed as the enormity of what her father was saying resonated inside her. She moaned and tears ran down her father's arms whilst his tears splashed on her hair. Eventually exhaustion overcame her, and heavy breathing replaced Hannah's shortened gasps for air as she drifted off to sleep on her Daddy's chest... which Mummy always said was "the safest place on earth".

CHAPTER THIRTEEN (UNLUCKY FOR SOME)

Sunday 4 December – 9.15am

Cup of tea.

How the English love their tea in a crisis and this was crisis of seismic and tragic proportions.

Harry left Hannah sleeping on the sofa and went to make Melanie a cuppa. Away from the familiarity of The Oast, and disorientated by grief, Harry opened and closed most of the cupboards in search of the mugs. He made two cups of English Breakfast tea which was left a little too long and brewed more orange than brown. Then he over-milked it and added two heaped teaspoons of sugar. Harry and Melanie had never taken sugar in their tea, but his shattered mind craved something sweet and milky.

Harry walked upstairs and perched uneasily on the edge of the bed balancing the two mugs of tea, just as he had the morning after they had made love for the first time in his hotel room in Brighton. It was endless, beautiful and passionate love-making, all night, over and over and with a symbiosis that revealed that these two souls were meant to be bound together, to become one flesh... forever and ever.

Melanie forced her red, swollen eyes open. Harry handed her a mug of tea and tenderly stroked his wife's hair. It seemed almost impossible to stop the tears from flowing, but she made an extraordinary effort to have a few moments with Harry without the tears. She slipped her hand into his.

Love you, she mouthed.

Love you too, he mouthed back silently.

He squeezed her hand and she squeezed back. Then he pulsated twice. She 'replied' with two more pulses. Then he came back with two rapid beats followed by three slow ones. She echoed the communication. They continued in their hand-to-hand 'Morse code' for several minutes – responding to each other with a new combination of short and long pulses.

It was a silent love language they had developed early in their relationship and one that they frequently reverted to – when words failed them. It was their wordless, secret connection and a code that no one else shared. Their eyes met through the haze of pain that clouded their vision and rational judgement. Somehow they both mustered a weak smile, for the sake of each other.

"Have they taken her?" Melanie could hardly bear to articulate the question.

Harry unable to verbalise that their baby's body had been removed for the post mortem simply nodded his head, his face winced with pain. Melanie lifted the mug under her chin and breathed in the woody tannin vapour that rose out of her mug and swirled around her face. She breathed over the mug to release more steam up and around her face.

⚘　⚘　⚘

Closing her eyes Melanie remembered the steam wrapping around her face and body as a child in the family sauna. It was a weekly custom that all the children took part in and remained unbroken throughout the Norwegian summers and endless and relentless winters.

The Henriksen's family sauna was a beautiful construction, lovingly crafted and honed by her practical father over many months. The interior cabin was surprisingly spacious, made from pine trees felled from a stretch of forest owned by three generations of her father's family. Three levels of wooden slats ran around the cabin, allowing each sibling to demonstrate their bravery. The hottest spot was on the top bunk closest to the coal fire. It was the place that Melanie, the youngest child, seemed most willing to inhabit – whether she ran to the water's edge through the sticky, hot summer air, thick with mosquitoes, or whether there was a deep layer of snow stretched across the lawn.

Melanie was always quickest to ladle more water onto the hot coals and loved to watch a wet and fiery cloud of heat fill the cabin, until she lost sight of her older siblings for a few seconds. The top level also gave the best view outside. Her father had created a long, high window at one end of the cabin and she often wiped a little peep-hole through the dripping condensation to give herself a teasing glimpse of the sweeping lawn leading down to the water's edge. The water was so blue and crystal clear that her father said you could dive forever and never reach the bottom.

Harry watched his wife, with her eyes closed, and saw a brief smile flash across her face. Melanie heard the squeals of pleasure and self-inflicted pain echo in a long-forgotten corridor of her memory. Melanie ran fastest, ahead of her brothers and sisters, bold, brazen and full of courage. It was a crazed shrieking procession of paper white arms and legs flying in all directions and steam emanating from every pore. The familiar journey continued along the jetty – the last chance for a reprieve – that none of them ever took. Then the flying leap and – WHOOSH – the ice-cold water hit like a concrete wall, utterly unbearable and yet inexplicably thrilling. It was a ritual that was strangely addictive and would be repeated again, without hesitation, the following weekend.

❀   ❀   ❀

Melanie opened her eyes, pulling herself back to shore again.

"It's going to be turmoil here for a long time to come," said Harry, as Melanie returned to the awful present tense. "The press pack is interbreeding outside. I counted 20 or more outside the front garden. We might want to think about moving to a secret location for a while."

"I can't Harry – I just can't move out. This is *our* home, *Hannah's* home. This is where I feel closest to Elizabeth. I can still smell her in the house, touch her clothes and hold photographs of her in my hand. It's all I have left of her."

Melanie's big blue eyes, rimmed with red, turned to water again.

Harry eased Elizabeth's dummy from his pocket, "Here you can kiss the place that her lips last touched."

"Oh Harry," Melanie gasped as she wept. She cupped the plastic dummy like a treasured piece of gold in her hands and touched her lips to the teat. "Where did you find it?"

"In the surgery… in the pocket of my white coat," said Harry.

"Really?" she said with incredulity. "Did the police let you walk outside?"

"Well sort of. I just marched over there… I needed some fresh air. Anyway I didn't go anywhere near the house. It's all tented up… I can't believe this is happening," Harry sobbed quietly as Melanie squeezed his hand again. He drew in a deep breath and continued, "Hannah watched the telly this morning… she knows her sister has been murdered. She went to look for Elizabeth in the freezer but her hands got stuck on the ice, so she was in a real state."

"Oh no, what sort of a mother am I?" Melanie gasped slowly shaking her head from side to side. "Hannah could have been hurt Harry… I didn't hear her!"

Harry lifted his index finger to Melanie's lips to still her.

"She's going to be fine – out of the three of us – *she* is definitely going to be fine. We cuddled and talked and she's deeply asleep now. I think Hannah found it easier to accept that Elizabeth's in heaven than all alone in that dreadful place in the basement."

Harry walked over to the front window as four police vans slowed up and parked in the sealed area in front of the house, a discreet distance from the grieving family being held in the guest-house. The van doors flew open almost in unison, as if their dis-embarkation had been rehearsed. Six police officers emerged in quick succession from each van and began assembling into their units with the sniffer dogs. Harry stared beyond the police search units, to the Georgian mansion that had been home to Darius. There were police and forensics going in and out of the mansion in their white suits like a trail of ants and he was also surprised to see a flurry of activity around Greenview Villa – the home to Miss Potts and her poodle.

But his eyes settled on the Sorokin home again, the home of his daughter's murderer.

"An eye for an eye, and a tooth for a tooth Darius, no tooth fairies this time," he muttered to himself.

The normally mild-mannered Harry, felt another wave of murderous anger bubbling at the pit of his stomach – as he gripped the old wooden window-ledge so tightly that he failed to notice a splinter had embedded itself deep in his right index finger.

Harry registered the swelling ranks of cameramen and jour-nalists behind the cordon and a few paparazzi shuffling restlessly, waiting to be thrown another juicy bone by Minky Sloane who stood in the place she felt most at ease – the limelight.

Dominica Sloane, of Sloane PR, had become the official spokesperson for her most lucrative and favourite client and 'the voice of Melanie Henriksen'. As soon as Elizabeth first went missing, Minky abandoned her offices in Sloane Street for a cosy country hotel in Cranhurst, so that she could be close to Melanie and Harry during such shocking and extraordinary times.

Whilst the detective superintendant from the Major Crime Unit issued the formal releases and held the official press briefings, it was Minky's unofficial press conferences on the grass verge outside the family home that the press really wanted to hear. It was the touching and personal details delivered so expertly in a blaze of publicity by Minky Sloane, that gave the nation an intimate and 'behind closed doors' glimpse into the world of Melanie Henriksen OBE. Today though, the morning after the discovery of the baby, not even Minky's outlandish outfits and over the top delivery could lift the gloom that hung over the green.

The most seasoned hack of all in the Weald of Kent, Douglas MacIntyre, temporarily moved his eyes away from the notorious Ms Sloane and looked up at the guesthouse bedroom window, where he spotted Harry standing at the window. Soon the whole media scrum had honed in on the 'dishy dentist' and the cameramen zoomed in on his outline through the glass.

Harry recoiled pulling back from the unwanted invasion, wondering if Melanie's 'expert publicity guru' was merely creating an insatiable hunger for news of his wife. He walked over to the relative tranquillity of the back window. His eyes meandered across the fields to the edge of the woods, which disappeared somewhere behind the Sorokin's household and were not clearly visible from his vantage point in the guesthouse. This was the place where Harry loved to walk every weekend with Melanie and Hannah and, for the last year, with Elizabeth strapped to his chest, like an African bush baby.

Harry's favourite time of year was spring – when the promise of better weather was tantalisingly close. It was the season when the forest floor was covered with the sweetest smelling carpet of bluebells. Their exquisite purple haze stretched out as far as the eye could see and impossibly brightened the darkest corners. Harry stared straight ahead as he spoke, looking intently now through the pane of glass.

"Do you remember what that family liaison officer said last night Melanie? Wasn't it DC Saunders who said they would be re-focussing their search around the village today? Well they're already gathering like storm clouds on the green."

He paced up and down like a frustrated wild cat, caged in a zoo, an animal that yearns to break free so that he can pounce and make the kill.

"We know Darius took the family car the night he disappeared, that much we have been told. But every line of enquiry has run dry. Think about it Melanie, the sightings in London, the airport and port checks following a supposed 'tip off' that he was heading back to Russia – it's been one blank after another. I know they can't really tell us too much, but it seems to me we're back to square one. I think the police believe Darius could be very close to home. Why else would they be doing such a big sweep of the area two weeks after the first search?"

Suddenly, he leapt across the room and grabbed both of Melanie's forearms.

"You remember you said you thought you'd heard something drop in the basement, just as you went to turn the light on yesterday afternoon? Well the window was pushed out, I might be going demented Melanie, but I saw the window was gone. Of course the police won't tell us now, not until the forensic team have done their job, but I have this horrid feeling that it was Darius. I think the little bastard has come home!"

"Oh God Harry how creepy," Melanie wailed.

A sensation icier than the water of the fjord seeped over her head. Melanie touched the dummy to her lips, as tears ran again down the familiar salt tracks.

"I know it and *they* know it," said Harry marching to the front window and jabbing a finger at where the police search units had gathered.

Harry mentally ran through the case notes which he'd poured over in the surgery that morning, paying special attention to his peculiar family history and his hobbies – the obvious fascination with knives, the obsessive fencing fixation, his love of the great outdoors, the garden and then further afield in the woods.

Suddenly Darius hissed into Harry's brain.

"Oh my God Melanie, he's in the fucking woods right under our noses!" Harry gripped Melanie's arms tightly. "Do you remember the times we were walking the dog and we'd bump into Darius in the woods, covered in mud? He was always playing in there – when he wasn't in the garden with Mr Morris, the old gardener. He once let slip when I was treating him in the chair that he had a secret underground place that he always went to in the woods, where he made himself like the 'invisible man.'"

He paused and gripped Melanie's hand so hard, she felt the blood stop flowing.

"Melanie he's right here – the fucking Judas Iscariot is sneering right in our midst, the bastard – the fucking bastard!" Harry shouted furiously.

Harry strode across to the bedroom door.

"Where are you going Harry?" Melanie said jumping out of bed.

"Don't worry," he reassured, returning to his familiar softness. "Just stay here for Hannah. When she wakes up she'll have so many questions, she really needs you this morning of all mornings."

Harry tilted Melanie's face upwards and tenderly kissed her on each tear-stained cheek.

"Are you going to call the family liaison officers – I've put their numbers somewhere, just give me a minute to think where? It's DC Jenny Saunders and… oh… what's the other one…?" said Melanie hazily, trying to think straight.

Melanie was worried by the alien look of venom in her husband's face, he didn't respond to her question and simply reiterated firmly: "Stay here for Hannah."

With that Harry left the room and ran downstairs to the boot room at the back of the guesthouse. The room was stocked with a good selection of walking boots and wellingtons for the stream of friends who came for a weekend in the country. Harry pulled on a pair of wellies that fitted almost perfectly. Next he reached for a hat which he lowered over his brow and flipped the flaps around his ears. Finally, he grabbed a full-length waxed coat, his right forearm still heavily bandaged. He turned up the collar, adding another layer of 'the country gent' to his disguise. Harry jumped up and strode across to the locked gun cupboard. He picked up the key from a high shelf, grabbed his double-barrelled shotgun and a handful of cartridges – which he pushed deep inside his pocket. Usually the gun was used for monthly clay pigeon shoots and the seemingly endless stream of rabbits that would hop tantalisingly out of range in the flower beds. Today, however, his target practice was his daughter's murderer.

Harry marched to the back door and he had his hand on the latch when he was momentarily distracted by scratching and whimpering on the other side of the laundry room door. Usually inseparable, but utterly separated by the extraordinary circumstances of the past fortnight, Oscar (a sleek, black Labrador Retriever) had been kept fed, watered and walked by a sympathetic neighbour and returned to the family the day they had been allowed back to The Oast after the initial fruitless search for Elizabeth. As Harry opened the door to release the hound, Oscar bound into the room with such force that he nearly knocked Harry off his feet and then twisted and jumped in the enclosed space like a Chinese firecracker.

Oscar was democratically called 'the family dog' but in truth proved to be Harry's four-legged friend from the outset. The two males in the family developed a special affinity in the very early days after his arrival at The Oast. It was Harry who took the gangly pup, the adorable runt of a litter of eight, to dog training classes. And it was Harry that got up to Oscar in the night when the young puppy howled through the night and peed his way across the kitchen in The Oast every night for ten days after leaving his mother.

If Harry's schedule didn't allow a daily cross-country walk, which was more usually reserved for the weekends, he always found time to throw a ball a dozen times or more on the green,

which the retrieve

feet, just as his gen

After two week;

self with the prospe

the back door was a

off-road walk and he

mally perfectly traine

developed into a sleek

his hind legs three or i

furiously at the door, wl

The usual chastisen

from Oscar's master. Ins ... for the lead, knelt down and held Oscar firm and still as he clipped the leash catch onto the dog's collar ring. Harry looked deep into his watery, treacle eyes, as the dog panted his hot, meaty breath into his master's face. His tail slapped from side to side, as his rear legs danced steps that were a close match to the Samba. Then Harry placed a firm and calming hand on his head and stilled the dog for a moment. The retriever held his tail sleek and straight and lifted his right paw onto Harry's thigh.

Harry cradled the dog's head very still between his hands.

"Let's go hunting Oscar."

※　※　※

Melanie heard the backdoor slam and rushed over to the bedroom window. She observed her husband crouching and running at speed down the back garden under his country disguise. He

d the hop huts and then she saw
scar racing by his side along the path
he woods beyond. She noticed something
er his coat which made the coat balloon up on
distort his shoulder with the gait of the Hunchback
Dame. She peered through the glass trying to make out
hidden shape under his coat.

"The shotgun!" she whispered in horror.

Melanie rapped on the glass furiously – hoping Harry would turn around to look back at her – hoping she might be able to persuade him to return. She struggled with the window latch – it had always proved sticky and stubborn her mother and father complained on the rare occasions they had flown over from Norway to see her. Then quite suddenly the window flew open.

"Come back Harry, don't be a bloody idiot," she yelled across the garden, but he'd already rounded the footpath running along the top end of the fields and was heading to Darius's neck of the woods. The astute local journalist, Douglas MacIntyre, spotted a man walking away from the rear of the guesthouse and decided to follow. He broke away from the media pack, sidled down a shortcut to the footpath out of sight of the police units and their dogs, and went in hot pursuit of Harry Maloney, armed with his long range lens and notepad.

Melanie was frantic now and her sense of imminent danger concentrated at the back of her throat like a ball of cotton wool. She ran to the bedroom window at the front of the house and was shocked by the scene in front of her. The village green, this tranquil 500 metre expanse of grass, hedging and mature trees, with its perfectly mown cricket pitch and pavilion, the manicured backdrop for the picture postcard village in the Weald, had been transformed into a macabre HQ for the search of the murderer of her baby. She wanted to rap on the window to catch Minky Sloane's attention, but saw that her publicity agent was stepping back into her Porsche having delivered the grim news of the morning.

Police vans, media vans and the cars of nosey onlookers were parked all around the green. The formations of police units and police dogs were lined up ready for battle, preparing to move out in a three-pronged formation. Several dozen 'extras' milled about the edges of the green, behind the police line, hoping to be part of the backdrop of any footage shot by the mushrooming camera crews.

Melanie's gaze dropped down below the bedroom window and she saw the helmet of a police guard standing below outside the front door, trapping her like a damsel in distress in the tower. Well beyond the picket fence, the police vans and the media, she noticed a group of ladies from the Women's Institute, arms folded deep in conversation, discussing the more salacious details of the case.

One lady, whom Melanie recognised as the postmaster's wife, was pointing to each window and describing the layout of the main house, having attended the Henriksen/Maloneys infamous, annual Christmas drinks party for several years previously. She took particular pleasure highlighting Melanie's silhouette in the window of the guesthouse, pointing at the exhibit with the excitement of a child seeing her first monkey at the zoo.

"There she is!"

The media men and women followed the squeal and pointing finger and the pack lit up like a Christmas tree, the long lens cameras flashing in quick succession through the grey December morning. Melanie pulled away from the window and ran downstairs. She pushed her head into the sitting room – Hannah was still deeply asleep. Melanie kissed Hannah on the cheek and then turned back to the kitchen to find the numbers of her family liaison officers. But her muddled brain couldn't find the contact details anywhere. So she grabbed a piece of paper and pen and scribbled:

> I need to talk to someone urgently – please come inside when I open the door.
> Ms Henriksen

Melanie folded the paper several times then ran to the front door and slid the security chain across. Standing behind the door she slowly opened it as far as the chain would allow and blindly stretched her hand into the open space waving the white paper like the last soldier standing – hoping his surrender will be honoured by the enemy. Melanie heard the cameras click again in quick succession and then a hand take the note from hers. She closed the door, counted to ten to allow time for the message to be read, slid the security chain off and then shuffled behind the door as she pulled it wide open. The cameras clicked to a crescendo, into the 'open sesame' space, but nobody from the house stepped into the void.

The gawky young policeman tucked the note in his top

pocket, painfully aware that the cameras were trained on him, and gingerly took several steps into the empty hall.

"Hello, can I help Ms Henriksen – is everything alright?" he called into the vacuum.

Melanie slammed the door behind him and the young man jumped inside his uniform, which looked rather baggy on his slim frame. He turned to see Melanie standing in a dishevelled night shirt, her ghostly white face framed by her wild dark hair and red eyes. More accustomed to seeing the 'kiddie cook's' striking oval face perfectly made up and her impossibly gorgeous hour-glass figure stretched across the front cover of one of his wife's magazines, the policeman enquired tentatively "Ms Henriksen?"

She grabbed the young man's arm: "You need to find Darius. I'm scared what might happen."

The voice of authority and procedure cut in: "Well Ms Henriksen we're certainly doing our best and we have several units scanning the area right now."

"I know I know – that's why it's ridiculous for me to dial 999 and I can't find the numbers of my family liaison officers. The police are everywhere but you need to look *now* in the woods and find Darius before my husband does."

"Don't worry Ms Henriksen your husband really mustn't join the search. It's best if you all just stay put for now in the house and leave the professionals to get on with the job."

Melanie felt trapped, pinned down by the officious young policeman's words. He woodenly lifted an arm to the nearest window, like a traffic officer: "I understand your reticence to come close to the window, but if you take a look from where you are standing, you'll see the police units are spreading out for a fingertip search as we speak."

"No you don't understand!" she said, her voice betraying her frustration. "My husband is *already* out there searching and I'm scared what might happen..." She gripped his arm tighter: "We regularly saw Darius in the same area of the woods when we were out walking. My husband thinks Darius might have created some kind of an underground hideaway. We often walk around the footpath from the back of our house – it runs all the way behind the properties to the opposite side of the green then you follow the footpath across two fields and swing a left into the woods. After that it's a right where the path forks. The trees and ferns are really thick there and you sometimes have to beat out the footpath again with a stick. Just before the woods open out again to views over The Weald, in the thickest area of brambles and vegetation – that's where we would see Darius emerge from the thicket. When I think back we saw him dozens of times over the years, always coming through the same part of the wood."

"Why didn't you share this information earlier Ms Henriksen?" the police officer enquired inappropriately, twisting the beam of suspicion back on Melanie.

Incredulous, Melanie felt anger boil inside her for the first time since Elizabeth's disappearance and now, confirmed death. She grabbed the young policeman's arm hard and assertively, "Look you horrid little man, my daughter was murdered two weeks ago and we found her body yesterday. Surprisingly neither my husband nor I have been thinking terribly straight, because we are just a little bit beside ourselves with grief right now! Do you have children PC…?"

"…Dawkins," he said, finishing her sentence for her.

He shook his head from side to side to reinforce the negative presence of offspring in his house.

"All I'm saying PC Dawkins is the idea only just occurred to us, the idea that there might be a link. And now my husband is ten minutes ahead of your *professional* search party and there's no accounting for what might happen if he finds our daughter's murderer first. So for pity's sake get back out on the green and tell the men where to search!"

The cloth-headed PC Dawkins reversed back towards the door kowtowing all the way and bumbled backwards, careful not to fly off the front step for a second time. The constable debated the best way to communicate this new piece of information. He knew he shouldn't leave his post and therefore felt reluctant to run across the green to talk to his colleagues. With endless cameras trained on his every move, PC Dawkins opted for radio control. The constable took on the demeanour of an undercover spy, half turning on the spot and surreptitiously lifted a hand to conceal his mouth to ensure his words couldn't be lip read by the journalists watching, as he radioed for a message to be passed urgently to the senior investigating officer.

Melanie hung back from the front hallway window. The message took some time to filter through the system and after ten minutes or so she noticed a sudden shift of activity towards the woods. She picked up a photograph of her husband on the hall table and ran her finger around his handsome face, as he cuddled

Hannah and Elizabeth on his knee with carefree abandon. Suddenly she was filled with a sickening feeling of dread and an awful impending sense of doom, for she feared that Darius Sorokin, her baby's murderer, would now kill her soul mate and tear away the other half of her whole.

CHAPTER FOURTEEN

Sunday 4 December – 9.28am

Harry heard Melanie rapping on the window as he strode along the footpath. He wanted to turn and reassure Melanie that everything would be alright, he longed to console her that the sheriff could return the rule of law to Cranhurst, but he knew to look back would be fatal. Those blue eyes, even dimmed by their red rims, would pierce his heart and dissipate the desire for revenge.

An eye for an eye, a tooth for a tooth.

So he strode along the path without turning, ignoring the sound of the window opening and the distant cry for reason, for self-preservation: "Come back Harry, don't be a bloody idiot."

Harry mechanically breathed in the winter morning deep into his lungs, using his bandaged right arm to steady the gun in position under his coat as he ran with Oscar on the lead. After two weeks of waiting and hoping for the return of Elizabeth, his body felt weakened, as though he too were recovering from the nanny's flu.

He sucked in the cold, crisp country air like a cooling balm and exhaled a cloud of condensation as he kept a steady jogging pace. His feet naturally connected again with the well-worn path of his familiar weekend walks... but his mind had already run ahead into the woods.

Harry reached the end of the footpath running behind the houses on the green. He turned for a brief moment to look up at the Georgian house that had held his daughter's murderer. Again the alien juices of revenge pumped into every fibre of his being and he spat on the ground outside the Sorokin's back gate.

An eye for an eye, and a tooth for a tooth he repeated the mantra in his mind. *There's no escape this time you bastard.*

The race to get to the woods continued and the orthodontist released Oscar as he shot into the distance, bounding wild and free. As soon as the retriever heard his name, he turned and sprinted back to Harry, skilfully circling his master at high speed, without ever quite touching his coat. The watery winter light glistened on the Labrador's thick black coat, as he shot away again disappearing out of sight into the thicket. After the scent ran dry the retriever returned again circling Harry three or four times. But the dog sensed a strange distance in his master and instinctively knew there was to be no ball or stick throwing this morning.

The local reporter tagging the orthodontist struggled to keep up with his fast pace. For each of Harry's long strides, Douglas

MacIntyre scuttled along like a crab and then paused to allow sufficient distance between the pursued and the pursuer. Douglas knew this was the biggest story he was ever likely to report on in his long and frustrated career in the media backwaters of Cranhurst and the Weald of Kent and he was determined not to blow the opportunity. He jealously guarded his subject matter, turning frequently in between his scuttling, to check that no one else was following.

It was Douglas who got the 'global scoop' on the discovery of Elizabeth's body in the freezer the day before. Sadly the 'scoop' would be lost on the world, as his 'exclusive' version of events would not be published till the following Friday. By the time The Wealden Weekly hit the local newsagents and supermarkets at the end of the week, the story had been crawled over by every national daily.

Douglas didn't pay much attention to the growing readership of the newly launched online Wealden Weekly and those consumers who casually clicked their way through the newspaper online... he saw no future in it. For this journalist it was all about holding a tangible newspaper in your hands, the readers he identified with were the ones who were interested enough in his stories to buy a newspaper for 45 pence. Although he'd heard various people refer to The Wealden Weekly as a bit of a "regional rag" Douglas consoled himself with the fact that it was still the biggest paid-for paper in the Weald – with a circulation of 30,000.

Douglas had made a lifetime habit of consoling himself, usually with a whisky bottle and a packet of roll-your-own cigarettes. The wiry, little Scot had shown great early promise, becoming the youngest news editor on The Scotsman and winning a coveted industry award by the time he was 25. A top job with a leading national paper based in London seemed the next impressive rung on the ladder.

But an early taste for whisky, acquired at 14 with his friends in a bleak high-rise estate in Glasgow, gradually deadened his razor-sharp ability to pursue a story. The intermittent late arrivals and pungent ether of whisky that hung in the air around his desk were ignored, as were the extended drunken lunches. As long as he continued to deliver his stories to deadline and effortlessly string words together like a fine string of pearls, his weakness for the fiery liquid was overlooked. But when Douglas smacked a 'Glaswegian kiss' across the face of a colleague to settle an editorial disagreement about the miners' strike it resulted in an instant dismissal.

Now in his early fifties and still alone, save for his whisky bottle, Douglas was determined that *no-one* would steal this part of the story. He had a front row seat and only he would be able to give the eyewitness account of the intriguing new angle that was unfolding in front of his eyes.

Douglas had taken to carrying a camera with him and stopped momentarily to zoom in close on Harry. With tightening budgets and improved digital technology, the 'flying Scotsman' (as he was known locally) often doubled up as the photographer and reporter on his stories for The Wealden Weekly. He stopped for a moment and focused in as tight as he could to capture the outline of the thing that was under Harry's coat.

What is that? Douglas said to himself, as he honed in on the peculiar lump beneath Harry's coat.

A gun... aye, it's a wee shotgun we have there. So where are you sneaking off to Dr Maloney?

His momentary pause had stretched out the distance between the tracker and the tracked, so he tucked his camera away and scuttled faster than before to close the gap.

Harry broke into a sprint over the second field then ducked into the woods, just as the teams of police and sniffer dogs began to move into place at the top of the fields outside the Sorokin mansion. The moment Harry entered the woods he felt the haunting hush of nature descend on him. The branches shrouded Harry from the winter's sky, whilst the mossy path below, with its thick mat of rotting leaves, deadened his footsteps. The air was stiller, more spiritual somehow and even the birds did not dare break the vow of silence that hovered over the wood.

❀ ❀ ❀

"I talk to the trees but they don't listen to me," Melanie sang as they walked through the woods, years earlier, laughing with carefree abandon, as the birth of Hannah drew near. They stopped to kiss, hot and breathless, still hungry for each other.

"They don't listen, but feel how they absorb something of us," Harry said as he gently leant with Melanie into the smooth trunk of a Silver Birch and they kissed one another tenderly. He felt himself swell against her swelling abdomen and then they both roared with laughter as the preposterous reality of making love standing up against a tree, with a seven-month bump between them dawned on them simultaneously.

❀   ❀   ❀

Harry shook the memory away as vengeance pumped through his veins again. He took the right fork where the path divided quite suddenly and continued striding at a pace down the narrowing track. He unbuttoned his coat clumsily as the bandage slowed his usual dexterity then slid his arm out and grabbed the gun from his shoulder. Pausing for only a brief moment to load two cartridges, one into each barrel, Harry closed and cocked the gun. Oscar ran back to his master, sensing the start of a rabbit or pheasant hunt and barked excitedly. Harry held a calming hand over the top of the dog's head and knelt down.

"Shush," he whispered. "We need to be very quiet Oscar."

He rested his forehead on the dog's head for a moment and then pulled back again.

"Find him Oscar, find Darius."

The dog shot off tail straight, with his head held high and his ears pricked up and alert. The flora thickened within a few paces, as rotting forest ferns and raging summer nettle beds were now choked by the dominant and virulent winter brambles, which caught Harry's trousers from time to time snagging the material. Harry slowed almost to a standstill and swirled low – his arms stretched out wide, his feet tapping the ground, like the Hualapai tribe of north western Arizona. Today he was happy to hang up his cowboy hat and replace it with all the hunting and tracking skills of the native Indians. He swirled around again, swaying from side to side tapping the ground lightly with each foot. Nothing... but he sensed he was close.

Harry turned to cover a new patch of the wood frequented by Darius as a teenager, marked by three giant horse chestnuts which stood in an almost perfect triangle. Harry turned slowly again and noticed Oscar scratching at the earth with his front paws.

"What you got there boy?" said Harry dropping to his knees, placing the palm of his hand on the soil. He noticed layer upon layer of branches that had fallen a little too perfectly to be the hand of Mother Nature.

Just then Harry heard the vow of silence broken. It started with a single muffled cough, somewhere below the bowels of the earth and then another deeper, rattling cough. Oscar whimpered and clawed the soil. Then the siren came. It was a hacking, frozen cough from a rib cage that had been dragged to the bottom of the lake and back. An uncontrollable phlegm-ridden honk that barked: "Here I am, come and find me."

Harry circled the dense area of branches and came to a carcass of tree trunk, its middle carved out. The father of one dropped low to peer inside the trunk, fatally placing the gun on the ground next to him. He pushed his head into the dark, dank space. Some sort of thick, black cloth hung over the end obscuring Harry's vision into the pit that held his daughter's murderer. Harry felt a panic grip his chest, as he saw an image of Elizabeth's frozen face before him in the dark, cramped space. The rising panic for oxygen screamed around his head as he tried to squeeze head-first into the narrow hole. Suddenly he bolted backwards gasping for the calming air in the woods.

From under the ground Darius cleared his throat, like a man preparing to deliver an important speech, an account perhaps of why he had committed such an unspeakable act of cruelty on a defenceless baby. And then the sound meandered, almost non-chalantly through the soil – Darius was whistling. The tune from Elizabeth's CD player mocked Harry and the company of trees, as it danced through the still, silent air taunting him.

Three blind mice
See how they run
They all run after the farmer's wife
Who cut off their tails with a carving knife.
Did you ever see such a sight in your life
As three blind mice?
Three blind mice

Harry's blood boiled now. The 'blind mice' were coming in for the kill. They had been blind, but now they could see. The mild-mannered orthodontist fermented inside like Mount Vesuvius, the angry lava and desire to avenge his daughter's murderer pulsed through every sinew, as his face flushed puce red and his body shook with the eruption of his fury. Without the premeditated plan of a cold-blooded murderer, Harry wildly and recklessly pulled at the branches and hurled the large heavy logs away, just as a Scottish highlander tosses the caber. The whistling came to an abrupt stop.

Oscar barked loudly and growled into the ground. Sensing the hunt was nearly at an end, the retriever's need to retrieve the thing that was being hunted, overcame the dog. So he ran to the narrow entrance and began shuffling through the confined space, barking and snarling as he smelt the foul stench of the wounded animal beyond the black curtain.

Harry neither noticed Oscar barking, nor did he hear his swift yet ruthless silencing when the dog slid into the pit with Darius, for Harry now roared and cried out with an unrepressed fury as he hurled each branch from the roof of Darius's pit.

"I'm coming to get you, you bastard! I'm coming to kill you Darius!"

Douglas MacIntyre edged closer, running from tree to tree to gain the best vantage point to observe and record the crazed orthodontist. He heard the distant hum of a helicopter and felt reassured that the police were closing in. Douglas edged in too, leaving around five metres distance between him and the new star of next week's story. He climbed the forgiving low branches of a Kentish cobnut and zoomed in with his camera to watch the wood hurling ceremony. Douglas boldly clicked his first shot as the camera released a bedazzling flash of light across the wood.

But Harry didn't notice, for his focus was elsewhere as he continued to rip the wood and branches up and hurl them to one side, even though his bandaged arm throbbed with pain. When all the wood was cleared, Harry's hands came to a large sheet of camouflage material which he threw to one side in disgust at the coward's attempt to hide. Then there were the layers of brown, corrugated plastic, he flipped the first one up and over on its end, the second he flipped the other way and it slammed to the ground as he came to the last physical barrier that separated Harry from his 'most challenging orthodontic case'. He ripped the waterproof sheet away and saw Oscar lying motionless on the floor of the pit, blood flowing from his main artery, his treacle eyes less syrupy now, staring motionless into eternity.

"NO!" Harry roared in horror and leapt down into the pit that was empty save for Oscar's body and a few remnants of human activity. Harry knelt down and picked up the dog's lifeless head, the pool of blood flowing all over his trousers and hands as he rocked 'man's best friend' on his lap. Harry returned to standing as the repugnant smell of rotting pond-weed mixed with the metallic smell of blood and the cold, damp earth filled his nostrils.

"WHERE ARE YOU DARIUS?" Harry yelled.

Then Harry saw that the end wall had a black cloth hanging over it. He stepped over Oscar's body and with his right hand, the hand that had spent eight years trying to transform the sneer into a smile, he lifted the curtain. He stood eyeball to eyeball with Darius, frozen like a rabbit in the headlights. Darius's ghostly white face and shaved head, was framed by the congealed wound that had bled and oozed pus down one side of his face. His rancid clothes clung to his tall, angular frame and his dark, black eyes of nothingness drilled coldly into Harry's face.

Nothing changed. The cowboy and his "brave little soldier" stood in the trench for twenty seconds staring at each other, absorbing the enemy before the duel commenced. Nobody could say how it would begin, let alone end. The third party, neutral observer in the trees was to remain passive – he was there merely to record events, not contribute to the outcome.

Then it started – the match that lit the fire. Initially it was the tiniest of movements no more than a twitch flickered across Darius's mean, thin lips... no more. But the twitch spread, drawing his lips thinner, out towards each ear and as his upper lid puckered up into a sadistic smile, his perfectly aligned white teeth flashed a moment of pleasure.

The sneering smile of his daughter's murderer was the trigger that released Harry's wrath. His shaking hand, more used to creating order out of chaos, and beauty from ugliness, now wanted to use his finely trained fingers and hands to destroy the vile thing that stood before him. His clenched fist and bandaged arm flew up from his side towards Darius and punched the Russian with such a force that he fell sideways, hitting his bald head against the edge of the pit. The ugly infected gash reopened and oozed puss and blood, as his former patient righted himself, staggering but still sneering.

Harry gripped the sides of Darius's face and wanted nothing more than to smash the enemy's head into a thousand pieces as he hammered his skull against the wall of the pit. Still sneering, Harry slid his bloody hands down and clamped them around Darius's neck.

Harry gripped tighter and tighter, shaking Darius's throat.

"Death's too good for you – you bastard," said Harry, as he spat into his face.

Darius just stood there limply, still smiling sardonically, his eyes black and devoid of emotion, as his face fermented red and his lifeless eyes began to pop grotesquely outwards.

"...I-I...know..." Darius said, giving his strangled, mocking reply.

All at once Harry felt the most fearful stabbing pain rip through his side – it was a long, sharp intrusion piercing under his ribs. The orthodontist slumped forward. Another slicing, searing wave of agony ripped across his right cheek and around his neck. He staggered backwards lifting his already bloodied hands to his face and side, trying to hold together the pieces of flesh that now swung apart.

Douglas MacIntyre caught each moment as the camera trembled in his hands. The police search units appeared at the fork in the path and a helicopter hovered above the canopy of trees, the cavalry arriving a little too late to prevent the first round of casualties.

The last thing Harry remembered before he slumped lifelessly to the ground was his 'most challenging orthodontic case' with his perfectly aligned teeth, sneering over him.

Then Darius clambered out of the pit and ran for his life with the police dogs snapping at his bony heels.

PART II

CHAPTER ONE

Sunday 26 September – 4.30pm

The first time Harry Maloney met Melanie Henriksen, it was the combination of Melanie's smile, and Harry's chosen profession that automatically drew his attention straight to her mouth. It was a mouth that held perfectly regular teeth, except for a cute 0.5mm gap between her upper central incisors, and a vulnerable mild Class II skeletal pattern, which, Harry thought, made her look like she needed to be kissed all the time.

Harry's long gaze into Melanie's mouth, a curious mix of business and pleasure, caused Melanie to self-consciously close her lips over her teeth, like a naughty schoolgirl, and bite her bottom lip for added security. And then their eyes met properly for the first time.

Wow those eyes, he thought.

It was Melanie Henriksen's tenacity, some said 'her balls' that brought about the unlikely union of this young, media savvy children's cook, food writer and food stylist and the slightly stiff, but endlessly warm and kind, consultant orthodontist Harry Maloney

FDS, M.Orth, MSC, BDS. Melanie's willingness to stick her head above the parapet for a cause she believed in, had certainly got her noticed, landing her an invitation to speak in Brighton, at the prestigious gathering of the top brains in the orthodontic world, the British Orthodontic Conference.

She first came to the attention of the dental and orthodontic fraternity with her single-minded battle to persuade mothers of the under fives to eliminate the consumption of sugar-packed soft and fizzy drinks in between meals. Her hard fought campaign, over a sustained two year period, ensured Melanie achieved a prime slot at the conference as 'Key Guest Speaker'. This elevated status was flashed all over the programme, next to a stunning photograph of the rising star.

Melanie's epic two year David and Goliath 'Lion's Drink' battle, created a seismic split between mothers and health specialists, and the soft drinks industry – the vociferous 'for' and 'against'. However, Melanie was not shy in publicly stating her views on the radio and in her popular magazine articles and she was soon picked up by the programme researcher on a popular early evening chat show, after he saw her publicity shot. Almost before Melanie knew it, she had landed herself a primetime slot on the 'golden sofa'. It seemed the perfect chance to take her campaign up a gear.

"I'd like to help young mum's convert their children to drinking water between meals rather than consuming high calorie, high sugar drinks that can contribute to them becoming overweight and suffering with tooth decay," said Melanie grinning a little too effusively, as tiny beads of perspiration formed across her otherwise beautiful face under the hot studio lights. "After carrying out extensive research with young families I've discovered you *can* slowly convert even the most addicted little ones to drinking water, by following my simple daily 'watering-down programme' for their juices and cordials. Every child who's taken part in the programme eventually asks for water unprompted!"

At this point in Melanie's twenty-six-year-old, single life, her willingness to put her head on the block with her carefully researched opinions on parenting, were based on observation rather than experience. This didn't bother the king and queen of chat shows – the king in particular chuckled like a schoolboy as he gawped at Melanie's impossibly blue eyes.

The royal couple didn't ask her for detailed and technical explanations. Neither did the floor manager who was shouting animatedly down the presenters' earpieces.

"Time's up, wrap it up!"

The 15 million viewers grew restless, waiting to hear who had won the three-week holiday of a lifetime to Australia. But Melanie was on a mission and so she continued, to the hair-pulling frustration of the floor manager and the suppressed yawns of the queen.

"If I could just explain to mums at home," said Melanie, smiling sweetly at the queen and then looking straight into the camera with her bedazzling blue gaze. "You see decay occurs with the sticky substance that forms on teeth called plaque, which combines with the sugars and starches from the food and drinks we consume. This combination produces acids that attack tooth enamel. So the more sugary the drink, the more acid you will produce, accelerating the decay."

At this point the floor manager's head fell into his hands. Apoplectic now, he screamed down the earpiece: "Time out, do the competition. Shut the bloody tooth fairy up!"

"But the problem is," Melanie continued earnestly, whilst still beaming nervously at the camera, "few people stop to think about the damaging effects that a perpetual stream of high sugar drinks can have on the environment in the mouth. Quite frankly you might as well give your child a bag of sweets to suck on all day! Water really is the..."

"Thank you Ms Henriksen, sorry we're out of time," said the king, taking one last look at his beautiful guest with the 'baby blue eyes'.

Melanie's self-esteem slipped through the studio floor, followed shortly after by her vivacious smile. Few would later associate her first live TV appearance with the sparkling girl-next-door 'kiddie cook' who achieved the much coveted, but hard to define 'national treasure' status before Elizabeth was taken.

❀   ❀   ❀

"Gosh that Melanie Henriksen has a lot to learn about live TV," said Minky Sloane to her PA, after watching Melanie's debut performance on the 'golden sofa'. "But there's something about that girl... all that passion and compassion of hers... and as for those eyes! She's got star quality just waiting to be un-wrapped by me."

Minky, the doyenne of food PR and publicist to a growing band of celebrity chefs, lit a slim line Panama cigar and had her PA track Melanie down to her brick-sized mobile phone in a wine bar, just off Piccadilly Circus.

"Dominica Sloane here, Sloane PR, but you can call me Minky, everybody does," said the deep, plummy voice. "Anyway darling, let's cut to the chase... I saw you on TV today."

Melanie visibly shrunk behind her large glass of wine, "I'm more used to appearing on the radio... and in magazines too," she added tentatively.

"I know, I know, I've heard you and read you and like you in both mediums," said Minky brusquely waving away Melanie's uncertainties. "Now about you and the beautiful medium of TV, I happen to think you've got huge potential darling. Let's talk. Tomorrow okay? 10.30 should suit."

And with that, the genie was gone. It was left to Minky's PA to explain that, like the company's namesake, Sloane PR could be found in Sloane Street, Knightsbridge.

Minky came straight to the point the next morning when they met, she wasn't in the habit of mincing her words. It took Minky a few minutes to explain why she was the perfect choice to guide and develop Melanie's career and another five minutes to explain her vision for a series of children's cookery books on healthy eating and a live TV mother and toddler cooking slot.

"Help to pay my goddamn extortionate fees darling!" she joked, the plum still firmly in place in Minky's mouth.

Melanie needed a few weeks to get used to Minky's style of speaking – her bang-bang-bang directness and the overuse of

'Melanie' and 'darling'. Then there was the omission of the connective words – the ands, buts, however – that gave a sentence its usual softness.

"Make it simple. Simple is powerful Melanie," said Minky as she stood up suddenly, turned on what appeared to be impossibly high heels, and without explanation disappeared into her private office. Melanie watched the clock at the other end of the meeting room as 12 minutes slipped by. Then just as suddenly as she was gone, the genie returned in a puff of cigar smoke.

"I've got it darling!" she said victoriously, slamming the paper down on the meeting table, with her perfectly manicured red nails.

"What do lions drink?"

"Pardon?" said Melanie hesitantly.

"What do lions drink Melanie? You know, bloody, big, strong roaring lions. What do they drink?"

"Water?" said Melanie, offering her response on a tray of uncertainty, unsure if it was a trick question.

"Exactly darling – WATER is 'lions' drink'. There that's it!"

Melanie still wasn't entirely sure what 'it' was, but the Sloane PR machine whirred into action immediately. Within a month Minky's media-friendly 'Lions' Drink' slogan, combined with Melanie's photogenic face, began to fill the column inches of most of the tabloids. Soon the 'Lions' Drink' campaign gained momentum, with hard facts and statistics for the broadsheet journalists to hang a properly researched story on. By the climax of Melanie's two year campaign, several leading health editors in the nationals reported on a marked drop in the proportion of five and eight year olds with filled primary teeth by 1993, which journalists dubbed the 'Henriksen effect'.

Minky, however, was less interested in facts and figures and believed the 'Lions' Drink' campaign 'grew legs' when she had an up-and-coming rap artist in London create a 'Lions' Drink' rap to a jungle beat. A nationwide tour of regional TV and radio stations followed and Minky conjured up a group of 'live under five' rappers to join in with the catchy 'Lions' Drink' theme tune of the campaign.

Lions' drink makes them big and strong
So don't have sugar drinks all day long
In between meals, stick to H_2O
Give your smile a lasting glow – yo

The rap finished with a huge 'ROAR' and that was the cue for Melanie and the children to lift their lion masks. It was also the first time Harry saw Melanie's mesmeric eyes and pretty smile, when she appeared on the London evening news at the climax of the campaign and lifted her lion's mask.

But for all the beneficiaries of Melanie's one-woman crusade, some noses were inevitably put out of joint. The attacks were especially strident from a politician with a double-barrelled surname, whose snout was firmly entrenched in the trough of vested interest. He put forward several spokesmen from the soft drinks industry to muddy the waters and cast doubt into the arena. Doubt over the food writer's 'researched figures' and doubt over the home economist's professional credentials.

There was even a rumour that he was behind the personal attack on Melanie's drinking habits and private life. Melanie was shocked to read of a *'former lover'* at university, a man who in reality had taken her out for pizza and left her cold after a cheap attempt at a grope. *'His girlfriend'* had apparently been completely addicted to one high sugar drink, he revealed in *'an exclusive'*. Her addiction was so bad that he often had to walk to the 24-hour garage in the middle of the night, after hours of *'frantic love-making'*. Somebody had even managed to get their hands on a picture of her dressed as a tart, and swigging a bottle of something or other, during a 'Vicars and Tarts' charity walk at university.

"God these people make me sick," said Minky spitting feathers. She ripped the article out of the paper and flushed it down the loo.

"Toilet paper Melanie, that's what this is darling, mere toilet paper. Leave this crap to me."

She hurled the remaining carcass of the newspaper into the bin and kicked her high heels onto the desk. Pausing to apply another layer of her stock-trade 'Siren' red lipstick, she picked up the phone and 'kicked arse'.

❀ ❀ ❀

In total contrast, the reception Melanie received in Brighton was warm and effusive. Like a preacher, preaching to the converted, the British Orthodontic Conference delegates rose to their feet to give Melanie a two-minute standing ovation. The president shook her hand warmly.

"Well done Ms Henriksen your presentation was balanced and informative. You have become a wonderful ambassador for dentistry and if I might say," he whispered, as his face flushed red, "a very glamorous ambassador too. The orthodontic community feels very lucky to have borrowed you for the day. Thank you so much for coming and enlightening us all about your tremendous 'Lion's Drink' campaign."

Melanie surfed on the wave of appreciation from the audience, who were still clapping enthusiastically.

"Now, come and meet your blind date for the gala dinner," said the president as his hand guided her through the crowds, before she had a chance to react.

*Blind date, did he say? What blind date? **That** wasn't in the briefing letter.*

The guiding hand of the president in the small of her back was like a toymaker's key. The mechanism had already been turned, her hands and legs moved stiffly forward.

I'm not 16, she wanted to say to Mr President.

But she smiled and nodded in all the right places, more mannequin like now, as the crowds politely parted leaving a clear path to the mystery man. It seemed the only person who wasn't looking at Melanie Henriksen in the room was her impending date. His back was facing Melanie and he appeared deep in conversation with a very attractive, female orthodontist.

Oh gosh this is horrid.

The wooden doll stood stiffly with her hands by her side, the toymaker's guiding hand had vanished.

What to do with my hands? I need a fag, she panicked.

But Melanie hadn't succumbed to the 'wicked weed' since she'd coughed up her guts in the girls' toilets with Samantha Tomlinson in Lower Sixth, when her mother had packed her daughter off to a boarding school in England.

Please let him be good looking, even okay she pleaded with cupid.

Her eyes slid down his broad, long back, while she waited with the matchmaker.

*Nice bottom, **really** nice bum.*

The president cleared the frog that had jumped into his throat, but the "A-hem" failed to invoke a response from her surprise date.

Can I just run now? If I'm quick, there's time to turn and run and he'll never know.

His conversation with the female orthodontist was clearly very interesting, thought Melanie, feeling a bit miffed now as her blind date remained deep in conversation with the woman.

"Dr Maloney," said the president tapping the date-with-a-name on the back. "Allow me to introduce Melanie Henriksen to you. Harry Maloney, meet Melanie Henriksen."

As Harry Maloney turned, she noticed the profile first, the square jaw line and then the open, honest face. She rapidly circled it like the hands on a broken clock speeding around the circumference in less than a second. Melanie grinned, embarrassed but pleasantly surprised.

Why is he looking at my teeth? She closed her lips over her teeth and bit her bottom lip.

*Stop looking at her mouth. She's biting that gorgeous lip of hers because **you** are making her feel self-conscious. Stop it Harry, look into her eyes,* the orthodontist mentored himself.

Finally his eyes jumped up into hers, splashing in the blue sparkle. At that moment the president slipped away.

There were no words, between them, just a big grin. They simultaneously exhaled a 'Huh'. His was a tiny burst of breath which said: *You are completely gorgeous* and her 'Huh' was one of disbelief.

I don't believe in love at first sight, she told her logical mind, but it was too late. Her heart was already in freefall.

"Please," he said, grinning broadly, "call me Harry."

He stretched out his hand to shake hers.

The thirty second handshake was exchanged in silence, as Harry and Melanie absorbed one another's faces and smiled inanely at each other. Almost immediately they forgot to move their arms up and down – as their hands simply interlocked and Melanie felt goose bumps run up her forearm.

❀   ❀   ❀

Neither could wait for the gala dinner to be over, both longed to be alone. At the end of the evening, the pair ran hand in hand, tipsy on wine and drunk on the rush of first love, giggling and kissing along the hotel corridors until they reached Harry's room.

"Are you going to invite me in for a coffee?" Melanie grinned broadly.

"No coffee I'm afraid, but how about a mug of love?"

She laughed and stepped inside the room. They stood at the foot of the bed absorbing each other – every minute detail, her curves, his strong jaw line, her liquid blue eyes, his broad shoulders. Several minutes might have passed, neither could be sure, but Melanie knew at that moment that she would never feel a greater love and desire for another man ever again, Harry Maloney was *the one.*

Every pore of his being lavished her with love and passion before they even held one another. They stepped closer and touched lightly, the ends of their fingertips their sole point of contact, as they both felt the thrill of excitement of what was to come. Then they slid the palms of their hands together, taking another step forward, and another, till Harry's body just touched Melanie's, brushing her nipples through her dress with his chest. He ran his big, strong hands under the back of her hair and gently caressed her head. Melanie dropped her head back into the palms of his hands, as he massaged her scalp and goose bumps sprang up along the length of her arms. His scent filled her with desire. Melanie felt the pulsing anticipation between her thighs, the swelling of the soft lobes of her vagina and the watery wetness moisten her knickers.

Harry bent and scooped the women, who he knew that night would be the love of his life, into his arms and lay her down on the bed. He had never wanted anyone this much and his heart beat fiercely in his chest. He straddled Melanie's feminine, hourglass frame and gently unzipped her dress, sliding the silky fabric down her body. Harry walked around the bed gazing again at the prize that he already treasured with an aching heart. Melanie held her suitor's strong arms, whilst he unhooked her undergarment. They kissed and smiled and kissed again as he placed his wine soaked lips over hers and plunged deeper into her with his tongue. He gently offered his hand and laid her back down, as her breasts parted and her nipples stood erect ready to be kissed. He peeled her knickers down her thighs and ankles, kissing and caressing the length of her body and leaving only her stockings and suspender belt around her tiny waist.

Harry gently parted her legs and he saw that she wanted him with every fibre in her body, her glistening wetness, dripping down her legs. As he moved up her body, waves of excitement and anticipation filled them both. Melanie smiled, closed her eyes and drew Harry into the hallowed court and they slipped away together in glorious oblivion.

By the end of the four day conference, Melanie knew she'd met the man she wanted to marry. Just one month later, Harry got down on bended knee to propose. Melanie had already mentally carved the initials of her married name onto an imaginary tree.

'MM & HM,' she cut into the bark of her imagination.

She smiled with the satisfied purr of a cat that knows she has pride of place on her owner's favourite chair.

"Melanie Maloney..." she murmured.

Then awakening from her 'Sleeping Beauty' fantasy, she pushed the imagined tree to the back of her mind and sat up.

"MELANIE MALONEY, baloney Maloney. Who would take *that* name seriously in my magazine articles or television appearances?"

She mentally flipped the two surnames: "Hi meet the new Mr and Mrs," she muttered to the clouds. "Harry Henriksen & Melanie Maloney."

She lay back down again under her imaginary tree, which was covered in pink blossom now, and laughed.

"All that is mine is yours, and all that is yours is mine," she whispered, "everything Mr Maloney, *except* your surname."

Chapter Two

September

In the very month that Melanie Henriksen and Harry Maloney's paths crossed for the first time at the British Orthodontic Conference, Darius and Natasha Sorokin moved to the exact same village that the couple would soon be calling 'home sweet home'.

A fresh start in the English countryside was just what the child psychologist recommended to Natasha Sorokin to help her six-year-old son recover from the trauma of seeing his 'pretend Daddy' gunned down in front of him in Moscow.

Boris Sorokin had been a brave and fearless man during his life (some said "ruthless and merciless") but when he stared death down the barrel of a gun, Boris whimpered like a baby. Then the man that Darius called 'Папа' (Daddy) for the first six years of his life; was shot into hundreds of little pieces. Boris Sorokin meanwhile, cowardly, gripped his son's hand till he fell to the ground, somehow hoping the presence of the boy (that he misguidedly thought was his genetic offspring) would save him.

Natasha observed three days of mourning after her husband's contract killing and on the third day, she rose again to a fresh start for the family that had been culled from three to two. The bereaved widow first decided to clean out the skeletons from her cupboard.

"I've always tried to tell the truth Darius," Natasha lied, as they sat by the large fountain in the centre of Sokolniki Park before their escape to Britain.

"I know this will come as a terrible blow sweetie."

No it won't.

"I don't know how to tell my boy this..." she stuttered.

Just spit it out then.

"...Boris isn't, I mean Boris Sorokin *wasn't* your real Daddy, your biological father. Mumsie wants to save you the trauma of grieving unnecessarily," she purred in Russian into Darius's ear, smoothing down his hair into a side parting.

Stop acting like my hairdresser.

Darius pushed his mother's hand away.

Mercifully, the heavy burden of grief never fell on Darius's shoulders. The long separations between Moscow and London from his money extorting, drug importing, pimp controlling 'father figure' made the grieving process considerably easier for the rich foreigner, with the dysfunctional family. Darius decided never to think of Boris Sorokin again.

"What was I to do sweetie?" she pleaded clumsily and defensively, as she twirled his hair like a baton in a street parade. "It was either pretend you were his son and marry my golden mafia boy, or abort you Darius. So what was I to do?" his mother said, seeking some latent contraceptive guidance from her six-year-old son. "You wouldn't have wanted to end your days as a foetus in a squalid little back street bin. Would you sweetie?"

Natasha used all her cunning and guile to extract substantial funds from her sugar Daddy's mafia millions and slipped anonymously through Moscow airport with her 'sweetie boy' to Heathrow airport. She spent some time with her dead husband's contacts in London, vanished again and re-materialised in the small, unassuming village of Cranhurst, in the Weald of Kent to begin a new life with her troubled young son in a beautiful Georgian mansion overlooking the village green.

As Natasha tucked her son into bed each night in the new house, sometimes she would return in the dead of night to watch him sleeping. She saw the pointy tongue that dropped out of his mouth as he slept and the right eye that never quite shut. She willed the sharp and harsh features in her imagination into the possibility of a handsome young man. Often she would place her hand on Darius's heart, for it was only in sleep that she felt she could draw close to the detached child and she felt a peculiar thrill feeling the boy's heart flutter between her fingers.

Darius was quick to embrace the country air. The big green spaces and open countryside gave him the chance to run wild and free. At night he filled his head with war films and combat games and by day he roamed across the fields and woods behind his house re-enacting scenes from the night's previous viewing. These were not the old black and white 'bang bang' Westerns that his future neighbour Harry Maloney favoured, but were the X-rated productions preferred by his pretend Daddy, where throat slitting and stomach exploding violence was the prevailing genre.

Natasha hired an English teacher to help the bright young boy perfect his second language and a Russian cook to fill the larder and fridges with her favourite delicacies and dishes. Darius enjoyed stealing the best knives from the chef's personal collection, so that he could practice his combat manoeuvres in the nearby wood. He ran from tree to tree – undetected by the opposition – and then wrapped his arm around an enemy sapling and stabbed it in the belly or slit its throat, with the accompanying sound effects.

But the chef's knives were designed to slice meat and vegetables and the knives quickly became blunt and some even snapped. Darius decided he needed to get his hands on a proper supply of hunting knives. Fortuitously for Darius, Natasha lavished a free flowing allowance to ease her guilt over the lies she had weaved about Darius's 'father' and his blood curdling murder. So with a fistful of notes, he went to buy a bike which opened up a whole new world that he couldn't easily access on foot. One Saturday he cycled into the village and rattled down a cobbled side street, following a small series of weathered, painted signs indicating the whereabouts of 'Backpack – the Outward Bound Supplies Store'.

He pulled up outside the shop, which was in desperate need of a lick of paint and looked at the hand-written slogan on the window: 'Backpack – for the young at heart'. The new kid in town leant his bike against the wall and pushed the door open with his muddy boot, which dislodged a large flake of loose paint. The door squealed louder than a frightened pig and a bell rang loudly to alert the hard of hearing owner that a treasured customer had stepped into his shop for some 'retail therapy'. As Darius meandered across the shop trying on a balaclava that caught his eye, he smelt a pungent mix of stale tobacco smoke and fried bacon from behind a curtain.

The little Russian boy stood behind the cash register and eyed an impressive collection of knives and penknives securely locked in a glass cabinet on top of the counter. Darius's head was barely visible above the counter and it was further obscured by the cash register and a large basket of moisture resistant walking socks. The sound of snoring behind the curtain was replaced by a phlegm-rattling cough, as the man pulled back the curtain and peered into the shop. Assuming the visitor had simply taken a look and left immediately – which had become an increasingly common occurrence, the shopkeeper farted loudly and filled the squalid little room with a putrid odour of sulphur and pork – betraying his penchant for fried bacon and eggs. The man had received repeated warnings from his concerned GP about his dangerously high levels of cholesterol, but the threat of imminent death had done little to dampen his insatiable taste for the great British fry up.

"Must be imagining things," said the shop owner, as he scratched under one of the folds of fat on his belly. The man looked across the empty, dusty room and cursed the day he'd turned down a good offer on the property, just before a new superstore nearby halved his turnover overnight.

Darius dropped a metal bowl and cutlery set on the glass counter and the loud clatter caused the obese man to jump, as his large, layered belly rippled and wobbled like jelly on a plate. He clutched his chest as the four chambers of his heart struggled to cope with a burst of cholesterol-laced blood now pumping through his vital organ. The shopkeeper looked down and jumped again, when he saw two eyes staring at him through a green balaclava.

"How much is this-sss?" said Darius, pulling the balaclava into a point at the top of his head.

"Oh my, you scared me half to death young man!"

The shop owner rested his fat infused body mass on a small wooden stool that creaked under the weight of his bloated frame.

"Five ninety five for one, fifteen for three," he said, wheezing loudly.

"I'll have three – green, black and camouflage," Darius said – his voice tinged with a strong Russian accent and muffled behind the wool and viscose mix. "What about the dinner sss-service?" he said sneeringly, feeling the material itching his lips.

Still holding his chest the shopkeeper said: "Nine, ninety nine for the whole set – bowl, knife, fork and spoon."

"What about the canteen?" asked Darius, as he held up an army style flask.

"Oh my you are a busy adventurer this morning," he said, laughing to himself, as his triple chin rippled under his swollen face.

"How much?" Darius repeated impatiently.

"Oh yes… um fifteen pounds and ninety nine pence," said the shopkeeper, clearly becoming excited by his largest potential sale in weeks. Then remembering that he'd read about the importance of creating a 'retail experience' for your customers he added: "Can I get you a bag to carry this little lot home?"

Darius swung round and without looking back at the man revealed a large camouflaged backpack he'd already slung over his shoulders, "Got one – how much?"

"My, my there really is no stopping you is there. That's a specialist one for trekking, so it's expensive I'm afraid."

"I sss-said, how much?" Darius said aggressively.

"Oh, um, thirty nine, ninety five – but it includes a waterproof inner lining, multiple pockets and there's a rescue blanket in the top pouch in case of emergencies."

But Darius didn't seem interested in the details of the design and began packing the items into his newly acquired backpack. Then the boy turned his attention to the locked display case of knives.

"Oh no," said the shopkeeper, "I can't sell those to a young lad like you I'd have the police after me! Now if your father were to come into the store… well… that would be a different kettle of fish altogether."

The two eyes that had scanned the knife selection lifted and bore into the back of the fat man's skull. The balaclava moved: "My Dad'sss dead, murdered by the mafia in Russia," said Darius without a hint of emotion, "and he wa-sss-n't my real Dad anyway, so don't *ever* mention him again."

A little bead of perspiration appeared on the middle of the man's forehead and ran down his nose, hanging off the tip. Silently Darius secreted two fifty pound notes from his pocket, which he'd neatly folded into small squares.

"Keep the change," said Darius and left.

By the time the man had eased himself up from his stool and unfolded the notes with his fat fingers, Darius had cycled to the end of the cobbled street.

Two weeks later, the boy returned to the 'young at heart' shop and saw that the words 'Closing Down Sale' had been sprayed right across the window in large white letters. Darius opened the squealing pig door, but saw that the bell had been taken down. The general demise of 'Backpack – the Outward Bound Supplies Store' seemed accelerated, as most of the merchandise had been hurriedly shoved into brown boxes of varying sizes. Somebody had written various sales prices on the sides of different boxes, whilst the combat clothing stood on a cheap rail with wheels, ready to be dispatched elsewhere. A man in his forties stood at the counter lifting out the hunting knives and penknives from the glass case and hurriedly pushed them into their original bubble wrap packaging.

"Where's-sss the fat man gone?" said Darius snappily. He felt irritated that the younger model standing behind the counter might have his wits about him.

"My uncle passed away a couple of weeks ago… heart attack," he added, a little too breezily to feign any sense of grief. "He died a happy man though, with a hundred quid in his hands. Anyway perhaps I can be of assistance young man? I'm Gavin."

Gavin stretched out a bony hand, rather too weakly to demonstrate he had a longer term future in retail than his uncle. Darius's eyes nonchalantly wandered down the man's long, skinny arm to his outstretched hand. The boy lifted his gaze, narrowed his eyes and out-stared the stand-in shopkeeper. Gavin let his limp, floating arm, return to his side and Darius beckoned the man closer.

"Got plans-sss for an ex-sss-pedition," Darius hissed in Gavin's ear. "Sss-so I'm depending on your shop to provide me with the provisions-sss."

The stranger in the village, with the foreign accent and the peculiar way of speaking read his list out in quick succession as the nimbler, but nervy shop assistant buzzed about the small space like a balloon accidentally released before it could be secured with a knot. He bashed into boxes that blocked his path and knocked a display tower over, stacked with walking boots, as he struggled to keep up with the list of items being fired out of Darius's mouth like a round of live ammo – fast and furious.

Darius seemed satisfied that he'd got everything he needed and paid the £283.30 bill in fifty pound notes, to the surprise of the middle-aged sales assistant. Darius turned on his heels, military style, and left without waiting for the £16.70 change.

Gavin, who hadn't achieved anything more than a grubby council flat and a paltry weekly income of benefits, held the three hundred pounds in his hand. He fanned the notes out and stroked each one like the hand of a suitor on a velvet glove.

As the fat man's only relative, Gavin was to be the sole beneficiary of the sale of the building and Gavin began plotting how he would spend his uncle's money. As he hurriedly swept the entire pile of knives on the counter into a box, with one careless and rushed swoop of his arm, he failed to spot that a dozen or so had been excreted from their bubble wrap.

CHAPTER THREE

October

After several weeks in the big old house in Kent, Natasha found she was struggling to run such a large property on her own and began to loathe the rural isolation. So in addition to the English teacher and cook, she advertised for and hired a cleaner, an ironing lady, a gardener and an odd-job boy in quick succession. Luke was a good looking man in his early thirties, with strong arms and a rugged face. He split his time between washing the cars, DIY, electrical and plumbing jobs and peeling Natasha's skin tight polka dot outfits off her body whenever the fancy took her.

Darius took an instant dislike to all the staff the dot had hired to run the Georgian mansion, but the jury remained undecided about the gardener. The first time Darius saw Mr Morris, a sprightly eighty-one-year-old man, he was skipping down the overgrown garden path pushing a wheelbarrow.

"Welcome my friend to your enchanted garden," said Mr Morris with a sense of Shakespearian drama, as he bowed grinning from ear to ear.

Dickhead, thought Darius, as he surveyed the weeds and brambles that covered the 'enchanted garden'. Mr Morris doffed his hat again.

"Well if you'll excuse me Master Sorokin, nature's calling."

Mr Morris continued down the old garden path and disappeared into the outside toilet, whistling all the while. Darius crept down the path and grabbed Mr Morris's spade. He made a dash for the back gate even before Mr Morris had pulled the clunky chain on the late Victorian cistern.

Darius disappeared deep into the local wood and identified a dense patch of sloped woodland for his newly dreamt up foxhole project. A rotting carcass from a fallen tree, a casualty of the great storms of October 1987, provided the perfect entrance to the dugout. Darius found it easy to hack out the soft wood interior with the aid of his newly acquired collection of sharp knives and the years of decay that had occurred inside the fallen section of tree. He rammed the metre length of trunk into the side of the slope to form the entrance to his camp and began digging a huge hole with the aid of the stolen spade. It was only when his stomach ached with hunger at the end of the day that he decided to return home.

Mr Morris searched for his spade everywhere and in the late afternoon, just as the gardener was preparing to leave, the elusive boy returned empty handed from the woods, covered in earth and leaves.

"Glad I could be of assistance Master Sorokin," he said, winking at the boy.

Darius glared at the old gardener.

"What do you mean?" he said defensively, holding a steady gaze with Mr Morris.

"The spade, of course, I'm so pleased it was useful."

He winked and bent down again to pull a weed he'd missed by his foot.

The next morning Mr Morris smiled to himself when he found the spade had been returned and was leaning up against the dilapidated greenhouse. Mid-morning Darius walked down the path towards the back gate and the fields and woods beyond. Mr Morris rested on his fork.

"Morning Master Sorokin," said Mr Morris, stepping out from his 1930s film set, as he courteously doffed his hat once more to greet the boy. Darius ignored him.

"Don't suppose my assistant could help you today?" said the gardener holding the spade up in the air and smiling.

Darius opened the gate, looking straight ahead, and had no intention of acknowledging Mr Morris.

"You're welcome to borrow it anytime Master Sorokin, just let me know," Mr Morris said.

As Darius disappeared across the fields he heard the distant sound of whistling dancing on the morning breeze.

Silly old bastard.

Mr Morris was known as 'the green fingers of the village green'. He lovingly tended the overgrown garden that he had first planted just after the Second World War, for the previous owners – the Davenports – and still tended the fruit cage behind The Oast for the last remaining member of the family, Florence Davenport.

Now almost five decades later the sprightly old gardener pulled at the weeds and brambles with the patience of a Saint, as he eventually tamed Mother Nature for Mrs Sorokin. He tied back, pruned and fed the unkempt rose garden and transformed it into a rose-scented haven within a year. He also rescued an overgrown vegetable patch, to provide fresh fruit and vegetables for the cook.

For many months Darius laughed at or ignored Mr Morris, who always came to work in his red braces and his big old leather hat.

Wanker.

Mr Morris was out in the garden in all weathers and Darius often watched the old man talking to the plants. The old boy looked like one of the garden statues when the sky turned black and it rained for hours on end. As the rain began to fall, Mr Morris stood still, transfixed, staring at the patch of earth he had most recently turned over with his fork.

One day, curiosity got the better of Darius and he decided to watch Mr Morris, watching the soil. He stared through the window for a while and then pressed his face flat against the glass and squelched his lips against it.

What are you looking at dickhead, he mouthed silently.

But the old gardener was too engrossed in the garden to notice Darius's weirdo, loner games. The young boy gave into his curiosity and he pulled on a raincoat and boots and went and stood alongside Mr Morris. The two stood there in silence, just how Darius liked it. Then he saw it. The earth started to move as an earthworm pushed through the surface of the sodden clump of freshly dug soil. Then another and another, until Darius counted 14 of the invertebrates doing a rain dance.

"How cool is-sss that Mr Morris-sss?"

"I'd say just about the coolest thing you're ever likely to see Master Sorokin. Nature's ploughs, that's what you're watching Darius – nature's ploughs. I can just rest on my fork for a while and watch the rain draw the ploughing team to the surface."

Little by little, Darius started helping Mr Morris in the garden. One morning as they worked in the green space together, Mr Morris shared his vision of a substantial legumes section that he planned to plant up in the spring of 1994.

"All legumes need plenty of moisture and I've got a little secret up my sleeve," he said, giggling like a child, as he pulled out a long roll of newspaper from the arm sleeves of his generous fitting waxed jacket.

Crazy old boy.

They dug a trench together, like a couple of war veterans, and filled it with garden compost and Mr Morris's trade secret – shredded newspaper. Mr Morris disappeared for a few minutes and returned with a tray of tea and cake.

"Hear Master Sorokin, come and enjoy a well earned rest."

Darius hesitated and then said: "Thank you for telling me your trade sss-secret." The boy paused again: "Do you know, I've got a sss-secret too?"

"Oh haven't we all my dear boy. But if you tell me – it won't be a secret anymore," mused Mr Morris.

"It could be *our* sss-secret," Darius said, fizzing excitedly.

"Okay then – you have a deal Master Sorokin."

Mr Morris held out his hand to shake on the pact.

"You tell and I'll zip it up," he said as he ran a pretend zipper across his smiling mouth.

"You'll have to come with me then if you want to sss-see my sss-secret," said Darius jumping up excitedly.

Darius ran ahead of Mr Morris, occasionally turning to check the coast was clear and placing his index finger over his mouth, to indicate the importance of moving quietly and stealthily across the fields to the wood. Darius picked his way across the familiar route and Mr Morris proved surprisingly sprightly for an eighty-one-year-old man.

After walking just over a mile across the fields and entering the trees, they eventually reached the thickest part of the wood. Darius bent down and lifted the camouflage to reveal a large round entrance through the trunk, leading into a dark space.

"Hold on a moment."

Darius slithered in backwards, his head being the last thing to disappear and then dropped out of sight. Darius flicked a match and lit a series of gas lamps and candles around the den. His face reappeared at the entrance, the pointed features somehow softened by his animated excitement.

"Welcome to my sss-secret hideaway Mr Morris-sss," said Darius, as his chest swelled with pride and he grinned from ear to ear.

Mr Morris squeezed through the entrance back-to-front, as instructed, with his eyes closed. His feet felt for the earth and wooden steps that Darius had fashioned into the side of the underground playpen. The gardener landed on the floor, drawing in the familiar smell of the freshly dug damp earth.

"You can open your eyes-sss now."

"My, oh my, this is fantastic Darius. Did you do all this yourself?"

Full of pride for the first time in his life, Darius nodded his confirmation. The intrepid explorer had staked the walls of the den, just as he had watched Mr Morris staking the roses in the garden. He'd even created little shelves for his survival kit, the torch, water bottle and the tins and packets of stolen food from the kitchen. There were books, candles and matches and a sleeping bag with a roll up mat.

"Looks like you're planning to move house Darius," said Mr Morris, winking at the boy.

The floor was covered with coconut matting, which Darius had scavenged from the greengrocer when he was serving a queue of regulars one Saturday morning. He'd even created a seating area with upturned crates and a table banged together with some pieces of old wood he'd found in the garage. A box stood in the corner of the den.

"What's inside that big, old box Darius?" Mr Morris asked playfully.

"Oh just some penknives and stuff," Darius said, brushing the question under the coconut matting.

"Hah... you've got a chimney," said Mr Morris, as he pointed like an excited child at the old piece of drain piping that pushed up through the corrugated and camouflaged roof.

"Promise you won't tell Mr Morris-sss?"

"It's our sss-secret Darius, forever and ever," and he gave the loner the most genuine hug of his life.

Having demonstrated his considerable DIY skills in the dugout, Mr Morris invited Darius to help repair and renovate the beautiful 1920s wooden greenhouse. One morning he arrived with a box of glass and he replaced the broken panes. Then the gardener-turned-handyman showed Darius how to rub down, fill in and undercoat the wooden frame.

"It's your choice Darius, what colour shall we paint the wood?"

Thankfully the boy changed his mind from Ox Blood Red to Hunting Green of his own accord, just as they reached the till at the DIY store.

"Well the 'hot house' is ready for action in the spring," said Mr Morris winking at his new assistant. "This is where you'll create some of your finest work Darius – it will be a real 'hot house' of horticultural genius. Just you wait and see. We can travel all over Europe, down through the glorious Mediterranean, over to the Caribbean and the Far East while we're at it. This is our very own tardis and we can go anywhere we please."

Just as a painter sees his completed canvas before the first stroke of paint, Mr Morris began to fill the blank space in the greenhouse with green and variegated leaves, purple tubers, red fruits and yellow flowers.

"We'll have hot chillies and peppers in the grow-bags and pots here. Then what about some beautiful aubergines?"

Darius liked the fact that Mr Morris was asking his opinion on something other than his mother's family planning issues and love life.

"We can get on and sow the aubergines next February then we'll transfer them into pots of compost over here. We'll need to wait till March or April to sow the Okra – that's a bit more sensitive to our colder climes – but at least it's not so demanding on the watering front."

Another seed of an idea germinated in Mr Morris's fertile mind and his face lit up.

"Why don't we have a race between Ceylon Spinach and Yams? Once we transfer them into the garden, you'll be able to watch them grow, they're two of the most vigorous climbers I know. The two of them might reach up to ten feet. It'll be a real 'Day of the Triffids' here next summer – you'll see Darius."

CHAPTER FOUR

Saturday 8 January – 2pm

Melanie and Harry got hitched in the New Year of 1994 in a 13th century church overlooking the sea in South Devon. Minky Sloane's choice of venue was a place the publicist assured the couple would ensure "the most beautiful goddamn day of your life is just that – beautiful and *private*".

Melanie's long dark hair, an unmistakable nod to her French grandmother, was weaved into a tumbling celebration of curls crowned with fresh roses. Even as she stepped into the back of the church, partly hidden by her veil, Harry could see the deep, blue Norwegian eyes, waiting to be unwrapped and the mouth asking to be kissed.

"You look beautiful," he whispered, as she drew level with Harry on the arm of her father. She lifted her veil.

Then he gave her the silent look that spoke of his eternal love and commitment to her.

Melanie Henriksen I love you with all my heart…always have… always will.

He paused, his gaze more quizzical now.

Do you love me too Melanie? Do you want to come and spend the rest of your life with me?

And her eyes danced across his face with *I do, I do, I do,* before the congregation had even picked up the order of service sheets.

❀ ❀ ❀

A few weeks after the wedding, Melanie felt a dark sense of foreboding as her dreams became punctured with images of her headstone marked with the date October 2008.

"I'm going to die young," she said one night, moaning in her sleep.

Drenched in sweat, she sat bolt upright in bed, freeing herself from the fearful, recurring nightmare.

"Shshshsh gorgeous."

Harry soothed his wife, kissing her crumpled brow, and his tenderness reassured her temporarily. But as the dream returned night after night, Melanie became overwhelmed with a desire to live a long life, beyond the 41 years being promised to her in her nightmare. More than anything else, she wanted to show Harry just how much she loved him and give him an extended bloodline of little Maloneys. She carried her beating heart, just as she would one day carry the beating, kicking, living Hannah and Elizabeth in her womb. Like a poet holds a new sonnet in his head, or a composer protects a landmark composition, Melanie carried her heavy heart around. It ached when Harry left her and beat faster when he came home at night.

They walked across the South Downs, wild and free, drugged up on love. The sky turned black suddenly and the heavens opened. Harry grabbed Melanie's hand and they laughed, on their futile race to beat the deluge. Tumbling over in the wet grass and moss, they fell on top of each other, rolling and laughing, first Harry, then Melanie, over and over. They finally nestled in a clump of long wet grass, with Melanie on top. Suddenly tears began to stream down Melanie's face.

"Why the tears?" Harry said, kissing her wet cheeks.

She looked at him smiling and crying, already longing for his baby to be inside her.

"Sometimes I love you so much it hurts – my heart aches. You *need* to know how much I love you Harry. I know it sounds ridiculous, but I'm crying because you make me so happy."

He cupped her face between his hands.

"My gorgeous girl," he said, as he reassuringly stroked her hair. "We've got a whole lifetime together. When we're cuddled up on a park bench someday, old and grey, we'll look at our big brood of children, our children's children and you'll see just how far this love you have for me reached, forever and ever Melanie. Your love for me will stretch into eternity through all the generations that started with you and me."

Harry rolled her over one more time with such tenderness and compassion and kissed her aching heart away.

❀   ❀   ❀

The next time Harry returned to the beautiful Devonshire church where they wed, was in 2009. He walked hand in hand with his nine-year-old daughter Hannah, clutching the words of his address for the memorial service 'To celebrate the life of Melanie Henriksen OBE – beloved wife, mother, cook extraordinaire, champion children's campaigner and charity fundraiser'.

Harry couldn't bear to speak publicly at the funeral of his wife in October 2008, but the passage of six months gave him the courage to climb the three steps of the ancient stone pulpit, to unwrap his love for her in front of family and friends, colleagues and politicians. Each fragile sheet was gently pulled away, layer by layer and laid before the people that had loved her the most and deeply respected her work.

"I fell in love with Melanie for her 'joie de vivre' and her gorgeous giggle. It was an impossible infectious laugh that made everybody else laugh too. And I'll *never* forget the first time I looked into her blue eyes…"

Harry stared blankly into the distance, over the sea of faces, to nowhere in particular.

"And who could forget the smile – that smile lit up her face and the whole room."

He smiled, and drifted again to another dead-end without her. He pulled himself back.

"Melanie's unflinching determination was legendary. She put healthy food and drink consumption in the under fives on the political agenda, whilst raising hundreds of thousands of pounds for children's charities in the UK during her numerous charity walks and marathons. Melanie never took the easiest or shortest path. I'm sure you'll all remember the time she ran the London Marathon dressed as a cupcake to raise awareness of the rising tide of childhood obesity."

There was a low hum as the congregation mustered a smile and savoured the shared memory.

"Through Melanie's articles, her books and TV appearances; she encouraged a whole new generation of young mothers to discover the joy of cooking with their children and the thrill of enjoying healthy, home cooked meals. And she did so much to reduce tooth decay in young children too – who could forget her first appearances on TV with that zany 'Lion's Drink' mask. We all know about Melanie's tenacity too, she made considerable personal sacrifices to fight for what she believed in and to support some of the country's best loved children's charities."

He paused and swallowed hard.

"But it was her love for two children in particular that took my breath away. Her enormous capacity to love our children often left me in awe. Her passion for Hannah and Eli-za-beth…" the voice cracked and trailed. But everyone understood what he wanted to say.

Each memory was gently folded into a neat pile at the end of the memorial. The congregation lovingly placed the tear soaked memories into a private drawer for safekeeping, hidden from the prying eyes and hungry news crews camped outside the church.

Harry slipped away from the church, down the winding path that led to the graveyard. He lay on top of Melanie, just as he had on the South Downs fifteen years earlier. Away from the crowds and cameras, the tears flowed fast and freely. He put his mouth to the damp grass and whispered to his wife.

"Melanie Henriksen I love you with all my heart…always have…always will."

And he lay his left cheek on the grass, revealing the deep and unsightly scar that ran across the 'dishy dentist's' right cheek and around his throat. He kissed the grass and his heart yearned to touch the lips that always needed to be kissed.

CHAPTER FIVE

Thursday 2 February – 6.17pm

Two coincidences were to draw Melanie Henriksen and Harry Maloney closer to the house that would one day be their baby's grave. The first was the fateful arrival of the property details of '*The Oast, in the well-appointed village of Cranhurst*' and the second was Melanie's urgent need to find a country kitchen setting for her first big break on television.

The onerous 'double celebration' started mundanely enough with nothing to alert the couple that they were just about to make the worst decision of their lives. At the time, Harry Maloney the young consultant was more preoccupied with his dash home from the tube station in torrential rain. For despite hearing the forecast of heavy wintry rain, he had hurriedly left the house for a full day at Guy's Hospital without an umbrella or raincoat. Now his best silk suit had degenerated into a soggy shadow of its former glory and his hair dripped haphazardly around his strong and handsome jaw line.

He fumbled for the key to the poky, rented London flat that

had been christened 'home' for the first year of their marriage. The rain fell so hard that it bounced three or four inches up his trouser legs, staining the pale grey material to a mud splattered charcoal. Pools of water ran around his feet on the uneven concrete path and seeped through the stitching of his shoes, permeating his socks. Harry tried to shield a large pile of patient files under his arm – he had at least two hours of dictation to wade his way through that evening, when all he wanted to do was kiss and cuddle Melanie on the sofa. He fumbled for his key in his suit pocket and berated himself for not sending it to the menders – the small hole had developed into a significant tear in the lining. This left him chasing his key around the base of his suit jacket with his free hand, whilst holding his briefcase between his knees to protect the leather from the small stream that now ran between his ankles.

It had been a particularly tiresome day – with a stressful meeting about budgets denying him a lunch break and a political wrangle with two heads of department looming gloomily over his afternoon clinic. Finally, he managed to jam the key into the sticky lock and wearily shoved the door open with his foot.

As the door opened he saw Melanie skipping towards him like a sixteen-year-old girl as she sprang into the air and threw her arms around the soggy scarecrow that stood in the doorway. This sent the papers flying in the air like confetti.

"Melanie!" Harry feebly protested between kisses as he saw his evening's work land on the floor in a muddled heap. Melanie wrapped her legs around Harry's tall, broad frame and rubbed her nose excitedly across his – side to side – Maori style.

"Sorry for the mess my gorgeous, I'll pick up your papers later... I promise," Melanie said as she jumped down grabbed Harry's hand and grinned playfully, kissing him again. Her hot, minty tongue wrapped his and melted the frustrations of the day away. Harry took one last half-hearted look at the pile of papers on the floor.

"Wait till you hear my news – it's not a night for working, it's made for celebrating," said Melanie, as she grinned widely and placed her index finger to her lips – as though she were the keeper of a great secret. Melanie led Harry into the small front room with its hand-me-down sofa and eighties chrome and black coffee-table. These recent additions stood strangely at odds with the tasteful wedding gifts and accessories that filled the room. Pride of place was given to a precious bronze 1920s lamp given to Melanie by her French grandmother at their wedding.

Melanie grabbed a towel from the airing cupboard and lovingly dabbed his skin dry, peeling off his suit jacket and shirt. She reached across to a bottle of champagne and poured two glasses.

"Well?" said Harry inquisitively.

"I've got two amazing pieces of news," she said beaming from ear to ear.

Her infectious joy spread across Harry's face and he touched her stomach in anticipation of her news.

"Oh no," she said, gasping, "I'm sorry darling...not that. Not yet, I certainly wouldn't be drinking champagne if my news was... *that*."

Harry's face slipped a little and he moved his hand to hers

and patted it reassuringly, straining not to run his fingers straight between her thighs.

Smiling gently, Melanie placed the details of The Oast in Cranhurst on Harry's lap.

"This is the one Harry, I just know it."

He tried not to show his disappointment and looked through the smart booklet, filled with photographs of The Oast, its out-buildings, a front view over Cranhurst village green to a large Georgian mansion on the other side of the grass and a rear view over rolling farmland and countryside.

"What's an oast house?" asked Harry, suddenly aware of his city surroundings and cloistered upbringing in his parent's Chelsea mews.

She giggled and kissed him on the forehead.

"I had to ask the estate agent too. They were used to dry the hops for brewing beer, but most have been converted now into private houses."

"Ah," he said absorbing the information and the flowery descriptions and embellished detail that was included in the house details. He smiled and laughed as he scanned and read aloud: *'The Oast is a spacious 19th century oast, with quadruple roundels, and substantial 18th century barn to create a unique and generous family home in one of the most sought after villages in the 'Garden of England'. This beautiful and well-proportioned quadruple oast offers tremendous potential.'* You know when they say *tremendous potential* it is code for loads of work and lots of money."

"I know," she said, stroking his hair empathically. "But it's a bit like when I first saw you – I knew you were the one."

Unable to think of any objections – he feebly murmured, "So where is Cranhurst?"

"Apparently it's the prettiest village in the loveliest part of West Kent," said Melanie in estate agent's patter.

"Kent? But that's miles away, how can we contemplate being so far outside central London?"

"The nearest train station is only seven minutes away and you've always dreamed of setting up a private practice from home. Little by little, you could reduce your consultancy post in London as the practice takes off. I know it's a big step, but I really believe in you darling."

Harry wrestled with the 'what ifs' and 'buts' that raced around the boxing ring in his head. He wanted to be able to deliver a knock-out blow that would dispel his worries about financing the project, but it was Melanie who would ride in to hold the financial reigns for her cowboy.

"That brings me on to my second piece of news. Minky Sloane called me this morning to say she's secured my big TV break-through – my very own TV series. It's going to be called 'Melanie's Munchkins' and I've been offered a fantastic fee Harry and there's a brilliant book deal on the back of the series too."

"Congratulations my clever TV cook," said Harry, as he wrapped his arms around Melanie's waist and hugged her as tight as a bear.

"Filming will start in mid-September and the production company wants me to cook in a 'wholesome country kitchen' set-ting. The producer says it will be a more appropriate environ-ment for a healthy cooking programme aimed at mothers and their young children. They are happy to fund the whole kitchen conversion and have sponsors for everything, from the paint to the kitchen units. It's going to be like working on one giant set of sponsorship, product placement and advertising! Minky says the more I let my fans feel part of my life the more they'll want my programmes and books, which fills me with both dread and excitement."

Melanie barely drew breath. "I've always dreamed of building my own home studio and when we manage to make a baby, how lovely will it be for us both to be close to our work and our children. All we've got to do now is get you to fall in love with the property, buy it and convert the studio by the autumn and get your surgery sorted almost as soon as we get there."

She smiled persuasively, caressing his hair.

"Okay, okay, but just slow down honey, one step at a time. Book an appointment and let's hope it will be love at first sight."

"Oh it will be Harry, just remember how you felt about me when you first saw me."

...And so their journey to the wrong side of town began.

CHAPTER SIX

Saturday 4 February – 11am

As the couple drew up outside The Oast Melanie felt the powerful and seductive pull of the house that was to draw her in and become home for the next thirteen years (unlucky for some). This was the house that would be her castle and protector. It would be the love nest for her procreation, the cradle for her young, the party hall for her family's anniversaries and birthdays, her retreat from the media's prying eyes... and the tomb for her second child. An artery ran somewhere between the building's beating heart, the four chambers of the roundels and Melanie's own heart. There was an inextricable connection, mere bricks and mortar cried out to be cared for again and transformed from that most inanimate of states – a house – into a living, breathing home. Melanie exhaled, slid her hand into Harry's and absorbed the property.

Home sweet home she mouthed silently. In her mind, Melanie had already bought The Oast before she had stepped across the property's threshold.

Harry scanned the length and height of the main building: "It's huge!" he exclaimed.

"What a handsome barn and oast, wouldn't you say, they don't come much more beautiful than this," said a rotund, port-faced, well groomed gentleman with a clipped accent.

The estate agent strode up the old brick garden path. The front garden was once richly stocked with poppies, Canterbury Bells, Chinese Lanterns, Lupins and Foxgloves, but now was a neglected wasteland of weeds and overgrown lawn. The man exited through a hole in a weather-beaten picket fence, where once the gate had hung.

"Henry Moseley," said the man, thrusting out a confident right hand to Harry.

He clenched a firm fist around the orthodontist's hand and shook it hard and bullishly. The agent's grip proved far too forceful for Melanie's petite, soft hand and after the encounter she slipped her right hand behind her back and massaged the palm.

The Oast was one of Moseley & Moseley's hottest properties and despite its dilapidated state, Henry was going to make "damn sure" he secured a quick sale on behalf of Miss Davenport, whether she liked it or not. He bragged to his brother that he would "seal the deal" by the end of the weekend, before "the old bat popped her clogs".

"Let me show you around the outbuildings before we go into the main house," Henry suggested.

With a magnanimous sweeping gesture, Henry guided the couple over to a single storey brick building.

"Welcome to the byre," he smiled smoothly.

"The byre?" Melanie quizzed.

"It means cow house, though funnily enough the Davenports used to keep pigs here. They ran a very successful pig business alongside the hop farm. Hop production ceased in the early seventies when the oast house and barn was converted into Miss Davenport's home. The byre is little more than a shell, but as you can see it has *enormous potential*."

Henry rotated his arms into a huge arc to emphasise just how much potential the former pig shed really had. Melanie and Harry caught each others' gaze and Harry saw his wife bite her bottom lip to suppress the giggle gremlin that was never very far from the surface.

"I'm obviously very familiar with your line of business Ms Henriksen, having seen you on numerous occasions on *Wake Up Britain*, and I understand Mr Maloney that you are a consultant orthodontist at Guys hospital," said Henry, oozing with charm as they walked through the outbuilding. "With so much space, may I be so bold as to suggest that the byre could be converted into a fabulous orthodontic practice and you'd be the first specialist orthodontist in the Cranhurst area I believe."

Having planted the seed of an idea, Henry drifted back outside to allow the couple time to absorb and get a feel for the space. Fired up and excited, Harry started to pace out the floor area and used the heel of his shoe to mark out imagined rooms on the dirt floor.

"This could be the reception area and waiting room here. The entire middle section would make a fantastic space for the surgery. Then we could have an x-ray room... here, filing room...

here, a sterilising room over there and a laundry room and toilet at the back here. It's a perfect size and just far enough away from the house to give my increasingly famous wife privacy from the stream of patients that will be beating a path to my door!"

The couple emerged from the byre smiling and chatting animatedly to one another. Henry folded his arms and felt rather smug with his first round victory. The seasoned estate agent usually knew within the initial ten minutes of a property tour, if he had a potential sale on his hands. The non-verbal signs were already looking good he thought.

"The second outbuilding would provide a great guesthouse with a little modernisation," Henry suggested.

The compact two storey weather-boarded cottage featured two small double bedrooms, a kitchenette/diner, sitting room, bathroom, laundry room and boot area – all of which were slavishly dated in a late seventies/early eighties time warp.

"If you've got any irritating relatives… I'd bung them in here, perfect place for the mother-in-law that's for sure." Henry chortled at his joke. "Whilst the décor is rather dated, I'm sure with your flair and good taste Melanie the guesthouse would look simply stunning." Henry had found flattery a powerful sales tool, when trying to woo couples to part with hundreds of thousands of pounds and so he laid it on thick for his first ever 'celebrity client'.

The estate agent led the couple around the expansive and overgrown garden, save for a beautifully cared for fruit cage, and pointed out a strange and unfamiliar building on the boundary, which looked like a row of animal stalls. Pre-empting the couples' curiosity Henry explained: "These were the hoppers' huts, where the hop pickers would sleep, eat and stay during the hopping season. The huts are listed now, so whilst you might struggle to get permission to convert them, they would make a very original garden shed to store your garden tools. Cleaned up they could also make a rather unusual playhouse for 'the children'... if I may be so bold as to assume that you are planning to have a family."

The couple both nodded in the affirmative, but neither dared catch each others' eye in case they betrayed their rising fertility panic, having both wrongly assumed that Melanie would fall pregnant straight after the wedding a year ago.

The estate agent explained that the hop huts had been built in brick just after the Brick Tax was abolished in 1850.

"The buildings were considered 'the height of modernity' by the poor, flea infested residents that annually flocked to the Davenports' farm from the squalor of Victorian London. With hoppers more commonly housed in corrugated huts for hopping in Kent, a hut on the wealthy Davenport's farm was considered a prize worth fighting for the families pouring out of the dark and dismal Victorian tenement buildings in the East End," Moseley waxed lyrically. "This apparently led to several unseemly scraps on the special hoppers' trains each September but eventually the 'wheat was separated from the chaff' and the hardest working, most loyal families were given the right to pre-book their chosen hut on the Davenport estate for the following season on the Costa Del Kent!"

Henry snorted like a pig in search of truffles in the wood, entertained by his own joke.

Many of the doors – which had once benefited from an annual coat of white paint – had now fallen into a poor state of repair, with just a few traces of paint clinging on to the rotten wood. Two of the twenty doors had given up their fight to hang onto the rusty hinges altogether and lay on the ground where they had dropped off over a decade earlier.

"Have a look inside if you want to," Henry invited.

Melanie was surprised just how small each hut was.

"How many people stayed in here?"

"Incredibly whole families of eight to ten people squeezed into these little rooms, with primitive sanitation and most of the cooking carried out on an open fire outside, it was pretty basic to say the least, certainly not my idea of camping!" Henry snorted again. "Right," said the estate agent rubbing his hands together and keen to close the sale, "Let's head over to the main house… though of course it wasn't originally the main house. No, if you look to the other side of the green, the Davenports' family home was that rather extraordinary Georgian house over there. In fact the Davenports owned the land that ran all the way around the green, whilst the farm stretched right back to the line of the woods. They were a very dominate force in Cranhurst and were hugely successful farmers in their Victorian heyday."

The three of them walked over to The Oast as Henry continued with his flamboyant storytelling.

"The Second World War decimated the family and, by all accounts, there was a bit of family scandal too, but I'm not sure of the details. The main house was sold off in the fifties for a song by the younger Davenport sister Viola who was apparently Florence

Davenport's younger twin. Florence Davenport – whom you'll meet shortly – lived in the guesthouse with her mother till her mum died, but Florence struggled to keep the hop farm going. It all folded in the late sixties I believe. Florence Davenport used the last part of the family fortune to convert the barn and oast into a residential property. By all accounts the poor dear ran out of money years ago, so the conversion is a bit half-baked I'm afraid."

Henry thumped on the front door of the oast house with his fist and then pulled down hard on a brass rod that linked to a large bell. The estate agent turned to Melanie and Harry and in subdued tones said: "I must just warn you that Miss Davenport is rather poorly. She has days when she seems very reluctant to leave the house and has been known to send buyers away after taking one look at them. But don't let that put you off. I think we can conclude that she is rather muddled and confused and her bark is worse than her bite! She lives entirely in the kitchen now and she can be rather territorial about that space. Follow me in – Miss Davenport's carer usually leaves the front door unlocked."

The couple stepped into a spacious entrance hall, which opened out into the spectacular main room of the house. The sitting room, with its Cathedral like proportions, ran the full height of the barn and Melanie and Harry let their heads drop backwards, to view the mesmeric oak beam roof that resembled the inner bowels of an upturned ship.

"It's beautiful!" Harry gasped.

Each piece of furniture was covered in old bed sheets or embalmed in a plastic casing and there was a strong and musty odour of mothballs. A thick layer of dust covered every surface and a blanket of cobwebs hung at each window, like Flemish woven lace marking the passage of time in the now abandoned space.

"A little spring cleaning would go a long way," Henry jested discreetly behind a hand held to his mouth. "However I think you'll agree that this is indeed a stunning room. Some of these pieces of oak will be up to 800 years old. Whilst the barn was erected in the early 1700s and the kilns were added in the mid 1800s, the builders tended to use reclaimed wood from the redundant ships of the 1500s. I guess they were into recycling even then!"

The only visual interruption in the entire cavernous space was a well-worn staircase which ran up the middle of the room to the upstairs walkway. The three of them climbed the old wooden steps, walking in the footsteps of a thousand hop workers before them. The enormous hop press still stood in the middle of the upstairs balcony, which had once formed the cooling floor for the hops to be dried. The worn winch handle bore testimony to the thousands of turns made by the workers as they pressed the dried hops into huge six foot high hop pockets, before each sack was lowered to ground level, stencilled with the Davenport stamp, and sent to the great breweries of Victorian Britain.

The bedrooms were entirely empty save for a commode and a walking frame in the corner of one room. Both of the bathrooms were filthy and the green slime in the baths and toilets indicated that neither had been disturbed for several years, whist the disabled handrails charted the demise of the once reputedly beautiful Florence Davenport.

"The whole of the upstairs would benefit from your creative flair Melanie, but I think you'll agree that this is a stunning blank canvas for you to make your mark. It's only cosmetic changes that need to be made. All the rooms are incredibly spacious and the view from the bedroom windows is stonking," said Henry, still stuck in an eighties' time warp.

The couple walked over to admire the 'stonking' views across the Weald of Kent.

"That's some view to wake up to every morning don't you think?" Henry suggested.

Melanie and Harry nodded in silence smiling, barely able to contain their excitement. It was indeed a breathtaking view.

"Now let's go back downstairs and move into the heart of the property. If you can look past the current state of the kitchen, I think you'll find that this could make the perfect kitchen studio for you Melanie. My brother mentioned you are looking to create an environment suitable for filming a *new* TV programme... how intriguing! My wife loves your appearances on *Wake Up Britain* and was thrilled to read in the papers that you will be hosting your own cookery show for mothers and children. For now you'll have to use your imagination, but without wishing to sound repetitive..." he snorted again, "the kitchen has *great potential*. Oh and there's also a large basement running under the kitchen which is ideal as a wine cellar and for additional storage."

Harry held Melanie's hand as they walked down the staircase together. He squeezed her waist and smiled his seal of approval.

"You're right, I think this is the one," he whispered in her ear.

He stole a kiss on the last step, as Henry Moseley strode across the vast sitting room ahead of them. Henry lifted the wooden latch on the oak door and led the couple into the kitchen. The sweet, repugnant odour of stale urine, mixed with a rotting cat litter tray and ingrained bacon fat swirled up into their nasal passages. Melanie instinctively lifted her hand to shield her nose from the foul stench, as her stomach turned and she retched behind her hand. Perhaps she was pregnant after all, she thought, until she looked across at Harry and noticed he too was struggling with the disgusting odour that filled the room.

Florence Davenport sat in the shadows, with the vague outline of a carer standing behind her wheelchair. The curtains were to be kept drawn at all times, the lady of the house had ordered, to blot out the daylight and the world outside. Miss Davenport's face was almost entirely obscured by a heavy shadow running across the darkest corner of the room. Only her swollen feet were easier to define, as they fell into a shaft of light that had escaped between one roughly drawn pair of curtains. Her mummified legs had been wrapped in bandages to control the hideous swelling and fluid retention that pooled in her feet. Above the bandages were bloated red and peeling limbs that were so deformed by their elephantine proportions, Miss Davenport's limbs appeared like the discarded legs of an oversized mannequin in an old curiosity shop. One foot had fallen off the rest plate of the old lady's wheelchair and slumped lifelessly at a peculiar angle, creating the optical illusion that it had become entirely detached from its owner.

Melanie and Harry suddenly felt self-conscious holding hands, awkwardly dropping them to their sides like rag dolls. The party stood in silence, save for the old lady's unsettled phlegm-filled breathing and the hiss of the oxygen tank.

"Turn on the light over there," said Miss Davenport hoarsely.

The woman waggled her bloated hand impatiently to the carer. The nurse in a crisp white tunic stepped out from the shadows and flipped the switch on an archaic lamp. Dull orange light stretched and settled across the face of the 71-year-old Miss Davenport.

"Who are these?" rasped the voice trapped in the dying rib cage.

A distended hand held the top of an ornamental cane. The lady twisted a dazzling diamond and sapphire engagement ring on her ring finger, but where the swelling was so pronounced, it seemed as though the ring might cut her blue-tinged finger off entirely. Quite suddenly, the end of the cane rose up from the floor and moved between the faces of the 'intruders' like a snooker player wondering whether to play the blue or the green.

"Who are these I say?" repeated Miss Davenport with her acerbic rasp.

The estate agent cleared his voice – preparing to speak.

"I didn't ask *you*!" she screamed at Henry.

The cane, come billiard cue, rose up in Miss Davenport's hand to Henry's eye level and 'potted the black' with a poke on his forehead between his eyes. Henry wanted nothing more than to snap the ornamental cane over his knee and throw it at the old bat, but he knew that a lucrative sale was almost in the bag.

"You girl," she said pointing at Melanie. "Why do you want to buy my house?"

"Well I'm not sure where to begin Miss Davenport," Melanie rattled off forgetting the importance of appearing cool, calm and collected in front of the seller. "I think the oast is absolutely beautiful. From the minute the details dropped through our door in London I… I fell in love with it!"

"And what about him," Miss Davenport spat out, pointing at Harry with the cane. "Do you love *him?*"

"Oh absolutely," said Melanie effusively, forgetting herself again. She paused and nibbled her bottom lip. "Actually it was love at first sight Miss Davenport, we both knew straight away that we'd found *the one.*"

There was a long dragging sound as Miss Davenport sucked in some more oxygen from the tank. Her wild but watery green eyes stared madly over the oxygen mask.

"I remember that, I remember that too," she mouthed through the mask sounding like an extraterrestrial creature. Melanie couldn't be sure whether the water flowing from her eyes was an infection or tears. An ill-fitting thick auburn wig clung to the old lady's shrunken skull like a dead cat. Miss Davenport let the mask drop to one side. Her lined face was covered in thick orange powder and her mouth was drawn into a tight, puckered grimace as though she had spent a lifetime sucking on the bitterness of life.

The sour and barbed low points of Miss Davenport's life were more acidic and biting than almost any other and had left her with a fatal wound that would not heal, even after five decades of nursing a broken heart. She wallowed in a cesspit of resentment and regret. It was a life that had reduced the sparkling beauty, painted and preserved at the age of 21 in a large portrait that now hung behind Miss Davenport in the kitchen, to a simmering and bitter old woman who had lost in love and lost in life.

CHAPTER SEVEN

23 August – 3.43am

If it were possible that one could be born with a silver spoon in one's mouth, then Florence Rose Davenport was born with a silver ladle between her exquisite cupid lips. For Florence had the softest of landings in the four poster bed of Mr and Mrs Davenport's bedroom, inside the beautiful Georgian family home overlooking Cranhurst green and surrounded by the profitable Davenport estate. Florence was the first twin to be born to Malcolm and Diana Davenport, in the early hours of the morning on the 23 August 1923, twenty four minutes ahead of her younger sister – Viola Geraldine Davenport.

The beautiful identical twins lived a charmed life on the farm until the outbreak of the Second World War. Adored by their parents and having the good fortune of a kind and Bohemian nanny, the girls were free to play on the farm for hours at a time, whilst their nanny refined their formal syllabus to focus on the girls' favourite subjects of art, geography, embroidery, reading and French.

The twins' older brothers (Edward, Charles and Arthur) had been carefully raised and groomed in the management and running of the Davenport estate, by their father. Edward the bright and aspiring businessman deftly handled the farm's accounts. He negotiated the best prices for the Davenports' hops and then, when the Hops Marketing Board was established in 1932 to set the prices of hops with the growers, Edward ensured that he had a seat on the board. He was bold and brave in his business decisions and the Davenports' eldest was also a masterful social chameleon. He seamlessly moved between the hoppers on the estate, to socialise with the sons of some of the oldest and richest brewing families in London.

Charles was intuitive and more comfortable surrounded by the familiarity of the farm, preferring to spend much of his time outside. He oversaw the hop planting and harvesting and ensured that the Davenports were the first hop farm in Kent to introduce hop picking mechanisation in 1934, ahead of their biggest rival in Paddock Wood. He was a great motivating force amongst the hoppers and always looked for ways to improve the pickers' working and living conditions. In a rare mixing of classes, Charles organised an annual cider and sausage party in the apple orchards each October to celebrate the end of harvesting.

The youngest son, Arthur, developed the pig farm first started by his grandfather into a thriving business. He introduced rare breeds not seen in the county since Queen Victoria's reign and discovered the optimum techniques to rear the best tasting meat. To his delight the happiest pigs made the tastiest pork and his pigs were never happier than when they were roaming free and foraging in the apple orchards. Arthur, meanwhile, was at his most content when he was surrounded by the pigs. More often than not, and especially on fine days, his mother could find Arthur sat in the corner of the orchard watching over the pigs, with a piglet on his lap and the sweetest look of contentment she had ever seen on a man's face.

The outbreak of the Second World War saw the slow unravelling of Florence Rose and Viola Geraldine Davenport's charmed life, as the seemingly inseparable bond between the devoted twins was cruelly broken. Despite the 1938 Schedule of Reserved Occupations, giving the Davenport boys the perfect 'get out of jail' card, Malcolm Davenport was determined that his sons should fight for 'King and Country'. Learning little from the senseless loss of a generation during the First World War, the fiercely patriotic Malcolm Davenport persuaded the local conscription office that the farm could continue to flourish under his experienced hand.

Edward was the first to sign up in 1939, followed shortly after by Charles and Arthur. Ironically it was Edward the bright, quick-witted businessman who adapted best to the theatre of war. His daredevil stunts, jumping out of the tree house as a child, were perhaps the earliest indication that Edward would head straight for the Airborne Division of the British Army. Indeed, the eldest Davenport boy was one of the first to train at The Central Landing School near Manchester when Winston Churchill ordered the creation of a British Airborne Capability in June 1940. But the paratrooper's luck finally ran out during Operation Varsity in March 1945. On entering the southern part of the Wald a sniper's bullet caught him clean between the eyes.

For the second son, Second Lieutenant Charles Davenport, the end came much more quickly even though statistics should have been on his side. With 330,000 allied troops successfully rescued during the Battle of Dunkirk in 1940 there was good reason to be confident that Charles would again see the white cliffs of Dover. In May of that year, Charles was part of the British Expeditionary Force that had become isolated from the French and Belgian armies near Armentières, as the Germans spearheaded their way up to the French coast on 20 May. Charles had shown an early and instinctive propensity to care for those around him on the farm in Kent, and the constant threat of death in France, merely amplified this noble character trait. When his best friend was left isolated by shrapnel wounds to his legs, Charles's decision to run back to his comrade under enemy fire was typical of his selfless-ness. The fact that he ran into an exposed area of combat, threw the soldier over his shoulder and carried him back to the relative safety of the unit would have been seen by many as heroic and sacrificial. His death the next day, however, was as unfortunate as his actions were brave the day before. An urgent 'call of nature' lured the Second Lieutenant (who should have known better) to step momentarily behind a farmhouse, out of view of his unit, and straight onto a mine.

Arthur, the youngest Davenport boy, survived the war, but when he returned from the Thai jungle his mother knew that the boy she had brought into the world was gone forever. The gaunt and tortured frame of her son was a shadow of its former self. Arthur's mind remained trapped on the railway tracks in 'Hellfire Pass'.

His nightmares were forever pinned somewhere under the 120,000 sleepers, which had cost the life of one man for every one lain. The poor boy's dreams would never be sweet again. They were punctuated by the screams of the POWs being ruthlessly whipped by the Japanese guards and the haunting, emaciated gaze of a thousand men who had lost the will to live another day in Hades. Perhaps it was little wonder that the soft hearted, youngest son, who had always felt more at home with his prized pigs, than in the company of men, could no longer stomach the mental torment of being a POW in Thailand. Arthur lasted little more than six months after his return to the 'Garden of England' and was found dead in the byre with the top of his head blown away, lying amongst a litter of Berkshire piglets.

Such catastrophic and momentous events in any family – could reasonably send it sliding towards self-destruction and despair. Initially all outward appearances indicated that the family was 'coping well'. Diana and Malcolm Davenport had the collective grief of a nation mourning their dead children. They had the unwavering support and loyalty of the local community, whose working people still reverentially doffed their caps to the much loved and deeply respected Davenport family.

The Davenports had also had a lifetime to prepare for this triple tragedy. For theirs was a buttoned-down and starched, 'stiff upper lip' upbringing, which would provide them with the reserve and stoicism to endure the most excruciating levels of personal pain – resolutely and without complaining.

So the fact that Malcolm Davenport began easing his pain with a bottle of wine at the dinner table each evening was indeed out of character, albeit understandable, given the loss of his three boys. These were the sons which he had fed recklessly to the slaughterhouse of war, when they could have remained by his side on the farm in Cranhurst.

The need for a night cap of port, to help the poor man sleep, could also be explained away. The early morning cups of whisky poured into his tea cup were more of a concern, as were the lunch-time tumblers of brandy disguised in coloured water glasses; whilst the all day drinking that followed soon after – linking breakfast to lunch, and lunch to dinner – marked a more sinister turn for his internal organs.

As it happened neither the drink nor the cigarettes turned Malcolm Davenport into the black sheep of the family, for that particular role was to be embraced by another member of the Davenport clan, who set their heart on a different kind of destruction altogether. For Mr Davenport's destruction was entirely of the self-destructive variety. The head of this particular household proved to be a good man and his intentions for the farm and his surviving family members remained entirely good and wholesome to the end of his life.

Weakened by the drink and the grief, a gash to his leg – sliced open on a piece of farm machinery – would normally have been dealt with efficiently by the local doctor. But Mr Davenport failed to visit Dr Watson even when the wound turned from red, to brown and black and emitted a foul smelling and unsightly fluid. Writhing in pain he eventually took his rotting leg to be seen to, but gangrene had already set in. Ordinarily the amputation of his gangrenous leg should have been enough to stop the physical slide towards a late middle-aged grave, but septic shock and the broken heart of a grieving father sealed his fate. A year after Arthur's suicide in the byre, the three Davenport women were left quite alone.

Chapter Eight

spring/summer

History determines that every great family delivers a black sheep into its midst. The greedy, irresponsible member of the family who squanders the wealth created by previous visionary generations and drags the family name through the mud. After the suffering brought on the Davenports by the death of four of its men, the remaining female members of the clan had not prepared themselves to recognise and deal with the vixen within their midst.

Diana Davenport was driven demented by the loss of her husband and three boys and the impending collapse of the farm and took to her bed for several months. However, she was a steely, intelligent woman and after languishing broken-hearted in her bedroom she emerged from her chrysalis of grief determined to rescue her daughters and the farm from an uncertain future. The beautiful and identical twins were dressed and pampered and dangled in front of a number of suitors, Florence Rose first – due to her 24-minute head start in life – and Viola Geraldine after that.

Throughout their childhood and teens, and particularly during the trauma of the war years, the twins were inseparable sharing every aspect of their lives together. There were the whispered secrets, the knowing looks, the special coded language, the exchanged outfits, the matching clothes, the swapping of roles and blurring of personalities. Any differences between them were quickly suppressed or honed. A divergence towards individuality was brought back into the common and unifying Davenport twin mould, which had enabled them to stoically and unflinchingly support their grieving parents during the war years, as they watched their brothers die one by one.

Their extraordinary likeness and similarity in character even confused their closest relatives and friends at times, whilst the girls took great delight in passing themselves off as the other twin at social engagements and events. However, their mother's attempt to find suitable husbands, amongst a much reduced pool of eligible young bachelors, triggered a change in Viola. Whilst physically Florence and Viola remained a mirror-image of one another, Viola's heart hardened and she became infected by the terrible and destructive emotion of jealously. Where once the girls had done everything together, the arrival of an outside male in the group, was viewed by Viola the vixen, as a threat, something to be pounced on and devoured at all costs.

Diana Davenport drew on her husband's business contacts and the brewing circles that Edward had circulated within in London. News of the eligible Davenport twins quickly spread around the social scene in London and Kent. Each potential suitor was meticulously studied and vetted by Diana to ensure that their family background, business acumen and character might restore some happiness and a steadying hand to the Davenport estate.

The son of a successful arable farmer close to Sevenoaks, who was two years Florence's senior, seemed the perfect opening gambit. However, his mop of carrot-orange curly hair and an unfortunate Roman nose covered in freckles did not provide the spark that Florence's mother had hoped for. Undeterred, Diana Davenport persisted with a string of other contacts. When each man was gently side-stepped by Florence, Diana would try to orchestrate a love match between the prospective husbands and Viola. But the boys were always casually and more ruthlessly tossed to one side by the younger twin.

"If they are not good enough for Florence, then they are not good enough for me!" she shouted at her mother.

Florence eventually found love of her own accord. She returned to the farm of the first carrot-headed suitor for a family drinks party, only to fall head over heels in love with Richard the debonair, younger brother, on the very first afternoon of their acquaintance. Viola watched from the corner of the room as her sister's heart melted with love and her face shone with joy and affection for Richard. Florence (the one half that made a whole) was being stolen from her.

Richard James Walker was warmly embraced by Diana Davenport and soon plans were put in place for the couple to marry the following year. It was agreed that Richard and his new wife would move into the Georgian manor, whilst Mrs Davenport and her younger daughter would move into the small guesthouse on the land. Although the farm had fallen into a state of disrepair, Florence and Richard were confident that with hard work and resolve, it could be restored to its former glory. Florence spent many months learning how to run the accounts and manage the hop farm, whilst her fiancé explored the latest and most efficient techniques for harvesting, storing and transporting the hops.

The couple decided to fold the pig business. With the floor of the byre tragically cradling Arthur's extraordinary knowledge, love and gift for the business, Florence found the prospect of continuing the pig farm too painful. Instead they kept a small drove of pigs to ensure the family would be stocked with bacon and pork for the year, with a modest parcel of hogs for the hoppers to enjoy an annual hog roast. Florence and her mother also wisely appointed a talented and respected market gardener, Mr Morris, to create a large kitchen garden for the Davenports so that the family could be self-sufficient in fresh, bottled and pickled produce.

Viola, meanwhile, sulked on the edges of every activity watching her older sister building her cosy new world with her husband-to-be. She sat on the margins observing her mother clucking and fussing like a hen around her firstborn daughter. *Florence* was the one who had saved the farm, *she* was the one who had brought love and joy and hope back into the house and *she* was the daughter who would bring her mother a longed for grandchild to fill the hollowness of grief.

Diana tried to replicate the newfound happiness in Florence's life for her younger daughter, but Viola rejected all of her mother's suggestions. *No* man, no matter how handsome, no matter how good his prospects appeared, could break through the film of green envy that enveloped Viola's heart. She now saw a world that would soon see her shunted out of the magnificent family home to a pokey, little guesthouse on the land in the shadow of her older twin who was to remain on the grand side of the green. Viola sat brooding in her room for hours, listening to the laughter of her sister seeping up through the floorboards, or watching the courting couple strolling through the garden hand in hand and kissing fondly. Her sister had been stolen from her by Richard James Walker.

After weeks of persuasion, and given Viola's considerable dressmaking skills, Viola finally and begrudgingly agreed to adapt her mother's wedding dress to fit Florence. But no matter how many alterations were made, the dress never quite seemed to sit very well on her sister.

A small engagement party was arranged in the summer of 1947 to announce the joyous news to the Davenports' close family and friends. It was the age of austerity and it would be an understated affair with a homemade punch, a simple finger buffet cooked by the twins and their mother, and singing around the pianoforte.

Florence was delighted to see her sister's mood lighten as the evening approached and Viola even agreed to help Florence prepare some food and make up the rum punch.

"This is just like old times Viola," said Florence, bubbling with excitement.

Viola turned to her twin and saw that Florence's face was no longer her mirror image, for Florence's face had changed and it now radiated contentment and joy and her eyes were alive with the effervescence that true love brings.

Florence looked up from the salmon she was dressing and saw that her mirror image now had a foreign, strangled look. It was a sour and bitter expression that Florence had not seen before in Viola – the other half of her whole.

Then Viola spat out her words contemptuously. "Things will *never* be like old times ever again!"

CHAPTER NINE

summer

Everything looked perfect as Florence descended the sweeping Georgian staircase of the Davenports' family home. Richard stood in the hallway and his mouth dropped slightly open, as he watched his wife-to-be descend the stairs. They kissed tenderly, both longing for their wedding day to arrive, so that they could finally be united as man and wife. Richard stepped back and admired the women who would publicly become his fiancé that night. He ran his hands down Florence's light blue evening dress and traced the line of the pale lemon bow, tied neatly around her tiny waist.

"Beautiful my darling – you are perfectly beautiful," he cooed.

"Come on my two love birds," Diana said as she swept into the hallway, clapping her hands as though trying to disperse the pigeons at Trafalgar Square.

"Everyone is *desperate* to see you both… and judging by the parcels on the piano I think there will be quite a few presents," Diana said animatedly.

Diana clucked excitedly behind the couple and then realised Viola was still missing from the room. She trotted back across the hall and stood on the bottom step of the staircase.

"Come on Viola – everyone is here now and waiting for *you*."

But there was no response.

Diana walked back into the reception letting the happy chatter, the singing and the piano playing envelope her. The sound of laughter and frivolity had seemed buried for so long. Now its release in the house was like the sun rising and lifting the heads of a field of sunflowers – the Davenport's house was coming back to life again. She stood for a moment absorbing the joy, as her heart longed for Malcolm, Edward, Charles and dear, sweet Arthur by her side.

A crowd of friends, cousins and other guests huddled around the young couple; the girls admired Florence's dress and the men congratulated Richard for his good taste in women. Richard picked up his cocktail glass and tapped the side of it with one of the teaspoons that had been laid out in a perfect circle ready for the trifle desert.

The pianist, who was halfway through 'As Time Goes By', effortlessly curtailed the song with the help of the una corda pedal. The hum of collective chatter and laughter fell silent.

"Ladies and gentlemen, girls and boys, the great and the good, it gives me enormous pleasure to welcome you all here this evening and thank you so very much for coming," said Richard heartily, beaming from ear to ear. "As you know Florence and I are to be wed next spring, thanks to the lovely and long-suffering Mrs Davenport agreeing to take me on as her son-in-law. I think you will all agree that my dearest Florence looks quite beautiful tonight and I have to be the luckiest man alive!"

There was a low hum of approval and Richard's carrot-topped brother yelled a hearty "Hear, hear" as the audience burst into applause. "Of course I was absolutely delighted that Florence said "yes" when I popped the question. But just to make sure she doesn't get away and all you other chaps know she is mine, I would like to present you... my darling Florence... with the sign of my love for you."

There was a gasp, a murmur, then spontaneous applause as Richard opened a small suede box and produced a sparkling diamond and sapphire ring which he slipped onto the finger of his betrothed. The family heirloom had been passed down three generations of the Walker family.

"Oh Richard, it's beautiful, it truly is, thank you from the bottom of my heart," gasped Florence.

"No thank *you* from the bottom of *my* heart. You have made my life complete Florence."

There was a long "Ah" and more applause as Richard kissed Florence fondly on the lips. Suddenly the guests parted like the Red Sea as Florence's twin pushed her way to the front of the gathering. The room was rendered silent. Everyone stood agog staring at the exact double of the bride-to-be. As Florence looked back at the silent crowd, Viola clapped zealously, long after everyone else had been shocked into silence.

Viola stood before the couple wearing the very same light blue evening dress, with a pale lemon bow. She grimaced cruelly and disingenuously at her older twin, as Florence wondered why, when and how Viola could have bought the identical party dress. Florence's bottom lip betrayed her inner turmoil and it was a fleeting display of disappointment and deep sadness that was only seen by Viola, the other half of the whole.

Viola threw her arms wide open and smiled theatrically, "My precious big sister, how very *beautiful* you look this evening." Then turning to the audience added, "Though I can't help thinking that perhaps I'm giving myself a back-handed compliment with such flattery for my double act!"

There was a tense and awkward pause as everyone absorbed the words of the vixen. Viola lured her sister into an embrace and the two peas were physically cocooned momentarily back inside the pod.

"I couldn't be happier for you darling," Viola whispered in Florence's ear.

Pulling back nose-to-nose, Viola smiled sweetly... sickly almost.

"Will you forgive me for being churlish earlier?" Viola pleaded insincerely. "*Of course* things can be *exactly* as they always have been."

Florence dropped her gaze and nodded her forgiveness, but her hurt over Viola's devious dress choice lay heavy on her heart for the rest of the reception. Viola lavishly held Florence's hand in hers and admired the ring, as everyone else in the room compared the twins' physical likeness.

"Richard," said Viola, now turning her attention to her sister's husband-to-be.

"*Con-gra-tu-la-tions!*" she said, louder than was really necessary.

She threw her arms around his neck, pulled him in closer than was appropriate and kissed him on the cheek.

"How about, we all raise a glass to the happy couple," she suggested to her audience.

The party murmured in perfect unison, "The happy couple" and after a clinking of glasses, the pianist launched into Cole Porter's 'I'm so in love with you'.

Diana's anger towards Viola was matched by the joy and pride she felt for Richard and Florence. She bustled past Viola, linking arms with Florence, as the photographer lined up the family and recorded the special occasion on his camera.

"Now let us all eat, drink and be merry," said Diana placing a protective arm around Florence and Richard, "for I think you'll all agree that we have much to celebrate."

And Richard's brother responded with another heartfelt, "Hear, hear."

※　※　※

The delightful evening was drawing to a close and the last dozen or so guests were gathered around the pianoforte, delivering raucous renditions of popular Billy Holiday, Bing Crosby and Duke Ellington songs.

"Alright, alright," said the pianist slurring his words, "Any last rekwests?"

Viola was swaying on her feet, together with most of the other guests. She'd taken charge of the rum punch and liberally filled the guests' glasses, as well as her own, throughout the evening, whilst topping up the rum on numerous occasions. Unused to the free flowing intoxicating liquid, with the stranglehold of rationing, the high-spirited group that had stayed till the end of the party were now determined to "sing until sunrise" even though the room appeared to be spinning around for several of them.

"How about 'You Always Hurt the One You Love' by the Mills Brothers," said Viola excitedly jumping up and down.

"Um… don't know that one," said the pianist, "sounds a bit downbeat though. Let's sing something much brighter. What about 'You are My Sunshine'?" the musician offered as an alternative. Immediately everyone launched whole-heartedly into the jaunty and popular song. Florence and Richard gave each other an affectionate and sloppy kiss.

"Back in a minute gorgeous, don't move a muscle," said Richard to his fiancé, feeling the call of nature.

Richard walked out into the hall and held the Dado rail, steadying his course down the passageway. He disappeared into the downstairs cloakroom to relieve himself. After washing his hands, he splashed ice-cold water on his face hoping to feel a little less fuzzy-headed. He peered at his reflection in the mirror, through his happy alcoholic haze, and noticed two bloodshot eyes staring back at the man who was grinning inanely.

"Ooo dear," Richard mumbled, "silly you," pointing at the ridiculous red eyed drunk in the mirror, who felt happy as a clown.

Richard held the wall again and negotiated a meandering and windy course back down the long corridor. Just then, the library door creaked. Richard stood to attention swaying.

"Halt, who goes there?"

Richard morphed into the part of a Roman soldier, holding his imagined shield and dagger.

"Me," squeaked the voice.

"Is that you?"

"Yes it's me," said the familiar voice.

A delicate, soft hand pulled the Roman centurion into the shadows of the library lit only by the haunting, white light of a full moon. The same hand caressed his back and then slid down and around between his legs.

"We said we'd wait darling 'till we are wed," Richard protested weakly.

"Let's just kiss then my love. I just want to give you a tiny taste of what you have to look forward to."

The twin took his hands and ran them over the fabric that covered her breasts, to the pale lemon bow tied around her waist.

"Unwrap me Richard, like a wedding present."

Richard pulled lightly on the bow and the ribbon tumbled to the floor.

"Peel the wrapping off darling."

Her soft, gentle hands caressed the swelling mound inside his trousers. He wrestled for a moment with his fuzzy-headed conscience. His hands pulled the fine and flimsy pale blue evening gown over her head. The pallid moonlight reflected off her pure white form and she lifted his hands to touch her pert and bud-like chest.

"We said we'd wait, till our wedding," he murmured again as he felt the soft, cupid lips slide across his.

"Just kiss me then Richard, just kiss me," as she gently pulled his hand across her pubic hair to her wet vagina.

She lay down on the chez-longue and Richard stood transfixed by his fiancé's beauty. The pale moonlight bounced off her angelic, white body. Her tiny virginal form, untouched by any other, looked as though it had been carved from the finest ivory.

"Take your trousers off," the breathless voice moaned. "Just lie on me and kiss me darling, save yourself for our wedding day."

His swirling head tried to reason with the stallion that was rising up between his legs. But from the moment he lay on her silky white skin, which seemed to him more fragile than tissue paper and smoother than the finest velvet, Richard was no longer able to resist the alluring bride-to-be that lay beneath him. And as the soft cupid lips enveloped his in warmth and passion, he entered her and the two became one.

After the sensual and erotic fusion of lust and flesh, the couple lay intertwined, panting, gasping for breath, Richard's penis still throbbing partially erect inside her pulsating vagina. Their hearts beat loud and fast knocking at the door of each others' rib cages as Richard stroked his fiancé's soft, sleek hair.

"I think I am going to like being married to you very much my darling," Richard murmured kissing her cheek.

But the youngest twin remained silent, smiling smugly to herself. The couple interlinked hands and Richard ran his finger over the place where he had slid the beautiful diamond and sapphire ring onto Florence's finger only hours before, but the ring was not there.

Chapter Ten

Friday 17 March – 11.34am

Miss Davenport sat in her wheelchair alone in the kitchen, staring across the empty space that had become her dining room, bedroom, toilet, bathroom and cattery over the past year. The last six boxes that held Florence Davenport's life within them stood by the kitchen door. Every now and then a burly pair of removals men would come crashing through the door to pick up another load. The taller, older and more experienced man was too embarrassed to acknowledge the sick, old lady in the corner. He kept his head down and, without looking up, flipped another huge box onto each shoulder and exited the room.

"Come on Kev, get a move on it's time for our tea break," said the older removals man to the new recruit.

The younger lad, unable to control his curiosity, lingered for a moment and snuck a look at the bloated, old woman in the corner of the room. The boy, who had failed in his childhood ambition to get into the fire service, and instead moved boxes for a living, shifted his gaze to a large portrait that hung on the wall behind the sick woman. Quite forgetting his manners, the boy gawped up at the painting and marvelled at the beautiful, porcelain, doll-like face of the young lady. He felt sure there had once been another person in the portrait, but the other human shape appeared to have been clumsily blacked out by the artist and was little more than an aberration, a shadow amongst the silhouetted trees. Curiosity eventually lured the boy's eyes back to the patient in the wheelchair and he found himself unable to pull away from her crazed glare over the oxygen mask.

"Didn't your mother teach you it's rude to stare," Miss Davenport hissed at the boy as she swung her cane wildly into the air. The strain of speaking, turned her eyes watery red and she returned the oxygen supply quickly back to her mouth to inhale deeply.

The boy, with his pumped up biceps and triceps hung his head and sheepishly apologised. He picked up a box and hoped to make a rapid exit to join his mate back in the lorry cab for the routine mid-morning tea break, which saw the daily dunking of two or three biscuits into overly brewed, sugary tea.

"Pretty wasn't I?" said the old lady.

The boy appeared to have lost his powers of speech and simply stared up at the beautiful oil painting and then returned to the invalid in the corner. He nodded furiously.

"Oh you weren't just pri-ey, you woz bu-i-ful Miss... sorry I dun't know your name?"

"Miss Davenport, Florence Davenport," said the lady softening for a moment.

"And you child, what is your name?"

"Kevin… but most people just call me Kev."

Indeed many of his mates called him 'Kev the rev' on account of his ability to take a blind bend at 60mph. It was this brave, but foolhardy desire to risk life and limb that eventually saw the young aspiring fireman fail one of the many rigorous entry tests.

"He's just too bloody reckless Barry," one of the examiners confided to his colleague. "He'll always try and be a hero and end up killing the whole bloody crew!"

Still unable to accept that his life was now inextricably linked to the business of lifting and lowering boxes, furniture and wretched grand pianos, he invariably slipped his imaginary fireman's helmet on during each removals job using his wild imagination and limited intellect. 'Kev the rev' estimated the weight of Miss Davenport and calculated how he would manoeuvre her onto the top of a fireman's ladder without the support of her wheelchair. The idea of carrying such a swollen and immobilised mass of human being on his shoulders, preferably from the top floor of the house with the flames licking at his feet, particularly appealed to the reckless hero trapped inside the removals boy. However Miss Davenport required a very different kind of rescue from the one that 'Kev the rev' imagined on the top rung of the make believe ladder.

"I need your help Kevin," said Miss Davenport, snatching for breath between each word, as a toad plucks insects from the air.

Miss Davenport curled one of her bloated sausage fingers as best she could and beckoned Kevin over. The new recruit glanced over at the door. He hoped the nurse might return to the room with Miss Davenport's next round of medicine, or his mate on the job might think to tell him that his cuppa was getting cold. But nobody came. As he drew nearer, the hiss of the oxygen mask seemed disproportionately loud and the boy could hear the phlegm rattling around the old lady's rib cage as she spoke.

"Please, please help me Kevin," Miss Davenport pleaded almost pathetically now through the mask. The lady's watery green eyes pooled and a viscose, pussy liquid ran down the woman's cheeks. She placed her engorged hand on his arm with a touch of desperation, engendering a turbo, fuel-injected burst of compassion in 'Kev the rev'.

"You remind me so very much of Arthur, he was the youngest of my three older brothers. There's that other worldly quality about you. You look like a dreamer boy... do you have dreams?"

"Well I hope to be in the fire service one day Miss."

"Good, a noble cause. You look very strong Kevin I'm sure you will make a very brave fireman indeed. Perhaps you could use your strength to help me pull this off?"

Miss Davenport slowly raised her hand like a resurrected life form emerging from the grave. Kevin stared at the beautiful and lavish ring, but was repulsed in equal measure by the seams of blue and red skin that floated around each side of it. The goodness in the wannabe fireman was ready to run to the dying woman's rescue, but 'Kev the rev' now wished he could turn on his heels and run.

"I fink it'll hurt miss," said the coward inside the failed fireman.

"I know," gasped Miss Davenport suddenly panicked by the lack of oxygen. She pressed the mask back over her mouth and drew in a deep, sucking breath. "That's why I need a strong, young man like you to help me. Please take the soap bottle from the sink... it's still there."

The removals boy compliantly followed her command. Kevin carried the bottle over to Miss Davenport and lathered her finger in soap.

"This'll really 'urt miss you do know that dun't you?"

"Yes I do," said Miss Davenport, her voice tinged with an aching sense of tragedy.

Tears sprang into her eyes, swirling the puss and blurring her vision for a moment, as she said the words "I do". They were the words that had been stolen from her mouth over 45 years earlier by her twin sister. They were the words that were, instead, spoken by Viola to *her* fiancé at a clandestine alter, to save the family's reputation. They were the words that were mumbled under duress by *her* beloved husband-to-be, as his heart still yearned for the one and only true love of his life, Florence Rose. They were the words that would spare the new generation that kicked and grew in Viola's belly from being labelled the "illegitimate bastard" that Florence knew the baby to be.

The shotgun wedding caused a rupture in Florence's heart that was so deep and heartbreaking it would prevent her from ever exchanging another word with her treacherous twin and the beloved, but foolish, love of her life who had been lured to have sex with the vindictive vixen on the night of her engagement party.

As Viola and Richard both lay on their death beds in 1967 and 1973 respectively, already separated by divorce in the 1950s, even then, no words of comfort would come from Florence's bitter, lined and puckered lips. For Florence's heart was one that was so shattered, that the pointed shards of her beating organ had been moulded and hardened into a knife's blade. It was a blade that would cut Viola and Richard's daughter out of her life altogether, the little lump of misery born out of her sister's treachery and her fiancés foolishness. And in her final act of revenge (for revenge was a dish best served cold) the now cold hearted, broken hearted Florence Rose Davenport would cut the last surviving relative out of her will and leave every last penny from the sale of her much diminished estate to a local cat charity.

Surprisingly tenderly 'Kev the rev' massaged Miss Davenport's finger, as she wept silently. She did not cry for the pain, but for the broken heart that still beat within her diseased chest and yearned for the man she still loved.

"Pull it off!" she commanded with a new sense of urgency. "Please... pull it off."

The man twisted and pulled and wormed the excess skin under the band of gold – finally freeing her finger from the ring that had turned the digit a bluish red. By releasing the lady from the band of white gold with its diamonds and sapphire, Miss Davenport felt strangely freed from the promise she'd made in her heart in 1947 to love, honour and obey till death us do part, even though she had been robbed of the chance of ever declaring her heart's desire in public to her fiancé.

"Thank you Kevin," she rasped holding his hand.

"Are you all right miss, I 'ope I 'aven't hurt you?"

"No... *you* haven't hurt me dear boy, someone else hurt me a long time ago. Now I'm free to leave, there's nothing more to stay for."

She coerced her lips into a smile, stretching out the tight, puckered parallel lines that betrayed a lifetime of resentment.

"Don't forget the picture, if you like it you can keep it – I have no use for it anymore," said Miss Davenport waving it away with her cane.

"Oh tar very much Miss Davenport, that's luvly of yer – don't mind if I do. Gosh you were a looker."

Just then Kevin's workmate popped his head around the kitchen door.

"Are you cumin or wot?"

The older and more experienced man finally achieved eye contact with the dying lady in the corner.

"Oh sorry miss I didn't realise you were still 'ere."

"*STILL HERE?*" Miss Davenport roared. "Of course, I'm *still* here. Until I leave, this is still *my* house."

The nurse bustled in behind the second man.

"Calm down Miss Davenport, don't upset yourself dear. Here let me give you your pills."

"I swear you're trying to kill me with all this medication," said Miss Davenport suspiciously eyeing the nurse. "I think Arthur had it right all along – get it over with quickly."

"Oh come, come Miss Davenport what's happened to that fighting spirit of yours," said the nurse soothingly.

But the fighting spirit had already been slain and Miss Davenport sat swamped by her wig looking lost and forlorn. A vacant, faraway look betrayed the fact that Miss Davenport had already departed from the farm that had been her home for over seventy years. She calmly stroked a wooden box positioned on her lap and caressed the object as though it were her favourite cat (though in reality Marmalade had already joined all her other feline friends in the charity cattery, that would soon be funded by Miss Davenport's last vestiges of earthly possessions).

There was a loud 'toot, toot' outside the front of the oast house.

"Sounds like the new owners," said the older removals man. "Come on Kev let's clear the last of these boxes out of 'ere."

'Kev the rev' winked at Miss Davenport as he lifted the picture carefully from the wall and manoeuvred the last box onto his shoulder.

"Well cheerio luv...good luck and thanks again for the picture!"

The nurse surveyed the empty room, satisfied that she could now wheel Miss Davenport away to her new life at the nursing home. She noticed Miss Davenport stroking the box on her lap.

"Looks like the contents of your box are pretty precious Miss Davenport do you want me to lock it safely in the car?"

"No thank you, it's a past life anyway," the invalid said coldly.

Miss Davenport listened to the excited hum of indistinguishable chatter and the infectious laughter of Melanie in the hallway. "Nurse, why don't you greet the new owners and I'll gather myself together. You can wheel me out of here for good soon... just give me five minutes on my own."

"Traditionally of course the sellers should really have left by now!" the nurse smiled and patted Miss Davenport's distended hand. She noticed the ring had been removed.

"I shan't be long, just leave me alone for a few minutes to say goodbye to the memories... the ghosts. Now you run along and welcome the new owners – their names are Melanie Henriksen and Harry Maloney."

Miss Davenport heard the excited distant chatter of the young lovers who had their whole life ahead of them. She recalled the couple who had bought her house, the beautiful girl with her piercing blue eyes and her handsome husband, who, like her, had known what it was to experience the thrill of love at first sight. She indulged her memory for a moment and thought back to the Walker's family party just after the war when she'd first set eyes on her beloved Richard.

"You beautiful, drunken fool, why didn't you realise it was the evil temptress... I would have loved you so much my darling!"

She kissed her fiancé one last time and slid the photograph from their engagement party into the box.

Focusing her last ounce of strength she wrote *To Melanie* on the envelope, slipped in a newspaper article with the note she had written to Melanie and then licked and sealed it. Though her hands suddenly trembled uncontrollably she negotiated the ring back inside its original packaging, the hand-crafted, salmon pink suede box. She placed the final chapter of her story inside the large oak box and wheeled herself over to the entrance to the basement. As she travelled along the top landing of the stairwell she found the hook that opened a secret hole in the wall and slid her life inside the void.

With her panic for oxygen now gone, her bloated body felt strangely light, as though she could float away. Her desperation to breath had passed. She paused for a moment to remember her mother and father, her three brothers, her fiancé – the man whom she had loved more than any other. Her mind rested for a fleeting second on the sister that had once made their two halves a whole, before Viola dropped the two halves from a great height, smashing them into a million pieces. Then Miss Florence Rose Davenport wheeled the chair to the top stair and shunted the wheels over the edge into the abyss below.

Chapter Eleven

spring

It was only when Melanie came to whitewash the walls of the basement that she stumbled across the secret hole in the wall created by Miss Davenport. Melanie had already tried everything to rid the basement of its onerous past. She began with an almost forensic clean of the dismal, dank space below the kitchen and added a new screed floor which she painted a light cream to brighten the place up. Fluorescent strip lights had been fitted by the electrician to flood the room with light, however, even their clinical luminosity failed to dispel the gloom in the basement.

Finally, she bought a large pot of masonry paint and a thick paint brush and began dabbing the paint vigorously onto the rough brick surface. After several hours of painting, her brush hit a small hooked handle cleverly disguised to blend into the brick-work. She slowly rotated the handle and was incredulous to see a section of the wall come away in her hands in the form of six false stone coloured, plaster of Paris bricks, no thicker than an inch that ingeniously disguised a deep and dark hole.

Melanie felt nervously into the black space and flinched as her hand passed through a sticky veil of cobwebs. She squealed and tried to pull the tacky web from her hand. The second attempted entry, now performed with her decorating gloves on, pushed through another layer of cobwebs and into the inner sanctum. Here her gloved fingers touched the surface of a wooden box.

Carefully she lifted the substantial oak box, with ornate brass trim, out of its hidey hole and turned the key. Trembling, though she knew not why, Melanie lifted the lid to discover a treasure trove of Miss Davenport's papers and photographs, an envelope simply addressed *To Melanie* and a small suede jewellery box.

Scooping the papers and photographs carefully between her hands she lifted them out of the vessel and positioned them reverentially on the kitchen island. Melanie was tempted to open the mystery jewellery box and letter first, but just as the child saves the best sweet in the bag till last, she placed them to one side.

Melanie picked up and studied an old sepia image, which was much fingered, with dog-eared corners. The picture showed a mother and father cradling two tiny and fragile looking babies, who were little more than three months old and were almost doll-like in their porcelain beauty. The parents were dressed in the height of 1920s fashion. The mother wore a simple coat and cloche hat with a fox fur draped around her neck, which was fashionably fastened by the animal's paw, whilst the father wore a twenties-style suit with Fedora hat and round horn-rimmed glasses. They cocooned the newborn twins in their arms with a hint of pride twitching under the father's moustache as they stood stiffly in the entrance to Cranhurst church. Melanie, the decorator, turned private investigator, assumed one of the babies must have been Miss Florence Davenport.

"So Moseley's estate agency patter wasn't fiction after all. You were a twin Miss Davenport," Melanie whispered to the photo.

Melanie marvelled at the identical likeness of the children. The beautiful christening gowns almost touched the ground and the three boys gathered around the adults, were, she presumed, the babies' brothers. Two looked stoically straight-faced at the camera, whilst the youngest boy seemed to be gazing up at something in the trees.

Another picture showed the Davenport family in *summer 1935* - picnicking by a river. The date was written on the back, as were the names of the family members. Melanie kept turning the photograph to and fro to match the names to the faces. *Mother and Father* identified by the writing on the reverse of the photo sat on director's chairs at the rear of the group. The mother's upbringing by rigid Victorian parents ensured her facial expression remained safely corseted under a bodice of stiffness. However, on closer inspection the detective noted there was also a look of warm contentment in her eyes as Mrs Davenport surveyed her five children.

The father, who had embraced the more relaxed fashions of the early thirties, now crossed his legs in the manner he had observed by the leading film stars of the day – though his expression retained the buttoned down modesty of his Victorian upbringing. *Edward* and *Charles* (again marked on the reverse of the photograph) looked well on their way to manhood, whilst *Arthur*, although approaching something close to 18, had a sweet almost 'other worldly' innocence about him and nuzzled into the Cocker Spaniel on his lap rather than looking up directly into the camera's lens.

The twins were sat at the front of the picnic blanket, their arms were linked and their heads were tilted towards each other. They wore the exact same dresses and their hair was braided into two plaits, each of which was tied in matching striped ribbon. Their eyes darted impishly sideways towards one another, rather than looking po-faced at the camera as Edward and Charles had clearly been trained to do. The girls were on the cusp of adolescence – neither children nor women. Melanie was struck by both their natural, effortless beauty and the fact that two human beings could look like carbon copies of one another.

If ever there were two peas out of the same pod. So which one of these girls are you Florence Davenport? Melanie thought quizzically.

The names scribbled on the back helped her identify *Florence* and *Viola*, but physically there was no distinguishing feature to divide or differentiate the twins.

A third picture catapulted the girls through 15 years or so, somewhere to their mid-twenties. The photograph captured what seemed to be a special occasion. Melanie picked out a pile of presents on a piano and a large crowd of smiling guests in the background. Both women were dressed in identical evening gowns that looked to be typical of the late 1940s, with the dresses nipped in at the waist and a bow accentuating their tiny waistlines. The two still retained the doll-like beauty of their infancy and early adolescence.

Melanie traced the front line-up with her finger. The mother, whom she had last seen in the picnic photograph, seemed to have aged markedly and she stood without her husband. Melanie wrongly assumed that he must be the one taking the photograph. It was difficult too for Melanie to ascertain which of the men in the crowd might be her brothers. One of the twins had linked her arm around a handsome young man. They looked very much in love as the sides of their heads tilted together and touched and they both smiled, dreamily at the camera, whilst Mrs Davenport also smiled broadly and had her arm wrapped protectively around the couple. Melanie's attention moved to the twin on the other end of the line, standing slightly aloof from the other three in the front line. Her eyes stared nonchalantly into the distance and she saw the beginnings of bitterness settling around the tight and puckered lips of the girl. It was a bitterness that Melanie has seen etched deeply into the acidic face of Florence Davenport, the day they had come to view the property. It was a mouth that appeared as though it had sucked on a lemon all its life.

Poor you Florence Davenport, she thought, touching the sour looking twin who stood alone.

Turning the picture over, Melanie was surprised and confused to see that the girl with the dreamy smile on the arm of the man was marked out as *Florence*.

Surely it must be a mistake, Melanie thought.

She flipped it back quickly checking she hadn't confused the names and faces. But it was unmistakable, *Florence* was clearly the happy sister named on the back of the photograph on the arm of *Richard* and it was her sister *Viola* who had the bitter, scowling disposition in the photograph from 1947.

She brought the image closer to her face, the diamond and sapphire ring was familiar. She remembered seeing a similar ring on the finger of Florence Davenport the day the couple had first looked around the property. Shrunken down by the elephantine proportions of the old lady's swollen fingers, it took a while for Melanie to realise that these two rings were one and the same.

You did fall in love Florence, so why so bitter at the end. Why did you remain Miss Davenport and what happened to your fiancé?

Hungry for an answer, the decorator turned sleuth picked up a pile of faded, yellow newspaper cuttings. But the papers only seemed to provide details of Florence's brothers. She turned to two pages cut from a newspaper, one from May 1940 and the other March 1945. Melanie picked up the 1945 newspaper cutting, hoping for a good news story so close to the end of the war. She gently ran a finger over the page unable to find stories related to the Davenport family. Then as she turned the paper over she saw dozens of entries in the *Obituaries* section, one of which was highlighted in black ink pen. She held her breath and read:

In loving memory and to honour the death of Edward Davenport, died 27 March 1945, killed in action in Schnappenberg, Germany behind enemy lines. He was the eldest son of Mr & Mrs Malcolm Davenport, owners of the Davenport Farm & Estate in Cranhurst, Kent. Prior to the war, Edward Davenport managed the hop farm with Mr M Davenport Esq. and was appointed to the Hops Marketing Board in 1932.

She scoured the second cutting from 1940, gloomily heading straight to the *Obituaries* section. The entry had been similarly marked with a thick, black ink border. It was coffin-like in its heaviness drawn regimentally around the words over and over again, with the aid of a ruler to ensure the neatness and symmetry of the box was maintained. She read of the details of Second Lieutenant Charles Davenport, whose life and death were even more sparingly reported than Edward's, with just the date and place of his death: *Died 23 May 1940, in Armentières in France under enemy fire.*

Melanie stumbled upon two more photographs, one a dashing picture marked *Second Lieutenant Charles Davenport*, staring proudly back at the camera in his uniform, with his top lip sporting a long, thin moustache made popular by the film stars of the day. *Edward the swashbuckling paratrooper* was lined up with two of his fellow troopers on the edge of an airbase, as they enthusiastically saluted the cameraman.

"What a waste," sighed Melanie as she felt her eyes prickling with tears. She traced the face of the two dead young brothers and shuffled back to the earlier picnic photograph and studied the picture again.

"So what happened to you Arthur?" she whispered to the innocent looking dreamer in the photograph.

She didn't have long to wait as the next envelope contained a Death Certificate. Wading through the official wording, she came to the last line of the certificate: Cause of Death – suicide by gunshot wound to the head.

Melanie gasped in horror at the violent nature of his death

and chewed nervously on the side of her finger. She picked up a small notepad which had been severely water damaged and muddied in places, though the inscription had survived intact:

To my dearest Arthur,
A sweeter, kinder boy there could not be. Keep safe my darling boy and keep
drawing – whether near or far.
With fond affection,
Mother

Some of the pages were missing altogether but there were several in the middle that had been perfectly preserved. Arthur had doodled cartoon pigs in the manner of Walt Disney, in every fanciful pose imaginable. There were pigs doing somersaults and cartwheels, winged pigs flying through fluffy white clouds, a row of pigs sat up on their hind legs each smoking a pipe and the three little pigs featured in the fairytale. Other pages depicted scenes from the farm with a drove of gilts in the apple orchards and the quadruple roundels rising up in the background. Another touching drawing showed a young sow suckling her litter of piglets.

The next pages took on a far darker, more sinister theme. One depicted a steam train riding over a long train track. Each buffer had been drawn as an emaciated soldier crushed by the wheels of the train. The cartoon clouds of previous pages had been replaced by steam curling out of the train's funnel, shaped into the word **DEATH**.

The last partly damaged image was the most haunting of all.

Arthur had drawn a narrow passage crammed full with emaciated men who hacked at the walls towering above them. They scrambled and climbed over one another in a fearful sea of human misery. Soldiers, drawn with slits for eyes, held whips in their hands and breathed fire from their mouths. A sign penned in the most exquisite calligraphy by the artist simply read *Welcome to Hell.*

Melanie reached over to the salmon pink, suede box and cradled it in her hands for a few moments, too scared to open it. As she lifted the lid she gasped when she saw the exquisite beauty of the diamond and sapphire ring up close for the first time. She turned it this way and that watching the gems sparkling in the light. It was then that she noticed the engraving and ran her finger across the wording RJW & FRD 1947. She placed the ring back onto the granite island and her hands reached for the envelope marked *To Melanie.*

There were two pieces of paper, an article snipped neatly out of The Wealden Weekly from November 1954 and a handwritten note. Melanie read the detailed article which sat under the damning heading '*Davenport's double shame as sham marriage heads for the divorce courts*'. The whole tangled and torrid story of the Davenport twins unravelled before her like a jumper whose thread is snagged and pulled as the wearer obliviously walks on. Shocked by the twists and turns of Florence Rose's life, Melanie paused for a moment to absorb the details of love turned to loss and joy turned to heartache.

You poor broken hearted lady Melanie thought as tears ran down her face.

Finally she turned to the handwritten letter and read...

Dearest sweet girl

I shall never forget your face and the love you radiated for your husband the day you came to view the last remnants of the Davenport legacy. In you dear girl I saw a kindred spirit – there was a familiar spark that once touched my heart. "It was love at first sight" you reminisced in the kitchen and likewise for me cupid once struck my heart in the exact same way.

This farm (or the small part that is left of it) has been the site of my birth, my happy childhood and the place where I courted my betrothed and planned our life together. But in 1947 this rural idyll decayed into the wretched prison that I could never leave, for although the memories have mocked me all my life they have become my constant and familiar companion.

When I instructed Mr Mosley to sell my house, how little he understood. It was not to realise my dwindling asset, no it was never about the money and it was not to find <u>any</u> buyer, but the <u>right</u> buyer. He brought me a stream of greedy and obnoxious viewers, saying ridiculous things and making absurd offers – but they would never wrestle this house from me. I am forgetful yet not stupid, dying, but not dead yet.

Then you and your husband breezed into the kitchen like a breath of fresh air. Your face lit up and I knew you loved this place as I once did. So I have found a new gatekeeper, someone who understands the strange yet mesmeric pull of this farm. I know you will cherish the oast as much as I once did, when my brothers ran the hop farm and Richard and I strolled in the apple orchards behind the kilns.

Treasure my ring and wear it to mark the most special moments of your life together with your husband. It is the circle that bound Richard and I together, though all too briefly. Let your beauty and the ring's beauty shine in equal measure, as it once did for me. Love it well, love the oast and your husband too, for love is the only thing that lasts forever.

Farewell Miss Florence Rose Davenport

CHAPTER TWELVE

spring/early summer

Whilst Melanie spent the first six months of her arrival at The Oast inside the house renovating it, on the other side of the village green Darius and Mr Morris spent every spare moment outside in the garden, working on the botanical haven they had created together. The 'green fingered' pair kept a constant eye on the weather forecast and in late March it was mild enough to sow the broad beans, carrots, parsnips, bulb onions and radishes. So they set to work.

Next the old man and his helper turned their attention to the runner beans. They weeded the trenches they had prepared the previous autumn and then Mr Morris showed Darius how to build the runner bean supports with bamboo sticks. Darius, with his practical flair for building things, proved a natural and the task was completed inside a few hours. The gardener ran under the arches turning his arms like the pistons on an old steam train and whistled "Ooo-ah-ooo" as Darius followed laughing behind.

At the end of the day Darius disappeared into the kitchen and emerged with a tray of tea and homemade biscuits that Darius had secretly baked that morning to surprise his friend.

"These are delicious!" said Mr Morris as he dunked one of the biscuits in his mug of tea. "What a multi-talented young man you are! Here, let me show you how to dunk without your biscuit going 'plonk' to the bottom of the mug."

They sat on a bench alongside the bird bath enjoying their well earned tea break, dipping their biscuits into the tea, and Mr Morris taught his trainee gardener the words of '*Underneath the arches*'. It was a song that Mr Morris had heard the London hoppers singing most nights around the fire outside the hoppers' huts, during the late forties and fifties, after a long and sticky day of hop picking on the Davenport estate.

"*Underneath the arches...*" they warbled together like a couple of songbirds.

The following weekend Mr Morris appeared with a large bag of fleece.

"Time to wrap the plants in cotton wool," he announced, holding the bag up like a medal won after a hard-fought campaign. "These little beauties are more sensitive than babies Darius, so you have to treat the tender shoots with love and affection. Lots of these vegetables will bolt if they're sown too early outside without protection. So let's wrap them up!"

Darius embraced the task enthusiastically and as he bent to wrap the young plants, Mr Morris was moved by the gentleness with which the boy carefully wrapped each shoot.

Towards the end of April, the gardener taught Darius how

to pot, plant out and grow four varieties of tomatoes and tasked the boy with keeping the tomato tubs moist enough to deliver a bumper summer crop. Darius watered the tubs every day rain didn't come and by early July the first ripened cherry tomatoes of the season swelled orange and red amongst the green leaves of the plants.

"Haven't you done well," Mr Morris exclaimed when he spotted the first fruits of Darius's labours. "They really are divine from the vine Darius. God's natural sugar!" he said with a glint in his eye, as Mr Morris popped a tomato into both of their mouths.

"They're ss*s-so* sss-sweet," said the Darius excitedly.

"A bit like you my dear boy," said Mr Morris patting his apprentice on the back.

Darius looked up at Mr Morris intently, "Can we always-sss be friends-sss."

"Always," Mr Morris promised, as he hugged the trainee gardener warmly.

One day Mr Morris and Darius decided to create a new bed for autumn planting and as they vigorously turned the soil over together, Darius accidentally split a worm in two with his fork.

"Oh no!" he cried.

His face dropped with horror as he thought he might have killed one of Mr Morris's "nature's ploughs", but he was soon smiling again when he spotted two wriggling ends of the invertebrate somersaulting in the soil.

"Wow look at that, Mr Morris-sss. I've made two of nature'sss ploughs-sss. Two!" said Darius as he burst into childish giggles.

Mr Morris didn't have the heart to tell his helper that the tail end would eventually die and the head with the saddle might perish too, so he simply patted the boy on the back and let the wriggling double-act captivate the boy's imagination.

Mr Morris demonstrated an incredible knowledge of spiders too and during the long, dry days of late July, when it was too hot to dig the garden they would often sit under the shade of a tree and watch the eight legged arachnids at work.

"Come and look at this one," Mr Morris enthused. "See under the leaf Darius, she's waiting for her prey underneath here. This is a Meshweb Spider, you can tell from the small robust web she's spun on this leaf."

Darius loved the Crab Spiders that crawled sideways across the garden path. Then the following weekend Mr Morris spotted a male and female Nursery Web Spider.

"Here Darius, quickly, come and look, before she eats him."

"Is that really true Mr Morris-sss?"

"Why yes of course Master Sorokin. You see she's sunbathing. If he wants to mate with her, he'll have to offer a present. A freshly caught fly always goes down well. He has to be quick though Darius. A moment of carelessness on his part and she will eat him without hesitation."

"That'sss sss-so spooky!"

The boy's favourite spider was the brown Wolf Spider and one day Mr Morris found some at the back of the garden.

"Come quickly Darius," Mr Morris called out enthusiastically. "I've found a group of Wolf Spiders." Darius counted four spiders gathered together. "That's quite remarkable for arachnids, because spiders can't usually stand one another. That's why they are known as the Wolf Spider, because they move around in packs."

Darius drew in closer to study the spiders as Mr Morris continued with his spider lesson, handing the boy a magnifying glass.

"They make the best mothers too. Look carefully Darius and you'll see they put their eggs in a cocoon, which they carry around till their young hatch. Some species even climb on their mother's back for one or two weeks when they are born, piggy-back style!"

The old boy smiled, his facing lighting up with a playful idea: "Here let me show you what I mean."

The thought of an eight-year-old boy climbing onto the now eighty-three-year-old gardener's back should have been ridiculous. But Mr Morris's insect lesson had captivated Darius to such an extent, that he looked forward to a practical demonstration of the theory. He climbed on board for the piggy-back ride and Mr Morris started trotting around the garden. The boy began laughing raucously.

His mother was so perplexed to hear the strange giggling noise rising up through the open bedroom window where she lay with the odd-job boy that she hurriedly wrapped a towel around her body and rushed to the window.

Darius laughed and tossed his head back in the most carefree moment of his life, as Mr Morris sang.

Incy Wincy spider
Climbed up the water spout
Down came the rain
And washed the spider out
Out came the sun

And dried up all the rain
So Incy Wincy spider
Climbed up the spout again

Mr Morris smiled and trotted down to the bottom of the garden again and rounded the corner for the final lap. It was only then that Natasha could see the look of agony on Mr Morris's face as he wheezed and gasped for breath, whilst her oblivious son roared with laughter enjoying the first piggy-back ride of his life. Mr Morris took his last few gallant steps and fell head first into the vegetable patch. His head twisted to one side, as Darius was thrown clear like a jockey at the Grand National.

Darius scrambled out of the rhubarb and ran to his old companion. He saw the frozen staring eyes and the dribble running from the side of his mouth. Darius threw himself onto the gardener's back, as he vainly hoped to hold the old man's soul within his body. He clung to his shoulders, in a desperate bid to prevent his spirit floating away above the cherry and apple trees they'd planted together.

He knew Mr Morris was dead. It was the third dead body Darius had seen in two years. The burnt one at the side of the road, the shot one that was supposed to be his father, and now his best friend who'd died of natural causes. Yet it was the death of the gardener, collapsing in front of him with a heart attack that proved the most terrifying to Darius. For this was the first and only time in his life that he felt the painful ripping sensation of separation from someone he loved.

He yelled up at the sky.

"Don't die, don't fucking die!"

And the dot just stared. She jerked out her neck, chicken-like through the window, to peer at the emotional outburst from her normally emotionally restrained 'sweetie boy' who hadn't shed a tear since she threw away his dummy when he was five. She was transfixed by the sight of Darius beating his chest in grief and rocking backwards and forwards on the back of the old man with the 'green fingers'. And for one brief moment, she thought she saw a single tear roll down her son's cheek.

CHAPTER THIRTEEN

early/midsummer

Darius knew he didn't have much time, he had to come up with a plan and he had to scheme quickly. The bereaved child locked himself in his room and lay prostrate on the bed; like the gilt copper effigy on top of the Black Prince's tomb at Canterbury Cathedral.

He 'saw' Mr Morris's face twisted around on the ceiling and clenched his eyes shut. In the blackness, behind his eyelids, Mr Morris skipped into view, smiled and held out a handful of strawberries in his hand.

"No," he screamed at the empty room, as he sat bolt upright. "No, no, no!"

Finally the sluice gates opened. After three years of desert eyes, the tears began to fall slowly at first, creating a salty track down each cheek. Then the flow increased. Tears and snot ran down his face, gathering on his top lip, splashing onto his thin, pointed chin and dripping down onto his trousers. The mucous and tears created an unfortunate pool of wet around the crotch of a boy who had been potty trained since the age of two and was too young to fill his pants or his mother with the product of puberty. His chest heaved and he cried out wailing like the paid mourners of the middle ages.

"It's good to gwieve, sweetie," Darius heard his mother's dulcet tones slide through the keyhole.

The interruption shook the boy. Darius threw a chair at the door and everything fell silent again. He didn't want anybody to know him, to see him or hear him. He turned onto his front and muffled his face deep in the pillow, coming up for air like a great, Blue Whale. On and on he cried, until finally exhaustion stilled him and Darius escaped into sleep.

Mr Morris was waiting for him.

"I'm so pleased you could join me," he said to the boy, doffing his hat and smiling broadly.

The garden looked extraordinarily beautiful. The cherry tree was weighed down under a bumper crop of cherries, the size of plums, and the strawberries glistened like rubies amongst the velvety leaves. There was a remarkable dawn chorus, as birds weaved between impossibly, fluffy clouds and the sky glowed, gold and red.

"You see Darius," said Mr Morris, smilingly, "everything's just perfect. See how happy I am here."

But as the old man smiled Darius saw tears streaking Mr Morris's face. He smiled again and handed Darius a basket, overflowing with every kind of fruit and vegetable. They were strange and foreign fruits, wonderful creations that he could not have imagined. There were rainbow-coloured pineapples, grapes that glistened gold and silver and a huge, shiny apple that glowed red and then green. Then he spotted the giant bananas that curled round and around, three or four times.

"They're beautiful," Darius gasped.

"Go on then, try one," said Mr Morris, as he winked at Darius.

Darius let his fingers run all the way to the top of the curly, whirly banana and then snapped back the stem and peeled away the skin.

"I'm so sorry I had to leave you, you know I loved you like the grandson I never had. I saw the potential in you Darius, you just needed to be loved," Mr Morris said soothingly and yet his voice betrayed his sadness.

Darius smiled at his friend through his own tears and then looked down at the intriguing banana. He broke off a few inches of the soft yellow fruit. His face fell down. It was black, rotting and festering, alive with worms and maggots. They seeped out of the fruit and crawled over the boy's hand. He screamed and looked up, but Mr Morris was gone, save for a puddle of tears.

Darius was covered in sweat and panted for oxygen as his eyes flayed open.

"WHAT?" he exhaled, confused for a moment, then comforted by the light that flooded his bedroom through the large Georgian sash windows. He catapulted out of bed and rushed to the garden window, hoping to find the beautiful, shiny garden, hoping to see Mr Morris leaning on his fork.

"I'm sss-o sss-sorry I had to leave you," Darius whispered to the glass, repeating the words of the dream and creating a circle of condensation on the window pane. "You don't have to leave me Mr Morris-sss, you can't... I promi-sss-e I'll get you back. I don't know how, but I'll find a way. I won't let them take you. Ju-sss-t give me time Mr Morris-sss, I'll find a way to bring you back to our garden and then we can carry on ju-sss-t as-sss we always-sss did, you'll sss-see."

He slammed both his hands on the glass.

"I'm going to get you back Mr Morris-sss – you're my only friend in the world."

For several days he lay on the bed, frozen in grief, unable to move, not sure how to bring his friend back to earth. On the fifth day, Darius looked at the new computer that had been delivered into the corner of his room only weeks earlier for his eighth birthday and ahead of most of the rest of the IT illiterate village. The dial-up connection, which he shared with the house phone line, was erratic and instantly slowed down by his mother's long phone calls to her 'special friends'. He turned the hard drive and screen on and clicked onto the world-wide-web. Gradually he became more familiar with the technology and search engines. He clawed his way around the globe to try to find a means to bring his friend back.

He clicked through endless websites, the spiritual, the medical, every place he could rest his desperate fingers on, the dirt-filled finger nails still bearing witness to his endeavours in the Garden of Eden only days earlier. As the clock past midnight and crept towards the morning of Mr Morris's funeral, he changed his search words to reincarnation and 'cryonics' popped up for the first time.

"What'sss that?" he whispered to Mr Morris, but the gardener didn't reply.

"Cryopre-sss-ervation – for those who want to make reincarnation a reality," he smiled slowly, his lip curled to one side. He jumped up from his seat and pushed the large sash window open.

"You see Mr Morris-sss. I told you I'd find a way to bring you back," but Mr Morris wasn't in a talkative mood.

After more searching for eternal life, he discovered a support and discussion group had just been set up over the county-border in Sussex, to help British citizens signed up for cryopreservation. He wanted to rush to the funeral parlour to retrieve the old gardener's body. He drew up a childish night-time plan to wheel Mr Morris home in his wheelbarrow and lovingly lay him out in the cook's cabinet freezer. This would buy him time, to figure out a way to get his friend back into his body.

But the clock was ticking for Darius's cryopreservation plan, the funeral was only hours away. Early that morning preparations were made to move Mr Morris's body from the refrigerated store and mortuary, which lay at basement level, under the unfortunately named Paine & Payne Funeral Directors. Mr Morris's remains were ceremoniously lifted into an ecologically friendly, biodegradable coffin, with a deep mahogany wood grain effect, chosen by his older sister Daphne. The eco-friendly box was placed inside the hearse and the entourage crept out of the village up the steep hill at a respectful ten miles an hour towards the 16th century church where Mr Morris had worshipped all his life. The bell ringers rang a depressing monotone *dong, dong, dong.*

Darius sat in the front row of the church, much to the irritation of his mother, who had wanted her son to keep her company in the back pew, behind the village congregation. Darius's front pew position, meanwhile, attracted sideways glances from the nephews, nieces and great nephews of Mr Edmund Reuben Albert Morris. They wondered how the strange little boy with the pointed face and the mean lips was related to their kind, round-faced uncle and great uncle. But the boy was oblivious to the sideways glances and just stared morosely at the coffin. He vainly hoped that by staying close to Mr Morris, he could somehow guard him and protect his friend from his final and inevitable destination.

It was a moving and surprisingly cheerful ceremony, thanks to Mr Morris's penchant for his Sunday school hymns and the love that everybody had for the kind old man with the 'green fingers'. But Darius felt a rising sense of panic as everybody stood at the end of the service and the grim reaper on the organ began his droning death march. The stony-faced coffin bearers stood at each corner of the coffin, preparing to raise the bio-degradable coffin onto their shoulders. However, the diminished frame of Mr Morris inside the lightweight box, flipped up onto their shoulders with too much ease and speed to achieve a truly dignified end to the proceedings.

The vicar took his first step behind the coffin and the pall-bearers. Darius placed a heavy hand on one of Mr Morris's nephews, who sat next to him, and pushed past the family to take second in command in the procession behind the vicar. Keeping just one step between himself and the vicar, the boy raised his eyes towards heaven and mouthed an incoherent mantra in Russian all the way down the aisle.

I won't let them bury you, I won't, prom-isss-e with all my heart Mr Morris-sss.

Many of the villagers presumed it must be a Russian Orthodox prayer as nobody could understand the peculiar babbling of the foreigner in their midst, who appeared to have fallen into a religious trance. The entourage passed out through the large, carved, wooden doors towards the graveyard. The weathered headstones marked the passage of five centuries of life and death, as the group drew closer to Mr Morris's final resting place.

The summer afternoon was heavy with a steamy humidity, making the air as thick as soup. The sky was a vivid dichotomy of bright blue sky juxtaposed with onerous clusters of black, threatening thunder clouds. Daphne, Mr Morris's elder sister, who had a serene, regal quality about her, sat quietly in a seat provided to rest her weary 86-year-old legs. Mr Morris's family had politely requested 'no flowers' in the funeral invitations that were hastily distributed throughout the village the day before the funeral and the order of service confirmed that any donations should be given to Edmund Morris's favoured charity – The Royal British Legion.

Daphne's simple floral arrangements for the burial reflected her sibling's humble tastes in life. She held a basketful of roses, which she had cut fresh that morning from her brother's beautiful English rose garden. The roses provided a brief moment of colour and brightness from the graveside ceremony that lay ahead. Daphne presented the roses into the hands of each mourner as they filed past her chair, like a dignified monarch bestowing grace and favours to a privileged few. The closest family members circled around the graveside with the vicar at Mr Morris's head and

Darius at his feet. Quite suddenly, Darius heard the droning and dramatic tones of his mother from the back of the group.

"Excuze, ev-er-y-buddy. I said, excuuuze me ev-er-y-buddy."

At first the close family and friends were reluctant to make way for the outsider, but after some moments, the crowd parted and Darius saw his mother standing in her hideous black and purple suit and hat, complete with a dated and ridiculous polka dot veil which failed to conceal the overly made up face of Natasha. In her arms she held an ostentatious and garish red carnation and purple lily wreath, the size of which was more befitting that of a state funeral.

Natasha knelt dramatically at the side of the coffin, bowed her head and placed the botanical aberration in the centre of the coffin. Nobody uttered a word, as the family lost the power of speech and stood with jaws dropped in disbelief. The regal crown of dignity slipped only momentarily from the head of Daphne, and recomposing herself quickly, she took the hand of Natasha between her two hands and thanked her for her enormous generosity. The coffin began its descent to its final resting place, with the ridiculous bouquet shrouding two thirds of the coffin.

"Ashes to ashes, dust to dust," said the vicar, trying to regain control of proceedings, as he invited family and friends to throw their roses onto the descending coffin. Mr Morris's roses now seemed small and paltry alongside Natasha's obscene bouquet.

As the coffin jerked and jolted down into the earth's crust, Darius bit his lower lip kneading it rhythmically with his teeth and restlessly rocking from foot to foot. He scanned each of the mourner's faces, his eyes silently pleaded with them to "do something"; to save his best friend; to stop the fearful descent. Mr Morris's remains were just a metre away from their final destination, when the boy could stand it no longer.

How can I save you if they put you down here? his brained screamed.

Without a rational thought left in his grief-stricken, sleep-deprived mind, he raised his hands to the thundery sky as though he had just received some divine intervention that required an evangelical response.

"NO..." he yelled, long and loud. "Sss-stop it!"

The sky turned black and there was a rumble of thunder. The sniffing stopped instantly as everyone stared at the strange, little Russian boy, who would never quite be considered 'a local'.

"I won't leave you," he said, bending his knees and arms and still looking at the black clouds. Then quite suddenly he dropped his head, swung his arms behind him and launched across the empty space, performing the most spectacular belly flop down on top of Mr Morris's remains.

The weight and force of his action slammed the coffin down the last metre of its descent and the box lid juddered and crumpled, revealing nothing of what lay below. However, a thousand wild imaginations 'lifted the lid' and imagined the fearful, decaying contents. Daphne let out a scream, inhaled sharply and fainted in her chair, whilst several others gasped in horror. Another young lady, quite without thinking, took the Lord's name in vain and was reprimanded with a glare from the vicar who dropped his service book.

At that moment, the heavy skies, pregnant with moisture, burst open and a deluge of rain fell. Without a thought for the deceased, the majority of the mourners turned on their heels and ran for cover, relieved to escape the dreadful scene. The torrent of water helped bring Daphne back to consciousness, with the aid of a gentle patting on her cheek from the vicar. Daphne sat bedraggled in her chair as the rain hammered down and reduced her crowning glory – the purple coiffed, bouffant hair-do – into sorry rat's tails that dripped around her forlorn face.

As Mr Morris's sister peered down into the chasm below, it was as though she sat on the set of a horror movie. The rain and mud splashed down on Darius and as he writhed from side to side hammering on the cracked lid.

The eight-year-old boy screamed like a toddler: "Come back, come back, come back Mr Morris-sss, before it's-sss too late. I think I know how to sss-save you, you can't let them bury you!"

The deluge had altered Natasha's garish purple and black ensemble into a dripping fashion disaster, which clung to her body, leaving little to the imagination of the pall bearers who stared at her exaggerated curvaceous form. Her thick eye makeup ran down her cheeks like fountain pen ink spilt across a blotter and the soggy polka dot veil clung grimly to her face.

The now ghoulish Natasha peered over the edge of the pit, careful not to slip over on the wet grass, in her high heels. She watched her son flailing from side to side, which looked to Natasha as though he was trying to learn to swim again, as the grave filled with several inches of water. To her horror, Natasha saw the flattened, soggy wreath of flowers being ground to a pulp by her son's writhing motion.

"Darius," Natasha said, crying out angrily as she dramatically held her hand to her mouth. "My flowerz. What 'av you done to my beautiful flowerz Darius? How will Mr Morris ever forgive you, you wicked boy!"

And with that she threw herself sobbing onto the shoulder of an attractive, young pall bearer. Jack, the local heartthrob, had only recently married the 'May Queen' and peeled the panda-eyed stranger off his shoulder.

"Is that your son?" Jack said incredulously.

"Is dat a trick question?" she said purring into his ear.

But the young man was in no frame of mind for Natasha's flirtatious games.

"Oughta be bloody ashamed of yourself," said Jack, as he pulled her lingering hand from his waist.

It was the first time Natasha's advances were rejected since arriving in the country.

"I 'ate funeralz," she said, huffing like a spoilt child.

She turned on her high heels and tottered home, knowing her son would be delivered back by the unfriendly pall bearer. Jack lay on his stomach and stretched down his big hands to the grief-stricken boy. At first, Darius ignored the means of escape from his current resting place with Mr Morris and clung to the coffin, with its crushed wreath. But eventually, wet, cold and exhaustion seeped into his body and Jack persuaded Darius to reach up and grab his hands.

The local village hunk lifted Darius onto the grass with ease and brushed him down. The deluge of rain finally softened to a light drizzle and the sun suddenly broke through the black clouds, as a rainbow was projected across the sky.

"Hey things are looking up," said the kind, young man with hands as big as plates, as he ruffled Darius's hair and patted him on the back.

"Come on little fellow, let's take you home."

Chapter Fourteen

midsummer

The next day, Darius sat bolt upright in bed – like a resurrected Frankenstein, exhausted and bruised from his spectacular descent into the depths of the earth the day before. His determination to 'do something' hadn't diminished. So he switched his computer back on and searched for more information on cryonics, running off endless printouts on his new bubble jet printer.

Darius yearned to be close to Mr Morris, so he stuffed the printouts in his rucksack and set out on his bike back to the graveyard, without telling the dot where he was going. The boy pedalled back to the place where Mr Morris rested in peace and lay on top of the freshly covered grave, with six feet of soil now separating him from his best friend.

He opened his backpack and pulled out the papers and veraciously began reading his way through strange and foreign words on cryonics, nanotechnology and liquid nitrogen suspension. But emotional exhaustion overcame him again and he slept fitfully for an hour or so on the grave, dreaming of Mr Morris's suspension and resurrection. A few spots of rain returned the budding young scientist to the land of the living. He reluctantly packed up his printouts and returned home.

"Sss-stay off the phone," he barked at his mother as he ran up the stairs and locked himself in his bedroom to continue his search.

Darius banged the keyboard in anger and frustration and waited for the sporadic dial-up connection and the world-wide-web to deliver Mr Morris from his grave. Then, quite by chance, Darius stumbled on the website of Alcor Life Extension Foundation where he read more about the science of cryopreservation. He scanned the screen hungrily for details, as each page loaded painfully slowly. Darius read how the organisation performed its first human cryopreservation in 1976 and that in subsequent years dogs had been resuscitated with '*no measurable neurological deficit after hours in deep hypothermia*'. As the technologies advanced and interest flourished he read that a further nine patients, including a member's pet, had undergone cryopreservation by the late 1980s, whilst the eminent scientist and one of Alcor's directors, Jerry Leaf, was cryopreserved following a fatal heart attack in 1991, shortly before the Californian-based organisation moved to Arizona to escape the risk of earthquake. Darius's mind whirred with the possibility of exhuming Mr Morris's body and flying his friend out to Arizona.

He looked again at the screen of words, but struggling to understand the complex terminology, he clicked onto the '*Frequently Asked Questions*' section and read on...

'*Cryonics procedures should ideally begin within the first one or two minutes after the heart stops and preferably within 15 minutes. Longer delays would place a greater burden on future technology to reverse injury and restore the brain to a healthy state, and would make it less likely that the correct original state could be determined.'*

His heart slowed to a sluggish thud when he read on...

'No adult human has ever been revived from temperatures far below freezing. Cryonics patients are cared for in the expectation that future technology, especially molecular nanotechnology, will be available to reverse damage associated with the cryonics process.'

At that moment, the terrible, final realisation hit him. It was all in vain, his search had turned to dust.

Ashes to ashes, dust to dust.

The metamorphosis of Darius's grief into an explosive rage was instantaneous. It boiled over into a raging hot pot of anger and resentment. He ran into the garden more wild than free now and picked up a pile of stones. He hurled them systematically at each pane of glass of the 'hot house', working his way around the entire 1920s structure like a professional darts player, section by section, grid by grid.

Smash – smash – smash – bull's eye.

As each stone shattered the panes, he vowed he would *never, ever, ever,* have another friend in his life. He vowed that he would never love again, so that *nothing* and *nobody* could hurt him like this again and with that he sealed his heart with a cold, cruel, hard casing, as he detached from everything and everyone around him. Then Darius ran and jumped at the door that had been painted a lovely shade of Hunting Green and kicked it in with both feet simultaneously like a martial arts expert.

BANG!

Next he turned his attention to 'nature's ploughs'. He knew he would never be able to watch the worms with his best friend by his side, so he decided to dish out his own justice system as the new head gardener. Darius dug up fifteen or so earth worms and they wriggled and squirmed over each other as he dropped them into a container and placed them in the freezer at -18 degrees Celsius. He decided to observe the changes at precise five minute intervals on his stopwatch which he recorded in his science notebook.

At five minutes he observed **the formation of crystals at either end of the Lubricus terrestris** but noted **full and lively movement**. By ten minutes **movement had slowed markedly and there were the first signs of stiffening in the worms**. By fifteen minutes he wrote **the worms were fucked, dead as Dodos, with no sign of movement whatsoever**. But he noted it took a further five minutes **for nature's ploughs to move from their semi-frozen state to frozen solid**.

The boy tossed the dead worms across the garden and made a second silent vow... his gardening days were over, dead and buried.

Despite an extensive search for a new gardener, Natasha failed to find a replacement for Mr Morris and eventually the nettles, thistles and thorns gradually throttled and squeezed the life out of Darius's and Mr Morris's Garden of Eden. Natasha noticed her son withdrawing back into his titanium shell after his "emotional outburst at the gwave", so she ventured into the local pet shop and purchased a black and white kitten to cheer her son up.

"Surprize," said the dot, as she waved her arms above her head like a can-can dancer. She bent down to release the kitten from a ridiculous pink basket she had purchased at the same time.

"Here's something to keep my little sweetie boy company," the polka dot purred, as she twirled his fringe.

But Darius didn't give the kitten a name and trained it to fight for her food. He teased her body with morsels of nourishment on an old fishing rod that Mr Morris had given him. Just as she tried to snatch the food, he'd whip it away. After a week of Darius's slow, systematic starvation programme, the kitten became so desperate for food that she would run the full length of the garden to chase the promise of a mouthful of sustenance. He spotted a thrush feeding her chicks at the back of the garden. After spooking the mother bird away, he laid the nest on the ground, loaded up the fishing hook with a piece of bait and cast the line down the long garden path, as the kitten frantically ran and jumped into the air, trying to hook it with her paw.

"Bingo," he said, snarling as the hook landed on top of the scrawny and vulnerable chicks, followed by the ravenous kitten.

When the kitten mysteriously disappeared, Natasha told Darius to make some posters to distribute around the village, despite the fact that he didn't seem perturbed by the animal's disappearance. Natasha shuffled through the most recent set of photos.

"Oh Darius, sweetie, you didn't take any photoz of your kitten and what'z her name?"

"Kitten," said Darius curtly.

Darius drew a Walt Disney grimacing black and white cat that looked like the character had stepped straight out of the set of the 'Alice in Wonderland' film, with its creepy grin from ear to ear. As Darius walked around the village with several photocopies of the poster, he noticed veiled conversations behind strategically held hands and long sideways glances. To his face, the shopkeepers and business owners went overboard with promises of help, sugar coated with saccharine smiles as they looked at the crude 'Lost Kitten' posters – with the generous promise of a £50 reward. Posters went up in the village shop, the dry cleaners and delicatessen.

Shortly after the kitten's disappearance, Natasha saw a stylish invitation drop through her door which said:

Celebrate the official opening of The Oast Orthodontic Practice

∞∞∞∞

Come and find out how to achieve the perfect smile for all the family

Natasha felt sure that her son's peculiar arrangement of teeth and unattractive profile could only benefit from such a visit and she was desperate to ingratiate herself into the neighbourhood after her son's embarrassing outburst at Mr Morris's funeral.

"Let's kill two birds with one stone, dah-ling. Let's go to the pah-ty and meet our new neiz-burs and then you can give them one of your posterz to find your little kitten."

But Darius wasn't listening to his mother and her words droned past him like traffic in the distance. Instead he engrossed himself in an arts and crafts session and took a copy of his poster, blotted out the face of the kitten with a thick red crayon and then cut off her limbs and head with a sharp pair of scissors and placed the disembodied picture under his mother's pillow.

CHAPTER FIFTEEN

early August

Planning for the official opening of The Oast Orthodontic Practice began in earnest in early August just a few weeks after the practice had opened for business.

Harry Maloney chose the last weekend of the August bank holiday for the party to attract the widest possible catchment of children and their affluent parents from the private school sector ahead of the start of a new term.

Harry's professional reputation preceded him all the way from Guys Hospital in London to Cranhurst and word spread quickly on the professional grapevine, as a number of local dentists saw The Oast Orthodontic Practice as the preferred referral route for the patients on their books who were in need of specialist ortho-dontic treatment.

"Of course technically speaking it's a bit of a fib isn't it Harry, wasn't the official opening meant to be in July?" Melanie teased, calling from the en-suite bathroom. She adopted a light and breezy tone, trying to cover up the bitter disappointment that she held in her hand. Melanie perched on the edge of the bath and willed the indicator wand to wave its magic, she closed her eyes waiting and hoping – hoping and waiting, but it was another dud, a false dawn.

She hurriedly put the used pregnancy testing kit back in its packaging, washed her hands and threw the evidence away in the bin. Her period was two days late and she'd just performed the test behind closed doors, whilst Harry chatted excitedly about the launch party from the marital bed.

Melanie had lost count of the times she'd excitedly peed on the pregnancy wand over the past eighteen months, only to have her hopes dashed with the test showing a negative result. Throughout the first year of their marriage (and still blissfully unaware of the fertility problems and gruelling treatment she would face in her bid to conceive), Melanie involved her husband in each pregnancy test.

"I really think I am this time Harry. I just feel different and I'm three days late."

"Well go on then, let's find out what the pregnancy kit thinks of your hunch."

Harry waited outside, pacing up and down like the expectant father unable to cope with the graphic close encounter of the delivery room. After two minutes he'd call through the door.

"Can you see anything?"

"No... not yet. Let's give it a bit longer."

The TV cook had longed to bake and cook for her own children, to trial new recipes on her own flesh and blood, to talk as the voice of authority from *real* experience, rather than relying on her imagination, careful research, or observation of other people's children. How she yearned to spoon one of her original 'first food for baby' purées onto a brightly coloured plastic spoon. How she desired to "choo, choo" the mix "*into* the tunnel...ooo-ah-ooo." How she longed for Minky Sloane to issue a press release to declare to the nation that Britain's favourite 'kiddie cook' was indeed finally 'with child'.

As the minutes dragged by and the longed for + sign appeared as another minus, she knew it was another 'phantom pregnancy' of her own making.

"Never mind gorgeous."

Harry always gave Melanie a consoling bear hug, but as the months rolled into years, she only had to take one look into his eyes to know that he felt the same crashing disappointment. After her first wedding anniversary, she decided to go solo with the pregnancy testing. Just one day overdue was enough for Melanie to see if *this time* the stork would deliver a baby to her door. Without the benefit of a crystal ball, Melanie was spared the knowledge that she would have to wait a further four and a half years into the new millennium for Hannah to be born. So Melanie smiled broadly as she emerged from the bathroom to disguise another heavy loss in their procreation battle.

❀   ❀   ❀

"I suppose *technically speaking* the end of August is a little bit of a fib for the *official* opening. But the July completion date for the surgery was ridiculously ambitious of me to announce to the local dental community," said Harry sheepishly. "Shack to surgery in a few months would have been extraordinary and don't builders always fall behind?"

Harry slid his arms around his wife's waist. "Anyway the most important consideration for the *official* opening was whether or not my celebrity caterer was free, I had to catch her between work on her kitchen studio and before she started filming 'Melanie's Munchkins'."

"So I'm your *caterer* now am I?" she said teasingly, hands on hips.

"How could I go to an outside catering company Melanie, when your food is the best I've ever tasted? You really are the *only* person I'd contemplate asking to do the food for the party."

"Flattery will get you everywhere this morning. I need you to make me feel good at something."

"Good at something?" said Harry incredulously. "You are good at *everything*."

Melanie tried not to think of the negative pregnancy test lying in the bin.

I'm good at everything Harry... except falling pregnant.

✿   ✿   ✿

Neither one of the couple wanted to mention the *other* reason for the delay for the official opening of the practice, the side show that prevented them from entering their new home for weeks afterwards whilst the emergency services and police did their work in the basement. The unfortunate, ill-timed and tragic 'accident' on the day contracts had been exchanged, the boxes were packed and the removal lorry had pulled up to transport the couple from London to their new life in the country. No, neither Harry nor Melanie was keen to drag up such an ill-fated incident which still hung like a dark shadow over the basement.

Harry had promised to make love to Melanie in every room as each one was converted or redecorated, and as a man who was true to his word, the basement would prove no exception.

"If we can't make babies straight away, we might as well get lots of practice in!" he grinned boyishly.

The couple christened each freshly finished space with a bottle of champagne and some 'procreation practice'. In the smaller, peculiar spaces, such as the surgery's x-ray and sterilising rooms, the lovemaking took on an almost comedic quality. The cosier the space the more arms and legs needed to be wrapped around each other and contorted into peculiar angles to perform their union. After many months, the basement remained the only room not to be christened by Melanie and Harry.

One evening when the couple was already rather tipsy from a shared bottle of wine, Harry appeared with the familiar, blow-up mattress under his arm and a bottle of champagne.

"Want to get some practice in?" asked Harry.

"Where to now cowboy?" Melanie giggled almost falling backwards off the kitchen stool.

Harry lifted his finger to his lips which were peeled into an inane banana shaped smile.

"Sssshhh," he slurred and looped Melanie's arm like the drunken line up on a New Year's Eve party.

"Come with me gorgeous," he grinned.

The couple staggered down the steps to the basement.

"Oh you've got to be joking darling, you know I don't like it down here, it's really spooky!" Melanie protested.

Harry lifted his finger again and rested it across her lips to placate her.

"Sssshhh gorgeous. Remember we have a schecret pact, we need to christen *every* room... Would madam care for her champagne from a glass or would she prefer to slug it from the bottle like an old drunk!"

"Cheeky so and so!" giggled Melanie, as she tickled her husband mercilessly.

"I have everything prepared for madam."

The butler in Harry magnanimously held out his hand and lowered Melanie onto the absurd, pink, blow-up mattress that was narrower than a standard single. It groaned and farted out an unglamorous squelching noise as Melanie lifted her feet onto the mattress.

Earlier that day Harry had rummaged around in the loft to locate a rare green leather gramophone he had bought in Portobello Market, years before he'd met Melanie. The avid amateur antiques' collector had set up the music box on top of one of the freezers (the one with a scratch that Melanie had got for a knock down price). Harry lit a couple of candles he'd dotted around the place to bring some warmth and atmosphere into the damp and 'spooky' place. Given Harry's inebriated state, it became something of a battle for him to wind up the gramophone quickly enough to achieve 78 revolutions per minute for 'I Can't Believe That You're in Love with Me'.

Harry picked up one of the champagne glasses which transformed into the crooner's microphone as he sang. Less sure of the second verse, Harry became hopelessly out of time with the vocals, but growing in confidence, he took on the alias of Frank Sinatra.

By the third verse, the Billie Holiday recording of the Gaskill/McHugh classic had slowed to a droning Marlene Dietrich rendition of the popular 30s song. Harry swayed theatrically from side to side, back amongst the New Year's Eve revellers in Trafalgar Square, as his voice adopted a Germanic guttural tone.

The gramophone ground into a – *hiss-pop, hiss-pop, hiss-pop* – as it hit the final groove on the disc. The crooner bowed theatrically to the sparse, yet enthusiastic audience.

"Bravo! Bravo!" Melanie clapped more furiously than a seal. "Encore! Encore!"

Harry turned and changed the disc winding the handle furiously again. This time he selected the genuine German article and placed the needle on a classic Dietrich hit 'Falling in Love Again'.

"There will be a short intermission in my performance whilst I lay with my gorgeous wife!" Harry announced.

Melanie rolled clumsily and noisily onto her back, as the mattress emitted something between a squelch and a squeak and she sipped champagne from the bottle as the 'butler' had suggested. The couple chuckled like children high on chocolate cake, as Harry lifted his leg over Melanie and the hopelessly narrow mattress morphed into a biological juke box.

"You're so funny Dr Maloney, you make me laugh," giggled Melanie.

"You're so beautiful Melanie you make me want to make love to you."

"Bad boy, more singing first, where did Frank Sinatra go?"

As Harry straddled Melanie's body his knees pressed into the hard, cold floor.

"We really *must* get a bigger mattress..." said Harry, "but then I guess we won't be in a hurry to christen this room for a second time."

Melanie looked anxiously at the ceiling above Harry's head which was covered in cobwebs, "No we won't be in a hurry to revisit the basement will we?"

Melanie thought of where she lay and the reason why they (and she in particular) had stalled 'christening' the basement. As she thought of Miss Davenport, she felt as though someone had thrown a large glass of ice water in her face to sober her up. Harry laughed raucously, still lost in the moment, and joined in with the dying flourishes of Marlene Dietrich's rendition of the song.

But the allure of unbridled lovemaking and champagne laughter evaporated for Melanie... POP!

Melanie sat up suddenly.

"Harry I don't know what we were thinking. Here of all places. I can paint and decorate as much as I like down here, but this room will always give me the heebie-jeebies. The *only* thing it's good for is for storing food in the freezers. Apart from that, I'll never have a good reason to come down here again!"

Harry lifted his wife off the floor that would one day hold the broken heart of Melanie and be the surface that would cradle the tomb of their second child. He swept her up into his arms and thought how small and vulnerable his wife felt in the hollow, dank basement.

"Come on my gorgeous girlie, let's take you to bed and practice upstairs," said Harry tenderly.

And Marlene droned that she couldn't help it.

❀　❀　❀

It was almost inevitable that Melanie would be the one to find Florence Davenport's body on the day of the move to their new home. For such was the 'kiddie cook's' excitement that it was Melanie who ran excitedly across the vast sitting room, as Harry chatted to the nurse. She skipped around the roundels of the kitchen like a schoolgirl.

Ring a ring a roses
A pocket full of poses
A tissue, a tissue
We all fall down!

The fact that the kitchen was empty (save for an oxygen

mask and tank) led Melanie to assume that the nurse had already taken Miss Davenport to the car to be transported away to the "delightful retirement home" the nurse had mentioned to Harry and Melanie, just before she slipped away to explore her new 'home sweet home' for the first time.

Whilst the kitchen was empty and dark, the door to the basement was wide open and the light spilled up from the stair-well drawing the new owner over to the space, like a lamb to the slaughter. A casual glance over the top of the staircase gave Melanie an uninterrupted and hideous view of the oast's previous owner.

For even before she screamed and ran towards the nurse and Harry, and shouted for an ambulance, her eyes were irreversibly exposed to the twisted, bloated form of Miss Davenport. Florence Rose lay tangled in her wheelchair on the basement floor, with the side of her once beautiful face smashed and trailing down the cruel, stone staircase that would one day lead to Elizabeth's grave.

CHAPTER SIXTEEN

late August

After threats of strong winds and heavy rain for the last bank holiday weekend in August, Melanie was relieved the weather reports had been downgraded by the morning of the party to light winds, with only a ten per cent chance of a shower in Kent, during the afternoon.

"Thank goodness for that," said the caterer as she flicked the TV off with the remote and checked her list of canapés, which were stretched across the newly converted kitchen. The marble island held trays of miniature buckwheat pastry cups with a Mediterranean pesto, as well as two trays of her favourite pre-dinner nibbles – devils on horseback. She opted to ditch the prunes by the third tray and wrapped pre-cooked parsnip strips with bacon; accentuating the sweet and savoury canapés with a delicious seasoning of honey and cinnamon that she roasted off to achieve a caramelised, toffee coating. Then there were the teaspoons of homemade duck paté which she had spooned delicately onto Melba toast; alongside Thai prawns, with ginger, coriander and sweet chilli wrapped in a twist of filo pastry.

For the sweet canapés Melanie made the most of a glut of summer fruit from the fruit cage that Mr Morris had lovingly pruned and cared for before his untimely death the previous month. As Melanie entered the cloistered fruit haven early on the morning of the party, she marvelled at the variety of soft fruits the old man had successfully cultivated for Miss Davenport over the years. Alongside the mini loganberry and white chocolate cheesecakes, Melanie prepared a huge bowl of whole strawberries dipped in alternating white and dark chocolate. The raspberry crop was mixed with crème fraîche and the seeds of a vanilla pod and sandwiched between two mini homemade almond macaroons, whilst she topped brown sugar meringues with a mix of whipped double cream and a crop of freshly chopped apricots and a dash of almond liqueur. Last of all, Melanie picked redcurrants and blackcurrants and baked dozens of miniature fruit tarts.

Exhausted but exhilarated from her marathon 24 hour baking session she went upstairs to get ready and then sat at the island in the kitchen and wrote a personal dedication to Mr Morris cutting out and sticking his image from The Wealden Weekly alongside the tribute...

In Loving Memory of Mr Morris – the 'green fingers' of the village green – we thank him for all the fruit in this buffet which was all grown under his tender and watchful eye.

"Shame we never really had a chance to get to know the old boy," said Harry as he walked across the quadruple roundels. "Apparently there was a bit of a commotion at the poor chap's funeral last month with a young boy falling into Mr Morris's grave. Sounds like something out of a horror movie."

"Ooo how creepy," said Melanie shuddering. "You'd better come here handsome and give me a kiss."

Melanie admired her husband who was immaculately groomed and dressed in a new pale linen suit ready for the reception. She kissed him hotly on the lips and as they parted Harry spotted the chocolate covered strawberries.

"Whatever happened to pineapple chunks and cheese on a cocktail stick?" said Harry, as he popped a chocolate strawberry in his mouth.

"Oh darling that's so 1970s!" Melanie giggled and then reprimanded the strawberry thief with a friendly nudge in the ribs.

"Sorry darling for stealing one of your strawberries," said Harry, as melted chocolate and strawberry juice dribbled down his chin, "it all looks and tastes *so* delicious! You're quite brilliant you know... I'm so proud of you!"

The waitresses dressed in black and white, began filing in and out of the kitchen like a busy army of ants. They carried the food over to the gazebo which had been deliberately erected in a highly visible location in the front garden, close to the practice and alongside a bouncy castle for the children.

"So how many RSVPs did we receive?" Harry said whilst trying to scurry the second and third strawberry he'd stolen into his cheeks, without his wife seeing. Melanie was too distracted by her final count to notice her husband's hamster cheeks.

"It could be as many as 130, but there will inevitably be the 'no shows'. Minky always says she counts on one third 'no shows' for any PR event she's ever organised. So as a guesstimate I'd say between 90 and 100. That would be super wouldn't it?"

"Absolutely... now let me give the beautiful hostess and caterer extraordinaire a thank you kiss."

Harry pulled Melanie close again and tenderly touched the lips that always looked as though they needed to be kissed.

"Emm yummy, I taste strawberry and chocolate!" Melanie teased.

Harry admired the beautiful floral dress his wife had bought for the party and despite her Norwegian and French inheritance today she looked every inch the English rose in full bloom. They interlocked fingers and Harry noticed Melanie had slipped on Miss Davenport's ring for the event. Harry ran his finger over the engraving RJW & FRD 1947 and quoted a section from Miss Davenport's letter, "'Treasure my ring and wear it to mark the most special moments of your life together'. So is this a special moment?" asked Harry, suddenly feeling anxious about the afternoon ahead.

"Of *course* it is darling," Melanie reassured him fervently, "I'm *so* proud of you."

A few minutes before 2pm the couple walked hand in hand across the front lawn to the gazebo. Immediately the locally infamous 'Cider House Rules' burst into song and began juggling an extraordinary number of strange and unusual homemade instruments. Melanie roared with laughter as she watched the theatrical, ruddy faced trio dressed in smocks delivering their raucous renditions of English and Kentish folk songs, from their stage made out of bales of hay.

The couple parted as Harry joined his nurse and receptionist to meet, greet and speak to the guests and dentists that began streaming across the lawn. Melanie soon lost sight of her husband as an enthusiastic group of young mothers surrounded the handsome consultant to be talked through the brand new brochure Dr Maloney had produced for the official opening.

The caterer's job now done, Melanie stood in the corner of the gazebo sipping a glass of sparkling wine. Interest in Melanie Henriksen usually followed a familiar pattern and the afternoon of the party went to script. Though none initially plucked up the courage to talk to Cranhurst's most famous new resident some of the couples threw furtive glances across the lawn trying to confirm if the stunning woman standing in the corner of the gazebo was indeed the lady on the television. Others were slightly less subtle and found an excuse to walk past Melanie even though she wasn't particularly en route to the food, drink or cloakroom. As a result, a few of the guests performed a peculiar zigzag approach towards Melanie, and then once happy that she was indeed the 'kiddie cook', they careered off at 90 degrees as though they had just slammed into an invisible pane of glass.

It was the unsuspecting Miss Potts who would open the rush of autograph hunters and mothers wanting a photograph with the glamorous TV cook. For although she'd seen Melanie on *Wake Up Britain* and had regularly stopped to chat to her new neighbour in the village, Miss Potts was oblivious to the 'celebrity status' that

Minky Sloane was creating for her highest income generating client.

Melanie broke into a broad smile as she spotted her elderly neighbour. Miss Potts, who usually ate like a bird, had heard of the 'kiddie cook's' culinary reputation and was piling a paper plate high with the tempting sweet and savoury canapés that were being circulated on the trays, whilst her poodle ran round in circles chasing her clipped tail and yapping excitedly. Miss Potts promised to take some nibbles back home to her sick sister, who was now too ill to venture beyond the front door of Greenview Villa with the rapid progression of her pancreatic cancer.

Miss Potts walked across the gazebo balancing a glass of wine, a plate of food and the ill-trained puppy. She had clearly gone to a huge amount of effort for this rare afternoon outing and had dusted off one of her best party dresses from the 1970s which had an unfortunate odour of mothballs and an equally unfortunate brown and orange floral pattern printed onto a static and crackling nylon/crimpolene material. Her face was covered with a thick application of pale powder and deep red lipstick, a beauty regime she had followed religiously since the 1940s, untouched by every fad and fashion throughout the decades.

The newly acquired poodle was dressed in a pink jacket and bow and the puppy swerved from side to side like a water skier yapping at every strange face in her wake.

"How lovely to see you," Melanie greeted her neighbour warmly. "I didn't think you would come."

"Oh I wouldn't have missed this for the world. Allow me to

introduce my new friend… Blanche this is Melanie… Melanie this is Blanche."

Melanie bent over to pet the dog, but the puppy began yapping wildly at the stranger's hand.

"Be quiet Blanche," said Miss Potts as she lobbed a devil on horseback straight into her mouth. "So did you wonder if it would be one Pott or two?" Miss Potts twittered at her own joke and began nibbling on a roasted, honeyed parsnip, wrapped in bacon.

"Oh of course I hoped for two Potts," Melanie reciprocated. "So how is your sister?"

Miss Potts shook her head gloomily.

"It's not looking good I'm afraid," she said brushing a tear away from her eye.

Melanie placed a steadying hand on her shoulder, "I'm sorry to hear she's so poorly."

Blanche yapped several times and ran around her mistress, encircling Miss Potts's legs like a strand of spaghetti on a fork.

"Oh you daft little thing," said Miss Potts cackling loudly.

The old lady swayed like the Leaning Tower of Pisa as she tried to balance her food and drink and another steadying hand from Melanie came just in time to prevent her neighbour from toppling over altogether.

"I really should have called her Lassie shouldn't I? Blanche always makes me laugh even when I'm sad. What a little imp she is though."

Miss Potts tossed another canapé into the mouth of Blanche.

"Anyway dear, these are delicious devils on parsnip backs –

what an original idea. Totally scrumptious, this is my third one already."

"Here let me help you find a seat," Melanie suggested diplomatically.

"Oh thank you so much dear. You're a lovely cook, very beautiful and kind too. What more could a neighbour ask for? Now you run along, I'm sure there's lots more important folk here than me, I'll catch up with you later. Have fun."

Melanie left her kind, elderly neighbour safely seated and the untrained puppy tethered to the chair. She turned back briefly and heard Miss Potts saying "One for you, one for me," as she alternately dropped a canapé into the tiny jaws of the much doted upon poodle followed by her own mouth.

The conversation with Miss Potts opened a floodgate of approaches as dozens of female guests asked the 'kiddie cook' to pose for a photograph, whilst others asked her to sign their newly acquired Oast Orthodontic brochure. Some came particularly well prepared and asked the 'kiddie cook' to write a personal dedication in a copy of her latest cook book 'Melanie's Melting Moments' which were miraculously plucked out of numerous large handbags.

Melanie looked up at the darkening skies and noticed that the ten per cent chance of a shower had turned into a 100 per cent reality as the heavens opened quite without warning. The deluge sparked an unseemly scramble into the newly opened surgery, whilst a few brave guests squeezed under the small gazebo, leaving the 'kiddie cook' ring fenced by her most ardent fans. By the time Melanie wrestled herself free from the adoring group and made it across to the byre, the waiting room was packed with people. The waitresses stoically attempted to continue circulating with the food trays, as they weaved and squeezed their way through the room. Elbows knocked and backs bumped together as the overly polite crowd of acquaintances apologised for the increasing amount of unintended personal contact and the inadvertent spillage of drinks and dropped canapés.

'Cider House Rules' decamped from their hay bale stage, still wearing their damp smocks and looked somewhat out of place surrounded by the clinical whiteness of the surgery and the orthodontic equipment.

The children, who had been entertained by the bouncy castle, eventually got wet through and started trickling back to the reception in twos and threes, covered in grass stains and mud. The warm, moist air became thick with the odour of wine, dank clothes, sweet perfume and BO, as the windows steamed up and thick lines of condensation dripped down the panes of glass. Melanie watched Miss Potts fold her fully restocked paper plate in two and slide it into her large patent leather handbag. She eased herself up stiffly from her chair and smiled broadly at the producer of the canapés whom she spotted tucked behind the reception desk. Miss Potts's poodle yapped a path through the throng. Her owner moved slightly woodenly feeling the first signs of arthritis in her hips.

"Délicieux Mademoiselle Henriksen, vraiment délicieux!" Miss Potts exclaimed.

"Thank you so much, I'm pleased you enjoyed the food."

"Yap!"

"Shush Blanche – be a good girl."

"Well that's my tea sorted," said Miss Potts as she patted her handbag.

"Yap!"

"Shshshsh-ush."

"Would you like a doggy bag too?" Melanie smiled cheekily, as Miss Potts's eyes fluttered with mischief.

"Oh I think there's more than enough for the three of us in here. It's a bit of a Mary Poppins handbag you know, I can squeeze an extraordinary amount in here!"

"Yap!"

"Anyway dear – I'd best be getting back to my sister." Miss Potts patted Melanie gently on the arm, "Thank you again – it was a lovely afternoon, goodbye dear."

"Goodbye Miss Potts."

Melanie left the reception desk and noticed that the large pile of promotional brochures had been whittled down to no more than a small handful.

Gosh you have been working the room Dr Maloney, very impressive.

Eventually Melanie found her husband 'talking shop' with three dentists at the back of the surgery.

"How lovely to see you gorgeous," said Harry as he wrapped his arm around Melanie's shoulder, "I wonder if you'll excuse us for one moment gentlemen, I just need to confirm something with my wife before the end of the party... we shan't be long."

Harry whisked Melanie down the back corridor into the x-ray room and locked the door.

"So what exactly was it that Dr Maloney needed to confirm with his wife before the end of the party?"

Melanie smiled impishly and clasped her hands behind her back.

"Well?" said Harry as he took a step forward and slid his arms around Melanie.

"I just wanted to confirm that you are looking particularly beautiful in that fabulous new dress."

He kissed her on the right cheek and she nodded, smiling broadly.

"And I also wanted to confirm that you simply are the best creator and maker of canapés in the world!"

She mouthed 'Thank you' and he kissed her left cheek.

"Oh and I just wanted to confirm that I *love* being married to you."

He kissed her on the forehead and she purred with contentment.

"Anything else to confirm?" she asked impishly, "or should we get back to the party Dr Maloney?"

"Yes one more thing gorgeous. I know it's been well over a year since we first started trying for a baby but – without getting ahead of myself – I just want to confirm that I can't wait to be the father of your children!"

He placed his mouth over the lips that always looked as though they needed to be kissed and they melted into each others' arms.

"I'm very tempted to peel your clothes off Ms Henriksen and re-christen the x-ray room right this instant."

"Now we don't want to risk a 'When Harry met Sally' moment do we?" said Melanie as the pair laughed and reluctantly parted.

On returning to the surgery the couple heard a loud commotion in the waiting room. Harry and Melanie walked across the surgery freely now as most of the party had moved into the reception area to ascertain the source of the hullabaloo.

"Scusie ev-ry-buddy, scusie, please letting us through," shouted the loud and alien voice, with the foreign accent.

A tall woman tottered on high heels across the waiting room, bumping and pushing her way through the various social groups packed into the reception area. The tall, athletic woman with her plunging neckline and dressed in a garish pink polka dot mini skirt that barely covered her knickers, temporarily rendered the party silent, as though someone had smashed a glass in a Michelin-starred restaurant. The foreigner in their midst was towing a small boy behind her by the hand. He hung his head down and buried his nose into a large tissue that obscured his face and was speckled with blood stains.

One guest turned to another and whispered, "Isn't that the boy who jumped into Mr Morris's grave?"

The other whispered back.

"It's hard to tell, with his face covered like that. Though the mother is not hard to forget is she. My goodness she looks like she's hot footed her way straight from the red light district in King's Cross!"

"Maybe she's the surprise kiss-o-gram!" joked one.

"Strip-o-gram more like, she's certainly dressed like a hooker!" said the other acerbically.

273

The two laughed haughtily, as they surveyed the stranger.

"Dr Muzloney, Mees Henerikzen."

The woman waved her invitation in one hand, together with another piece of paper, which seemed to have a child's drawing on it. The boy simply buried his face deeper into the tissue, which was almost soaked through now with blood.

"Dr Muzloney, Mees Henerikzen, how luvzly to you meet."

Melanie and Harry temporarily lost the power of speech.

"Zankyou so much for ze luvzly invitation," said the woman, as she fluttered the card excitedly in front of her face like a geisha with a fan. "I'm your neighbour across ze green over high wall. Please let me introducing us... Natasha Sorokin and my son Darius Sorokin."

Natasha tugged on Darius's hand as his cue to lift his head and say hello, but the boy kept his head down and buried in the tissue.

"I'm so sorry for nozebleed and my English, I slowly improve. My son was fluent almost straightaway, but it's harder much for my head with ze older brain. The nozebleed is happening ever since Mr Morris died, you know ze man they call ze 'green fingers'."

Melanie nodded sympathetically for she too missed the wise old man's presence as he tended her fruit cage behind The Oast. Natasha leant forward between the party hosts and dramatically raised her hand to conceal her mouth from her son.

"He duz the nozebleed for attention, I've seen him pick his nose to set it off, hez just a big attention seeker like his father, but hez dead now anyway, so we don't have to worry about him!"

Melanie's mouth opened several times like a gold fish, as she struggled to find the best greeting or response for her new neighbour. Natasha plucked one of the last glasses of sparkling wine still circulating and drained it.

"Sorry for that – I'z dying of the thirst. Anyway I won't beat the bush about. We have three reasons for coming to your party. First to say hello to the new neighbour... so hello. Second for my son's teeths. Dr Muzloney the big ones that has come through iz horrible and I think they will be very much work for you. Thirdly, my son has lost his kitten and has made a poster to try and finding she. If possible would be luvzly to display in surgery if you are agreeing."

"Well... hello back... and... um... lovely to meet you too," said Harry, as he eventually found the most appropriate response. "I'm sure we can help your son achieve the perfect smile once I've had a proper look in his mouth and we'll certainly try everything we can to help him find his kitten too."

"Good it's a deal then," said Natasha resolutely. "Darius show ze nice doctor your teeth."

Darius's mother tried to lift the boy's chin up but he snapped his head firmly onto his chest.

"Really Mrs Sorokin, it's not necessary for me to look at Darius today," said Harry. "It's best if you book an appointment at the reception desk and I can give you an informed opinion during a proper appointment session on the best way forward. I'd want to take x-rays, photographs and impressions and would need to take a few days to give you my professional opinion as to whether Darius even requires treatment."

"Dr Muzloney I can say you right here and now my son will definitely need treatment, his teeth iz really horrible," said Natasha.

Harry dropped down and crouched to Darius's level.

"Mrs Sorokin I think the most important thing to do right now is to get this wounded little soldier cleaned up. Howdy partner!" said Harry warmly as he held out his hand to shake the young boy's hand. But Darius kept his face buried behind the large tissue that had turned crimson.

"Never mind cowboy, let's clean up those wounds shall we? We'll have you back on your horse before you know it," said Harry, as he called the nurse over.

The nurse led Darius over to the sink. "Pinch your nose here and here," said the nurse as she demonstrated how to stop the blood flow. Darius mechanically followed her instructions but kept his face hidden behind the tissue.

"If you just lift the tissue away from your nose now I can clean you up."

But Darius refused her offer of help and instead snatched the two cotton wool plugs that she was holding and pushed one up each nostril. She persuaded the boy to swop his bloodied tissue for a fresh one and as he did so, the nurse could see that his face was still covered in freshly running blood and darker, dried patches. A little frustrated by the child's incompliant behaviour, the nurse took Darius back to his mother.

"I'm sorry he seemed a bit shy and didn't want me to touch his face," said the nurse tactfully.

Natasha, however, appeared disinterested as she plucked

a second glass of wine from the last circulating tray and flirted wildly with the handsome orthodontist.

Melanie bent down to Darius, "Let's find a good place to hang your lost kitten poster shall we?"

The boy reluctantly held the hand drawn poster of his kitten with his spare hand and rigidly followed Melanie to the reception desk whilst she found some double-sided stickers. She carefully peeled the plastic backing off the first double-sided sticky pad and passed it into the hands of the boy who would one day murder her second child.

Melanie giggled as the first few pads became stuck between their fingers, twisting into a gummy mess and rendering them redundant.

"Oh well I guess we'll just have to throw those ones away and start all over again," she said.

Melanie helped Darius peel the sticky substance off his fingers, giggling as their fingers became stuck to one another once more.

"Let's try again shall we?"

Darius narrowed his eyes, sly as a fox, to focus on fixing the sticky pads to the four corners. Melanie saw the boy's peculiarly pointed tongue push out like a slug between his unfortunately arranged teeth. He grunted like a gagged hostage victim, frustrated that such a fuss was being created for a kitten that he'd never asked for and didn't want.

Silly fuckers he laughed internally, as he thought of the kitten that was already dead and hidden with her neck slit at the bottom of the cook's cabinet freezer.

He applied each sticky pad methodically to the paper with none of the sense of fun or humour that the effervescent woman crouched next to him seemed to be experiencing.

"So where shall we hang your poster Darius?" asked Melanie cheerily as she stood up and looked around the room for the ideal spot.

Darius stared stubbornly at the floor and Melanie suddenly felt foolish, holding the animated cartoon picture of a kitten in her hand. Then Darius slowly raised his gaze for the first time. His eyes lurched their way up Melanie's body and locked onto her eyes. Her dancing, vivid blue gaze was overwhelmed by the menacing darkness of the boy's eyes which were so lifeless that the pupils seemed to have spilled rivers of nothingness into his irises. The two bloodied cotton wool plugs hung out of his nostrils like a pair of fangs, whilst his nose and thin, mean upper lip was caked in dried blood. Melanie stood rooted to the spot as she looked into the eyes of the boy's soul and could only see a big, black void. Clearing her throat from the ball of awkwardness that was now lodged in her windpipe, she shuddered herself free of the young boy's glare.

"Right well I think the best place for the poster will be above the receptionist's desk. Everybody stops here to make their appointments, so if anybody has any idea where your poor little kitten is – this will give her the best chance of being found."

Melanie stuck the paper to the wall, suddenly craving the warmth of Harry's arm around her.

"There, that looks good doesn't it Darius?"

As she turned around, she jumped, not realising that the boy was standing right behind her now.

"Yes-sss that looks-sss really good Miss-sss Henrik-sss-en."

The mechanically and perfectly enunciated words and strange hissing 's' slithered its way around Melanie's head for the first time and she sensed a cold, creeping sensation run up her spine.

"We should find my kitten now, Miss-sss Henrik-sss-en," said Darius.

Then Melanie watched the boy's upper lip curl up into something resembling a smile, but she couldn't help thinking that somehow it was closer to a sneer.

PART III

Chapter One

Saturday 11 December – 6.20pm

"How are you Melanie?"

"Oh you know... a bit weak."

"You lost a lot of blood," said Joshua Haverstock as he curled the phone lead tightly around his finger, wondering if he should have spoken so directly about Melanie's haemorrhage.

"Yes... apparently it was touch and go for a while," said Melanie.

"Sophia and I were worried sick when we heard how ill you'd become after the delivery," said Joshua as he heard some gurgling in the background, "Is that Elizabeth?" asked the photographer.

"Yes," said Melanie, as the weakness in her voice was dissipated by her smile.

"We've just got your birth announcement card. Oh my days Melanie, Sophia and I thought twins were extreme enough, but 10lb 8oz for one baby, poor you!" Joshua hesitated before continuing, "Harry told me you won't be able to have any more children, I'm...I'm so sorry for you Melanie. Harry always used to joke about wanting a football team."

"I know we're devastated, but Elizabeth was worth everything I've been through, she's such a beautiful baby."

"I couldn't agree more I'm looking at Elizabeth's photograph now, what a cutie... just like her Mum!"

"Thank you very much you little smoothie! Our photo of Elizabeth is probably not quite up to your standard of photography," said Melanie.

"Ah photography, that's another reason I'm calling. I just want you to be really sure you still want to go ahead with 'The Art of Food' book in January. Of course I'm really excited about working with you, but if it's one project too far I do understand, even if Minky Sloane won't," Joshua insisted.

"No absolutely I'm still on schedule for the New Year. Of course I need to hear the details of the project and financial deal before I sign on the dotted line, but I know Minky wouldn't let a newborn baby and near death experience stall her plans for her highest earning client!"

They both laughed.

"There's only one thing, or should I say, one *little person* that could scupper our plans," said Melanie almost apologetically.

"Go on?"

"I want to bring Elizabeth with me during the photo shoots – I've been through too much to dump her with a nanny. Hannah's at school from nine to three each day from January so sadly she has to stay in Kent whilst we work on 'The Art of Food' project, but at least we've found a super local nanny to do the school runs and tea times. As you know I'm not militant about anything ordinarily, but I absolutely can't compromise on this one Joshua. Elizabeth is part of the 'kiddie cook' package."

"It will be a pleasure to have another baby in the apartment, as you know the flat's right above my studio. The more the merrier, I'm sure Sophia won't mind."

"But you've got twins Joshua, Sophia couldn't cope by herself with three babies under six months!"

"I guess another pair of hands would be helpful," said Joshua, as his mind raced... *who to ask?*

"Leave it with me Melanie I think I know just the right person to help Sophia for the assignment. Anyway I just wanted to wish you and your family a very happy Christmas."

"You too Joshua, say hello to Sophia and give the twins a kiss from me... happy Christmas and see you in the New Year!"

CHAPTER TWO

Monday 3 January – 10.30am

Joshua Haverstock anxiously flitted across the studio tidying and moving items around, despite the cleaner's immaculate six-hour clean of the space on the previous Saturday. Sophia brewed a cafetière of coffee and placed a basket of warm pastries from the deli downstairs on the huge coffee-table which had been fashioned from a reclaimed industrial steel panel from an old wharf building. Alongside the mid-morning refreshments Joshua placed his large sketchbook, opening it at his favourite sketch, and then covered the two easels with sheets. He sat down again tapping his foot against the table and drumming his fingers on the armrest.

"Relax sweetheart," his wife said reassuringly, as she turned the baby monitor on to check the twins were still sleeping peacefully upstairs. "Melanie loves the sound of 'The Art of Food' book and she's already agreed in principal to doing the project, even before Minky Sloane has confirmed the financial deal."

The bell reverberated loudly across the studio and Joshua jumped out of the king size sofa and ran to the top of the staircase.

"Just take a deep breath," said his wife calmly, "remember Melanie's been through a hell of trauma, since we last saw her. Let's make the next hour as relaxing as possible."

Just then Melanie's publicist impatiently pressed the bell again at street level and held her perfectly manicured finger on the bell.

"Maybe you spoke too soon about being relaxed," said Joshua, as he leapt down the stairs two at a time, whilst Sophia shuffled down the steep staircase as quickly as she dared in heels. Joshua threw the door open.

"Minky I know you're keen to see me but that's just ridiculous," he said with an ironic grin.

Finally the publicist lifted her finger off the bell.

"Oh darling, you flatter yourself," said Minky loftily, as she stood on the pavement dressed in an electric pink, fake fur hat and coat. She pushed past Joshua and Sophia and shielded Melanie and Elizabeth with her golfing umbrella – despite the fact that the day had delivered a clear blue wintry sky over London.

"Bloody paps, anyone would think Melanie is the first woman on earth to have a baby."

Minky ushered her client indoors behind her and opened the door again, as several photographers caught the infamous publicist gesticulating in front of Melanie, Joshua and Sophia.

"*Yes* she has had baby and *no* Melanie Henriksen does not want to make a comment! As you can see my client is NOT dead! Now sod orf and come back in November when Ms Henriksen and Joshua Haverstock are ready to announce their joint collaboration. Until then mum's the word!"

She slammed the door dramatically and cackled loudly at her coup d'état.

"Sorry about that but the nation's 'kiddie cook' fixation is getting out of hand. I guess I only have myself to blame for creating such a media sensation – I just can't help being brilliant!" said Minky without a hint of irony. "Now, let's start again shall we darlings."

The PR smacked her customary *MWA, MWA* air kiss either side of Joshua and Sophia's shoulders. Joshua and Sophia turned to Melanie, excited to catch their first glimpse of Elizabeth.

"Well, come on then, let's meet the cause of all the commotion outside," said Sophia excitedly.

The 'kiddie cook' radiated joy and serenity and peeled back Elizabeth's hat to reveal her newborn baby's plump, rosy face.

"She's even more beautiful than her photo," the photographer cooed.

"Oh come on you three, let's get this mothers' meeting over with," said Minky, who had sidestepped the maternal instinct in her early twenties in favour of a thrusting career to the top of the PR tree. "Come on troops, we've got work to do," she ordered and marched up the stairs.

Once they had settled into the studio, Joshua hovered around Melanie like a matron on a hospital ward as she tried to make herself comfortable in the low slung sofas, with Elizabeth still tied into her baby carrier.

"Sorry about the seating, it looks really trendy, but they're hellishly uncomfortable even if you haven't got a baby strapped to you," Joshua apologised. "Would you like a cushion for your back?"

"Oh for God's sake Joshua, she's had a baby she's not bloody dying!" said Minky impatiently.

The three of them winced. Minky clearly hadn't grasped just how close to death her most successful client had come.

"Coffee, pastries anyone," Sophia said, cutting in diplomatically.

"Just a glass of water thanks and a Danish. It's amazing how many calories you can get away with consuming when you're breastfeeding," said Melanie.

Minky looked impatiently toward the ceiling and shuddered at the thought of Melanie feeding Elizabeth in front of her.

"Oh just pour me a goddamn G&T darling," said Minky as Sophia offered the publicist a drink.

"It's only 11am Minky," said Sophia, raising her eyebrows.

"Well that never stopped me before darling. With the morning I've had I need all the sustenance I can get. Alcohol's always been *my* primary source of cals and I'm not planning on changing my wicked ways anytime soon."

"How are the twins?" Melanie enquired, spotting a photograph of the babies on Joshua's desk.

"Just adorable," said Joshua.

"Hard work," Sophia interjected, "but adorable all the same."

"Sophia it's so good of you to let Elizabeth stay in the nursery upstairs – whilst I work on this fantastical project with your husband," said Melanie appreciatively.

"No problem, it was Joshua's idea to employ my younger sister to help me out. She is taking a gap year between school and uni to give her time to recover from the death of our mum last summer. It was bad enough for me, but at least I've had eight years more experience of life than her and I had the almighty distraction of the birth of the twins and the support of Joshua. Mum couldn't have died at a worse time for Angelica she was just about to sit her A Levels."

"I'm so sorry to hear that Sophia, I only hope Elizabeth's crying will be a *healing* experience!" said Melanie, smiling doubtfully.

"Genuinely Melanie, Angelica is really looking forward to the experience," said Sophia, "and the gap year will give her time to focus on her fencing career too. She's currently number one in Great Britain and has won every competition over the past year, so she's going great guns. Well I'll head upstairs to check on the twins, whilst you three talk business. Angelica should be here soon."

Melanie turned to Joshua.

"So tell me some more about 'The Art of Food' book Joshua – what sparked the idea?"

"Well it might sound a bit crazy but it was mushrooms... actually."

"What magic mushrooms, you rascal," said Minky, after downing half her G&T in several large gulps.

"No Minky, Portobello mushrooms," Joshua corrected po-faced. "I'd decided to take a few days out of the studio last summer, just after Sophia's mum had died. We both needed some fresh air and a change of scene. So we visited my favourite fruit and veg market where we stumbled upon the most amazing Portobello mushrooms, a bit like these."

Joshua placed a handful of fungi in front of Melanie who

picked them up and started to study the mushrooms as the photographer continued with his story, animatedly pacing up and down the studio.

"I was transfixed by their curving trunks and parasol canopies, somehow they transformed from everyday fungi into sci-fi trees on a lunar landscape."

"Now you really do sound like you've been on the magic mushrooms darling!" said Minky, as she drained her glass.

"I know I might sound mad, but from that moment on it was as though I'd been given a fresh pair of eyes. Everywhere I went I started to see ingredients and food in a new way as part of an edible 3D world... a kind of food landscape if you like."

Joshua whipped the cover off one of the easels to display the mushroom-scape.

"Gosh Joshua – it's fantastic," said Melanie, smiling broadly.

The photographer paused to sip his coffee.

"My second extraordinary moment came with smoked salmon."

"Really?" said Melanie incredulously.

"After a Finnish food company spotted my work with mushrooms they commissioned me to create a tropical foodscape out of a typical Finnish meal. When they presented me with a rather unglamorous collection of ingredients including a salmon fish, some new potatoes, dill and soda bread – I knew I'd have my work cut out. The seascape was to be shot over a huge area and I'd been pondering the challenge of creating a tropical sea effect out of whole salmon for days. It became a real stumbling block – I just couldn't see how I could get the salmon to look like the tropical waters they were looking for. I was close to turning the commission down when I decided to break for lunch and headed over to the pub. I guess I had salmon on the brain so I ordered a pint of ale and a plate of smoked salmon. As the waitress walked across the bar, it was my 'eureka' moment Melanie. Shafts of light poured into the old smoky pub through the long high windows, dancing across the surface of the smoked salmon. 'That's it' I cried out to the poor waitress, 'Hold it right there'. She definitely thought I had a screw loose, but I realised I'd found a way to make the tropical sea."

Joshua threw the sheet off the second food landscape and Melanie gasped.

"It's beautiful it really does look like a Caribbean beach... quite extraordinary Mr Haverstock," said Melanie wholeheartedly.

"You're not the only one to say that – one of the directors at the company insisted he'd visited the exact same beach on a recent Caribbean cruise!"

Melanie eased herself out of the low slung sofa, careful not to wake Elizabeth and stood transfixed by the photograph, laughing out loud as she identified the foods behind each part of the seascape.

"So how do you see me fitting into 'The Art of Food' concept Joshua?" Melanie asked.

"Well darling," Minky said lunging out of the sofa. "I think it's probably best if I take it from here. We've let Joshua do his wafty creatives so why don't I explain the commercials. Despite Mr Haverstock's meteoric rise in continental Europe over the past six months, he's never developed the concept into a book. So he approached me and then of course I approached you and voila I believe we have the perfect ménage à trois."

"Understood Minky," said Melanie, "but whilst our friendship with Sophia and Joshua has blossomed recently, perhaps there was a reason our professional paths haven't crossed until now. My recipe books are so utterly different from a photographic food book... I just can't see the synergy."

Joshua boldly took Melanie's hand. "Ah but Melanie that's where you are so wrong," he said in the sweetest, softest way that took any note of patronisation from his words. "Working with food and ingredients is like second nature to you, as it is to me. You are utterly creative in the kitchen, whilst I know what is photographically possible and achievable. I think our combined talents would be an exciting and intoxicating fusion of food creativity and 'The Art of Food' would be a genuine work of art."

"Oh God Joshua, now you sound like a bloody poet as well a photographer! The thing is darling," said Minky clinking her glass with her long red nails and holding it up to Joshua for a refill. "The thing is – it's shaping up into an uber exciting commercial deal. I've already got a satellite TV company interested in filming the project over six months to make a television programme, and a lucrative publishing deal in the offing for 50,000 open editions and 5,000 limited edition books and a 10 per cent cut each for the two of you. We're only looking to produce 24 images by the end of the summer so we'll be all wrapped up in six months. Don't forget it's a coffee-table book: code for lots of white space and hot air darling!"

Melanie smiled patiently whilst Joshua cringed internally,

terrified that the publicity powerhouse was frightening the 'kiddie cook' away with talk of a six month schedule, only two months after her near death experience giving birth to Elizabeth. However, Joshua's fears proved unfounded as Melanie turned warmly to the photographer and her publicist and shook hands with them both.

"As you say Minky, it sounds like we have a wonderful ménage à trois. So let's get started early next week."

Joshua audibly exhaled a sigh of relief just as the front door bell rang again.

"Ah that must be Sophia's sister Angelica, I won't be a minute," said Joshua. He ran downstairs and threw the door open enthusiastically, "how's my favourite sister-in-law and Elizabeth's nanny to the rescue?" he chirped, warmly embracing Angelica Mayhew.

As he pulled back his face fell into a worried look of concern. Angelica's usually flaming red hair and vibrant green eyes were dulled, having lost all their luminosity, and her cheek bones pushed through a hauntingly white complexion.

"Gosh Jelly, what happened to you, you've lost so much weight. You look terrible sweetheart," said Joshua.

"Well thanks so much for the vote of confidence Joshua. You can blame my coach for my leaner, meaner frame, he's been working me ridiculously hard in training," Jelly said unconvincingly, as her hollow, drawn cheeks reformed into a broad smile. "Bradley's been talking about me being a possible reserve for Beijing 2008, can you believe it?"

"That's fantastic Jelly... but don't drop anymore weight they'll be nothing left of you and you won't be able to pick up your sabre, let alone fight with it."

Joshua embraced his sister-in-law again, more protectively this time, and felt her shoulder blades press against his hands. He pulled back, still deeply perturbed by her skinny appearance.

"How are you coping without your Mum?" he asked as he gently rubbed her forearms, alarmed to feel a downy layer of hair had formed on her skin.

Jelly smiled bravely and closed her eyes trying to shut the last image of her once beautiful mother out of her mind. But it was always waiting for her, the image of her mother's skeletal frame covered by paper thin yellowing skin, her hair plucked like a chicken by the cocktail of chemotherapy drugs and the fragile, bony hands that could no longer protect Jelly. Joshua watched his sister-in-law wince with pain and tears seep through her closed eyelids and decided diversion was the best tactic.

"Race you to the top!" he said as he began running up the staircase.

Despite her painfully thin frame, the ambitious perfectionist in Jelly always rose to a physical challenge and nimbly took the stairs three at a time. Pushing past her brother-in-law she stood at the top of the stairwell smiling triumphantly, as Joshua's chest heaved up and down from the exertion. The dash up the staircase had failed to even raise the pulse of the young athlete standing next to him.

"Melanie Henriksen this is my very fit younger sister, the junior fencing champion Angelica Mayhew," said Sophia as she reappeared from the apartment upstairs with a twin on each hip.

"Oh *please*, call me Jelly... *everybody* does," said Jelly as she grimaced at her older sister.

Minky pushed between the women and smacked an air kiss either side of Jelly's head. "So you're a junior fencing champ already Jelly, well I'd say we're looking at a future gold medal Olympiad from what I've heard from your sister," said Minky.

"That's terribly generous of Sophia, but I think a 2012 Olympic *hopeful* is more realistic," Jelly suggested. "If I make the fencing team at Beijing 2008 it's only likely to be as a reserve."

"Well don't go into PR darling, I find it's *always* best to talk things up in our business," said Minky loftily.

Elizabeth began to stir in her harness, snuffling into Melanie's breast, seeking her next feed.

"Well thank you *so* much for hiring me to be Elizabeth's temporary nanny," said Jelly as she stretched out her hand to shake Melanie's.

"You came with a very good recommendation," Melanie confirmed, smiling warmly at Sophia.

"Can I hold Elizabeth?" Jelly asked enthusiastically, as Melanie untied the baby harness.

"Of course you can," said Melanie, "you'll probably want to get some practice in before we all get going properly next week on 'The Art of Food.'"

Jelly instinctively lay Elizabeth on her front, across her forearm and rubbed her back.

"You're a natural Jelly, that's Elizabeth's favourite position," said Melanie, "I can see you two are going to get along famously!"

"I guess I've had quite a bit of practice with my sister's twins,"

Jelly said, as she felt the baby rubbing her mouth across her hand in search of milk. "It looks like Elizabeth's ready for her next feed Melanie. Let's go upstairs and you can make yourself at home in the twins' nursery."

"Well if it's feeding time at the zoo, I guess that's my cue to leave," Minky said dispassionately. She slipped smoothly into her pink coat and hat ensemble, inappropriately lit a cigar, kissed the air twice – *MWA, MWA* – and then the PR genie disappeared behind a puff of cigar smoke back onto the streets of London.

CHAPTER THREE

Monday 10 January – 9am

On the first full morning of 'The Art of Food' project, Melanie delivered Elizabeth into the care of Angelica Mayhew's loving but skinny arms. Jelly gently placed her new charge across her forearm in the baby's favoured cuddling position, like a lion cub on the branch of a tree.

Almost as soon as the sisters had agreed to Joshua's suggestion to take care of Elizabeth, the photographer seemed amenable to extending the nursery to house three babies, rather than two. Sophia and Jelly cheerfully shopped for the additional equipment together, grateful of a happy distraction from the raw and recent memory of their mother's death the previous summer. The pair hit the sales and added a travel cot, an additional nappy changing area and a chest of drawers filled with spare clothes and toys for Elizabeth.

"You've gone to so much effort!" Melanie gasped as she walked into the nursery only a week after the initial planning meeting.

"I just thought it would save you having to drag everything up and down between Kent and London," said Sophia, as she placed a beautifully wrapped parcel into Melanie's hands, "Here Melanie, this one's for you."

"More presents? You really have been so generous already, thank you so much," Melanie said warmly, kissing Sophia on each cheek.

Melanie pulled the ribbon and peeled away the layers of pink and cream tissue paper eventually coming to a soft pink leather book entitled '*Mother's & Baby's First Year*'.

"Sophia it's gorgeous, you really are so kind, thank you!" said Melanie, as she hugged Sophia.

Melanie thumbed through the leather bound album, filled with exquisite handmade paper. There were sections to record her baby's weight and height progression and a delightful milestone of 'firsts' – first word, first smile, first food, first steps. Then Melanie came to a diary section for her to write a detailed account of Elizabeth's first year of life. A look of anxiety flashed across Melanie's face.

"You haven't got one already have you?" said Sophia, noticing Melanie's facial expression.

"Oh no, not at all it's *such* a special gift... really I *love* it," Melanie reiterated.

"You don't like pink then?" offered Jelly.

"I *love* pink Jelly. It's just I hope I'll be able to keep the monthly diary section up to date, you know with my schedule being as mad as it is this year. It's funny I still regret not having done anything like this for Hannah. So this is my solemn vow... and you two can be the independent witnesses!"

Melanie placed her hand on the book, as though standing in

court (though her real court appearance, following Elizabeth's murder would follow much later).

"I Melanie Henriksen promise to keep this diary up-to-date for a whole year... no matter how busy Minky Sloane makes 2005 for me," she grinned at the sisters. "Thank you again, it's beautiful and it'll be a lovely treasure trove of memories to give to Elizabeth on her 18th birthday."

Then glancing at the clock she turned her attention to work, "Anyway I'd better get down to the studio, your husband will be wondering where I am. Don't hesitate to come and get me Jelly when Elizabeth needs a feed."

Sophia left the room with Melanie leaving Jelly on her own with Elizabeth. Jelly rocked Elizabeth in her favourite position on her front and softly sang the nursery rhyme her mother had sung to her as a child.

Two little clouds, one summer's day,
Went flying through the sky.
They went so fast they bumped their heads,
And both began to cry.
Old Father Sun looked out and said,
"Oh! Never mind my dears,
I'll send my little fairy folk,
To dry your falling tears."

Jelly saw the baby's eyelids grow heavy and placed her gently in the cot, stroking her cheeks to the melody.

One fairy came in violet,
And one wore Indigo.
In blue, green, yellow, orange, red,

They made a pretty row.
They wiped the clouds-tears all away.
And then from out the sky,
Upon a line the sunbeams made,
They hung their gowns to dry.

Jelly finished the song that was so familiar to both sisters just as Sophia popped her head around the door and whispered, "That was lovely... happy memories hey? Breakfast is ready."

Jelly followed the sweet, salty aroma of bacon and the comforting smell of toast down the corridor. Having avoided all temptations to eat in her apartment and refused all offers of food from friends for the past 24 hours, Jelly's stomach growled loudly. She pressed a fist into the gripe to silence it.

"I don't remember asking you to make me breakfast. Are you trying to fatten me up?" said Jelly defensively.

Sophia tried to sound as natural and flippant as possible, "Oh I just thought it would be nice to make a special effort on our first day together looking after the children. Trust me we won't get many times when the three babies fall asleep at the same time!"

Jelly smiled weakly trying to hide her anxiety about eating a full English breakfast in front of her sister. She walked over to the sink and drank two large glasses of water in quick succession to fill her empty stomach.

"Gosh you're thirsty," said Sophia, blissfully unaware of Jelly's tricks to suppress her appetite. Sophia bulldozed her way through two rashers of bacon, a sausage, tomatoes, toast, two eggs and some mushrooms.

"I can't believe how ravenous I feel now that I'm breast

feeding the twins," said Sophia, in between a mouthful of toast and tomato.

I can't believe how ravenously starving I make myself, thought Jelly... but she kept her thoughts to herself.

Jelly chased the breakfast around the plate, cut it up and slid as much as she could beneath one of the slices of toast. The corner of poached egg that she pushed into her mouth slithered down the back of her throat like a slug, as did the mushroom and half of a tomato.

"Have you got any ketchup?" Jelly asked, to create a diversion.

"I'm sure I have," said Sophia helpfully as she went in search of the ketchup, whilst Jelly slid some of the plate's contents into a paper napkin.

"This is delicious," said Jelly.

Sophia was delighted to see how much her sister had eaten when she finally located the bottle of ketchup. Sophia sipped on her tea, whilst watching protectively over Jelly, but felt sad and helpless to see how painfully thin her younger sister looked. Jelly's jaw bones pulsed in and out through the skin below her ears, as she ruminated on the remaining food congealing on her plate.

"How are you doing?" said Sophia tentatively, almost too scared to ask the question.

"I have good days and bad days," she said stoically as she pushed the plate away, still half full with chopped up and mashed food hidden under the slice of toast.

Dark shadows ran under Jelly's eyes and her lips trembled as she tried to resist the tears that were pooling. Sophia wrapped her arms around her younger sister, she felt thin and brittle, like a dried out twig that would snap in two if she hugged her too tight.

"It's *so* much harder for you," said Sophia gently. "I have Joshua and the twins and you are still so young."

"Yes but at least I have Dad," Jelly said sarcastically.

They both smiled knowingly at one another.

"How is Father QC?"

"Oh... just the usual... you know... pompous, aloof, work obsessed. In fact since Mum died I barely see him. He's always working on some important case or another, so it's great to have this temporary nanny job which slots in very well with my fencing training."

Jelly felt a repulsive mound pushing over her tight jeans. The food she had consumed sat like cement at the pit of her stomach... she knew what she had to do.

"I'll just pop to the loo... leave the washing up for me... and thanks again for the breakfast, it was yummy," said Jelly breezily.

Jelly picked up her bag and walked back down the corridor towards the toilet. She checked on Elizabeth who still slept soundly and then disappeared into the family bathroom. Morosely, Jelly unbuttoned her jeans and shirt and folded them neatly on a chair. She stepped in front of the full-length mirror. Her nudity was only thinly veiled by a see-through bra and knickers and she stepped onto the electronic scales. The scales shrieked 2lbs past her new target weight of 7 stone 8lbs.

"Fat, too fat Jelly!" she reprimanded herself quietly.

Jelly stepped anxiously back in front of the mirror and looked again at her body, then turning sideways she pinched at her tiny buttocks. She looked at her bud-like breasts, which still gave away the tell-tale signs that she was no longer a girl and wishing them away from her body, she covered her chest with her arm. Finally her eyes fell on the repulsive mound that had formed above her pubic bone after breakfast. Jelly delved into her bag to retrieve the kit she used daily, a hair tie, tooth brush and tooth paste, a bottle of foundation and cotton pads – all stored for the ceremony that she performed religiously. She washed her hands in hot soapy water, till they stung from the heat. Ritualistically the hands were dried, first between each finger, then over the backs and palms. She stared hard into the mirror, which was distorted now like the fun fair's hall of mirrors. Her stomach had grown by monstrous proportions, as had her thighs which blubbered and oozed with lumpy fat deposits. The skin seemed to swell over her knees and even her wrists and ankles appeared bloated like the carcass of a dead cow floating down a river. But most heinous were the womanly curves, which she wanted to eliminate, so that she could become childlike once more. She grabbed at the cheeks that her mother had once held so tenderly in her hands.

"Sorry Mum," she whispered to the mirror as tears streamed down her cheeks. She dropped to her knees by the toilet. She was exhausted and lonely and didn't want to do it, but there was no escape... just as there was no escape from the boy who had followed her into the woods... there never was.

Jelly pushed her tongue out wild like a Maori haka. She slid her fingers to the grainy, fleshy area at the back of her tongue, gagging. Then it began... the rhythmic pumping. Her nails were kept ruthlessly short, but her fingers hit the back of her throat, which was still sore and red from the day before... and the day before that. She gagged and choked, retching, as her body recoiled against the self-inflicted pain, but her mind drove her on.

Come on – come on she mentored herself silently rocking backwards and forwards on her knees, as she choked and retched determined to starve away her femininity, her attractiveness to creepy boys who crept behind her, greedily taking a piece of her burgeoning womanliness.

Finally the reward began to flow, the sweet bacon-flavoured saliva passed with an acidic, volcanic vengeance over the sorest part of her throat. Her fingers returned pushing again, jabbing unrelentingly, desperate to rid her body of the food that still lay within her belly. She wretched and gagged on chunks of mushroom and tomato as they jettisoned themselves out of her mouth and into the toilet with such force that her face was splashed with an odious mix of puke and toilet water. She grasped the edge of the bowl panting, as snot ran over her lip.

After some time, she wasn't sure how long... she pushed herself shakily to a standing position. She stepped in front of the mirror, the beautiful Jelly that her mother had loved, that the boy had hunted down in the forest, had flown away. Instead her normally pure complexion was red, blotchy and bloated. Thick smudges of black makeup streaked down her cheeks and she appeared wild and ghoulish with bloodshot eyes, whilst her nose and mouth were swollen with an unsightly purplish hue. But Jelly only looked at her stomach, examining it from the front and then the side, then repeating the movement four or five times, front, side, front, side – always the same routine, always in the correct order. Satisfied that it was flat again, she reached into her secret store for a handful of diuretics. She knew she would be exhausted and drained by the end of the day, but her stomach would be concave again and she would be a step closer to achieving an androgynous childlike form – devoid of the sexual siren that made it okay for unhinged boys to slam naive girls against trees and violate them.

Jelly stepped back onto the scales.

"Seven stone, eight pounds – better, much better."

When Jelly stepped back into the kitchen, she realised that she must have been gone for at least 15 minutes as the washing up had been done and the table cleared. She picked up a tea towel and began drying the dishes.

"Oh you beat me to it, let me at least dry up and put away," said Jelly. "I'll make you a cup of filter coffee too, if the babies don't wake up in the next ten minutes that is."

With the use of a powerful mint mouthwash, Jelly had managed to hide all lingering traces of the acidic, musty smell of vomit, but there were telltale signs of her anorexic episode with a cluster of red veins in the corner of each eye, whilst her face looked strangely bloated and blotchy. Still unfamiliar with the vagaries of an eating disorder, Sophia naively assumed her younger sister had been crying heavily in the bathroom.

"You look so sad Jelly, please don't lose any more weight – it's not what Mum would have wanted," said Sophia.

"It's *nothing* to do with Mum!" Jelly snapped reverting to the highly strung teenager that she was. But the pout soon crumpled as her bottom lip quivered and Jelly began to howl from the core of her being.

"Oh my goodness Jelly, what on earth is it. I've never seen you in such a state. You do know Mum loves you even though she's not here anymore, no one can take that away from you," Sophia said as she rubbed her sister's back tenderly.

Jelly sobbed violently.

"It's not about Mum... I can't tell you Sophia what it's really about. I can't tell a-ny-one!"

Snot and tears ran down her face, as she sobbed between each syllable. Sophia ran for a box of tissues and gently wiped her sister's face clean, as she curled an empathic arm around her shoulders.

"A problem shared is a problem halved Jelly. Whatever your secret is, you don't have to carry it around on your own."

"Everyone thinks I've lost the weight because of Mum dying... my coach, my friends they all think it's that too. I just don't want to be a woman, I want to be a child again. I don't want boobs and hips and I don't want men to look at me... you know, like that."

"It's okay Jelly we all grow up at different speeds and in different ways, but starving yourself free of your curves isn't the way to do it sweetheart, especially if you want to go all the way with your fencing career. It was really tough on you loosing Mum whilst you were still in school, but I'm sure there's a very special boy out there that will want to love you one day."

"Oh stop it no!" said Jelly, her voice filled with terror, "That's exactly what I *don't* want to happen, I *never* want a creepy boy to touch me ever again."

Jelly closed her eyes but saw the boy with the sneer slam her against a tree.

"Again?" Sophia said with a whisper, hardly daring to continue, "D...did someone do something bad to you Jelly?"

"YES!" Jelly wailed.

"It's okay Jelly you can tell me in complete confidence," Sophia reassured.

"I'll only tell you if you promise, on your life, never to tell *anyone* else," said Jelly trembling uncontrollably.

Sophia held her sister's face gently between her hands, just as their mother had done.

"I promise sweetheart."

Jelly's face contorted again as she screamed: "I was raped on the fencing camp in Budapest. I was RAPED!"

Chapter Four

January to November

JANUARY

So this is what you call just-in-time delivery. It's the very last day of January and I'm only sitting down to write your diary, a few minutes before midnight — I made a promise to the lady who gave me this book (her name is Sophia Haverstock) that I would keep up with my entries for one whole year. As you can see (well once I teach you to read) you were born on 1st November 2004 and have a big sister Hannah Mary — she'll be five in February. I've filled in everything up to this point and yes that birth weight is 10lb 8oz. You were born pink and perfect and I LOVED YOU the minute I saw you. Sadly I don't remember much after that (a few complications which I won't bore you with till you've had children of your own).

So my little princess Lilybet it's a very Happy New Year from your Mummy. The days are dark, dreary and cold, but life is simply heavenly now you have made our family complete... we waited a long time for you to arrive. Love you and see you next month... promise xxxxxxxxxxxxxxxxxxxxxxxxxxxxxxxx

FEBRUARY

You won't remember this when you are older, but we are shuttling to and from Kent to London at least twice a week to work on this fun picture book I'm making with a very clever photographer called Joshua Haverstock. You have completely bonded with your lovely nanny Jelly Mayhew and her big sister Sophia Haverstock who is married to Joshua.

Daddy thinks you have lungs big enough to bring the house down some nights. But seeing you smiling is the best tonic in the world, particularly as Mummy is rather sleep-deprived at the moment. Oh and I definitely think you know I'm your mother... you gave me a very knowing look with those piercing blue eyes. Love you xxx

MARCH

Well who's the little joker Elizabeth? You've been blowing raspberries on and off for about two weeks now and find the whole thing very amusing. Now you have the entire family at it, we blow raspberries on your neck, your cheeks, your arms and (best of all) your tummy. This is obviously cutting-edge comedy when you are five months old. Daddy filmed you in fits of hysterics and your laugh is very infectious (your father always says my laugh is very contagious too). Your giggles fill the house and make up for those moments when you still scream the place down. Love you the whole world x

APRIL

Well it was the big move this month from a cot by my bed to your very own nursery. I remember feeling really sad when we moved Hannah into her bedroom for the first time and I have to confess to padding down the landing five or six times during the night. Oh dear I was meant to look glamorous the next day for filming, but the makeup lady had a tough job on her hands!

You showed your first case of 'stranger anxiety' when a lady called Minky Sloane popped into the studio where Mummy's working in London. I'll have to explain to you what PR is when you grow up. Anyway your reaction to Minky probably wasn't the best bit of PR on your part, but it was certainly a memorable publicity stunt. You did one of your 'scream the house down' cries when she attempted to pick you up (I'm not sure if Minky has ever held a baby before). She did try to placate you by turning you onto her shoulder. Unfortunately Minky tapped a little too vigorously and your last feed reappeared all over the back of her smart black jacket. That was certainly a show stopper darling! See you next month xxxxxx

MAY

You've started eating solids and already I can tell you will be a 'foodie' – join the Henriksen/ Maloney Club. However, I think you are teething, because you are dribbling every- where and we are back to lots of broken nights. Maybe you could try to sleep a little bit more soon?

Your favourite game is bouncing at the moment and the other day I caught you bouncing and giggling on Daddy's knee to the theme tune of Bonanza. Just to warn you, your father has a rather strange obsession with cowboys and Indians and those ghastly black and white Westerns. So don't appear too keen... you'll only encourage him and could find yourself stuck in front of endless 'Bang Bangs' when you are a teenager... very un-cool! Lots of love, Mummy xxx

JUNE

So this is the month you've really learnt you can move, it all started with a cheeky bottom shuffle and then you realised you could slide around on your tummy too... you now have your commando crawling down to a fine art. One day I watched you get from one side of the nursery to the other by rolling, so you could pick up Chocolate the bear— how very inventive of you! You've also started pulling yourself up to a standing position by determinedly heaving on the nearest available piece of furniture. Thankfully you haven't managed to destroy anything yet in Sophia and Joshua's apartment but the twins are having a jolly good go on the furniture front! Love from Mummy x

JULY

You've turned into a water baby this month and just in time for the arrival of the new paddling pool last weekend and some wonderfully warm weather. Hannah kept inviting you for a swim "in the swimming pool 'lizabeth". How nice that we only had to spend £15.99 rather than £15,000 to provide you with a pool in the back garden!

We've been producing the last few food landscapes for the photographic food book and were working on a Nordic fjord-scape which brought back all my childhood memories of growing up in Norway.

The model maker (yes that really is a proper job) made us a brilliant pontoon out of breadsticks and crackers, it was just like the one I used to run along after our weekly sauna. The film crew was in and out of Joshua's studio for most of the month finishing off filming 'The Art of Food' – so it was pretty crowded and busy. You were such a good girl this month... thank you for being so gorgeous. Jelly, your nanny, loves looking after you. She's got a pretty voice, and is always singing songs to you when it's time for your nap – you really love nursery rhymes. Night, night, sleep tight xxxxx

AUGUST

You've suddenly realised that knees bend and have learnt how to sit back down again after standing. Each time you seem startled and amazed by your knees, which is very amusing.

Sophia, and Jelly in particular, have said they are going to miss you when we've finished work on the book, so I'm inviting them to your birthday party in November.

Minky Sloane (the PR lady who you were sick on a few months ago) has started coming to the studio now 'encouraging' us to get the last picture done as quickly as possible – we were meant to have finished at the end of July... oops! I persuaded Joshua to do a cowboy valley-scape out of food which I know Daddy will like very much. The model maker took all morning to build a wagon out of bread-sticks. He made the wheels out of onion rings and pretzel sticks and then I suggested a tor-tilla flour wrap for the wagon cover – which worked brilliantly. Maybe I'll become a food model maker when I retire, it is such fun. It's going to be very difficult for me to tell you off for playing with your food ever again! Love your Mummy x

SEPTEMBER

Your baby babbling is starting to sound like proper words now. Of course I think you said "Mama" first and Daddy insists you said "Dada". Hannah was so excited when you said "a-nna" for the first time. I think the 'H' might take a while to come and Chocolate is much too much of a mouthful — you simply call the bear 'Ocut'.

Minky Sloane is busy planning a very glamorous book signing and VIP party in November in Oxford Street, London (no less)! If only you and Hannah were old enough to come, you would definitely feel like princesses that night. Apparently Minky is even planning to have a red carpet, very Hollywood! Much love your Mama (yes Ma-ma-ma, not Da-da-da!) xxx

OCTOBER

Your desire to explore is stronger than your desire to listen to my warnings and I found myself saying "No" a little too often this month. You certainly understand what I mean, but sometimes choose to ignore me.

You're crawling at lightning speed now and pulling yourself up to standing all the time. Mummy's doing the autumn season of

'Melanie's Munchkins' and 'Henriksen's Half Hour' my weekly TV chat show, so I'm sad how much time we are apart again. I must get Daddy to take us all on holiday once the book launch is over.

You are very sweet with Oscar (apart from when you pull his tail). Thankfully he has the gentlest nature. The other day I caught you crawling over to him and lying on his stomach. Hannah joined you and here is the loveliest photo of the three of you together. xxx

NOVEMBER
(1 November 2005 – HAPPY BIRTHDAY PRINCESS LILYBET)
How's this for efficiency getting my entry in on the first day of the month. Well I had to really, because today is a very special day – you're one year old – Happy Birthday darling!

You gave me the best birthday present this morning when Hannah and I were finishing the food for your birthday party. Out of the blue you pushed yourself to standing (still fascinated by your knees) and then took ten or so determined steps towards me, arms out – stretched and squealing with delight.

I hope you like your teddy bear birthday cake, here's a photo. It was lucky I took a picture

because the cake is all gone now! Daddy, Hannah, Joshua and Sophia all had seconds and Jelly even managed two small slices, which was great to see.

It's been a beautiful first year and I love you very, very much.

Happy Birthday Elizabeth xxx

CHAPTER FIVE

Friday 18 November – 4.10pm

Melanie sat in the corner of Elizabeth's nursery adding the final touches to her makeup and nails as the hotly anticipated evening launch of 'The Art of Food' book drew nearer. She watched Hannah playing on the nursery floor and Elizabeth sleeping fitfully in her cot. She wanted to be close to both her daughters before it was time to leave for the book launch – unaware that these would be the last 35 minutes she would ever spend with Elizabeth.

Hannah was immersed in a complex game of "hostibles" on the nursery floor. The hospital had been grouped into wards of sick teddies and dolls, and "ree-ally" sick patients who were swaddled in bandages. Some lay in shoe boxes, whilst others had yet to be allocated a bed by the nurse who was dressed in a peculiar mix of floral pyjamas, a nurse's apron and a white cap, which sat on her head back to front.

"How are the patients feeling today nurse?"

"Oh they're reee-ally sick Mummy," she said shuffling along

the line of toys spooning imaginary medicines to some and vigorously jabbing the less fortunate toys with her plastic syringe. She placed her stethoscope on one rag doll's midriff, "This one's got a bad tummy, this one's got a bad leg and this one," said Hannah walking over to her sister's cot, "this one is the worst of all. She keeps getting ree-ally hot and crying all the time."

"Well Nurse Maloney it's a good job your little sister has you to watch over her, you make a wonderful nurse," said Melanie, smiling warmly Hannah.

"She's not my sister silly, she's my patient Mummy."

"Oh yes, of course, very silly me. All the same your *patient* is lucky to have such a kind and good nurse to look after her this evening."

Melanie walked across to the 'critical unit' and held her hand to Elizabeth's forehead.

"Hot enough to fry an egg!" Melanie exclaimed.

"That's not very nice Mummy," Hannah retorted.

"Oh it's just an expression darling – it doesn't mean I would actually fry an egg on Elizabeth."

"Oh..." said Hannah, who began to lose interest in her sickest patient and went back to the 'main ward', dotting chickenpox with a red felt-tip pen onto a group of plastic dolls.

Melanie pushed Elizabeth's bedding to one side. She'd already removed her baby grow, in an attempt to bring her body temperature down, and after hours of screaming and writhing the baby slept fitfully for the first time that day. Melanie knelt by the cot watching Elizabeth's soft round tummy rise and fall as it met the waistline of her nappy. She stroked her silky red cheeks and touched her lips – instinctively Elizabeth began to suckle in her sleep.

Tat-tat-tat.

"Car's here darling," Harry popped his head around the door.

Melanie got to her feet and turned around. Harry let out a long low wolf whistle.

"Wow Ms Hepburn you look sensational, very 'Breakfast at Tiffany'. Come here so I can really appreciate you," said Harry.

Melanie negotiated her way around the hospital in her stilettos and Harry pulled her onto the landing and slipped his hands tenderly around his wife's waist.

"Have I told you lately?" Harry asked.

"Oh I don't think so," Melanie responded teasingly.

"Well at the risk of sounding repetitive, I love you so much Melanie Henriksen... always have... always will."

"And I love you too, always have, always will," said Melanie as she kissed Harry gently on his lips.

"Anyway before I got distracted by my bedazzling wife, I came to tell you the van's just left with the signed limited edition books. I'll distract the chauffeur with a cup of tea as he's a bit early and Darius isn't due till 4.30."

"Oh good, there'll be quite a lot to run through with him darling," said Melanie. "After you've shown him where things are in the kitchen, could you send him upstairs, so I can go over everything up here? I'd like to spend my last half hour with the girls."

"Only the last half hour tonight gorgeous," Harry corrected, "we should be back by 1am."

Melanie smiled at Harry as he disappeared downstairs again. She opened her jewellery case and selected a matching set of pearl earrings and necklace given to her by Harry at Christmas and was just about to close the jewellery case when she spotted Florence Davenport's ring.

"So Miss Davenport, if this isn't a special occasion then I don't what is!" she said admiring the ring and slipping it on her finger.

"Who are you talking to Mummy?" asked Nurse Maloney.

"Oh myself darling... first sign of madness!"

"You're not mad Mummy, your lovely."

"Thank you poppet," said Melanie.

The doorbell rang and the muffled low hum of her husband's voice and the unfamiliar voice of the babysitter rose up through the floorboards. She looked at her watch, 4.28pm.

Great, thought Melanie, *sounds like Darius is here a couple of minutes early.*

Melanie placed the pearl necklace around her neck and fiddled with the clasp and security chain. Peering intently into the mirror, she slid the right earring in with ease, but her left lobe had become infected and, given her enormous workload, she hadn't taken care of the infection. She winced as she pierced through the inflamed, crusty hole.

"Ouch!" Melanie whimpered.

"Mummy what's the matter?" said Hannah, looking up from her game.

"Oh nothing darling... my ear's a bit sore that's all."

"Would you like some medicine to make it better?"

Hannah stood up shaking a tube filled with buttons.

"I'd love a magic kiss and cuddle from you most of all," said Melanie, throwing her arms open.

Hannah dropped her patient on its head (a knitted doll) and climbed onto Melanie's lap, linking her hands around her neck. The little girl smacked a loud, sloppy kiss onto her mother's neck.

"Now it's time for your medicine Mummy."

"What colour would you like?"

"Red please, to match my dress," said Melanie.

Hannah took a red button from the medicine tube and pretended to feed it to her mother.

"Well I feel so much better now, that's very good medicine you have Nurse Maloney," said Melanie, play-acting the part of the recovered patient, "but just remember you mustn't ever give your button medicine to Elizabeth because she would choke on it."

"Don't worry Mummy I'll look after 'lizabeth till you come home tonight," said Nurse Maloney.

They smiled and kissed each other. Hannah nuzzled into her mother's neck.

"Emmm... you smell lovely Mummy," said Hannah.

"Well so do you," Melanie reciprocated.

Hannah traced her finger around her mother's face.

"Mummy you look sooooo pretty tonight!"

"Oh thank you poppet, you are such a sweet daughter, do you know that?"

Melanie looked back up to the mirror to apply a last layer of red lipstick, as Hannah rested on her knee... her focus shifted from the reflection of her image in the foreground, to what lay behind her in the corner of the room. She jumped out of the chair, as Hannah bumped onto the carpet.

"Ouch Mummy, that hurt. You dropped me!"

Melanie scooped her daughter into her arms and rubbed her coccyx.

"I'm so sorry poppet," said Melanie apologetically as she spun around with her daughter in her arms jumping again as she came face-to-face with Darius, who stood motionless in the corner of the room. One half of Darius's face was blackened by the shadows that lurked in the darkest part of the nursery, whilst the other appeared a haunting white exposed by a sharp shard of light from the side lamp. Dressed entirely in black leather, as though he'd just stepped off a motorbike, Darius's scarf was wrapped around his chin and mouth.

"Goodness gracious Darius, you made me jump!" said Melanie indignantly. "How long have you been standing there?"

"Only a few sss-seconds-sss," the voice slithered through the scarf.

Melanie rubbed Hannah's back as the girl stared wide-eyed at the stranger in the room. She clung furiously to her mother.

"Sss-sorry to sss-spoook you," the babysitter said in an unrepentant voice.

"That's okay Darius," said Melanie defensively unconvinced by the boy's apology.

"BOO!" shouted Darius randomly, as he curled his gloved hands into bear claws. Melanie recoiled, clutching Hannah. The little girl buried her face into her mother's neck, away from the man with the hissy snake voice.

"That's not funny Darius," said Melanie sharply.

"What's not funny?" said Harry as he appeared in the door-frame whilst negotiating his arms into his evening overcoat. Darius dropped his arms back by his side, just as Harry looked up, flashing an ingratiating smile at his longest serving patient.

Fucking dickhead sneered Darius silently.

"Are you all done gorgeous, we really need to be going?" Harry asked.

"No we haven't even started have we Darius. Just *how* long have you been standing in the corner spying on us?" Melanie asked pointedly.

"Come on Melanie I know you're feeling anxious about the launch tonight, but let's give our new babysitter a break. Remember this is the young man that gets the record as my longest serving patient, he pretty much grew up in my orthodontic chair, isn't that right Darius?"

"It sure is-sss," said Darius, slapping his thigh cowboy style, as though he were just about to join the Sherriff for a cool beer in the saloon. Then turning to Melanie Darius added coyly, "I'm sss-sorry Ms-sss Henrik-sss-sen I didn't want to break up that sss-sweet little moment between you and Hannah."

Darius pulled the scarf under his chin with his gloved hand to reveal the thin, mean lips. His eyes crawled coldly up Melanie's dress and he licked his lips with his pointed tongue. Melanie looked across defensively to Harry for support, but the lone ranger was preoccupied with buckling his boots.

Harry returned to a standing position.

"Darius was just telling me how he regularly looks after his young cousins for his aunts and uncles in London, so he's very experienced with taking care of toddlers and babies – isn't that right Darius?"

Trusting moron, they're all in Russia.

Darius nodded, as his lip twitched at the side. Melanie felt a cold draft on the back of her neck.

"I'm sorry Darius," Melanie offered reluctantly.

She was wrong-footed by her husband backing the joker with the sneer whilst her mind screamed – *don't trust this stranger with your children!*

Darius fixed his eyes on the bundle of flesh that lay in the cage. He remembered the chicks in the nest (before he fed them to the kitten) their featherless pink skin, puckered and exposed like the one-year-old baby that now wriggled and squirmed behind the bars of the cot.

Melanie handed Hannah to Harry and fretted around the nursery showing Darius where Elizabeth's spare clothes were stored, the location of the nappy changing mat, wipes and nappies, how to operate the baby monitor and how to use the thermometer if he had any concerns about Elizabeth's temperature.

"Now most important of all Darius is Elizabeth's medicine," Melanie continued. "She had her last dose two hours ago, so she's allowed one more spoonful anytime after six and before midnight. We hope to be back by one o'clock at the very latest. If you could give Hannah her tea before 5.30pm, she normally goes to bed by 6.30. Please leave her door open and her nightlight on, as Hannah is afraid of the dark. She loves a bedtime story and if you know any nursery rhymes – you can sing those with her before bedtime

– she's got a book by her bed with all the words in and there's a sing-a-long CD. Elizabeth loves nursery rhymes too and there's a CD player by her bed. Right then... here's my mobile number and Harry's number. Actually we'd appreciate a call around 9.30 when the book signing should have finished, just so as we can hear how Elizabeth is doing. Can I have your mobile please?"

"It's all done Melanie," Harry reassured. "I've got Darius's number and he's had a tour downstairs. He knows how to warm Elizabeth's bottles, I've shown him where Hannah's tea is too, so that's everything covered," said Harry, massaging his wife's neck which felt stiff from the cold chill that ran down it. "Now if we don't leave in the next five minutes, it will be off with our heads when we see Minky!"

"Yes-sss off with your heads-sss..." Darius repeated sardonically, smiling oddly at the host of 'Henriksen's Half Hour'.

Melanie looked across to Harry deeply perturbed by the babysitter's demeanour, but Harry was distracted kissing Hannah and Elizabeth.

"Night night Hannah, Daddy will see you in the morning. Come on Melanie, we need to go. Thanks for offering to babysit so last minute Darius it's really good of you. You've really saved the day!" said Harry wholeheartedly.

I didn't offer dickhead, the dot volunteered me.

Melanie questioned her internal gauge which was whirring hysterically inside her.

Something's not right Harry, something's not right.

"Don't go Mummy!" Hannah cried rushing over to her mother and clutching her legs to prevent her from leaving.

"Come on poppet, Mummy's only going to be gone for a few hours. Why don't you go and show Darius some of your toys," but when she looked up at Darius she saw that the sarcastic smile had inverted into a pronounced sneer. She looked down again quickly closing her eyes as she kissed Hannah on the top of her head. But the stored memory of the grimacing eight-year-old boy, with the bloodied nose plugs hanging out of his nostrils, flashed in front of her mind.

He's always been a bit strange, why am I leaving my children with an oddball?

Melanie squeezed Hannah tightly in her arms trying to push her worries back down, like the last unpalatable mouthful of cold spinach on a plate.

"Night night darling I love you," said Melanie to Hannah as she sobbed fitfully.

Harry's voice drifted up from the bottom of the stairwell, "Hurry up gorgeous we're going to be late."

Melanie walked over to the cot and knelt down. Elizabeth turned her face to one side and without warning opened her eyes, wide and blue and bright. She grinned broadly at her Ma-ma, as Hannah clung to her mother's back. Melanie stroked her baby's cheek, as Elizabeth gurgled contentedly.

"Ma-ma," said Elizabeth.

The mother of two lowered the side of the cot and kissed Elizabeth's cupid lips one last time.

"Night night princess Lilybet, I love you..."

Chapter Six

Friday 18 November – 6.26pm

The black Mercedes pulled up outside Oxford Street's 'Flagstones' (the independent book company's flagship store in London) twenty six minutes after the agreed arrival time. Minky stood at the edge of the red carpet with a stony expression, dressed in an electric purple dress coat and puffing furiously on a cigar. She tapped on the window and Harry pressed the electric button as a blast of cool, metallic air flooded through the window carrying with it the excited squeals of fans and the deep, throaty grumbling of passing buses and taxis.

A long queue of people clutching a copy of 'The Art of Food' snaked all the way from the revolving door leading into the bookstore along the glass-fronted length of 'Flagstones' and around the corner into Duke Street. After an hour and three quarters of travelling inside the soundproofed, temperature controlled back seat of the Mercedes, the vibrant ambiance on Oxford Street seemed just as unreal as the atmosphere inside the chauffeur-driven car. A group of photographers sprang into action with their cameras, even before Melanie stepped onto the pavement.

"Look at the queue Harry, can you believe they're all here for us," exclaimed Melanie.

"No gorgeous, they are all here for you," said Harry.

Minky folded her arms on the edge of the window frame like a nosy neighbour preparing for a salacious gossip over the fence.

"You're late darlings!"

Harry realised he was best placed to smooth Minky's ruffled feathers. He gently took Minky's hand, kissed it and smiled.

"Fashionably late I think you'll find Minky... judging by the queues," Harry said smoothly.

"Now just because you're handsome, don't think I'm not furious with you," said Minky. "Joshua's been here since six sharp (as instructed) but it's *you* they're queuing to see Melanie... some of them have been here since four o'clock."

Melanie mouthed a silent and apologetic *Sorry*.

Minky left the chauffeur redundantly clutching his cap as the PR opened the door just ahead of the driver. The couple stepped out onto the red carpet to be greeted by a sea of photographers, ardent fans, autograph hunters, curious shoppers and those simply passing by. The crowds were contained behind red and gold roping and two burly bouncers, who wore sunglasses, even though it had been dark for several hours. They stretched out their arms to restrain the most exuberant fans of 'Melanie's Munchkins' and 'Henriksen's Half Hour'. Minky smacked two fabulous PR kisses into the air around Melanie's head and repeated the performance with Harry who bent down to whisper in Minky's ear.

"Be a bit gentle tonight Minky, Elizabeth's gone down with a fever and we've left the girls with a new babysitter, so Melanie's a bit on edge. She's got nothing to worry about I've known the guy for eight years for goodness sake."

"*Boysitter* hey, now that does sound interesting!" cooed Minky.

"Seriously Minky, the boy's only 18 years old and he doesn't strike me as your type."

"When did that ever stop me darling," she said, whispering in Harry's ear flirtatiously.

Minky swept in a dramatic, sympathetic semi-circle around Melanie.

"Darling I'm *so* sorry Elizabeth's unwell. Let's get tonight out the way and you can have a quiet countdown to Christmas. How about I back off with the pre-Christmas bookings so you can spend time with the girls?"

"That would be fantastic – it's been an exceptionally busy year," said Melanie.

"By the way darling, I don't know if you know it, but you look absolutely fabulous tonight," said Minky, "and as for that 'dishy dentist' of yours – well it's lucky he's married to my best selling client, you make quite a pair!"

The cameras flashed in quick succession as Melanie began the much anticipated red carpet walk between the car and the entrance into 'Flagstones'. Melanie intuitively turned, smiled and paused as the photographers called her name and she patiently responded to every request for an autograph. This seemed to disproportionately irritate the bouncers, who looked anxiously from left to right, as though they had just been privy to a death threat hanging over the 'kiddie cook's' life, when all the time it was her daughter lying in her cot in Kent, who was in mortal danger. As the couple came to the end of the line Melanie slipped her hand into Harry's and they smiled tenderly at one another.

"Give her a kiss," shouted one of the photographers.

Harry, who was traditionally shy in front of the cameras and happy to let the spotlight fall on his wife, quite spontaneously picked Melanie up in his arms and kissed her on the lips, as the flashbulbs furiously devoured the dream picture for the next day's papers. The Saturday papers ran with *Henriksen knows 'The Art of Food' and love* whilst by Sunday the headlines took a more onerous turn, with the smiling picture appearing alongside darker headlines including *Nation's 'kiddie cook' in baby snatch nightmare* and *'Henriksen's Half Hour' horror in double disappearance mystery*.

The last picture to be taken of the golden couple, before Darius murdered Elizabeth, helped to achieve a macabre iconic status and rich pickings for the photographer who had quite coincidentally stood in the best vantage point outside the bookstore. It was a photograph that was to divide a nation, as the man and woman on the street, and TV chat show hosts alike, debated the wisdom or folly, and the naivety or selfishness of leaving a sick child with an unknown babysitter. It became the picture that was endlessly shown across international media channels and the final picture to be held up alongside photos of Melanie at the end of her life, when she had been reduced to a drawn and desperate woman, a broken-hearted and bereft mother, racked by grief and guilt.

But for now the mother of two, the domestic goddess of day-time TV and popular primetime chat show host laughed freely as her husband spun his wife around and carried her through the revolving door like his new bride. The crowd impulsively burst into a round of applause as the very last moment of carefree abandon between the nation's 'kiddie cook' and the husband she adored, was captured on camera and frozen in time forever and ever.

CHAPTER SEVEN

Friday 18 November – 8.05pm

An hour and a half of signing books left Melanie and Joshua feeling as though they had just completed an English essay. Joshua massaged his hand and Melanie tried to wipe the ink that had leaked from the pen onto her middle finger.

"It is years since I've had an ink bump," laughed Melanie as she held out her right hand and surveyed the raised area around her top finger joint on her middle finger that had been coloured blue by her fountain pen.

'The Art of Food' duo leant back in their chairs to rest for a moment.

"S'pose we ought to go upstairs for the VIP reception? Minky will want to extract maximum value out of us," said Joshua, warmly patting the other half of the creative team on the back. As they pushed their chairs back simultaneously from the signing table and stood, Joshua turned to face Melanie.

"Actually there is something else I wanted to ask..." said

Joshua, his deep resonant voice as familiar and comforting to Melanie as Elizabeth's nursing blanket.

"Oh yes?" said Melanie.

"Well... there's no easy way to tell you this but Sophia and I are expecting our third child."

Melanie yelped like an excited puppy and threw her arms around Joshua.

"Congratulations. Wow, three babies in less than three years, that's some going Mr Haverstock. I think Harry and I will leave the football team to you guys."

"We felt a bit awkward telling you, with your situation..."

"Well don't be, I'm *thrilled* for you both... I mean it," Melanie reassured the photographer.

"Sophia and I wondered if you would be the godmother, we're expecting a girl," said Joshua.

"Oh Joshua of course the answer is 100 per cent yes, I'd *love* to be the fairy godmother, as long as you let me spoil her endlessly. It's wonderful to see how much Elizabeth loves the twins. Being your third child's godmother will give me another excuse to buy baby's clothes again. If I can't have any more children of my own, I'm happy to gather a great brood of godchildren around me!"

The two hugged and then climbed the broad glass and steel staircase leading to the VIP reception. As Melanie and Joshua stood at the top of the stairs, the guests spontaneously burst into applause, as the creators of 'The Art of Food' smiled and waved like a royal couple on the balcony. The lofty space swirled with canapés, champagne and familiar faces as Joshua and Melanie identified a string of well-known faces from the world of TV, music and film.

"Minky really is the best connected PR in the business isn't she," said Melanie.

"She always comes up trumps," Joshua acknowledged.

Harry was chatting to Minky at the far end of the reception and Melanie and Joshua resigned themselves to a half hour crawl through the packed space to get to the stage at the front of the room. Melanie spotted Sophia and Jelly deep in conversation and mouthed *Congratulations* over the sea of heads when Sophia looked up smiling serenely.

"Your wife looks ridiculously happy Joshua... being pregnant again really suits her."

"Oh trust me she is on cloud nine and I'm not sure she'll let us stop at three!" said Joshua.

"Now that's just greedy," said Melanie teasingly.

Melanie looked across the crowded room again and caught Jelly's eye, she smiled warmly and waved.

"I do believe your sister-in-law has managed to gain a bit of weight, what a relief I was worried how frail she looked, even though she seemed to love looking after Elizabeth."

"You're not the only one, Sophia was climbing the walls with anxiety, but she slowly seems to be finding her feet again since their mum died. Sophia says there's something else behind her weight loss, but she's sworn to secrecy. Jelly's winning all her fencing competitions still, both in the UK and overseas, so we're really proud of her."

"Jelly really was a wonderful nanny to Elizabeth," said Melanie appreciatively.

BOO!

The single word echoed through Melanie's head, like a ball rolling down a bowling alley. Melanie shuddered as she thought of the bazaar encounter in the nursery with Darius, her gut twisted. Voicing her concerns out loud, Melanie turned to Joshua, "I wish I'd asked Jelly to babysit tonight, but we were only let down by Rachel this morning when she called in sick with the flu and I wanted Jelly to be part of tonight."

"Well that's really good of you. As you can see Jelly *loves* being here, she's been chatting excitedly about the launch party for weeks. I think she's got her eye on a few celebrities to go autograph hunting after the speeches."

You picked the joker with the sneer, Melanie's mind taunted her. Feeling the tension rising inside her again, Melanie said, "Joshua I'm really not sure about this new babysitter... Harry knows him pretty well after treating him for eight years in the surgery... but I have a *horrid feeling* about tonight."

"Wow... *horrid feeling*... that's pretty strong stuff that's tumbling around that pretty head of yours Melanie. Come on, you just need to relax and enjoy yourself. You are such a good mum, it's *okay* you know to have *one* night off duty. Come on, let's get you a glass of bubbly, you've certainly earned it tonight," said Joshua.

Eventually they arrived at the front of the stage where Minky was holding a glass of champagne, with a Panama cigar between her lips, and flirting outrageously with the 'dishy dentist' under a 'No Smoking' sign. Joshua picked up two more glasses of champagne from a circulating tray and handed one to Melanie.

"Thanks Joshua, just what the doctor ordered," said Melanie as they clinked glasses.

Melanie turned to Minky.

"Could I borrow Harry for a moment?"

"Of course you can darling, if I can borrow the photographer," Minky replied.

Melanie and Harry slid behind a pillar.

"Have you managed to get through to Darius?" Melanie asked anxiously.

"Yes, he phoned bang on time at 9.30 as you requested. He said that everything was fine, in fact to quote him verbatim he said: "Everything's cool, so you don't have to keep phoning". He's not the most talkative fellow is he? I guess I never noticed when he was in the chair with my fingers in his mouth, but he's very quiet."

"Introverted you mean," Melanie retorted anxiously.

Melanie heard her voice sounding more pointed than she had meant it to and bit her bottom lip sheepishly, as Harry spoke.

"Darling I've known Darius for years. Okay he's a bit shy, but he's always so polite with those over enunciated s-es. I think he's just a bit overwhelmed by his ghastly mother and all those polka dots!"

They both laughed wryly. Harry kissed his wife on the cheek.

"Just relax and enjoy the rest of the evening. Look around you Melanie, this is all for you."

"...And Joshua," she added graciously.

"Yes... but mostly you gorgeous, there's a lot of love out there for Melanie Henriksen. It's incredible what you've achieved in less than a year with Joshua and Minky... and after everything you went through after giving birth to Elizabeth. I'm *so* proud of you."

"Thank you darling, forgive me for being a little jumpy. I've just got this irrational unsettled feeling," said Melanie.

Harry and Melanie rejoined the others.

"So Minky," said Harry, turning to the publicist, "didn't you promise me that you're going to relax your punishing schedule after tonight and give my lovely wife a chance to take a well earned rest."

"Abso-bloody-lutely. No more projects till the New Year," Minky said categorically.

Harry squeezed his wife around the waist.

"So I think that leaves me free to pick up the phone tomorrow morning and book the four of us on a two week, pre-Christmas break in the Caribbean."

"Harry that sounds heavenly, I can't wait!" said Melanie, as she threw her arms around her husband's neck and kissed him tenderly on the lips.

"Oh put him down Melanie. Now before you two love birds go swanning off, there's one last job tonight... the speeches," Minky reminded her most lucrative client.

Minky led the stars of the book launch up onto the stage like a 'Sale of the Century' girl, grinning wildly from the four glasses of champagne she had consumed in quick succession and buoyed up by the evening's book sales and the room full of celebrities and VIPs. After a flowery introduction from the publicity guru, Joshua ably entertained the crowd with stories about his 'eureka moment' with smoked salmon, but it was Melanie they had all come to hear speak. When she stepped up to the microphone there was an almost reverential silence as the now highly respected TV chat show host of 'Henriksen's Half Hour' regaled the audience with a perfect combination of wit and charm. Melanie stepped off the stage to rapturous applause and Harry embraced her.

"You were wonderful," he said and then leaning in whispered into her ear, "Just as fantastic as you were all those years ago at the British Orthodontic Conference when I first fell in love with you."

"Thank you Harry, but, I'm only wonderful because of you and the girls. You all make my life complete."

Suddenly distracted again Melanie glimpsed at her watch, *10:10*. Her mind turned homewards.

Elizabeth how is your fever darling?

As the applause faded, Melanie kissed her husband's cheek, made her excuses, and disappeared into the ladies, locking the door to one of the elegant powder rooms behind her. Melanie dialled the pre-programmed number and was surprised when Darius picked up almost immediately.

"Yes-sss what d'you want?"

"Oh Darius, I'm so pleased I've got through to you I just wondered how Elizabeth is?"

"Ha, ha, ha tricked you... leave a message..."

"Pardon...? Darius?"

Melanie hung up confused and unnerved. She dialled again.

"Yes-ss what d'you want?"

"Darius are you there or is this recorded, because if it is it's not very fu..."

"Ha, ha, ha tricked you... leave a message..."

"Darius this is Melanie Henriksen. It's um 10.13 and I'd really like a quick call from you if you get a moment. I know you spoke briefly to my husband, but I'm just wondering if Elizabeth is okay. I expect Hannah's been fast asleep for hours now, but call me please it would just be good to touch base. Thank you."

Melanie washed her hands and splashed cold water on her face. She touched up her makeup and added a new layer of concealer under her eyes, noticing the dark rings.

Time for a break Ms Henriksen – you've been over doing it.

She promised herself the next day she and Harry would spend the whole morning in bed playing with the girls, looking at holiday options to the Caribbean. She loved it when the four of them piled into the same bed...

There were four in the bed and the little one said...

Melanie rotated her lipstick and was just applying the colour to her top lip, when she saw her phone buzz and vibrate across the dressing table surface like a fly covered in insecticide – spinning around in its dying moments. She grabbed the phone and clicked the green button.

"Darius?"

Melanie heard someone breathe for a moment at the other end and then the line disconnected. She fumbled back through the list of recent calls – *Darius Sorokin* was at the top of it. Feeling the rising and unspeakable tide of alarm that she first felt in the nursery, she jabbed at the redial button.

"Yes-sss what d'you want?"

"Darius stop it," Melanie cried helplessly at the recording.

"Ha, ha, ha tricked you... leave a message..."

She swallowed hard and steadied herself on the sink as her head swam and swirled in panic.

"Darius, **please** call me. I would dearly like to speak to you... **please**. I wonder if you could change that message too, it's very... confusing and upsetting. Thank you."

She hung up... and put the phone back in her handbag. Melanie shakily powdered her face to absorb the beads of perspiration that had gathered across her face. She was desperate now to flee the VIP party through a back door, to run home and gather up her two precious lambs into her arms and protect them from the wicked wolf that she feared had crept into their pen.

Little Bo Peep has lost her sheep
And doesn't know where to find them
Leave them alone
And they'll come home
Wagging their tails behind them
Little Bo Peep began to weep
And lay down to rest for a while
She fell fast asleep
While counting her sheep
Then dreamt they came home with a smile

Melanie closed her eyes and felt her handbag vibrating. She frantically opened the clasp and scavenged through the layers of makeup, tissues, business cards and keys and grabbed the phone, which had fallen to the bottom of the bag. *Darius Sorokin* flashed up on her mobile again.

"Darius thank God you've phoned. How's Elizabeth?"

But her worst fears were realised as she heard Elizabeth screaming feverishly in the background.

"WHAH-WHAH-WHAH!"
Then the babysitter spoke.
"BOO!"
And the line went dead.

CHAPTER EIGHT

Friday 18 November – 10.34pm

Harry was the first to notice that something was seriously awry with Melanie when she emerged from the ladies room, ashen and shaking.

"You look like you've seen a ghost," said Harry

"We need to go home, something's wrong," said Melanie solemnly.

A few heads turned to look at the star of the evening and then twisted back into the huddle to mutter to one another.

Melanie began frantically scrambling through the crowds, as her panicky demeanour alerted the guests that all was not well. Harry followed in Melanie's wake of panic and fear, trying to thank everyone on behalf of his wife and smooth over the waves of surprise and alarm she was causing during her departure. The party gossips and society columnist whispered to one another with such speed that by the time Melanie had reached the top of the staircase at 'Flagstones' it seemed that hundreds of guests had turned to stare at the TV host and celebrity cook. The volume in the room fell to a concerned whisper. Speculation was rife about what had caused the sudden change and unfamiliar behaviour of the usually sparkling 'kiddie cook'.

A couple of paps hung around to catch some of the VIPs rolling through the revolving doors or falling out of their dresses (they didn't mind which it would be that evening). Instead they snapped a frozen-faced Melanie Henriksen running to the door of the car shielding her face with a copy of 'The Art of Food', followed shortly after by Harry Maloney who appeared preoccupied and withdrawn. Even before the car door was shut by the chauffeur (whose familiar role had been reinstated with Minky otherwise engaged upstairs with a bottle of champagne and a TV producer) the photographers phoned through their hunch to the late night news team that something was seriously wrong with Melanie Henriksen.

"She looks like she's cracking up," muttered one freelancer to another staff photographer.

The car pulled away silent and morgue-like, as though the couple had been hermetically sealed inside the back of the Mercedes. Melanie was grateful for the seclusion of the darkened glass and the discretion of George the chauffeur, who closed the privacy panel behind him, so that their private conversation remained confidential. Only his darting eyes into the rear-view mirror revealed his concern for one of his favourite clients.

Harry tried to soothe his panic-stricken wife and placed his hand on her knee.

"What's the matter darling, why do we need to dash home? You created quite a stir in there. Look if it's Elizabeth, I understand your concern we both know we wouldn't ordinarily leave her when she has a fever, but then this is *no* ordinary night. I spoke to Darius and he assured me everything was fine. Okay he turns out to be a man of few words, but he said everything was fine Melanie."

But his wife shook her head like a three year old, her lips pressed tightly together, as tears began to stream down her face. "You've been working at such a pace this year gorgeous, I think you're wrung out," Harry continued. "Maybe your body's crying out for that Caribbean cruise with Hannah, Elizabeth and me!" said Harry jokingly, as he nudged Melanie jovially in the ribs. But his little quip failed to distract his wife and instead the mention of Elizabeth's name caused her to howl louder than before.

"I can hardly bear for you to say her name Harry."

"Look darling let's get home before you work yourself up like this, seriously Melanie... I've never seen you in such a state!"

Melanie cradled her arms around her body and rocked backwards and forwards.

"When I finally got through to Darius, Elizabeth sounded really distressed and, by the way, I am *not* working myself up," said Melanie angrily.

"I'm sorry gorgeous, that came out wrong, it must have been very distressing hearing Elizabeth crying."

"*Screaming* Harry, she was screaming hysterically, and Darius wasn't doing a thing to comfort her."

Her face split in pain and anxiety and thick black lines of mascara ran down her cheeks giving her the fractured appearance of Picasso's 'Weeping Woman' painting.

"Elizabeth's got such a healthy pair of lungs on her darling," Harry continued, trying to lighten the mood, "remember how we often joke that she'll scream the house down one day!"

"Harry this is *not* a joke, something's really wrong. And there was a really creepy message on Darius's phone... sinister even..."

"Let's try calling again," said Harry trying to reason with the unfamiliar character sat next to him on the back seat of the Mercedes. He flicked Melanie's phone onto loud speaker.

"Yes-sss what d'you want?"

"Oh my goodness Harry – it's the same sick message," said Melanie.

"Ha, ha, ha tricked you... leave a message..."

Harry switched the phone off, without leaving a message and chuckled to himself. "Actually I think it's quite clever... I really thought it was him on the line for a minute. I wonder how many of his mates have fallen for *that* trick. Maybe he's just a typical 18-year-old boy Melanie who likes to play the odd prank on his friends."

"Emphasis on *odd*," said Melanie, "He's weird – you should have seen him in the nursery."

"I did."

"Yes but you weren't looking Harry, you were too preoccupied to notice. He stood in the corner spying on us and did you see what he was wearing, he looked like a motorcyclist dressed for a bank raid in all that black leather... and why was he covering his face behind that scarf, what was he trying to hide?"

"It's a really cold night Melanie and he's just very shy. Have you thought that perhaps he waited quietly in the corner of the nursery because he didn't want to interrupt you chatting to Hannah?"

"Shy? Creepy you mean, he was sneering at me Harry."

"Melanie that's just his face, he can't help how he looks," said Harry defensively, thinking of the year's of investment it took to treat his 'most challenging patient'. "He's got a really unattractive expression, I'll give you that, but he had such a mouthful of braces for all those years that the weird smile has just become a habit."

"It's not a smile Harry he has a leering, snarling sneer."

"Okay gorgeous, come on, stretch out on my lap and try to get some sleep, I'll wake you when we're home."

As Melanie rested her head on her husband's lap, he gently massaged Melanie's neck and shoulders.

"So what did Darius actually say to you when you finally got through to him?"

"BOO!"

2005

Chapter Nine

Friday 18 November – 11.13pm

The moment the Mercedes pulled up outside The Oast, Melanie sat bolt upright like a death row prisoner on the electric chair awaiting his execution. The chauffeur turned discreetly and slid the privacy glass panel open and was concerned to see his usually glamorous client looking frayed and distressed.

"Is everything alright Ms Henriksen? Would you like me to see you to the door?"

"No George, that's fine. Harry's right I've probably just been working too hard and am being a little hysterical."

"Well at least let me open the car door for you Ms Henriksen."

But Melanie had already bolted out of the vehicle and was disappearing into the night.

"Sorry about that George, we're going to book a much needed holiday tomorrow."

"Good for you, thoroughly deserved I'd say. Your wife has been working her socks off this year. Well... good night then."

"Good night George."

Harry tripped up the path, struggling to pick his way up the uneven stones as his eyes slowly adjusted to the moonlight.

"What's happened to the porch light," he called ahead to Melanie.

Harry lifted his head and saw that The Oast was entirely cloaked in darkness. It was a blackness that seeped into his stomach, bringing the first twist of anxiety. The 'dishy dentist' wrapped his arm around Melanie's shoulders as she sobbed quietly. He thought of 'the brave little soldier' who'd grown up in his orthodontic chair and the young man whom he'd willed to be on Harry's winning team during the last difficult years of treatment, whilst Melanie scrambled around her bag to locate the house key. She turned on the miniature torch on her key ring and pushed the key in the door.

"The key's not turning," said Melanie jumpily, her hand shaking with the impending sense of doom that hung heavily over her frame.

They pulled on the doorbell rod and banged on the door, but the house was as silent as a funeral parlour in the dead of night. Harry jammed the key in the door forcefully, but again the lock wouldn't engage. Melanie clung to her husband – her shrunken frame diminished by the dread of what she feared awaited them inside the house. The vivacious, dynamic beauty who had delivered a sparkling and entertaining performance, only a few hours earlier, now possessed the haunted look of an old woman with dementia. Her terror was infectious. Harry's hand began to shake as he tried in vain to turn the key over and over. Melanie fell to her knees and rocked backwards and forwards once more.

"Seriously Melanie, stop scaring me... you're acting mad!" Harry snapped as he felt a horrid tension snaking through his guts. Melanie looked up at him, kneeling on the front step as more black mascara streaks ran down her face.

"NO I'M NOT MAD!" she shouted, sounding uncharacteristically snappy to Harry. "Whatever he's done to our children has already happened."

"I can't stand this Melanie I'm going to smash a window. The door won't open," said the sheriff banging loudly again... but the law enforcer had forgotten to bring a warrant for Darius's arrest.

Harry staggered around the garden fumbling for a large rock but was only able to find a stone. He threw the weapon hard at the pane several times but it simply bounced off the surface. On the fourth attempt he heard a cracking noise like the sound of a child walking across a frozen puddle.

"Come on break will you," he yelled stabbing at the pane of glass in frustration. Without warning the glass fractured and plummeted downwards as a large shard of glass, the size of a dagger embedded itself into his right forearm. Harry screamed in agony.

"Harry no," Melanie cried.

The sheriff swayed wildly as the blood drained from his head and the pain seared up his arm.

"I feel sick... help Melanie, I think I'm going to faint."

Melanie shone the torch on her husband's arm, "Oh God Harry, you're bleeding so much."

Melanie fell to her knees and vomited from the shock and the

351

sight of the blood, as Harry moaned frozen by the horror of the glass embedded in his arm.

"We have to pull it out Melanie or I'll bleed to death," said Harry panicking.

Melanie pushed herself to a standing position, "I'll do it. I'll pull it out," she said, feeling calmer after throwing up.

Blood seeped from his arm as Melanie gripped the large dagger of glass and yanked it out. Harry screamed again as more blood spurted over the two of them.

"Quick get my tie off and wrap it round as tight as you can," said the wounded sheriff.

Melanie sobbed quietly as she whipped off her husband's tie and lassoed his wrist tight to stem the flow of blood. Harry grimaced in pain.

"What's happening to us Melanie, tell me this is a bad dream and we'll wake up."

But Melanie already knew that the bad dream had turned into a nightmare and there was no escape. She was on auto-pilot now.

"I'll climb through and open the door, keep your arm up like this, and hold it firmly here just above the elbow to stem the flow of blood. I'll be as quick as I can."

Melanie hugged the father of her two children and pulled herself through the window, catching numerous splinters of glass in her hands as though she had brushed past a cactus. She ignored the pain and shone the beam of light from her miniature torch into the black void.

"Darius... Hannah... Elizabeth," she called into the chasm, but her voice boomeranged back. She fumbled for a light switch with her blood-stained fingers.

Click - nothing.

"The lights don't work Harry," Melanie yelled.

"Try to open the door," Harry said weakly, his voice barely audible through the thick panel of oak.

Melanie directed the beam of light onto the front door and noticed that the bolts had been pulled across by the foreigner's hands and the dead-lock turned. She rattled through the locks and pulled her wounded cowboy into the fortress.

"Harry let me call an ambulance... and the police."

"No, let *us* find *our* children."

They held on to one another in the doom and gloom stumbling across the sitting room, neither able to call out the name of Darius Sorokin.

"HANNAH, ELIZABETH!"

Silence.

"HANNAH, ELIZABETH!"

The cry for their children wrenched at their hearts, and breast milk dripped into Melanie's bra – Elizabeth's late night feed was due.

"It's like a greenhouse in here, it's so hot," said Melanie.

"Let's go to the fuse box and try to get the lights on, so we can see what we're doing," Harry suggested.

They clung to each other and staggered into the kitchen, as a wall of hot air hit them.

"It's sweltering. Why is the house so hot?" said Melanie breathlessly.

They made their way over to the fuse box.

"Shine your torch Melanie," Harry instructed.

Harry flicked the tripped switches and almost immediately The Oast burst into a surreal electrical storm as every light in the house shone an interrogatory light onto the crime scene, revealing a gory trail of blood across the downstairs rooms and all over the fuse box. Meanwhile, the CD player boomed Purcell's Funeral Music for Queen Mary, whilst the empty washing machine spat water around the drum and the tumble dryer roared at 95 degrees. The coffee filter gurgled and chuckled, the liquidiser spun furiously, the microwave turned and the dishwasher hummed as every inanimate object in the house mocked...

We're alive.

"What the hell's going on?" shouted Harry over the din.

"I don't know, but let's go and find our children," said Melanie morosely.

"Oh God.... please let them be here!" Harry pleaded with the heavens above.

They grasped onto one another as each light in the house shone a beam of light on their journey to the end of the world. The couple climbed the stairs, slowly... deliberately, dragging each other up one step at a time, as Harry's path across The Oast was marked out by the slow relentless drip-drip-drip of blood from his lower arm.

A late night comedy show dribbled canned laughter and vacuous banter at full blast on the TV below them. As the couple reached the top landing a jolly nursery rhyme danced down the corridor from Elizabeth's nursery. They came to Hannah's door first, which had been locked. Trembling Melanie turned the key and pushed the door open. The darkness of the room stood in total contrast to the Gestapo lighting that now flooded into Hannah's bedroom from the landing.

Melanie's heart immediately contracted, *Hannah is afraid of the dark Darius, I told you that.*

"Hannah," cried Melanie, gasping for oxygen as she ran across to Hannah's empty sleigh bed. "Oh God, she's gone!"

"Hannah," said Harry, moaning his daughter's name as he stared at the empty bed.

A faint whisper emerged from the corner of the room "... Da-ddy?"

"Oh darling my little elf what are you doing behind the door?"

Both parents rushed over to Hannah and encircled their first-born, showering her with kisses and blood.

"It's sooo hot Mummy," whimpered Hannah.

"I know poppet, I'm sorry, I'll open some windows," said Melanie as she ran to the windows and threw them open. Melanie wiped the beads of perspiration from Hannah's face as Harry held Hannah in his arms, rocking her with joy and relief.

"I don't like the man with the hissy voice, he's mean Mummy," said Hannah.

"Did he hurt you darling," Harry felt a wave of fury burn up his oesophagus.

"No, but he was horrid because he wouldn't let me have my light on and he locked me in. I was wee-ally scared."

"I'm so sorry my little elf," said Harry. "Go to sleep now. Mummy and Daddy will protect you."

Melanie stroked her face, as she tenderly tucked Hannah back into her sleigh bed.

"I love you Hannah."

"Love you too Mummy."

"Night, night Daddy..." said Hannah turning to her father, "what have you been painting?"

Harry looked down at his body and saw that his shirt, his right trouser leg and shoe were dripping blood red and that his daughter's nightclothes were now smeared in blood too.

"Oh... lots of red things... I'll clean up the mess in the morning little elf. I love you."

"Love you too."

As he smiled she closed her eyes and fell immediately back to sleep. Melanie and Harry relaxed for a moment and then gripped one another again as they turned, exited Hannah's room and walked down death row to Elizabeth's room. Light blazed out of the open nursery door and a merry little rhyme rang out from the CD player.

This old man, he played one,
He played knick-knack
On my thumb.
With a knick-knack, paddy whack,
Give a dog a bone,
This old man came rolling home.

Melanie clasped her hands around her husband's arm and she noticed that his pink tie had now turned a deep shade of crimson. They paused and turned the corner.

"ELIZABETH!"

Melanie screamed, ran to the empty cot and fell to her knees. She smashed her head back and forth against the bars and as she did so, caught a sweet yet agonising scent of her baby. Harry checked behind the door and then panted in horror at the vacant cot and the empty medicine bottle hurled on its side on the carpet. His head swam and his vision blurred in and out of focus just before he crashed to the floor, falling amongst the sea of broken toys and chopped up baby clothes strewn across the nursery.

❀   ❀   ❀

"So Ms Henriksen, let me repeat the question. When you dialled 999, why didn't you ask for the police?"

"I-I don't know."

"You don't know. Members of the jury doesn't it strike you as a little odd that Ms Henriksen had the presence of mind to dial 999 to ask for an ambulance, and yet it didn't occur to her to ask for the police to come at the same time. Was it perhaps because you had something to hide?"

"No, not at all!"

"Ms Henriksen you have already described how you entered a 'darkened and silent house', you crossed the drawing room to the kitchen, got the lights working again and went upstairs with your husband who was already bleeding profusely from his injuries. You then established that your oldest child was in her bedroom and that your youngest child was missing from the nursery. So why did you simply ask for an ambulance for your husband, with no mention to the emergency services that your one-year-old child had been 'kidnapped', as you say you thought at the time."

"I was in shock, confused..."

"Indeed you were confused, because members of the jury you realised the full horror of what you had done to your own daughter and you realised you were going to need more time to concoct an elaborate and convincing story to cover your tracks."

"No... no it wasn't like that at all, I wouldn't hurt Elizabeth, I loved her... with all my heart."

"So you keep telling us Ms Henriksen. So if you *really* loved your daughter yet already suspected she had been 'kidnapped', why did you waste valuable time by not asking for the police as soon as you saw that she was not in her cot?"

"Because... because I still thought I might find her... do you understand? I just hadn't looked properly... there was still a chance. I *had* to believe there was still a chance I'd find her in another room in the house, so I went in search of her, calling for her, I checked every room and opened every cupboard and then the ambulance arrived for my husband."

"Every room? Or perhaps there was one room you didn't check, because you already knew your baby was down in the basement Ms Henriksen, because it was *you* who murdered your baby and placed her in the freezer."

"No... never! I *did* go into the basement... I just didn't think to open the freezers. The idea is so repulsive, so utterly repugnant that the thought would not have occurred to a right-minded person to look for their child in a freezer."

"*Right-minded* person indeed, are you taking any medication Ms Henriksen?"

"Yes but I don't see what that has to do with..."

"Just answer the question yes or no."

"Yes."

"Yes members of the jury, yes. In fact Ms Henriksen has been prescribed a 'veritable feast' of anti-depressants in recent years. First there was Fluoxetine, which is more commonly known as Prozac, then Citalopram or Celecoxib to give it its over-the-counter name, and more recently Sertraline otherwise known as Lustral. Yes you are quite the mobile pharmacy aren't you Ms Henriksen."

The jury hummed with derisory laughter.

"Objection Your Honour," said the prosecuting barrister, leaping to his feet.

"Objection sustained, might I remind counsel for the defence that you are not here to *entertain* the court, rather to question the witness," said the judge throwing a steely glare at the defence barrister. The judge turned to survey the 12 members of the jury, who collectively withered an inch or so.

"Might I also remind members of the jury of the seriousness of the matter in hand. There is *no* place for laughter inside the court, so please refrain from doing so."

"Your Honour I was simply trying to illustrate Ms Henriksen's dependence to prescribed anti-depressants," said Darius's defence counsel. "Now, if I could turn the court's attention to the psychiatrist's report to the prosecution which pronounced my client, Darius Sorokin, 'of sound mind' whilst the mother of the deceased is reported by her general practitioner to be suffering from, and I quote, '*profound depression and prone to bouts of hysteria and panic attacks*'. Is that not the case Ms Henriksen that you are suffering with both hysteria and panic attacks?"

"No! I wasn't suffering from anything before Elizabeth was murdered. I didn't take *any* medication before my baby was killed!" Melanie blurted out hysterically.

"Ms Henriksen, I put it to you that when you got back to the house, Darius was still inside The Oast performing his duties as a trusted babysitter and both children were safely asleep in their beds. You thanked Darius, paid him for his services and my client set off across the green to return to his house," said Darius's defence barrister with streamline efficiency, allowing no chance for Melanie to defend herself. "Almost immediately Elizabeth woke up and began screaming again and she continued to scream. Tired and emotionally frayed you went upstairs to stop the baby crying, but instead of comforting her, you silenced her forever and killed your own baby."

"NO, I didn't, that's a lie!" Melanie shouted, tears streaming down her face.

"Perhaps it was a temporary moment of madness, or perhaps you were simply unable to cope with the enormous workload and constant media attention you were under after the traumatic delivery of your second baby. Isn't that so Ms Henriksen?"

"No you have to believe me, I loved my baby!" Melanie begged, turning to the jury.

"Almost immediately you were filled with remorse and pleaded with your husband to help you conceal the baby's body in a place, and I quote, "so repulsive, so utterly repugnant" that this hidey-hole "would not have occurred to a right-minded person". So you set about creating a lavish cover story that would shift the blame to my client, didn't you Ms Henriksen?"

"No, that's not how it was..."

"After you had murdered Elizabeth you encouraged your husband to smash the window (which closely missed his main artery), to make your return to the house look like a forced entry. You wanted it to appear as though Darius Sorokin had already fled the house, that *he* was the one that had murdered Elizabeth, rather than the baby's own mother. Isn't that correct Ms Henriksen, you staged the whole scene?"

"Yes... I mean no... it was Darius, not me, I didn't *stage* anything."

"You then compelled your husband, who you said and I quote "would do anything for me" to trail around the house whilst he bled profusely. Only when you went back into Elizabeth's nursery, after Harry had lost a huge amount of blood and collapsed on the floor, did you finally call the emergency services. Isn't that so Ms Henriksen?"

"Yes... I didn't call 999 till we got to Elizabeth's nursery, but you're twisting everything..."

"And then... *even* then, you still panicked, because you needed more time to cover your tracks to erase any trace of fingerprints in the basement and to work out the fine detail of your story. So as your husband lay on the floor bleeding to death *for you*, and your baby lay murdered in the freezer in the basement *by you*, you simply said and I quote "An ambulance, I just need an ambulance"."

❀   ❀   ❀

"NO!" Melanie screamed as Harry crashed to the ground. Panic-stricken, Melanie knelt by her husband and kissed his face pleading with him not to die.

"Don't die Harry, I love you, don't leave me."

She dialled 999.

"An ambulance, I just need an ambulance... The Oast – Cranhurst Village Green – please hurry!"

Melanie lay on her husband's chest, the safest place in the world, sobbing fitfully as he drifted in and out of consciousness.

"Harry darling, stay with me, the ambulance won't be long. I'm going to try and find Elizabeth... hold on precious the ambulance will be here any moment."

Melanie gently lowered her husband's head onto her coat and then ran from room to room, screaming Elizabeth's name, searching every corner and cupboard, upstairs and downstairs.

Wee Willie Winkie runs through the town,

Upstairs and downstairs in his nightgown,

Tapping at the window and crying through the lock,

Are all the children in their beds, it's past eight o'clock?

Finally Melanie came to the empty kitchen, where the air dripped with heat and a cacophony of noise emanated from the kitchen equipment. She opened and closed every cupboard as she cried, "Li-ly-bet, come back princess Li-ly-bet."

...But the cupboards were bare.

Melanie opened the door to the basement, staggered down the stairs and ran past the frozen grave that suspended her child in eternity. She trailed bloodied fingerprints down the basement handrail on top of where the gloved hand of the babysitter had smoothly and anonymously glided only hours earlier, carrying the feverish baby to her final resting place.

Breathless and broken, and running back past the cabinet freezer for a knock down price, the mother of one returned to where she had set out, Elizabeth's nursery. She collapsed at the side of her wounded sheriff. Alone and desolate, the nation's favourite 'kiddie cook' dialled Darius's number hoping to plead with the creepy, sneering loner to return her baby.

As the message played out she could hear Elizabeth screaming feverishly in the background: "WHAH-WHAH-WHAH!"

"Sss-so you want me to change the message do you bo-sss-y boots-sss, well how about a little sss-sing-a-long

WHAH-WHAH-WHAH!

Hey diddle diddle the cat and the fiddle

The cow jumped over the moon

The little dog laughed to sss-see sss-such fun

WHAH-WHAH-WHAH.

And the dish ran away with the sss-spoon

Ha, ha, ha tricked you."

...And the line went dead forever and ever.

Amen

PART IV

CHAPTER ONE

Tuesday 1 August – 9.06pm

JM: Sophia I've just heard some awful news

    SH: What's the matter Jelly?

    JM: I've found out who Dad's defending

    SH: Who?

    JM: Darius Sorokin

    SH: Oh no not him

JM: Yes, Dad's defending the creep in the 'Frozen Baby' case, the bastard who murdered Elizabeth

    SH: That's terrible – I can't stand it. How will we tell Melanie? I'm so ashamed

    JM: I know it's horrific but that's not all

    SH: What do u mean?

    JM: He's the guy

    SH: What guy?

(pause)

    JM: I can't text it...

Sophia Haverstock flashed up on Jelly's phone.

"Jelly what can't you say in a text?"

"You know I told you in confidence that I was raped on the fencing trip... but I couldn't ever bring myself to tell you who it was," said Jelly hesitantly. "Well I can now, after what the bastard did to Elizabeth Maloney. Our Dad is defending the murdering bastard that raped me!"

Chapter Two

Friday 8 September – 6pm

Andrew Oliver Clarence Mayhew QC had sharpened his tongue to perfection over several decades in the courtroom. The high profile barrister, who was revered as an advocate of outstanding ability, had achieved silk within 14 years of call and built a formidable reputation for his cutting intellect. The shrewd tactician was universally admired and feared in equal measure as he left no stone unturned and had been victorious in over 30 murder trials and numerous serious fraud cases.

He was notorious for twisting and turning the knife, for rolling up a witness like a piece of spaghetti, tying them in knots, as they orally slipped and tripped their way through their eyewitness accounts of a gruesome or distasteful event that had happened sometimes several years earlier. Not even the tragic early death of his wife from breast cancer blunted his razor sharp tongue. If the QC was defending, Mayhew painstakingly and ruthlessly backed the prosecution witnesses into a corner, a blind alley or a dead-end, with a long-suffering and weary...

"Just answer the question, yes or no."

His verbal superiority was reinforced with an intimidating and stony faced glare over his half-moon glasses, whilst the thick brooding lips of the courtroom bully made the large and solid frame of the QC seem all the more intimidating. The inevitable stuttered vocal slips and sweaty brows induced by the infamous Mayhew cross-examination, was painful to observe – like a cat cruelly playing with a wounded mouse. Members of the jury shuffled uncomfortably in their seats or cleared their throats, whilst others nervously chewed on their finger nails or hid behind a tissue. Slowly, almost imperceptibly, Mayhew's eyes narrowed over his glasses – till they appeared no wider than a fox and the orally incompetent witness sensed the tightening of the noose around the neck of their testimony. His pointed tongue began to tease out the flaws in their account, the silly slip ups and inconsistencies. Then jab, the spaghetti wriggled and squirmed as Mayhew, the victor, triumphantly declared "No further questions".

The worn down witness, whose only crime was to be in the wrong place at the wrong time, or to have foolishly allowed the wrong babysitter to watch over her children, slumped out of the witness box dumbfounded and silenced... guilty your honour, verbally inept and emotionally destroyed, as charged.

Yet despite this verbal brilliance in the courtroom, the bombastic Andrew Mayhew QC found communicating with his daughters surprisingly difficult, for although he loved them both, the emotionally constipated father of two found it almost impossible to articulate his affection for either of them. So when news first reached the QC that both Sophia and Jelly were planning to attend the 'Frozen Baby' case, Andrew Mayhew realised he had a problem on his hands. He would have to sit down and talk to his daughters openly and frankly about such a decision.

"Angelica I know we don't often sit down and talk, your mother was so good at that sort of thing," Andrew said stiffly, focussing on a photo of his daughter on his desk, rather than looking directly at her. "However, I really would question the wisdom of you and your sister coming to court during the Darius Sorokin trial. You've been through so much with your mother's cancer and I'm concerned it will be a distressing case for you and Sophia."

"Yes I'm sure it will be distressing," said Jelly trying to temper her anger and revulsion for the murderer and rapist that her father was defending. "But don't you understand – Sophia and I *have* to be there, it's the least we can do to support Melanie and Harry. I did look after their baby for nearly six months in case you have forgotten. I really love her dad."

"No of course I haven't forgotten, this whole *messy situation* must be very awkward for you, as indeed it is for me."

There was a pregnant pause as Jelly considered the enormity of the mess. Andrew shuffled awkwardly in his chair piercing his thick, brooding lips together in an attempt to form a smile.

"Angelica I've been meaning to ask you... of course I don't want to pry, but did you ever come across Darius Sorokin in competition or on any of those fencing training camps you attended in Budapest each summer?"

"I saw the creep from a distance, but the boys and girls trained separately, so our paths never really crossed," Jelly lied.

"Well that's a relief anyway," said Andrew. The QC longed to cross over into his fatherly role and hug his frail looking daughter, but a lifetime of buttoning up his emotion prevented him from showing the love he kept hidden from her. "Look Angelica I'm sorry it's worked out that I'm defending Sorokin... strange twist of fate really seeing as you looked after Melanie's baby and the couple were such good friends with Sophia and Joshua, yes unfortunate really, most unfortunate," he said ponderously, but a little too flippantly to give his words any sincerity. "When I get to court, I promise not to try *too* hard, ha, ha," he said laughing hollowly, but the attempt at humour fell flat on the floor.

Jelly longed for her father to wrap his arms around her, but the last time the crusty, old QC had cuddled her was on her 12th birthday, just ahead of puberty. Jelly looked at her father long and hard and considered the man that would be defending the defenceless, as a desolate feeling that was dryer than Death Valley swept through her.

"It's nothing personal Dad but I really hope you lose," said Jelly, spitting the words out. "Darius Sorokin is evil to the core I just hope you know that. Yes, he is evil through and through and I hope he rots in hell!"

Chapter Three

Tuesday 12 September – 10.15am

"All rise."

The tense hum of whispered conversation was instantly silenced by the two word command of the usher as he led the judge into the packed courtroom. Melanie and Harry sat in the public gallery their hands tensely interlinked so that the blood ran out of their taut knuckles. The jury stood and looked up to the place where the 'kiddie cook' was sitting in the front row of the gallery. Some were visibly shocked at the dishevelled and drawn appearance of the once glamorous and beautiful TV cook and chat show host, who now floated above them in the gallery like a lost soul that had already departed this world.

Sophia and Joshua Haverstock sat alongside Harry and Melanie, as Sophia gently stroked the hand of the godmother of her recently born third child – Emily Haverstock. Jelly Mayhew linked her hand around her older sister's arm as the two of them held on tightly to the terrible secret they kept locked between them, safely hidden from the defending barrister and their father Andrew Oliver Clarence Mayhew QC.

Minky Sloane sat slightly detached from the main group, unable or unwilling to connect to the emotion and sadness that clung heavily to the atmosphere surrounding the front row of the gallery. Instead, the PR preferred to turn her attention to the defendant and glare at the "Bloody bastard who had destroyed her highest earning client."

Andrew Mayhew QC turned to acknowledge his daughters in the public gallery, attempting to form his mouth into a smile. The women returned a begrudging nod accepting the cruel twist of fate that had led their father to defend the most hated man in the country – R v Darius Sorokin – in the 'Frozen Baby' case.

The QC glanced across to the mother of the deceased. He'd last seen the 'kiddie cook' several years earlier in one of his wife's glossy magazines, before her untimely death from cancer. Seeing Ms Henriksen in the flesh for the first time shocked even the Teflon coated barrister. Almost unrecognisable, he saw that the dark circles under her eyes matched the black of her dress and that Sorokin's neighbour was already destroyed... defeated... even before she'd taken one step towards the witness box for the QC's notorious cross-examination.

Melanie's black and grey dress loosely hung on her frame, like a scarecrow guarding the fields from the magpie that had stolen her chick. Funereal black was the colour of choice since Elizabeth's murder and burial. All other garments – the frivolous ball dresses, the eye-wateringly expensive designer outfits for the now suspended 'Henriksen's Half Hour', the red Hepburn inspired book launch dress and the jaunty summer frocks – had all been donated to one of her chosen children's charity, for an upcoming auction.

❀   ❀   ❀

The final two bin liners filled with her black wardrobe were reluctantly bundled away to a local charity shop by the 'dishy dentist' several months after Melanie's body had been laid to rest in the beautiful 13th century churchyard overlooking the exquisite South Devonshire coastline. But the wounded cowboy foolishly repeated the same fatal error that his wife had made shortly after Elizabeth vanished from her cot, as he choose to seek out his wife's scent one last time before he loaded the final tragic chapter of her life into two bin bags.

The overpowering desire to inhale Melanie's beguiling fragrance overcame him as he unlocked the wardrobe that had, until that moment, remained firmly under lock and key. The black dresses processed in a Victoriana cavalcade of grief, together with the dark cardigans, the sombre jumpers and trousers and the ebony shoes and boots. Harry stretched out his arms and wrapped them around half a dozen of the outfits, burying his face into the black and grey dress that his spouse had worn for the opening day of Darius Sorokin's trial. But just as his wife had discovered before him, the pain was too great to bear, the loss too searing to contain, as the coil of grief unravelled inside his heart and soul, whipping and kicking everything in its path, until Harry slumped to his knees and the fearful earth splitting moan of eternal loss emerged from the pit of his stomach.

Eventually he found escape at the bottom of the wardrobe, the scent of his wife subliminally punctuating his fitful sleep. When he stirred in the early hours of the morning, his face salty and dry from crying, his neck stiff from the cramped space, he found Hannah asleep beside him, with her hand curled around her mother's soft black cashmere jumper.

Darius Sorokin remained standing in the dock, between two burly dock officers, as everyone returned to their seats. He lifted his gaze for the first time, staring directly at Melanie in the gallery as she felt the dark pools of never-ending nothingness swirling lifelessly around her like a flooded quarry pit.

He mouthed a silent *BOO* just as the judge busied himself with the case papers. The edgy and jumpy 'kiddie cook' gripped her husband's right hand so tightly that the blood flow was constricted for a moment and the deep scar that ran up his forearm twisted into an angry reddish purple ridge.

The defendant rolled his eyes dismissively up and down the sheriff, who had failed to keep the peace in his corner of town, and rested his interminable stare on the ugly scar that ran across the orthodontist's right cheek and neck, spoiling the handsome jaw line of the once 'dishy dentist'. Harry saw the corner of Darius's mouth twitch momentarily with pleasure and the lone ranger imagined lassoing his daughter's murderer from where he sat across the court and dragging him to the lynch mob that stood outside. He was certain that the crowd baying for a summary execution and the return of the death penalty had already reached their verdict... "guilty as hell!".

Finally Darius's eyes turned to the crotch of his teenage puppy love and the dumping ground for his first ejaculation (before he discovered the ready availability of the dot). Jelly crossed her legs and Sophia shielded her younger sister protectively.

"Don't look down whatever you do Jelly," Sophia whispered into her ear. "Don't let him win, remember he can't hurt you now, keep staring at the evil sod, don't back down!"

Titillated by the girl's flushed demeanour, Darius rubbed his crotch rearranging his erect penis under his boxer shorts. The clerk walked solemnly over to the dock focussing on the defendant's face.

"May I ask the defendant his name?"

"Darius-sss SSS-Sorokin."

"Do you understand the charges brought against you?"

"Yes-sss."

"And how do you plead, guilty or not guilty?"

"Not guilty."

Chapter Four

Friday 22 September – 2.05pm

"Your Honour I now call the defendant, Darius Sorokin…"

Andrew Mayhew QC hooked his right and left hands around the top of his court coat and breathed in deeply through his flared nostrils as he prepared to defend the defenceless.

"Mr Sorokin would you explain to members of the jury, why you were at The Oast Orthodontic Practice during the afternoon of Friday 18 November 2005?"

"Yes-sss ccc-ertainly," Darius hissed compliantly. "I'd been for one of my final review appointments-sss at Harry Maloney's-sss practi-ccc-e."

The jury, unfamiliar with the alien hissy 's' that slithered out of the defendant's mouth, stared hypnotically at the cruel lips delivering the serpent's account of the day.

"How long had Dr Maloney been treating you?"

"Oh a long time, eight years-sss in fact."

"My goodness eight years, so Dr Maloney had virtually seen you grow up?"

"Yes-sss he always-sss cracked a joke about me being his-sss mo-sss-t challenging orthodontic patient and he calculated I'd sss-spent more hours-sss in his-sss orthodontic chair than any other patient."

Harry massaged his forehead trying to relieve the migraine headache that was shooting between his temples.

"How well would you say that Dr Maloney knew you?"

"Very well, I mean obviously it was-sss hard to talk very much with his hands-sss in my mouth mo-sss-t of the time," said Darius in a jocular fashion as he grinned at the jury, though not one of the twelve reciprocated.

"I see and where was The Oast Orthodontic Practice in rela-tion to your house."

"Right oppo-sss-ite, across-sss the green."

"So you were neighbours too?"

"Yes-sss and he invited us to his party."

"Us?"

"My mother and I – she always-sss came with me on appointments-sss."

"I see. Would you describe yourself as enjoying a close rela-tionship with your mother?"

"Oh yes-sss very clo-sss-e."

The dirty, sleazy, fucking whore.

❀   ❀   ❀

Darius rarely cursed out loud. It was the criminal psychiatrist to the Crown Prosecution Service who picked up on the schism, between the venomous swamp of bile and vitriol that raged and festered in his head and his outwardly impeccable manners with the smooth 's' and the sneering smile.

The psychiatrist uncovered his 'Top dog' – the righteous, perfectionist side of his personality and the manipulative and ingratiating 'Underdog' during a Gestalt session talking to the imaginary polka dot on the 'Empty Chair'. Therapy would never bring harmony to the two sides of his personality. His internalised parent, the judging and bullying 'Top dog', and the deceitful and rationalising 'Underdog', had already ripped each other's heads off. This left Darius Sorokin "entirely sane, but utterly detached," the psychiatrist concluded in her report to the CPS.

❀ ❀ ❀

"So not only had you been treated by Elizabeth Maloney's father for eight years, you were practically next door neighbours and both you and your mother socialised with the family too?"

"Correct."

"Why did Dr Maloney accept your offer to babysit his children?"

Because the dot volunteered me.

"I wanted to be helpful, a good neighbour if you like. I knew everyone el-sss-e had let them down including their regular babysitter and their nanny, who had the flu. Dr Maloney knew he could tru-sss-t me."

"Indeed if we look at your last school report you were quite the model student, your housemaster said, and I quote, '*Darius*

Sorokin is a self-motivated, self-contained, hard working young man. His perseverance and outstanding academic achievement has been rewarded with offers to study at both Cambridge and Oxford. He combines all these character traits with a quiet determination and great sporting promise in the fencing arena'. Very impressive Mr Sorokin."

"Thank you."

"Mr Sorokin let us turn our attention to the point at which Dr Maloney and Ms Henriksen arrived back at The Oast. Can you tell me what time the couple returned home?"

"Much earlier than I'd e-xxx-pected. Melanie sss-said they would be home before about 1am, but in fact they came home ju-sss-t after eleven."

"Did this early return catch you unaware?"

"No I was-sss completely rela-xxx-ed, everything was-sss under control. If anything it was-sss Ms-sss Henrik-sss-en who sss-seemed like she wa-sss-n't in control."

"I see, not in control, so why did Miss Henriksen come back home almost two hours before she'd intended?"

"She was-sss really jumpy before she left, because of Elizabeth'sss fever," *lecturing me, patronising bitch,* "but I felt confident that I could handle the evening, I'd already run through everything with Dr Maloney and I had their numbers-sss to call if there were any problems-sss."

"There's a record of four calls being made from Melanie Henriksen's phone during the evening."

"Yes-sss as-sss I sss-said Melanie was-sss pretty jumpy, she kept phoning becau-sss-e the baby hadn't been well," *WHAH*

WHAH, fucking WHAH all night. "Melanie a-sss-ked me to phone them at 9.30pm, sss-so I did. I didn't want them to worry even though the baby had a temperature. I sss-spoke to Dr Maloney and told him everything was-sss fine."

Dickhead cowboy, fallen out of your saddle now haven't you?

"What happened when they arrived home?"

"I apologi-sss-ed about the lights-sss, they kept tripping and it was-sss dark when they got back. It was-sss-n't a problem though, Harry and I went to the fu-sss-e box to sss-sort out the lights-sss. I'd managed to get Elizabeth to sss-stop crying by comforting her and she fell back to sss-sleep, but the minute Melanie was-sss home the baby sss-started sss-screaming again, because of the fever. Melanie looked really sss-stressed and di-sss-appeared off upstairs-sss. The crying sss-stopped quite sss-suddenly, but I didn't think anything of it at the time."

"Liar, the snake is lying," Melanie muttered under her breath, leaning her head on Harry's shoulder.

"Harry paid me and I headed home across-sss the green."

"What time was that?"

"About 11.15."

"Did anybody see you?"

"No it was-sss pretty late. It's-sss a very sss-sleepy village not a lot happens-sss after nine o'clock in Cranhur-sss-t," Darius grinned again at the jury.

"What about your mother, did she see you come in."

Drunken dot, half comatose in the bath, always up for it.

"She called out goodnight from her room, but didn't get up."

"What did you do next?"

"I sss-started getting ready for bed and after a while I sss-saw an ambulan-ccc-e and then a while later sss-several police cars-sss appeared. I wondered what on earth was-sss going on?"

"So why didn't you wait to find out. If you had nothing to hide, why run away?"

"Because I was sss-scared, I panicked. I'd lived a very sheltered life with my mother, up until that point. All I'd known was-sss village life and boarding sss-school. I was-sss totally out of my depth."

"Clearly though you didn't feel you had anything to hide because you returned home on Saturday 3 December 2005?"

"That'sss right I knew I had nothing to hide and I wanted to," *fuck*, "sss-see my mother and tell her I hadn't done anything wrong. As-sss I sss-said we were very clo-sss-e."

"Did you know Miss Rebecca Potts?" Mr Mayhew continued, peering over his half-moon glasses.

"No I've never sss-spoken to her in my life."

"Didn't she come to the house looking for her dog?"

"My mother an-sss-wered the door whilst I was-sss having a bath. I overheard her sss-saying she'd sss-seen the dog running towards-sss the woods-sss. When I looked out of the bathroom window I could ju-sss-t make out the outline of the old lady walking towards-sss the lake, where I used to keep a rowing boat. It was-sss only later I found out Miss-sss Potts-sss had drowned. She must have u-sss-ed my boat in an attempt to re-sss-cue her dog. It was-sss a very tragic a-ccc-ident."

"Why did you run away from the house for a second time?"

"It was-sss unbelievable I'd only been home for an hour or sss-so, when an ambulan-ccc-e and more poli-ccc-e pulled up out-sss-ide Elizabeth's-sss hou-sss-e. I didn't want to leave and sss-so I decided to sss-stay clo-sss-e by and went to my childhood den in the woods-sss. I hoped the truth would come out quickly as-sss to the true identity of the murderer and then I could get back to my normal life."

"I understand that Dr Maloney and his dog were the first to find you in your den ahead of the police. Tell the jury exactly what happened next."

Darius looked up at Harry and stared at the father of the deceased.

"Dr Maloney went crazy... ber-sss-erk and unleashed his-sss dog on me. The dog was-sss out of control and leapt on top of me. He sss-snarled and lunged at my face and I thought it was-sss going to kill me. I reached for my penknife in sss-self defence, it was completely terrifying. I didn't mean to hurt the dog, I love animals-sss. Dr Maloney went in-sss-ane with rage I tried to calm him down but he ju-sss-t wouldn't lis-sss-ten, then he lunged at me and began choking me round the neck."

"What did you do to try to defend yourself?"

"I don't remember, I pa-sss-ed out and as-sss I fell back-wards-sss, my penknife caught his fa-ccc-e and neck. It was an a-ccc-ident."

Several members of the jury looked up to study the unsightly 'accident' across the right cheek and neck of Dr Maloney, whilst Melanie bowed her head weeping silently.

"No further questions."

Andrew Mayhew QC sat down self-satisfied, smug even, like

the cat which licked the cream from the milk. Just as Mayhew's ample ego returned to a seating position, the tall and wiry prosecutor Henry Jackson QC sprang to his feet.

"'*Self-motivated, self-contained, hard working and academically outstanding'...*" said Jackson, repeating the contents of Darius's school report, "all *very* noble qualities I'm sure the court would agree. But perhaps there is *another* side to Mr Sorokin that his school report didn't touch upon."

Jackson QC slammed a book on the table and then triumphantly waved it above his head as the judge began leafing through his copy of the damning piece of evidence and the prosecution handed Andrew Mayhew a copy. The jury strained forward trying to inspect the lurid front cover.

"This book, members of the jury, is the journal that was found in Darius Sorokin's rucksack following his arrest and perhaps it shows another aspect to Darius's character, a side that he would prefer to keep hidden from us all. Indeed, I would go so far as to say that the shocking contents of this journal reveal the scheming, secretive, obsessive and bitter thoughts that ferment in this young man's mind. It is a mind which appears to possess a twisted penchant for gratuitous violence and sexual degradation wouldn't you say Mr Sorokin?"

Darius smirked, but said nothing.

"Answer the question Mr Sorokin," the judge commanded.

"No I wouldn't sss-say sss-so... not at all," Darius snarled.

The judge directed the usher to hand out copies of the journal to the jury and as he did so each of the 12 jurors recoiled, one after another. Mayhew sat comatose, dumb-struck with horror as he looked down at the front cover. It featured a crude hand drawn skull and bones picture on the front of the book with the design encapsulating the words *First Fuck* in thick, black writing that dripped with red ink and formed a pool of red below the skull. A photograph of Jelly had been superimposed onto a pornographic model with a sabre sword cut out and stuck between her legs.

Next Jackson turned the jury's attention to a picture of Jelly mid-competition, lunging towards her opponent covered with graffiti-like blood slashes down her lamé jacket and breeches. Then he flicked rapidly through a series of pages that tracked her progression through British and overseas competitions, the dates and locations of her whereabouts, her likes and dislikes and intimate details of her life that tracked the girl like a heat-seeking missile right up to the time of Darius's arrest.

Jackson turned the page again to display a photograph of Jelly in a bikini taken by Darius on the annual summer training camp in Budapest, but he'd chosen to chop the image up and display the rape victim as though she had been hung, drawn and quartered. The final heinous graphic compilation featured Jelly's head attached to another image of a pornographic body image tied to a tree. The girl was marooned on the page by the defendant's glue stick and ensnared by the words *Jelly's pussy is HOT – Summer 2003* as a naked cut-out of Darius, with his erect penis pressing into her, was glued beside the ensnared fencing champion.

Jelly froze in horror in the gallery recoiling at the images, whilst her father, who was usually so erudite and verbally victorious in court, sat dumb-founded, his mouth flapping open and closed in rapid movements, like the fish on the quay gasping for its last breath.

The counsel for the defence felt a volcanic fury bubble up in him. The QC shot a thunderous glare at his client but Darius was oblivious of the violent anger that was fermenting inside Mayhew, as the defendant had already lifted his eyes to find his 'first love' on the balcony.

Angelica, Angelica wherefore art though Angelica you pussy... you warm, juicy pussy.

Cornering the girl with the irises that ran into pools of black nothingness, Darius squeezed his pointy tongue through his teeth to reveal the slimy snake that had gagged Jelly's screams as he raped her. He ran the tip of his tongue over his thin, mean upper lip.

"Don't look down," Sophia whispered again, as she held onto Jelly protectively in the gallery. "Don't let the creep win!"

Jelly tried to endure the steely, staring dual by launching a compound attack, which was parried by Darius, whilst his riposte was too quick and accurate for Jelly, as the fencing champion looked away, knowing she was defeated.

Andrew Mayhew QC felt sick to his stomach. He turned to see his precious youngest daughter looking thin and drawn and crying on the shoulder of Sophia. He turned again to stare at Darius Sorokin and felt a pyroclastic fury flowing out of every pore and orifice of his being. The moment of blind rage, the point of no return for Andrew Mayhew, came as the defendant smirked meanly and sardonically at his barrister. Like a red rag to a bull, the animal which is unable to curtail his genetic disposition to charge, the QC leapt to his feet risking his whole brilliant career as he vaulted up the witness box and wrapped his hands around the throat of Darius Sorokin, in defence of the one he had left undefended, his youngest daughter.

Chapter Five

September to September

Time was on his side. Time had become his comrade, silent, stealthy, predictable and crawling on its belly. One, two, three hours on his back reading, absorbing the outside world... until he felt the urge to piss or wank – sometimes both.

With an IQ just short of the top two per cent of the population (that would have guaranteed him membership to British Mensa), Darius's brain needed constant nurturing and feeding, like the wild kitten he had once owned. He had discovered almost immediately that he could absorb the world, the *whole fucking world* from the confines of his cell, as he veraciously consumed science, politics, religion, more science and sport.

Only once did a fellow prisoner attempt to cross him, by shoving some of his highly-prized reading material down his cell toilet, creating an unlikely papier-mâché mush consisting of the 'History, Origins & Progression of Cryogenics' by Dr Angus Jones and 'The Oligarchs in the driving seat of modern Russia' by Miranda Green.

The *fucking little maggot* found his head down the same toilet bowl two hours fifteen minutes and 27 seconds later, gasping for air, between the piss and shit. Nobody bothered Darius after that. No inmate dared to mess with his books borrowed from the prison library, nor did they touch the journals and specialist magazines.

From the moment Sorokin stepped outside his cell, he left behind the bile that ran around his head and charmed the prison librarian, who now bent over backwards to obtain some of the more obscure titles for the charming, well-spoken bookworm. He stuffed news of medical breakthroughs, human endurance and outstanding achievements into his brain, like a fat kid pushing doughnuts into his bloated body. He greedily chewed on war zones around the globe, natural disasters, political intrigue and space exploration. At times there seemed no end to the variety of facts and figures he could shove into his mind in one 24-hour cycle.

The misfit inmate (X7980XXSOROKIN) who should have been hounded, bullied or beaten up for being a "fucking book-worm oddball" or a "nerdy weirdo cunt" didn't bother his fellow inmates and neither did they bother him, as he choose to asso-ciate with nobody during evening 'association'. Leaving the going nowhere crowd to watch TV, play snooker, smoke and chat banality, the loner with the menacing sneer sat alone in the recreational areas or in his cell, escaping into the outside world through his books and newspaper articles, his thoughts effort-lessly switching from the Queen's English to fluent Russian.

The reading, the clock watching, the wanking – the world was his *fucking oyster*. He built a giant fortress around him, which none of the *dumb-fucks* around him could penetrate. Not one of the tabloid turning, porn consuming inarticulate Neanderthal prisoners possessed the mental gymnastics to even try to engage in conversation with this educated oddball... so no one tried.

No one... except the prison officers... to whom he was wit and charm personified. Unused to such a well-spoken, well-educated inmate, the officers were beguiled and hoodwinked by the deceptively immaculate manners of the High Public Interest Cat A prisoner, the "yes-sss guv", "no guv" allure disguising the internal simmering of the *three fucking bags full you kanga, you screw – you screw cunt.*

His daily work output was exemplary, as was the effort he put into his hourly exercise regime, making the athletic prisoner X7980XXSOROKIN a model inmate; settled and seemingly ready to embrace his three decade detention at Her Majesty's Pleasure.

A quarter of the way round the globe, Natasha Sorokin followed her son's trial from the safety and obscurity of the murky underworld in Moscow and under the cover of her new identity. Her priority was always self-preservation, but as the separation evolved from weeks, through months and years, the desire to splash in her gene pool, began to chip away at the dot's flaky conscience and her twisted moral compass. Her son, the foetus, which she had already spared from the back street abortionist knife 21 years earlier, now pulled at her maternal strings and her knickers'

elastic. She longed to see her flesh and blood once more, to feel his warmth beside her and to free the caged bird... the magpie trapped by a minimum tariff of 30 years.

Two months into Darius's sentence, Natasha began to pull on the rotten strings that had once connected her with her murdered sugar Daddy, the sleazy mafia man who had turned out to be her golden ticket out of the country over a decade earlier. She bribed, seduced and prostituted her way around the seedy channels and back passages of the international criminal world in Moscow, until 'uncle' Vladimir Sorokin was conceived and perfectly formed. Vladimir was paid a substantial sum of cash, which would spare him from the need for further employment for another decade or so, and then he was packaged and dispatched to London with his false passport and carefully contrived story to release the caged magpie. The long lost 'uncle' began visiting Darius six months into his sentence and it was a false identity so convincing, so utterly watertight, with a trail of flawless documentation, that not even the most sophisticated criminal record check or credential verification could throw up the whisper of suspicion.

Each layer of the complex escape plan was laid out carefully and methodically, brick by brick, month by month, as the pair cemented and fine tuned the smallest details, expertly secreting the vial and syringe between visitor and prisoner during a single prison visit, with the exchange carefully timed to fall just two days after the officers had completed the Cat A cell search. The pair engaged in banal banter as the officer passed their table during Vladimir's visit, returning to a muffled exchange in Russian as the officer proceeded up and down the line like the lion prowling in the cage, backwards and forwards.

"You'll be placing yourself into hypoglycaemic shock at the very least and almost certainly a hypoglycaemic coma," Vladimir said in Russian, barely moving his lips like a ventriloquist.

Vladimir Sorokin saw the officer returning, "So tell me Darius, what book are you currently reading?" he asked exuberantly in English. The officer past by again and Vladimir continued in muffled tones in his mother tongue, "The low blood sugars will cause you to sweat, you'll experience extreme hunger, your pulse will become very rapid and you'll appear confused, drunk even... and with no alcohol in the house, the screws will notice, ha ha," he said, laughing wholeheartedly, as his belly shook against the table. "Before you blackout you need to be sure that the screws know you are suffering with hypoglycaemia, even if you just mutter the word as you pass out – but be sure to squirrel the syringe and vial away before you exit the cell, we need to cause confusion and keep them guessing as long as possible. That way you'll be kept in hospital for a couple of days of investigations, which will give you time to recover and regain your strength ready for your escape."

Vladimir slapped his thigh as though he had just thrown a shot of vodka to the back of his throat. Returning to English again as the prison officer approached, he said loudly: "So, 'War and Peace', it's a good read, a long one too, but then I guess you have a lot of time on your hands. Ha ha."

The officer smiled to himself as he walked past. They drew closer again across the table, without touching, and returned to Russian. "Your vision will blur and you'll black out, all being well the next thing you'll know is when you wake up in hospital. You do understand that this is extremely dangerous Darius don't you – brain damage can occur and the worst case scenario is death. Are you sure you want to go ahead with this my favourite 'nephew'?"

"Yes-sss," the serpent hissed in English to his fake uncle, "it ccc-certainly is a long read. I think I'll sss-still be reading it ne-xxx-t year," he said, laughing hollowly, as the officer slowed, then moved on.

They returned to their mother tongue... "And Angelica Mayhew, I need her confirmed location for the day of the hospital breakout?" Darius said urgently.

"Sure, sure... but I advise against any contact or diversion from the main plan," Vladimir warned.

"It's *my* e-sss-cape, and it'sss part of the main plan. She was my fir-sss-t love you know," Darius said smiling sarcastically. "I want to sss-see her one more time. You're being paid by my mother to do as-sss I sss-say, sss-so work her location into the e-xxx-it route to the coa-sss-t."

That evening the magpie pecked his way through the collection of saved articles about Angelica Mayhew, he'd managed to gather and squirrel away during his time in prison. He fingered the newspaper and magazine pictures of her, running his nimble and bony hands over the words describing her victories, the enchanting details of her life as one of '*Great Britain's Golden Girls*' and one of the country's brightest gold medal contenders for London 2012.

He lingered over a picture of his QC and his daughter celebrating a win at the British Youth Championship Finals. He stared at the pompous oaf who had failed in his dismal defence of Darius in court and stared at his daughter, the girl who had spurned his advances, and so needed to be punished. Pausing for a moment he ran a finger across both of their necks.

On the night of Tuesday 30 September 2008, having memorised every last detail of Angelica Mayhew's life, he tore the papers to shreds, wiped his shitty arse on them, and flushed them down the cell toilet. The magpie circled Wednesday 1 October 2008 in his mind but left no written evidence that his cage would be unlocked once and for all that day.

Chapter Six

Wednesday 1 October – 5.30pm

Darius lay on his bed, watching the clock shift round to 5.30pm, he heard the distant – click-thud, click-thud, click-thud as the officers began 'shooting the bolt' on the cell doors, releasing the men for their evening 'association'.

"Evening Darius," said Darius's favourite screw, as Mr Everett opened the door.

"Good evening Mr Everett," responded Darius, with immaculate politeness.

The click-thud, click-thud, click-thud continued along the corridor. Darius leapt to his feet and grabbed the loaf of bread from the table in his cell and disappeared behind the screened toilet. There was always an excess of bread at breakfast, the hotplate overflowed with the stuff – white sliced loaves, loaf upon loaf, multiplied like the feeding of the five thousand, so scurrying one loaf away in his cell was made easy. He lifted the slices away from each end and pulled out the syringe and insulin vial which he had burrowed into the middle section of the loaf – a safe hiding place that had not been picked up by the screws on the daily superficial Accommodation Fabric Check.

First he flipped the flat plastic cap on the top of the vial to reveal the rubber stopper and then pulled off the cover on the needle of the syringe. It was a procedure he had observed the dot perform hundreds of times, lowering her polka dot knickers to inject herself in the stomach with insulin, after wiping her skin with a sterilising pad. Darius pulled the plunger back to the desired number of units – a life-threatening 10 units to be delivered by the apprentice doctor of death.

"Would you believe that bubblez can kill you sweetie," the dot droned repetitively at the same point in her insulin ritual, as she tapped the side of the syringe.

No.

The boy didn't know, nor did he care.

However he had paid just enough attention to the wellbeing of his mother to know to push the insulin back into the vial and draw back on the plunger for a second time to get the required dose, minus the lethal bubbles. Darius lifted his top and pinched his skin just above his hip bone, plunging the needle all the way into the subcutaneous tissue. His mouth twitched at the corner, as the novice injected himself for the first time releasing the overdose of insulin into his body, neatly and cleanly at a 90 degree angle. He liberated the pinched skin and pulled the needle out, methodically disposing of the evidence quickly and surreptitiously back into the middle of the loaf of bread.

The sick magpie left the bread table and fluttered out onto the walkway outside his cell, filled with the voices of too many men crowded into the decrepit space, the clatter of metal on metal, the endless jangling of keys around the grim, hollow space, where some tried to throw themselves onto the netting below to escape to the other side.

But Darius, the magpie who had taken to stealing other mothers' chicks, would not take a weak suicidal flight path neither would he fly along a self-destructive, self-harming slipstream. For this little bird would soar straight along the thin line of purgatory that runs between life and death itself in his bid for freedom.

CHAPTER SEVEN

Saturday 4 October – 3am

Darius lay in his hospital bed faking sleep. His head felt groggy from the massive overload of insulin to his system, but his mind began to race with the fight or flight of adrenaline that began to surge into his body. Tonight he would be called upon to both fight and flee.

The senior prison officer and one of the juniors guarding him succumbed to sleep within twenty minutes of each other, somewhere between 2.30 and 3am. The youngest prison officer, who was on his first 12-hour bed watch, sat bolt upright trying to resist the seductive allure of closing his eyes in the dead of night, as the hot, close air in the single ward hung soporifically around him like a warm duvet.

Darius rubbed his stomach and groaned quietly, as the cuffs and chain that ran between prisoner and prison officer clanked in the still night air.

"Is there something wrong?" enquired the young prison officer.

"Yes-sss," the snake hissed politely, "I don't feel too well. Would you mind awfully accompanying me to the toilet?" he said without a hint of irony, morphing into the role of the Eton-educated Englishman.

The inexperienced officer, who liked to stick to the rules, hesitated – he wanted to wake up the senior officer and his colleague who were now snoring loudly in unison. The guidelines explicitly stated that a SO and two further officers were to accompany a Category A prisoner at all times during a hospital stay. He was a man who liked to play by the rulebook, even if his charge was about to shove the rules down his throat. The officer reached over to the most senior of his colleagues.

"I shouldn't wake him if I were you," Darius suggested helpfully, "you'll show him up for falling a-sss-leep and the loo'sss only ju-sss-t down the corridor."

"Okay then, let's be quick," said the officer nervously.

It was the first time Darius had left his bed since being admitted unconscious, double-cuffed and further anchored to a drip of 10 percent dextrose for 24 hours after an initial bolus injection to bring him back to the land of the living. Now freed of the IV cannula in his wrist, he pushed to a standing position and his head spun wildly as the kind, 'by the book' officer steadied Darius on his feet.

"Are you okay there?" he asked.

"Yes-sss thank you guv, ju-sss-t a little dizzy," Darius reassured.

The two walked down the deserted corridor cuffed to one another, the harsh, fluorescent panel lighting bouncing off the clinical laminated floor and plasticised wall and ceiling surfaces.

They passed a lone hospital porter in blue overalls and hair net pushing a trolley. The pair walked through the bathroom door and the officer locked the door behind them. Darius shuffled past the bath, gripping his tummy and groaning dramatically, as the shackled prisoner moved inside the toilet cubicle.

"Hold on Darius," said the officer running through the guidelines in his head, "let me just secure the cubicle."

"SSS-Seriously governor? We are on the third floor and it'sss pitch black out-sss-ide, do you really e-xxx-pect me to sss-squeeze through that tiny window and jump, when my sss-stomach's turning over on sss-something that feels-sss like a rotten vindaloo?"

"Okay, everything appears to be in order, I'll just wait here," said the officer, after methodically checking the cubicle despite Darius's insistence to the contrary. The officer fed the ratchet chain through the crack in the door just above the sliding bolt, giving Houdini six feet of manoeuvrability.

Before long a loud groaning noise, interspersed with violent retching sounds drifted through the thin panel that divided the two, Darius flushed the toilet and the groaning began again, this time louder than before. The hiss of the cistern and the groaning effectively masked the sound of cold running water as Darius contracted the warmth out of his left hand with the ice-cold water. He lathered the cuff, which had mercifully been left loose by the officer... though Darius had no intention of returning the act of mercy.

CHAPTER EIGHT

Saturday 4 October – 3.13am

Three rapid knocks, followed four slow ones.

"Добрый вечер (Good evening)," Darius called through the door.

"ты свободен (You are free)," Vladimir responded.

The agreed code words saw Darius respond by unbolting the door, as Vladimir Sorokin glided into the bathroom pushing the trolley.

"What do you want me to do with that?" asked Darius.

The young, wet behind the ears prison officer, sat like a sack of new potatoes slumped against a wall in the green-grocers. His hands were trapped under the closeting chain wrapped around his neck and his eyes popped wide open and frozen in his skull.

"I'll deliver it to the incinerator. Now be quick Doctor Johnson, get changed."

Darius held up his left hand, as his thumb jutted out of its socket at a ghoulish angle.

"We'll have to get that back into the socket. Here... bite into this towel and don't make a sound."

'Uncle' Sorokin crunched the thumb back into the socket, a poker-hot rod of pain shot up Darius's arm, as the triple murderer staggered backwards.

"Будь сильным (Be strong)," the 'uncle' mentored impassively. "Here let me bandage your hand – you'll need the support for driving."

As soon as the first aider was done, Vladimir Sorokin morphed back into the phony porter and peeled back the sheet, revealing Darius's change of clothes. The former prisoner wrestled the medical disguise on with speed and agility, given the trauma to his metacarpo-phalangeal joint and ulnar collateral ligament during his Houdini-style escape from the handcuffs. He pulled on a white coat over the top of the suit.

"Very smart Dr Johnson," the 'uncle' said wryly.

Vladimir clipped a fake ID onto the doctor's coat and fitted him with thick black glasses and an auburn wig.

"Every inch the junior physician on night call," said Vladimir. "Right doctor help me load your first patient onto the trolley. Only use your good hand."

The medical team lifted the dead weight onto the trolley and covered his body in a sheet.

"Car park 3, row N, red Saab, three sets of car keys, exit parking ticket is here," the porter-come-uncle rattled off in quick-fire succession pressing the ticket and keys into Darius's hand. "Money, passport, driving license and suitcase are in the boot. The Sat Nav is keyed in to take you to your car swap five miles away in the underground car park we discussed – it's a white van and there's a new identity for you to adopt. Then your third switch is the green Ford Fiesta parked in Battle town centre. If you have any problems, the addresses and postcodes are in the glove compartment of the first car so make sure you empty it before you do your car switch. If you have to take the diversion you spoke of, be quick... but I advise against moving off script to give your first love one final kiss goodbye.

"The Serpentine leaves Simmons Quay, Rye harbour as soon as you get there, fishing overalls, boots, hat are in the trunk of the Fiesta. Make sure you put them **all** on before you board the boat. You need to be unrecognisable by the time you leave. All three cars will be picked up and destroyed as soon as you abandon them. The two man crew on the boat are our men. They'll take you along the Straits of Dover and there'll be a switch to a sailing boat off the north coast of East Anglia, then you'll hug the coastline up the North Sea for your next rendezvous on Orkney. Your mother will charter a private plane and you'll be briefed on the final leg of your transfer and re-assimilation back home. Now go, before my patient gets too stiff to feed him into the incinerator and before anyone realises how long it takes my 'nephew' to take a crap. См. вы в Москве (See you in Moscow)."

CHAPTER NINE

Saturday 4 October – 8.15am

Joshua Haverstock stood behind Sophia, his arms stretched around his pregnant wife's stomach as their three younger children played in the nursery.

"Feel it?" Sophia asked.

"No I missed it again," said Joshua.

"Well how about down here."

Joshua laid his hand on the side of his wife's stomach.

"Ah, felt that one," Joshua confirmed.

"Ouch... so did I!" said Sophia.

"I'll miss you darling," said Joshua as he turned Sophia around to face him.

"I'll miss you too, but I have to confess it will be nice to escape nappy duty and have a girlie weekend by the sea with my sister."

Joshua picked up her weekend back and checked his watch.

"You'd better go sweetheart or you'll miss your train... and don't worry about me... leaving me up to my elbows in dirty nappies, washing up and broken nights."

"*One* broken night Mr Haverstock!" Sophia corrected.

"I know, I'm just being a drama queen... you know us arty types. Actually I've cheated for lunchtime and have invited Harry and Hannah up for a Dads and daughters pizza lunch in Covent Garden."

"What about Melanie will she be joining you for lunch?" Sophia asked.

"No luck I'm afraid, Harry says she never leaves the house anymore and is rarely out of bed before lunchtime."

"It's just so sad, Melanie was incredibly radiant and beautiful, she had such a gift with food – everyone loved her TV shows and books," said Sophia soulfully.

"Hey less of the past tense sweetheart, Melanie's not dead, she's just profoundly depressed."

"I'll give her a call on the train to see if we can arrange to get together soon. Maybe I could take Emily down to see her god-mother, so Melanie's not too overwhelmed by travelling up to London."

❀　❀　❀

Melanie willed her body out of bed to kiss Hannah and Harry goodbye, before the pair headed up to London to rendezvous with Joshua and his three girls.

"How about I bake you both your favourite cakes for when you get home tonight," Melanie suggested, as Harry saw the blue sparkle in his wife's eyes return for the briefest of moments. "Don't tell me, don't tell me, let me guess!" said Melanie giggling childishly. "Something choc-o-let for Hannah and, ooo let me see, that gorgeously moist fresh coconut cake for my darling husband!"

Melanie threw her arms around her family and hugged Hannah and Harry tightly, as though her life depended on it. She waved them goodbye from the front door, blowing kisses down the garden path.

Time slurred after that, maybe one hour, two hours as she returned to her bedroom to top up her medication. Eventually Melanie shuffled down the stairs dressed in a baggy tracksuit, her hair tied roughly in a ponytail and her sunken and sallow skin devoid of makeup. Her pale blue eyes were framed by dark circles and the red eye liner of a thousand tears, as her head swam with a fuzzy, groggy fog induced by the sleeping pills and anti-depressants that were prescribed to hold her sanity together.

The former 'kiddie cook' robotically broke eight eggs into the stainless steel bowl of a state-of-the-art duck egg blue food mixer, a gift from the leading manufacturer of the day, when 'Melanie's Munchkins' had first risen to a weekly audience of six million. She spooned in butter, sugar and flour instinctively measuring out the correct amount, without the need for scales, and then pushed the power button on.

The whirr of the mixer masked the sound of the house phone and on the third ring it flipped to the answer machine. The recorded message, the one which Melanie could not bear to erase, pirouetted freely around the kitchen undetected by the 'kiddie cook' as she stood comatose, watching the balloon whisk beat through the ingredients in a hypnotic figure of eight until they amalgamated into a smooth, golden paste. She followed the track of the beaters whirring round and around as she began planning the division of the mixture into two – one for Hannah and one for Harry – one chocolate and one coconut.

As Sophia sat on the Charing Cross to Battle train listening to the recording of Elizabeth and Hannah laughing down the line, she allowed herself to be caught up in the jollity of the moment, even though Elizabeth had been dead for almost three years. After ten seconds or so of riotous frivolity Melanie and Harry managed to deliver the message almost in unison, but still punctuated by the gurgles and chuckles of Elizabeth.

"Welcome to the house of fun. You know what to do... leave a message after the beep."

"Hello... Melanie? Are you there?" Sophia said falteringly.

She hoped her long lost friend and the absent godmother to her third child might pick up. "I hear the boys are getting together for lunch today and I thought how lovely it would be to come and see you soon," said Sophia. "Maybe I could bring Emily down to see you, you know, just the two of us. I often tell her about her beautiful fairy godmother. If you are up to it I'd love to take you out, just something local, maybe an afternoon tea in Cranhurst at those lovely tea rooms. I'll call again on Monday... I'm actually on my way to see Jelly for the weekend which will be lovely. She sends her love by the way. Anyway Melanie, you look after yourself... we are all very fond of you... I hope you know that... bye for now."

Melanie turned the food mixer off just as Sophia hung up. Having missed the call and a rare and fleeting opportunity to connect with the outside world, Melanie continued robotically in glorious isolation. She picked up a coconut from the fruit bowl and hammered a skewer into the two eyes of the shell and drained the coconut milk into a glass. She mechanically walked over to the door leading to the basement and hesitated for a moment, before descending the stone staircase. Gripping the coconut tightly in her hand, Melanie imagined it to be the head of her baby's murderer and hurled it violently onto the cold, cruel floor below, smashing it into dozens of fragments as the rain pelted against the lone high window – replaced with wood-effect pvc and a secure grill to keep the baddies out.

❀ ❀ ❀

Jelly kissed Sophia on the cheek as she walked through the front door of Battle Fencing Club.

"Thank you so much for coming to watch me," said Jelly excitedly.

"I've been meaning to escape London for months and come and see you. I know you told me on the phone, but tell me again; how was Beijing?"

"Incredible, I was only a reserve... in case of an injury in the main squad, but I was really lucky to be able to go and watch. It was an unforgettable experience and great to take part in the training and build up too. Dad generously funded the whole thing. Sadly only three of our fencers qualified and of course the American's completely dominated the sabre competition winning gold, silver and bronze in the individual category, but I won't let that put me off. I'm completely focussing on sabre and I can't wait till London 2012, my coach thinks I'll be coming to my peak just at the right time."

"And I think it too. I read the article on 'GB's Golden Girls' in The Times after the Beijing Olympics. How exciting that you're part of a growing group of female medal hopefuls for 2012. The next four years are going to be a very exciting test for you," said Sophia.

"That's for sure. I'm working on every aspect of my game, my fitness, speed training, footwork, technique, sleep and my diet. Oh and I've just gone teetotal too by the way – but it's a price worth paying."

"Join the club," said Sophia patting her tummy. "Well you look fantastic on it Jelly and I see there's more muscle now and less skin and bone. How's everything inside that head of yours?"

"The team psychologist has been building up my self-belief, there's no room for doubt or self-destruction now. I've been able to put the rape behind me at last, knowing that bastard is behind bars... and it doesn't hurt so much when I think about Mum anymore."

"I know, me too," said Sophia as she hugged her sister warmly.

"The funny thing is I actually believe for the first time in my life that I really can go all the way, that I really could be a medal contender in 2012."

"And so do I," said Sophia emphatically.

"Are you still okay for dinner and staying over?" Jelly asked

"You bet, it's not often I get away from the nappy changing, feeding, kindergarten routine, so it will be a real treat to stay over. So where is your new house?" Sophia quizzed.

"Rye, it's absolutely beautiful, you're going to love it. It's a 16th century cottage with great views over Rye harbour. It's close enough to visit Dad a couple of times a week, but just far enough away to escape. He just sits around moping, feeling sorry for himself since his suspension from practice by the Professional Conduct Tribunal. I feel so guilty sometimes... for what happened... he was only trying to protect me."

"Well don't! It just shows how much he really loves you, even if he doesn't always articulate it," said Sophia.

They smiled a mutual understanding.

"He's got so much time on his hands now, but he can't seem to shake himself out of his black mood. I'm so grateful for all his financial support, but I just wish he took a bit more interest in my fencing career."

"Well I'm interested and I have every intention of cheering you all the way to London 2012."

Sophia looked around the mirrored practice area, intrigued by the alien strips that ran down the length of the gym. She waddled over to the back wall and studied a series of huge framed photographs, featuring Jelly and other top fencers from the Battle Fencing Club.

"What great facilities you've got here, I feel terrible that I have only been able to follow your progress from a distance. Once number four is born, I promise that will change and I'll come and support you as often as I can. I love your outfit and your sabre too."

Jelly passed her fighting weapon to her sister. Sophia ran her hand over the bell guard and wrapped her fingers around the French grip handle, pointing the blade out in front of her.

"Gosh it's straight out of the three musketeers. It looks dangerous."

"Oh it can be, that's why I'm wearing all this protective clothing, it very rarely punctuates through, but it can happen. Of course Dad got me all the top of the range equipment. The club's been really fortunate too, we got Lottery Funding a few years back, given the strength and number of fencing hopefuls we have here in Kent and East Sussex for London 2012."

Just then Jelly's phone rang and her coach's name flashed up *Bradley Kingsley*.

"Hey Jelly I'm running a little late," said Bradley breathlessly. "Make a start on your warm up and I should be with you in the next half hour. I want to work on your balestra today so make sure you are nice and loosened up so we can get cracking as soon as I arrive."

"Will do coach," Jelly said.

Jelly flipped her phone to silent and slipped it into her bag.

❀ ❀ ❀

Harry held hands with Hannah and skipped down the front garden path as she clutched the ribbon of her prized helium balloon from Pizza Park, Covent Garden.

"Can I do it, can I do it Daddy?" Hannah pleaded.

"Don't you think you are getting a bit big for this my little elf?" said Harry.

"I'm only eight I'm not even double figures. You can stop picking me up when I'm ten, then I'll be too big and you'll be too old!" said Hannah giggling like her mother.

"Cheeky. Well hold on tight to that balloon or it'll fly away."

Harry slipped his hands around Hannah's waist and lifted her into the air as she pushed the key into the lock with one hand, gripping the balloon ribbon with her other hand. After several attempts to turn the key she gave up.

"It won't turn Daddy, it's jammed."

Harry's heart froze as his memory unravelled back to the jammed lock, the bolted door, his arm bleeding profusely and Elizabeth... gone, suspended... forever and ever. The father of one shuddered momentarily and gently placed his hand over Hannah's. They turned the key together and to Harry's relief the door opened.

"Melanie we're home," said Harry, as he helped Hannah unbutton her coat.

But the house was deathly quiet. Harry stood up slowly and felt the emptiness of the house hang heavy on his shoulders – deadweight.

Hannah sniffed the air, "I smell chocolate.... Mummy's been baking, just like she promised!"

"Race you to the kitchen," said Harry.

Hannah scampered across the sitting room, pushing past her father, but in so doing she caught the edge of a coffee-table and knocked Melanie's art deco lamp over, whilst losing her grip on the balloon as it floated up towards the vaulted ceiling.

"My balloon... Mummy's lamp... oh no!" said Hannah, as she burst into tears.

"Shit," Harry cursed as he looked at the shattered lamp.

"Daddy, that's a nawty word."

"Sorry darling," he said, picking up the pieces of the wedding gift from Melanie's grandmother.

She loved that lamp and she really loved the person who gave it to her, he thought.

Harry grimaced and his sorrow was infectious as Hannah burst into tears with the guilt of the broken lamp and the sadness of losing her balloon.

"Hey come on little elf. I'm sorry. It was my fault for racing," said Harry as he picked Hannah up again and said gleefully: "I smell ca-ake."

He opened the door to the kitchen and they both gasped with delight.

"It's buuuuuuutiful," said Hannah.

Melanie had filled the kitchen with flowers and silk butterflies. A huge floral and fruit arrangement flowed over the marble island, with curls of ribbon tied around every available hook and door knob. A childish banner with a stick family of four hung from the Victorian inspired utensil hanger, with the multi-coloured words

I LOVE YOU FOREVER & EVER...
always have... always will

Two recently baked cakes sat on the curved dresser, their 'welcome home' aroma still floated in the air. The home baked fragrance was made all the sweeter by the scent of lilies, roses and freesias that filled every available vase the couple had collected during their marriage.

"Oh isn't Mummy lovely,"

Harry nodded as a tear silently rolled down the ridged scar on his right cheek.

"Yes she is, *very* lovely."

CHAPTER TEN

Saturday 4 October – 11.42am

Andrew Mayhew sat listlessly in his now redundant home office shuffling through old papers, sorting them into three piles active, stagnant and dead. The clearout was long overdue, he knew, but the dismantling of the hallowed space marked the end of an era, a lifetime of outstanding advocacy cut short by one reckless act to protect his daughter, to avenge the foul deed of his client. He rubbed a cloth over the pictures of his dead wife and distant daughters, whom he longed to draw near to but didn't know how. Then turning the radio on in search of some classical inspiration to drown his sorrows, he wallowed in the thunderous melancholy of Beethoven's 5th.

At the top of the hour, the headline bulletins commenced with a breaking news story...

"Convicted double murderer, Darius Sorokin, who escaped from hospital in the early hours of the morning last night, by killing a prison officer during his escape, is still at large warn Kent Police. The man who was convicted in the notorious 'Frozen Baby' case was

caught on CCTV cameras leaving the hospital grounds disguised as a medic and driving a red Saab, with stolen number plates FL10 XRL. Police say the man is extremely dangerous and may be armed and should not be approached under any circumstances. Kent Police believes Sorokin is hiding somewhere in the county and the police have issued a reward for information leading to his arrest."

Andrew froze for a moment, paralysed by the news. He scrambled for his mobile phone and hit his daughter's contact details. Jelly's phone vibrated in her kitbag, as she worked her way up and down the metallic piste warming up for her training session, but the vibrations were absorbed by her towel and the phone went straight to voicemail.

"Angelica listen to me, as soon as you get this message phone me immediately. I've just heard the terrible news that Darius Sorokin has escaped from hospital. Where are you? Are you fencing or at the cottage? I'll be on my mobile and am driving straight down to Battle and then on to Rye. Please phone me – Darius may be armed and, as we both know, he is extremely dangerous. Oh God darling please be careful... I know I don't really say it often enough but your grumpy old father loves you very much. Phone me."

Jelly completed her tenth set of short-burst sprints up and down the practice room, as she heard the front door of the training centre open and close, its distinctive metal bar mechanism reverberating loudly around the entrance hall.

"Hopefully that'll be my coach at last," said Jelly, as her chest heaved up and down from the tough, self-imposed warm up. The door to the practice gym opened and Jelly's coach stepped into the room looking flustered and distracted.

"Sorry about that Jelly, my car decided not to start, brilliant hey and it's only just been in for a service," said Bradley. "Give me ten minutes to change Jelly and I'll be with you. Finish off your stretching and then start your footwork practice."

The coach noticed a pregnant woman sat in the corner.

"Oh hello, who are you?"

"This is my big sister.... Sophia Haverstock," Jelly cut in. "Sophia meet Bradley Kingsley – my coach extraordinaire and the man who'll help me get to gold in 2012."

"Very nice to meet you Bradley," said Sophia, "you should get used to seeing me around once I've delivered number four. I'm planning on supporting my sister all the way to the Olympics."

"No pressure then Jelly," quipped Bradley.

The two strangers shook hands and Bradley headed off to get changed as Jelly ran through her stretches. After five minutes or so Sophia asked if there was anything she could do.

"You could call out for me," suggested Jelly. "Start with 'advance' and then 'retreat' and throw in the occasional 'lunge' after some of the advances, mix it up, make me work Sophia."

"En garde," said Jelly taking up her start position. Sophia watched the champion smoothly and elegantly bending her knees into the start position, her front foot pointing ahead of her, her back foot pointing outwards in a graceful 'L' shape. She lifted her front arm forwards before her and her back arm curved into the air.

Jelly moved forwards and backwards, switching effortlessly from advance to retreat at Sophia's command and lunging with the grace of a ballet dancer and the aggression of a pouncing tigress.

"Gosh it's beautiful to watch you Jelly you are like a balletic Zorro. I can't wait to see you in competition."

Sophia felt the baby press on her bladder as the front door clattered open and shut again.

"There goes the front door again. I'll go and see where my coach has got to... sounds like he might have had to pop out to the car," said Jelly, checking her watch and seeing that she had already been warming up for close to 40 minutes.

"Not to worry Jelly, I'm dying for a pee, so I'll go and find the ladies. Why don't you just do some sedate stretching and I'll see where Bradley's got to, see you in a few minutes," said Sophia.

Jelly dropped to the floor and moved into her stretching routine as Sophia headed out to the foyer to find the toilets. She pushed open the front door to see if Bradley was in the car park, but there was no sign of life outside. Sophia stepped back into the foyer and spotted the sign for the men's changing room and knocked on the door... nobody answered.

She knocked again... silence.

Sophia pushed gently on the door opening it no more than a crack, "Hello...Bradley... are you there?"

She pushed the door open a little wider not wanting to disturb the coach, nor wishing to catch him if he were still in the process of getting changed. But her concerns were redundant, dead and buried, for Bradley had already been stripped of his breeches, plastron, white jacket, lamé and electronic mask, as he lay the other side of the lockers strangled by his own sabre, which had been pressed against his throat, choking the life out of the south east's most inspiring coach.

Sophia felt her baby roll again. Now desperate to empty her bladder she bolted to the ladies changing room, locked the toilet, slid her pants down and sat on the toilet – relieved that her pelvic floor had held out with her fourth child pressing down on her bladder. The ladies changing room door squeaked open and shut and Sophia heard footsteps approaching.

"Jelly is that you?"

But no answer came. The stealth-like footsteps were only just audible and Sophia gasped as a pair of men's fencing trainers appeared at the base of the cubicle door. She leapt off the toilet as though she had sat on hot coals, scrambling to pull up her underwear and tights and drop her dress back down to its below knee modesty.

"Bradley is that you?"

Sophia laughed nervously trying to push away the fear that knotted at the top of her stomach above her baby.

"Yes-sss it is-sss, why don't you come out and join us-sss?"

Sophia recoiled backwards away from the familiar hiss of the serpent and felt the cold ceramic edge of the toilet rim press into the back of her legs. She placed the palm of her hand over her mouth to prevent herself from screaming.

Darius Sorokin... oh my God please help me dear Lord Jesus, she prayed silently.

The feet stepped away from the base of the toilet cubicle.

Sophia trembled in terror as she heard an almighty metal clattering across the floor and then – *BANG* – the light below the cubicle door disappeared.

"I'll sss-see you when I've dealt with your baby si-sss-ter," the muffled voice slithered through the barricaded door.

All fell silent and Sophia was momentarily paralysed, her hands shaking uncontrollably over the flimsy bolt that had separated her from Jelly's rapist and Elizabeth's murderer. She opened the toilet door and found herself completely trapped, ensnared by the row of lockers pushed across the doorway. Sophia banged on the metal wall before her, screaming Jelly's name hysterically, but her voice and beating fists were swallowed up by the fortification. The knot of fear that had lodged itself at the top of her stomach now spread across her womb, gripping her and her baby in a vice of terror. Sophia cradled her stomach as her womb convulsed violently and she dropped to the floor in agony as blood oozed into her knickers.

"Well about time Bradley," Jelly smiled broadly as she saw her coach appear in the frame of the gym door. The imposter was dressed and ready for the assault, his mask pulled down over his face, black and anonymous.

"I thought maybe somebody had gobbled you up," said Jelly as she pulled on her gloves. The fake coach held up his hand, as if appealing for mercy (though none would be given by him) and he remained silent.

Jelly was expecting her coach to start with the usual lesson before sparring with his star pupil, but she saw the man she mistook to be Bradley heading straight to the metallic piste.

"You're mixing it up today then coach, keeping me on my toes?" said Jelly cheekily.

But no response was forthcoming from the 'south east's most talented fencing coach'. Jelly's face was flushed red from the warm up and she wiped away the perspiration that had formed around her cheeks before pulling on her mask and picking up her sabre. They both clipped one end of their body wires onto their electronic lamés and anchored the other end to the spool at their respective ends of the piste.

The sparring opponents plugged in their sabres and walked towards one another standing behind the en garde line before the battle commenced. But there would be no jury to raise the carton noir, the black card that might have a chance of protecting the young fencing protégé from the man who planned to rape her one more time before killing her. They saluted one another and Jelly called out "En garde" as she dropped with balletic elegance into her ready position.

It was only as "En garde, ready, fen-ccc-e " slithered through her opponent's mask and the sabreur lunged recklessly and wildly towards Jelly that the awful realisation as to the identity of the man behind the mask hit Angelica Mayhew.

Gaining the initial element of surprise, Jelly's attacker slashed viciously and illegally at her legs and she reeled backwards falling to the floor. But little did Darius know or understand that he was now playing a game of Russian roulette – a lethal game of chance

– with the golden girl of fencing. For the sabreuse expert, who had spent the past two years honing her skills as he languished in prison, vowed to 'fight to the death' if she had to, and play by Darius Sorokin's rules... mean, ruthless and dirty.

Melanie looked towards the horizon stretching out across the sea. The sunset danced over the water, catching reflections of pink, red and gold in the ripples. She hadn't turned on the radio and so was blissfully unaware that her daughter's murderer was on the loose, fleeing towards the very coastline where she sat for the last few minutes of her life, the date set in her dream long ago – October 2008. The afternoon rain had washed the pebbles clean and she watched the sun turn a deep red and melt towards the horizon. She wound the window down and breathed in the cold, fresh, salty air.

Harry frantically dialled Melanie's number, but it switched straight to voicemail.

Text. I'll text her, he thought.

What to say? Then without hesitation, the words he had said a hundred times over.

HM: I love you so much Melanie Henriksen ... always have... always will...

He hit the send button... but it was only the next morning that Harry found Melanie's phone under her pillow.

❀ ❀ ❀

Melanie picked up her favourite photograph of the family, before it was culled from four to three, and kissed Harry and Hannah goodbye. She turned the picture over and wrote.

> My darling Harry & Hannah
> I love you with all my heart, forever and ever, but I can't leave Elizabeth alone any longer. I miss her so very much. Forgive me.
> All my love
> Melanie, Mummy xxx

Melanie opened a copy of her number one best seller 'Tummy Love' and tucked the photograph inside the front cover. Picking up Elizabeth's teddy, she walked towards the sea and filled her pockets with pebbles. As she walked into the water, she tasted the salt and moisture of the sea, mixed with the saltiness and wetness of her tears.

"Mummy's coming princess Lilybet," she said with a whisper and Melanie Henriksen disappeared under the waves, forever and ever.

Amen

About the author

Sarah Orton was born in Islington, London in 1964, to the eminent consultant orthodontist Harry S Orton OBE and to mathematician and practice manager Shelagh. The third of four children in a very close family, Sarah was dubbed the 'arty' child with her love of creative writing, penchant for dressing up extravagantly and theatrical cooking which earned her the reputation as 'The Pudding Queen'.

The family moved to a big, rambling house in Surbiton, Surrey in the late Sixties and Sarah was raised on what she later affectionately described as the "original set of 'The Good Life'" with sheep and chickens on their 'Suburbiton' lawn, an awesome kitchen garden tended by her parents and cupboards and freezers filled with fresh produce, pickles and jams, to complete the visionary, self-sufficiency dream ahead of the hit TV show in 1975. As Sarah's father treated his orthodontic patients in the front of the house (with pop stars and princes amongst them), her mother (a talented homely cook) rustled up a fantastic evening meal made with the home grown produce. This sparked Sarah's lifelong passion for home cooking and sharing food around the table with family and friends.

Sarah wrote a recipe book in her first job and then went on to become the youngest editor at Reed Business Publishing in the late 1980s, editing a baking magazine. After a brief spell in consultancy PR, Sarah set up her own PR agency 25 years ago with her husband. Specialising in food and art clients, Sarah has worked with many of today's well known celebrity chefs and edited one of the industry's leading art magazines.

She has lived in the Weald of Kent with her husband and two children, Sophie and Harry, for the past 22 years. Sarah describes her children as her "raison d'être" and "my greatest achievement in life". Although her two grown up children have 'officially' left home, she can still tempt them home with the promise of some great home cooked food.

Tummy Love is Sarah's debut novel and the realisation of a lifelong dream to become a published author. Sarah says, "As long as people want to read my stories I'll keep writing them" and she is already working on her second book *Room to Let*, a psychological thriller set in 1970s London.

www.SarahOrton.co.uk

Acknowledgements

Thank you to my husband Steven, who gave me the time and space from a busy life to realise a lifelong dream to write this book. Your belief in my writing and story-telling ability has been unflinching. Also thank you too to my darling daughter Sophie, who whilst reluctant to read a book written by her mother ("how weird is that!") was glued to the manuscript till the early hours of the morning. Similarly I would like to thank my cousin Karen who was so gripped by the first draft that she cancelled numerous social engagements so that she could read the story and give me reams of invaluable feedback. Thank you to my adorable son too. It was lovely of you to agree to do the creepy 'Darius experiment' and freeze a garden worm, because I was too scared to! A huge thank you goes to my younger sister Siobhan for her endless positivity and love. For me, you make the planet a sweeter place to dwell. Thanks too for the effusive support of my sister-in-law Gina who was full of praise and glued to "the scary bits" and to my brother-in-law Chris for your literary observations.

There are several experts that helped me with all sorts of technical details too. First of all to my gentle brother Julian (Dr JJ) who helped me with all the medical jargon and to my wise older sister Dr Sharon Orton-Gibbs at Walpole – The Orthodontic Specialists – for assisting me with the orthodontic terminology.

And how could I write my acknowledgements without mentioning my beloved Daddy (or to give you your official title, Dr Harry Stanley Orton OBE). Although you are long gone and with it your brilliance as an orthodontist, I will never forget your fatherly adoration of your 'Tussie' and 'Middley'. Thank you too to my incredible mother, for your rock like support and love throughout my life and your wonderful Christian faith that shines like a light in your family and community.

Enormous thanks go to my Christian friend and talented photographer Carl Warner, who inspired the character Joshua Haverstock in the book. In real life, Carl is the originator of the creative and brilliant 'food landscapes' and Joshua's mushroom and smoked salmon story is loosely based on actual events in the Carl Warner studio!

My thanks go to the Prison Reform Trust and a wonderful prison officer who gave me a fascinating, insider's view of prison life – thank you Mr E! My heartfelt thanks go to the fencing expertise of four times Commonwealth medallist Marc Bengry and former British number one and silver Commonwealth medallist Jo Maynard of One Two Six Fencing Club. I am also indebted to legal expert Paul Jefferson for guiding me through court procedure. However I do confess to adding my own 'artistic licence' and hope the lawyers amongst you will indulge me this digression for the sake of the dramatic effect of the story. Also to sisters Naomi and Sam W. Thank you Naomi for your insight into the workings of the police and Sam for your friendship and initial read of the manuscript. I would like to acknowledge Alcor Life Extension Foundation in the USA for allowing me to use their name and a chapter in their company history.

Finally, I would like to acknowledge and thank all my readers. I hope you enjoyed the ride and please let me know what you think. Find Sarah Orton at www.SarahOrton.co.uk, sarah@SarahOrton.co.uk, as well as Facebook and Twitter.